GW00578264

Tell me a
long, long
story

Tell me a long, long story

12
MEMORABLE
STORIES FROM
INDIA

edited by

Mini Krishnan

ALEPH

ALEPH

ALEPH BOOK COMPANY
An independent publishing firm
promoted by *Rupa Publications India*

First published in India in 2017
by Aleph Book Company
7/16 Ansari Road, Daryaganj
New Delhi 110 002

ISBN: 978-93-86021-14-4

Printed and bound in India by Replika Press Pvt. Ltd.

1 3 5 7 9 10 8 6 4 2

Dedicated to the spirit of Indian literature in translation

*For my part I deem those blessed to whom,
by favour of the gods, it has been granted
either to do what is worth writing of, or to
write what is worth reading...*

Pliny the Younger
Translated by John Delaware

CONTENTS

EDITOR'S NOTE

I'd like to thank all the writers, editors and publishers who generously allowed me to use their works in this collection. These include: Bolwar Mahamad Kunhi and Keerti Ramachandra for 'Period of Mourning', Naveen Kishore and Ipshita Chanda for 'Seed', K. R. Meera and J. Devika for 'The Deepest Blue', Usha Gopikrishnan and Vasantha Surya for 'A Place to Live', Aniruddha Pendse and Shanta Gokhale for 'Jumman', Chetan Raj Shrestha for 'The King's Harvest', Kamalakanta Mohapatra, Leelawati Mohapatra and Paul St. Pierre for 'The Witch', Women Unlimited and Tahira Naqvi for 'Lingering Fragrance', Waryam Singh Sandhu and Nirupama Dutt for 'The Fourth Direction', Gagan Gill and Pratik Kanjilal for 'Signs', Kolakaluri Enoch and C. L. L. Jayaprada for 'Hunger' and Azad Ahmed and Neerja Mattoo for 'Bulbuls'. I also thank Isabel Fernandes without whose diligence and consistency of purpose this book would have taken another year.

Having chivvied and bullied hundreds of writers and translators into submitting and redrafting scripts I suddenly found myself at the writerly end with two guardian angels at the other end of my invisible lifeline—Aienla Ozukum and David Davidar. To them I owe a debt I do not intend to repay except by saying that this book is as much theirs as mine.

Mini Krishnan
Chennai
July 2017

THE LONG SHORT

MINI KRISHNAN

This anthology is put together by an editor who has always looked for the best story never told.

Some years ago, casting about for something from Indian languages that hadn't been held up to the light frequently enough, I made a simple discovery: nearly every famous writer had memorable short stories and novels, and though many outstanding translations of both genres were available, there were hardly any Indian language *novellas* available in translation. Had they flown so low that they had escaped the radar? I persuaded Oxford University Press to publish a series of Indian language novellas translated into English. Some renderings were published and received well by critics and readers—a few of them even made it to study courses. My ambition for our writers (and their amplifiers) is that they should not only be read and enjoyed but also studied. While shopping for novellas, I noticed but impatiently pushed aside another literary creature—the long short story—because it failed to make the word count I'd marked off for the Oxford Novellas series.

The long short story. Flashes from a lighthouse, appearing and disappearing with puja and festival specials: 8,000 words, 10,500 words, up to around 20,000 words. While the novel depends on the proper development of characters, the short story allows no time for a slow unfurling. But when a 'story' runs to twenty pages, the reader expects to see excellent characterization as well as propulsive narrative action.

This collection of long shorts came about because I was unable to publish these stories on their own. Nevertheless, because they are such exceptional pieces of fiction, I thought that they would work well as part of a larger collection. It was in this way that *Tell Me a Long, Long Story* was born.

∽

Before we get to the stories themselves, I'd like to give readers some background to fiction in Indian languages, how it is shaped, and makes its way, through translations, to readers in languages other than those in which it was originally created.

My immense and astounding country (into which the area of Britain would fit several times), has a god beneath every stone, a god of Fire, a god of Air, a god even of Death. This Truth and the myriad lesser truths of India present a formidable challenge to anyone who sets out to study the essence of the country, the essence that drives its creativity and informs its fiction. Layered with the secrets of antiquity, Indian society had, by the second millennium after Christ, already acquired all its essential features. Many empires had risen and fallen in this religious and superstitious society, leaving behind their stamp on their one-time subjects; the division between cities and villages had been established; the pleating of a rich mix of genetic pools into subdivisions had taken place, and, with it, the economic hierarchy of the production and distribution of wealth and its management which gave rise to the disgraceful social inequalities evident even today.

For 600 years, from about the eleventh century onwards, powered by the Bhakti Movement, there was a literary and philosophical outpouring that militated against the policy of exclusion which was the social expression of Vedic Brahminism. When the languages spoken by the ordinary people of India in different regions began to be heard, things changed forever. These new bhashas (modern languages) came clothed in regional aspirations and fused into a protest against the hegemony of Sanskrit and the culture it stood for. However, it must be remembered that while this literary expansion was taking place, what prevailed was still a largely oral tradition.

On a parallel track to these developments came the Islamic invasions, bringing about a civilizational change. While the conquering Turks, who established the Delhi Sultanate in the early thirteenth century on the plains of north India, ushered in a new era of political domination, they also enriched the region culturally through the introduction of Arabic and Persian. India not only 'nativized' both these languages but, when the Hindi family of dialects mixed with the Islamic languages, it produced a hybrid language, namely Urdu. What is less well known is that long before the thirteenth century, thanks to the Arab traders on the Konkan and Malabar coasts, and their peaceful penetration into the land of the Cholas (modern-day Tamil Nadu), there was a rich mingling of Tamilized Arabic, Arabi Malayalam and Arabi Tulu. Meanwhile Tamil, the oldest language of the subcontinent, continued to grow and flourish in south India, having developed sophisticated structures and systems of poetics and philosophy long before these invasions and upheavals.

The great cultural struggle for the psyche of India began with the British 'discovery' of Sanskrit in the eighteenth century. Prior to that, British officers had studied Persian (the court language of the Mughals). However, as the traders became rulers it became necessary not merely to conduct trade profitably, but also to rule justly (and to appear to be doing so). This need to understand the historical complexity of India in order to control the natives naturally led to the rise of translation and a unique area of scholarship—Indology. How else could Indian forms of knowledge be converted into European objects of study?

The eighteenth century Indologist's admiration for what was possibly a romanticized view of a glorious Indian past gave the study of Sanskrit a great leg up. The privileging of Sanskrit and its meteoric rise in the eyes of Europe as the Ursprache of the subcontinent was because Governor General Warren Hastings (1732-1818) was keen on Indians being tried according to their own laws. One of the consequences of this was that many of the important Sanskrit texts needed to be translated. These decades, therefore, saw the earliest translations of Sanskrit texts of philosophy and laws into English. Most of them were executed with the help of Brahmin pundits who explained and interpreted to Muslim scholars of Persian. These language brokers then translated what they had absorbed into Persian for the benefit of the Englishmen waiting to translate into English what they in turn had understood. With a few exceptions, these translations were of dismal quality. When all the footnotes and explanations had been peeled away, what was not badly translated was wrongly translated or presented in discouragingly ponderous language. It set the foundation for a certain mistrust of the profession of translation which contemporary translators are still struggling to overcome.

In the century that followed, public prejudice in Britain began to affect the way in which India was ruled, and the manner in which Britons comported themselves. Hinduism was attacked by English evangelists and administrators whose careers and self-esteem depended on feeling racially superior to the natives. Missionary activity and translations of the Bible into Indian languages led to the preparation of dictionaries and the establishment of printing presses. Print culture altered the public sphere. Curriculum development and the preparation of textbooks knitted with the spread of journals, magazines, and newspapers in the local languages generating a middle-class readership that wanted to read something other than stories and poems about gods and goddesses; they wanted to read about people like themselves. So during the late nineteenth century, forms and models found in English literature were quickly adapted by Indian writers.

Meanwhile, Hindu reformists and revivalists, sensing the danger of having their traditions submerged by a seductively attractive alien influence, which also offered privileges and a livelihood (through English), began to mount counter-attacks. These initiatives were led by Indians who had by then mastered English. Unsurprisingly, Indians who studied English understood English people better than the rulers did the ruled. In this ironic and unstoppable manner, a language that had no indigenous base in India, became one of the mediums of our intellectual discourse and the means by which we began to communicate with the outside world. 'The English language,' to quote G. N. Devy, 'was grafted onto India's linguistic banyan tree.'

That, briefly, is the backdrop against which this compilation of long short stories needs to be placed. The tradition into which the stories in this book can be slotted—translations of Indian works into English—had an auspicious start: a portion of the Mahabharata. It was the first text to be translated directly from Sanskrit into English without intermediaries and by someone who knew the original language. The title, *Bhagvat Geeta*; the translator, Charles Wilkins (30 May 1784). Today nearly every publisher contributes to this stream, this third language made up of an Indian soul and an English body.

Some of the stories in this collection celebrate the creativity, intelligence and practical wisdom of the non-lettered, and all of them drive home the importance of bhasha writings for our intellectual lives, encouraging us all to becoming critical insiders.

I can confidently assert that the enlarging of horizons that translation makes possible affects not only readers and writers of a language, but the very nature of language itself. The more a language absorbs elements and turns of phrase from another language, the stronger and more flexible it becomes. It is safe to paraphrase Goethe who believed that a literature exhausts itself and its resources if it closes itself off to the influences of other language worlds.

Can this be said of the vigorous culture of translations in India? Every one of the writers in this volume was influenced not only by the different movements in their own languages but by the different streams that ran into their literature, including the rivulets from translations of European writers into Indian languages. Thus, 200 years ago, the multilingual ethos of India was forever infiltrated, hybridized and energized by Western languages and their histories and, more recently, by all the socio-linguistic and scientific advances and discoveries that accompanied India's contact with Britain, including the impact of an agrarian nation struggling to be reborn as an industrial one.

In my opening paragraphs I made a reference to various forms of the Truth. There is another truth and it lies in fiction. It lies in immersing oneself in tellings loaded with spices and a pinch of salt, a process which has an amazing power to arouse feelings and therefore to change lives.

I hope that readers of literature who lead relatively predictable lives will be startled, maybe even unsettled, but ultimately rewarded by the depth and complexity of these twelve stories, their masterful use of rhetorical devices, the sweep of their insights, and the lustrous expanses of emotional detail. I hope that these stories will enable readers to experience the many different lives that dwell within the pages. But, more importantly, to experience their own lives differently.

SEED

MAHASWETA DEVI

Translated from the Bengali by Ipshita Chanda

The land north of Kuruda and Hesadi villages is uneven, and so arid and sun-baked that there is not a hint of grass even after the rains. You might see the occasional erect serpent hoods of cactus plants, and a few neem trees. In the middle of this scorched wasteland, where no cattle graze, is a low-lying boat-shaped piece of land. Around half a bigha. You can spot this bit of land only if you climb a high embankment; the splash of green, from the wild aloe bushes that grow on the land, presents an eerie sight.

Even more sinister is the machan in the middle of the field, a platform on wooden posts topped by a thatched hut. A hut on the land is most unsettling for anyone who sees it, because such a hut is generally built to guard crops. Only stray aloe plants grow here, with leaves as thorny as the plant of the pineapple. Even buffaloes don't eat them. Elsewhere in the world, the fibre from these plants makes extremely strong ropes. In India, they are dismissed as wild bushes.

The most eerie scene occurs as evening falls. A man comes striding along from Kuruda village. As he approaches, you can see that he's old, his skin gnarled and knotted, a loincloth wrapped around his waist, a quilted bag hanging from it. He carries a stick and raps the aloe barks at random as he approaches the machan. He climbs the rickety ladder fastened to the branches of the tree. He strikes a flint stone, lights a beedi and sits down on the machan. Every day. When night falls, he spreads a mat and goes to sleep. Every night.

At this time, every day, in Kuruda village, the old wife of Dulan

1

Ganju yells curses at him. This is her right. Because this old man is Dulan Ganju. Her son, daughter-in-law, and grandchildren dislike this yelling and cursing, but can't do anything about it. If they protest, they'll be abused too. And in these parts, Dhatua's mother's abusive powers are legendary. In every dispute, she is called upon to exhibit her professional squabbling skills. She takes the field and starts by cursing the first of the adversary's seven previous generations. Generally, by the time she reaches the third generation, the opposition flees the field.

She is widely respected. When there was trouble at Tamadih during the Emergency, the police had come to this village asking questions. Dhatua's mother's fiery tongue had forced them to leave. One of the fugitives the police was seeking was hiding in the loft of the cowshed. Dhatua's mother's strident commands to 'Come, search every room, you vultures!' conclusively proved that the whole village was completely innocent.

She didn't stop there. 'Look,' she said, 'there are only children and the elderly in the village. Want to examine them? Want to arrest them?'

Once the police left, Dhatua's mother bloodied the fugitive with her sharp tongue, 'Rotoni! You've always been a halfwit! Less sense than a nanny goat! So you axed a Rajput mahajan? Excellent, well done. You should've despatched the devil by giving it to him in the neck. Why didn't you hide in the jungle? Which idiot returns to his village? Go, go to the forest!'

Dhatua and Latua don't have the guts to tell their mother, 'Don't curse our baba.'

If they do, Ma will explode. So, the old man is now his sons' darling, and their mother a worthless old she-goat! Do the sons know their father's true character? Only she knows.

Ma had been married at the age of four. At fourteen, after the gaona ceremony when she attained puberty, she made her husband's family her home. Ma knew the old man through and through. Lord of a thorny wasteland, guarding his land alone. After all, who would be widowed if a snake bit him or a tiger dragged him off? Dhatua and Latua? Could they fool the government into giving them seeds every year for that barren piece of land? Collect government fertilizer and sell it off? Extract money from the government for the maintenance of a plough and buffalo borrowed from the pahaan, the village priest, year after year?

The sons fall silent. Ma puffs away at her hookah and, delivering her final, unanswerable line, 'You'll never know my true worth till I'm dead,' goes off to sleep. The daughters-in-law whisper to the sons, 'Well, another day gone.'

Ma addresses the darkness, 'One day he'll lie there dead. I won't even be here.'

The sons know it is abnormal to guard the aloe plants every night. But they don't consider their father a normal person by any standards. Baba is a dark character, complicated and impossible to understand. The trade of the Ganju caste is skinning dead animals. Baba poisoned a few buffaloes that belonged to the powerful Rajput mahajan, Lachman Singh, owner of ten rifles. This in Lachman Singh's own village, Tamadih. Then he sold the skins. Characteristically, Lachman suspected his traditional rival, his brother and coheir Daitari Singh of the crime. The resultant family feud is still raging.

Despite this, Baba survives, proving that he is a man of a different measure. Always busy with such strategies of survival, he had never had time for his sons or grandsons.

Ma is no less. Her mature old bones have such stamina, bear such stubborn courage and resentment, that she, too, is beyond the ordinary measure of a human being.

Their sons had never seen their father and mother seated together chatting. But when Baba is planning something important, he asks Ma to come and sit in the courtyard. Lights her hookah and says, 'Eh Dhatuake ma! Advise me. Give me your advice. Everyone in the village consults you, even the police are scared of you.'

'What mischief are you brewing now? Who're you planning to cheat or rob?'

Ma's voice is loud, but without rancour. Together they plot and plan in low voices. Such an event occurs once a year or every year-and-a-half.

At other times, Baba doesn't pay any attention to Ma. She says,

'I might as well go back to my father's house.'

Baba smiles slyly and quietly tells the breeze, 'Yes. To that huge mansion of your father's in Tura village.'

Ma has no father-mother-brothers. Yet she gives Baba the opportunity to smile crookedly and pass mocking remarks.

This is what Latua and Dhatua's parents are like—and there's nothing to be done about it. Just as you can't help the fact that the hill lies to the west, or that the Kuruda River flows nearby. Sanichari says, 'Your father and mother are both mad. Your father, of course, is completely crazy. Why else would he guard that land without ever farming it? Why?'

There's a proverb which says that what you pick up free is worth fourteen annas. The land was free, but there wasn't even fourteen paise profit from it.

The land belongs to Lachman Singh. Quite a few years ago, activists belonging to the Sarvodaya movement, which sought to redistribute land from the rich to the poor, had gone from door to door to every landlord in this area. About them too, Sanichari used to say, 'These are madmen of the babu caste. They'll make the landlords feel deep regret and spontaneously admit, "Tch, tch! We have so much land, and they have none at all?" And they'll give away the land. The day they do this, I'll sit on a divan, eat butter and cream, and cook rice twice a day.'

But some landlords did begin to give away little bits of stony, barren land to provoke their fellow landlords into doing the same. Everyone had 500 or 700 or 1,000 or 2,000 bighas of fertile land. Everyone harvested paddy or maize or maroa or mustard or arhar. Groundnuts earned large profits. So it didn't really matter much if you gave away some land.

The Sarvodaya leaders and workers had become the butt of their countrymen's mockery. The gifts of land saved their face. Didn't the uppercaste Rajput and Kayastha mahajans, jotedars who owned or controlled the land in the Kuruda belt give up their lands? Didn't that mean they had had a change of heart? Certainly. Bas. The Sarvodaya mission was successful. Immediately after this, the activists would go off to change the hearts of the dacoits in Madhya Pradesh. Their mission would not be complete till they filled the hearts of two classes—the landlords and the dacoits—with remorse

The gifting of land has many uses. It is a way of getting rid of barren land and buying over its recipients. It strengthens one's position with the government. Above all, like a rasgulla after a meal, there is the added satisfaction of knowing one is compassionate.

Dulan Ganju gets this land. He didn't want to take it. But Lachman Singh is too powerful. His eyes grew red with anger and he said, 'Typical of you low castes! Today I'm feeling generous, so I'm giving you this. Fool, do you think I'll feel this way tomorrow?'

Dulan said, 'Hujoor is my mai-baap.'

'Then? Low-lying-land floods every monsoon, sow whatever you like and you'll get high yields.'

During the monsoons, reddish water streams down the embankment and collects in the field. But all around lay barren, stony ground. Who'll go all that way to plough that land? If it was fertile land, would Lachman Singh have let it lie fallow? Dulan had gone to borrow money. He came back a landlord.

Everyone in the village said, 'It's a rich man's whim! He eats parathas soaked in ghee, and the heat's gone to his head. He'll forget all about it tomorrow.'

'Suppose he doesn't?'

'Just let the land be. In Ara-Chhapra, this is the kind of land they gave at the behest of the Sarvodayis. Those who got it sold it back to the mahajan or mortgaged it to him. You'll do the same.'

'Who'll take that land? The mahajan's buying himself a good name, and at the same time getting rid of it.'

Dulan would have said more, but the pahaan who was part of his audience gave him a mighty tongue-lashing. People had so many problems to deal with, what was Dulan's land trouble in comparison?

Dulan mutters and grumbles.

His wife says, 'Oh! He's busy calculating how to make a profit from this land, but just look at the fuss he's making! No one's ever seen through his wiles.'

'Profit from the land?'

The next day, Sanichari hears all about it and says, 'Why? Eh, Dhatuakemaiya! If he gets land, Dhatuakebaap can go to Tohri! To the block development office! The government will bear the expenses of farming, seeds, everything!'

Only when he heard this did Dulan smile. His eyes glazed over with dreams. Even a man like Dulan had not realized how barren land could help him run his household. In some fairy tales, cows yield milk even though they haven't calved.

∽

One day, the land came into Dulan's possession in the form of documents and deeds. They had two adjacent rooms and a corridor in the Ganju neighbourhood: rooms that served as a living room, kitchen, everything. This was his world. Barricaded, one end of the corridor turned into a bedroom for husband and wife. Someone so bereft of support generally has no backbone. All around him were Rajput jotedars and mahajans; the Brahman priest Hanuman Misra of Tahar was particularly influential in these parts. Living in such an area, continuously under the thumb of the higher castes, would naturally break the spirit of people like Dulan who belonged to the lower Ganju and Dushad castes.

But the drive for survival prompted him to exploit situations by using his natural guile rather than force. He fooled his powerful adversaries not by strength, but by wit and cunning. All the stratagems of survival were at his fingertips.

Dhatua's mother says, 'It's a large piece of land, very fertile. Oh, Dhatua, tell your baba to build a granary for his crops. Oh, Latua-re, your father's become a zamindar, yes, a zamindar!'

She said all this, but the villagers and she continued to wait to see what Dulan would do.

The villagers were appreciative witnesses to Dulan's one-man strategic warfare. Everyone knew about the business of Lachman Singh's buffaloes, but no one told on Dulan. He sold a pumpkin to Daitari Singh's household and took money from both Daitari's wife and mother. When the bananas and radishes were brought in a bullock cart from Lachman Singh's house to the banks of the Kuruda River during the Chhat festival, he walked beside the cart, shooing away imaginary birds, and continuously stealing things. Not once had he ever given a single thing to the other villagers. Yet, they treated him with respect. He could do what they dared not do.

As soon as he got the land, Dulan touched Lachman Singh's knees and said, 'Malik, protector! You've given me land, but how will I farm it? I won't get a thing from the BD office. A-ha-ha, such a good piece of land! I've got it, but I can't use it.'

'Why? The BD office will give you everything.'

'No, Hujoor, I'm a low caste.'

'Of course you are. It's because you don't remember this that you get kicked around. Sure, you're a low caste! But how can they refuse to help someone *I'm* giving land to? Who's the BD babu?'

'Kayastha, Hujoor. Says the Rajputs are stupid country bumpkins. Listens to the radio all the time and uses his left hand to drink water, tea.'

'Arre Ram Ram! Chee, chee, chee.'

'I've seen it myself, Hujoor.'

'I'll write to him.'

Lachman Singh is no learned mahapundit. He keeps a vakil. The vakil writes a strong appeal in Kayathi* Hindi advocating that Dulan get money in instalments to buy a plough and bullock, seeds and fertilizer. The BDO might live in Tohri, and it's true that Tohri is far from Lachman's village Tamadih, but he has only one life. The SDO himself has warned him to avoid conflicts with Lachman and Hanuman Misra. So he immediately agreed to everything. He explained to the loincloth-clad Dulan in a very gentle voice that he would get seeds and fertilizer. But he wouldn't get the entire amount for the plough and bullock at one go. If he could pay an advance and show that he had bought the plough and bullock, he would get the rest of the money.

Dulan returned to the village and said to the pahaan, 'The sarkar

---

*Local variant of Hindi, used for legal documents

makes laws, but doesn't understand anything. People buy ploughs and bullocks with cash. Who will sell to someone who pays in instalments? Lend me your plough and bullock.'

Dulan got the money by displaying that plough and bullock every alternate year. Every time he asks the BDO for the money, he says, 'The bullock died, Hujoor.'

He takes the money. Collects the fertilizer and sells it at Tohri itself. Hoists the sack of seeds onto his shoulder and brings it home.

He eats the seeds.

It's no easy task to boil paddy seeds and make rice. But he does it. The first time, his wife had said, 'So much seed! How much land do you have?'

'You can't measure it even if you try.'

'What do you mean?'

'Our hunger. Can hunger be measured? The land of the stomach keeps expanding! You want me to farm that barren strip of land? Are you crazy?'

'What'll you do, then?'

'Boil it, grind it, we'll eat it.'

'Are you going to kill yourself eating seeds?'

'We haven't died yet. Didn't we eat rats during the famine? Why should we die from eating seeds? If we do, at least we'll have died eating rice! We'll go to heaven.'

It took Dhatua's mother just one meal of rice made from the seeds to realize that she had never eaten anything so sweet in her life.

She proudly told everyone in the village about this tasty food. Can any other married woman in the village boast of how brainy her man is, of how cunningly he fooled the gorment so that his family could eat paddy-rice seeds?

Everyone in the village was pleased. The gorment has never protected their interests. The gorment's BDO never helps them with farming. Their children never get to enter the gorment's primary school. Lachman Singh or Daitari Singh force them to harvest their crops for four annas a day or a single meal, at gunpoint. There was a lot of tension over this, because the Ganju-Dushad-Dhobis of the neighbouring block were getting kicked and fed for eight annas daily. The villagers wanted a raise of twenty-five paise. Knowing all this, whenever there was trouble, the SDO brought in police reinforcements and picked up the labourers. Lachman Singh and Daitari were let off without a word.

The gorment belongs to Lachman Singh. The gorment belongs to Lachman Singh, Daitari Singh, Hanuman Misra. If such a gorment is fleeced by someone who happens to be a Dulan Ganju, then the villagers are bound to appreciate it.

Like the mythical Kaamdhenu, the cow that never ceased giving, the land continues to yield Dulan about six hundred rupees annually. But Dulan continued to sleep outdoors. At the corner of the covered veranda, on a platform beside Dhatua's mother, who coughs and wheezes as if she has asthma. They tie a billy goat beneath the platform when they go to sleep. A son to a room, each with his wife and children. Wheat, maroa, corncobs by the sackful, pots and pans, firewood, everything stacked in the same room. The earnings from the land cannot see them through the whole year, so father and sons work as field labourers, or search the forest for wild potatoes, or carry headloads in Tohri, or work in Misraji's orchards. Like everyone else.

One day, Karan Dusadh of Tamadih arrived in the village. A glamorous personality who used to work as a labourer in Lachman's field. He had a dispute over wages with the owner-manager, the malik, and went to jail at Hazaribagh where he made friends with prisoners from other parts of Bihar. They didn't shrink from him because he was a low caste Dusadh. They respected him as a fighter. They were amazed that with no organizational help at all, 200 labourers had turned against an ocean of exploitation and set fire to the powerful Lachman Singh's fields of ripened wheat. They explained to him the importance of battles like theirs, burgeoning everywhere. The need to fight in an organized way. The need to fight from their own base.

The repercussions were swift and merciless. They were tortured. They were beaten up by the authorities. Many were even beaten to death. Despite all this, they told Karan, 'You're a fighter, you did the right thing, never give up the fight.'

Hence, there was turmoil in the layers of Karan Dusadh's mind. The Karan who had rebelled only when Lachman Singh had driven him to the end of his tether, now came out of jail and said to everyone, 'Conditions are unchanged. Why wait till he forces us to resist, get shot at, get jailed? Let's organize in advance. Talk things over with him. Ask the police to be present during harvesting. Our demands are very few. We're Harijans and Adivasis. We won't get good wages in these parts. We'll fight for eight annas. Women-men-children, eight annas for everyone. He's giving four annas. This will be our "twenty-five-paise battle" for an additional four annas.'

As soon as Dulan heard about this, he called Karan to Kuruda. Suspicious by nature, he insisted they talk on the embankment at the edge of his land, away from everyone. Karan Dusadh is middle-aged, scrawny, a tiny man. After two years with the prisoners in Hazaribagh, he is like a new person.

'All this caste business is rubbish. It's the Brahman and the wealthy who have spun these tales about untouchability.'

His words startle Dulan. For a moment he is speechless. Then—he's an old fox, after all!—'Oh, the babus who can read and write have always said that. Now let's get down to business. That Lachman Singh and the BDO, SDO and daroga, the police chief, drink together. First, go to the Adivasi office and the Harijan Seva Sangh at Tohri. Keep them informed. Let them go with you to the thana and the SDO.'

'Why? Are we that weak?'

'Yes, we are, Karan. Make no mistake. The entire sarkar will help Lachman. He can open fire and they won't notice. But you raise a stick and they'll catch you. Madanlalji of the Harijan Seva Sangh is a good man. Everyone knows him. Get him to back you.'

Karan takes this advice. Madanlal can garner a powerful pool of votes. So the SDO and daroga secretly consult with Lachman Singh. Then they agree to what Madanlal says.

The harvesting and gathering of the corn goes on without incident. Eight annas as wages. Karan Dusadh becomes a hero. A fairy tale come true.

Then, abruptly, Lachman tells Dulan, 'Stay on your land tomorrow.

If anyone gets to know that I've told you this, I'll kill you.'

When this 'tomorrow' turns into 'today' at daybreak, the SDO suddenly goes off to Ranchi and the daroga to far-off Purudiha, chasing bandits.

As evening turns to dusk, in the radiance of the setting sun, Lachman Singh, accompanied by his Rajput-caste brothers, attacks the Dusadh quarters in Tamadih.

Fires rage, people burn, huts collapse.

∽

At night, the newly risen moon reveals an unearthly silent scene before Dulan's eyes. Lachman Singh on horseback. Two horses tied abreast, a plank across their backs, laden with two corpses. Ten of Lachman's men escort the landlord.

At the point of Lachman's gun, Dulan buries Karan and his peaceable brother Bulaki in his land. Terrified, head bowed, he digs deep holes with his shovel. Lachman stands on the edge of the field, supervising and chewing paan. Then he says, 'Breathe a word of this to anyone, you cur, and you'll join Karan Dusadh. We can't trust the jackals and wolves not to dig up the corpses. Build a machan here tomorrow. Stay on guard at night. I'm the son of a Rajput! Karan lit this fire—from now on, there'll be more dead bodies.'

Dulan nods. In order to survive, he says, 'As you wish.'

The police came the next day to investigate the attack. A lot of hullabaloo. Ultimately it was learnt that Karan wasn't even present during the disturbance; the reporters' attempts to write 'A True Harijan Story' at all costs were totally foiled. No one said a word against Lachman Singh. One of his henchmen spent a few days in jail for arson. The government gave a pittance in compensation to those rendered homeless for the construction of new huts.

From then on, Dulan sleeps on the land. At first, this is seen as a sign of insanity, and his sons try to dissuade him. No advice penetrates Dulan's ears at this stage. When questioned, he glowers silently at them with bloodshot eyes. Then, shaking his head, he threatens them with his stick, 'Don't talk to me, Dhatua! I'll break your head.'

A great explosion, a landslide, occurs in the strata of his mind, ending in mental upheaval. So easy! Is everything so easy for the Lachmans? Dulan had thought that just as a man's life is linked to so many rites and rituals, so is his death. But Lachman Singh has proved that these time-honoured customs are meaningless. How easy! Two corpses on horseback! And these corpses must have been carried off arrogantly, from right under the Tamadih Dusadhs' noses. Lachman knows there's no need to hide them. Witnesses won't say a thing. They have read the warning in Lachman's sharp, silent gaze. He who opens his mouth will die. This has happened before. And will happen again. Once in a while it is necessary to rend the sky with leaping flames and the screams of the dying, just to remind the Harijans and untouchables that government laws, appointment of officers and constitutional decrees are nothing. Rajputs remain Rajputs, Brahmans remain Brahmans and Dusadh-Chamar-Ganju-Dhobi remain lower than Brahman-Kayastha-Rajput-Bhumihar-Kurmi. The Rajput or Brahman or Kayastha or Bhumihar or Yadav or Kurmi is, in places, as poor as, or even poorer than, the Harijan. But they are not tossed into the flames because of their caste. The fire god, having tasted the flesh of forest-dwelling, black-skinned outcastes during the burning of the Khandav forest[*], is fond of the taste of the untouchable poor.

All this causes havoc in Dulan's mind. Before this, his was a surface cunning. Aimed at survival. Now he has to conceal two corpses beneath his heart. They begin to rot within him. Buried in the earth, Karan and Bulaki grow lighter as they gradually lose the burden of flesh. But in the realm of Dulan's mind, the corpses weigh heavy. He looks wan, hardly speaks. He can't confide in anyone. The constant burden he bears makes him feel as if he is tied to a whipping post. If he opens his mouth, the Dusadh quarters of Kuruda will go up in flames, ashes will scatter in the air, along with the stench of charred flesh.

Slowly time passes. Everyone is forced to forget that two people,

---

[*]Forest in the Mahabharata

Karan and Bulaki, went missing. From Tohri to Burudiha on one side and Phuljhar on the other, rail tracks are laid. According to area and jurisdiction, the thana and the SDO are given special powers to immediately investigate, take action, prepare cases for court, in instances of atrocities against Adivasis and Harijans. A panchayati well is dug in Dhai village. Dhai is a lower caste and Adivasi village. In this fashion, the area attempts to limp towards modernity.

The result of all this is to make Lachman Singh more powerful. He pooh-poohs government dictates and pays field labourers forty paise as wages, gifts a golden cobra to crown the Shiva idol in Hanuman Misra's temple, buys the BDO a scooter and the daroga a transistor radio, and takes over the bigha-and-a-half of land belonging to Karan and Bulaki as repayment of an old loan.

Everyone accepts all this. But all at once, there is a government circular about field labourers and with it comes a new SDO. This man is suspected of being left-of-centre, and because it is the administration's pious intention to drive the final nail into his coffin and suspend him, he is transferred to Tohri one-and-a-half months before the harvesting season begins.

The field labourers in the Tohri area are Harijans and Adivasis. The landowners, jotedars and mahajans, are upper caste. The particular problem of the area is the deep distrust of the labourers for the masters. This explains the lack of progress in agriculture or increase in individual incomes. Income, expenditure, health, education, social consciousness, everything continues to remain at a sub-normal level. An enlightened, sympathetic, humane officer is needed here.

The SDO realizes that he's in deep trouble. He tells his father-in-law, you win. Look for a bank job for me. I'm a student of Afro-economics, I might even get it. Else, where they're sending me, your only daughter will definitely end up a widow.

Having made alternative job arrangements, the SDO tells the impatient field labourers, 'You have the right to get five rupees eighty paise as wages.' He officially informs the jotedars of this. Lachman Singh's land and crop and labourers are spread over a vast area, including villages like Tamadih, Burudiha, Kuruda, Hesadi, Chama and Dhai.

The son of the Burudiha village headman, Asrafi Mahato, says, 'We still remember Karan. We haven't forgotten him these three years. But this SDO is a good man. Why should we harvest crops for just forty paise and a meal? Five rupees eighty paise! We don't want the meal, let him give us five rupees forty paise as total wages.'

As he had once explained to Karan, so Dulan now carefully explains to Asrafi, 'Karan made a big noise. As a result, Tamadih's Dusadh quarters went up in flames.'

'Where's Karan? Where's Bulaki?'

'Who knows?'

'They're dead.'

'Why do you say that?'

'They've been killed and buried in the jungle.'

'I don't know. But keep the hakim, the village doctor, with you when you act.'

'All right.'

'Get the hakim to help you later, too. That time, they paid the wages. But later, they lit the fire.'

'I'll tell him.'

⌘

In every area, every conflict has a characteristic local pattern.

Lachman Singh says, 'I won't pay that much. Just two rupees and tiffin.'

'Give us the wages, Hujoor, protector.'

'Should I?' Lachman Singh's eyes are terribly gentle and sympathetic. He says, 'Let me think about it! You do the same.'

'Even a donkey knows that those wages are fair. But you know what? You mentioned the SDO, right? Go tell him, in these parts, Makhan Singh, Daitari Singh, Ramlagan Singh, Hujuri Prasad Mahato, no one is giving these wages. Why should I alone be ruined?'

Asrafi offers a timid but stubborn smile, 'Ruined, Hujoor? You own the flour mill, your mansion can be seen from miles away—how can you be ruined?'

To Lachman Singh this smile is arrogant mockery. He says, 'The rate I mentioned is what we decided amongst us. Because we own land, the sarkar treats us like thieves. Yet you get sarkari aid for whatever little land you have. I've given Dulan land. The bastard doesn't farm it, but he collects seeds every year. Animal! He eats them. So let him. And what aid do we get? Fertilizer, seeds, insecticide, we have to buy everything ourselves. Tell the SDO what I said.'

Asrafi tells Dulan, 'Be careful, Chacha! The bastard knows that you don't farm the land or harvest crops.'

The corpses weigh even heavier on Dulan's mind. Lachman Singh has warned him, 'Don't sow or plough the land for a few years, Dulan.'

Dulan, sorrowfully and with deep concern for Asrafi, says, 'Don't trust him, beta. Your father performed the birth rites for my Dhatua-Latua.'

'No, Chacha.'

Asrafi keeps shuttling between the SDO and Lachman Singh. Dulan grows increasingly depressed. Fearing some calamity, he growls at his sons, 'The son of the lowborn will always be lowborn. You eat whatever I manage to wring from the soil. Someone else would have gone off to a nearby colliery. Why are you hanging on here?'

Dhatua raises his calm, dreamy eyes and says, 'This time we'll get double wages, Baba.'

Dulan says nothing further. He goes to the block office at Tohri, says, 'This time I want to sow rabi after the harvest. I need help.'

∽

The BDO seems to know the irrefutable reason for continuing to supply seeds for land that will never be farmed. He, too, joins Lachman and Dulan in this conspiracy and, smiling toothily, says, 'I'll look into it.'

Dulan notices the huge trees in his compound. Such tall papaya trees are rare.

He says, 'How did this papaya tree grow so tall, Babu?'

The BDO gives a deeply self-satisfied smile, 'This area became a part of the office compound later. During the summer they would shoot mad dogs and dump them in the hole there. Trees are bound to grow well if they're fertilized by rotting bones and flesh.'

'Does it make good fertilizer?'

'Very good. Haven't you seen how flowers flourish on the burial mounds of poor Muslims?'

These words cause the corpses to weigh lighter in Dulan's mind. Returning to his village, Dulan goes to the land in the middle of the afternoon. Yes, true enough! Karan and Bulaki are now those putush bushes and aloe plants! Tears strain at his eyes. 'Karan, you haven't died even in death. But these putush bushes and aloe plants are of no use to anybody, even buffaloes and goats don't eat them. You fought for our rights. Why couldn't you turn into maize or wheat? Or, at the very least, china grass? So we could eat ghato made of the boiled seeds?'

Sorrowing and bitter, he goes to Tamadih. Nobody is around, so he dismantles the fence protecting Lachman Singh's vegetable patch. He rounds up a few buffaloes and clicks his tongue 'Har, har, har' and drives them into the vegetable patch. Then he goes the long way around to the front of the house and says to Lachman Singh, 'Malik, protector, write me a letter. I want admission into hospital. Cough and chest pain.'

'I'll give you the letter after the harvesting.'

'Very good, master.'

Once more, the corpses weigh Dulan down. He returns to the patch of land, digging into the depths of his mind with the pickaxe of anxiety. Tells Karan and Bulaki to move over and make space.

After the harvesting is over? Is someone coming to keep Karan and Bulaki company?

The harvesting is underway. After much debate, two rupees fifty paise a day and a snack are decided upon. Lachman Singh supervises the harvest on horseback. The police ceremonially make an appearance and confirm that the harvesting is peaceful. On the seventh day, everyone gets their wages.

Heaving a sigh of relief, the SDO leaves with the police.

On the eighth day, the storm breaks. Lachman Singh brings in outside labourers to harvest the paddy. Asrafi and the others feel threatened, and, though scared, they speak up stubbornly.

'You can't do this.'

'Who says so? I am doing it. Sons of bitches, see for yourself—I can do it.'

'But—'

'I let you work. I paid you your wages. Bas—the game's over!'

Seeing Asrafi and the others on the verge of creating trouble, the outsiders lower their scythes and huddle together. Shots are fired. The outside labourers flee.

Shots are fired.

There is no account of the number shot dead. According to Dulan and the others, eleven. According to Lachman Singh and the police, seven. Asrafi's father loses his sons. Two sons, Mohar and Asrafi, both missing. Mahuban Kairi of Chama village and Paras Dhobi of Burudiha—missing. Cries of mourning in almost every home. When the SDO arrives, the fathers, mothers, wives, children of the dead and missing fall at his feet. The SDO's face is as if hewn from rock. He promises the villagers that he'll file a police case against Lachman Singh. He's telling the reporters the whole story, escorting them around. Until the warrant comes, Lachman Singh is not to leave home.

ॐ

On a moonlit night, when there's a nip in the sweet-scented air, Lachman Singh arrives. Everything in these areas follows a pattern, and the noblest animal is the four-footed horse... Four horses carrying four corpses. This time, Lachman's men help Dulan. Deep, deep pits are needed. The land is soaked with monsoon rain and autumn dew. Four corpses piled one on the other. The burden within Dulan grows even heavier.

Dulan becomes increasingly strange. He picks quarrels at the BD office to extract more and more seeds. Money for a plough and buffalo. Then, before the month is out, a few aloe plants bring solace. Very healthy, very green aloe plants and putush bushes accept the salutations of the sun each dawn during the Emergency in neglected southeast Bihar, silent testimony to the murder of field labourers cum Harijans. Lachman is released without being charged. Emergency. The SDO is demoted for undermining the harmony between the labourers and the landowners by inciting the former to revolt. Lachman and the other Jotedars and mahajans offer puja at Hanuman Misra's temple with savage fanfare and a hundred and eight pure-silver bael leaves, and announce that only those sons and daughters of curs and bitches who are willing to work for one rupee without food or water, need bother to show up. They can bring in outside labour.

The Emergency has caused widespread calamity in the region. Congress musclemen have contracted to get outside labourers. Now the game hots up, becomes even more cruelly entertaining. Four annas out of each days' wages have to be given to the contractor. Whether you are contracted by him or not. These musclemen have vowed that they'll get the crop harvested at gunpoint, and anyone who dares object will be doused in petrol and set on fire, so that matters are settled once and for all.

Dulan wanders around with a heavy mind, and looking at Dhatua-Latua, wonders if they should flee. But where can they go? Where will a Dulan Ganju be safe in his motherland of southeast Bihar?

Is there a place without Lachman Singhs?

During the Holi festival, he doesn't even listen to the songs carefully. But suddenly the joyous celebrations are interrupted by a strange song. Dhatua, intoxicated with mahwa, plays the tuila and sings, his eyes closed:

Where has Karan gone?
And Bulaki?
Why is there no news of them?
They are lost in the police files.
Where is Asrafi Hajam?
And his brother Mohar?
Where are Mahuban and Paras?
Why is there no news of them?
They are lost in the police files.
Karan fought the twenty-five-paise battle.
Asrafi fought the five-rupees-forty-paise battle.
Bulaki and Mohar

Fought alongside their elder brothers.
Mahuban could brew the best mahwa
Paras was the best Holi dancer
All lost in the police files, lost.

The song ends. Everyone is silent. The colours of Holi turn to ash, the intoxication wears off. Dulan stands up.

'Who made up this song?'

'I did, Baba.'

Dulan broke into deep sobs. He said, 'Forget that song. Or you too will get lost in the police files.'

Dulan returned to his land. Climbed down the embankment, into the middle of the patch. In an eerie whisper he said, 'You've become songs. You hear? Songs. Songs made up by my son Dhatua. You've become gaan, song, not dhaan, paddy, not china grass—now get off my chest, I can't take it any more!'

Under the full Holi moon, the fresh leaves of the aloe plants and the rough-barked putush bushes shook with laughter. They had never heard anything so funny. Dulan's heart was filled with an unnamed fear for Dhatua. As soon as he climbed the machan, he heard Dhatua's song. Now everyone was singing it. But they were not lost in the police files. Dulan would never be able to reveal everything. The power of Lachman Singh.

৵৹

One day, the Emergency ends.

One day, the Liberation Sun of India gets off the gaddi, her seat of power, to watch the fun, and then, regaining her breath, a little later, begins agitating to regain the gaddi. One day, Lachman Singh's crop ripens, once again.

After two years of drought-famine-crop destruction, this year the earth generously floods the land with paddy. Paddy fields disappearing into the horizon, punctuated with rows of machans. Birds feed on the ripening paddy day and night.

He who was a Congressman and muscleman and field-labour

contractor two years ago now expunges the title 'Congress and muscleman' from his name and appears as the Contractor of Field Labour. With him are a Terylene-and-dark-glasses-flaunting, gun-toting foursome, all exactly like him. In an Amitabh Bachchan voice, this mercenary tells Lachman Singh, 'Your days are over. Now, strike-breaking, supplying contract labour and harvesting is managed by professionals. I provide mercenary services in southeastern Bihar. This service is compulsory. Five thousand bucks. Advance.'

'Five thousand?'

'Are you willing to pay the sarkar's fixed wage rate?'

'No, no.'

'By not paying those rates, you stand to make a profit of eighty thousand. And you don't want to pay five thousand?'

'I'll pay.'

'Bas. Give me the names of the villages and the labourers. Any troublemakers?'

'No.'

'All right. I have to provide services to Ramlagan Singh and Makhan Singh, too. I'll come at the appropriate time. And yes, pay them five sikka as wages. My share is four annas.'

'One rupee.'

'Five sikka. Amarnath Misra doesn't waste words.'

'How are you related to Misraji and Tahar?'

'Bhatija. His brother's son. The seed capital for my services was provided by Chachaji himself.'

Thus everything is settled. Later, Hanuman Misra says to Lachman Singh, 'Yes, yes, he's my bhatija. I bought surface collieries for my sons, and asked him, "Shall I get you one, too?" But no, he didn't want such tiresome work. Very competent and efficient. Election candidates use his services, as do owners of factories on strike. He supplied labour for surface collieries. Very efficient! Three wives. Keeps them in different towns. Built a house for each one. The previous sarkar knew his worth. Not one of my sons turned out as clever as him.'

Lachman Singh, a ruthless Rajput, is all-powerful in his own territory. But even he accepts that this time he has no choice but to accept the services of the mercenaries who are being forced down his throat. If he doesn't, Makhan and Ramlagan will score over him by availing of the services of the gunmen, while his own work will not be done.

Harvesting begins. No outside labourers. Dhatua and the others are doing it themselves. A snack of corn sattu, chilli, salt and five sikka daily wages. Dhatua's mother packs some pickle of wild karamcha for her two sons to go with the snack.

Dulan sits on the machan. Sits and waits—for what? Harvesting is going on. In the distance, the women are singing as they reap. It sounds like a lullaby. But Dulan can't sleep.

Who has stolen the sleep from Dulan's eyes?
His sleep is lost in the police files.

Dulan waits at home for Dhatua and Latua to return. Then he goes to his land. In the monsoons, wet with showers and the autumn dew, the aloe plants and patush bushes stand arrogant, like a rampant jungle. The bushes are bursting with flowers. Sleep eludes Dulan's eyes.

The expected trouble begins on pay day. Amarnath demands his share. Lachman says, 'No bloodshed, please. You and I have no agreement about cutting your share from the wages. Settle it with them.'

'With all of them?' Amarnath laughs like a hyena. '*You* pay me.'

Dulan's son, Dhatua, resists the most. That's why Lachman Singh doesn't want to get involved. He knows only one way of dealing with the untouchable and that is a bullet from his gun. This is one person he doesn't want to shoot. Dulan is too useful to him.

Amarnath says, 'Talk to these curs? Five sikka for five hundred people. One sikka per day per head works out to one thousand eight hundred seventy-five rupees for fifteen days. Hand it over.'

'No Hujoor! We won't,' Dhatua protests.

Lachman sighs. Once again, he will have to work according to his usual pattern. Once again he will have to pick up his gun. Karan went, Asrafi came, Asrafi went, now there's Dhatua.

'How can we take home fifteen rupees for fifteen days? Shouldn't we get eighteen rupees twelve annas? Wasn't that agreed upon? We haven't delayed the work, have we?'

'Watch it, Dhatua.'

Lachman Singh hands over the money to Amarnath. Then he says, 'Don't say a word, Dhatua. Just leave.'

Karan was raucous with his demands. Asrafi was aggressive. Dhatua had never known that he could protest so stubbornly over this matter of cutting Amarnath's share from their wages. Stepping out, he tells the others, 'You carry on. I'll settle things before I leave here.'

He returns to face Lachman Singh. Says, 'If you don't settle the account for the remaining twenty-five paise, we won't come to work tomorrow. The best fields are not yet done. We won't work, and we won't let anyone else work, either.'

'You're lucky the police are here for their cut, Dhatua. You're safe this time.'

'Why? Do the police scare you?'

Dhatua leaves, but this last barb enrages Lachman Singh. Even so, since Dhatua is Dulan's son, and Dulan is necessary to his secret, Lachman Singh gives the lower castes a day's time.

The next day, everyone comes, but no one works. Lachman is enraged and frustrated. The mercenaries are not available. They have gone to help Makhan Singh and Ramlagan Singh. Outside labour is not available at short notice. As the light fades into evening, Lachman gives his men the necessary instructions: if threats do the trick, don't open fire. Lachman's men ride their horses through the ripe paddy. Having seen several films on the Chambal dacoit gangs, they too have donned khaki green uniforms. They advance. The other side rises and waits.

'Listen here, you whelps, you sons of bitches!'

'You're the son of a bitch!' Someone shouts.

They raise their guns. This side storms into the field at amazing speed. They vanish into the paddy. First, verbal missiles speed back and forth.

Then the inevitable bullets fly. Lots of them. Flocks of birds leave the ripe paddy and take flight. In the field, someone gargles blood deep in his throat. A familiar sound.

Then, sharp scythes and iron choppers slash the horses' hooves, keep slashing. The horses and their riders thunder on. The others steal out and flee. Latua and Param run off towards Tohri.

A long, long, agonizing wait for Dulan. Evening turns to night, and the night is far gone when Latua returns.

'Where is Dhatua?'

'I haven't seen him. Hasn't he returned? I went to the police thana.'

'Where is Dhatua?'

'We fetched the police. They'll come here as well. The same SDO, Baba. He's back. He'll come too.'

'Dhatua!'

Why are the corpses stirring deep within Dulan? For whom are they making place? For whom? Realization hits Dulan. He starts up.

'Where are you going?'

'To the land.'

'The boy is missing, and you...you...are you mad, or are you a ghost?'

'Shut up, woman.'

Dulan walks out, begins to run. Dhatua's song, Dhatua's song.

Where has Karan gone?
And Bulaki?
They are lost in the police files.

Dreamy eyes. A birthmark on his hand. Don't you get lost, now, Dhatua, don't you get lost. Oh, you aloe plant, you putush bush, don't you laugh at me tonight.

Dhatua is alive, alive.

Lachman Singh. A man. With bloodied face and eyes. Lachman is hitting him. Kicking him. The man falls to the ground.

Two of them, three horses.

Lachman looks at him.

'Come close,' says Dulan.

'Dhatua?'

'Sorry, Dulan, I forbade them, but still these beasts opened fire.'

Lachman kicks the man again. Curses, 'Trigger-happy tough!'

'Dhatua?'

'Buried.'

'Who buried him?'

'This animal.'

'Him?'

'Yes. But don't open your mouth, Dulan. Or else your wife, son, son's wife, grandson, no one will be spared. Take, I'll give you money, lots of money. Your son called the police. I'll buy them off, of course. But remember that I'm sparing Latua only because he's your son. I haven't fired a single bullet today. I could have felled Dhatua with a single shot. I didn't.'

They go away. Dulan can no longer stand there with seven corpses. He falls onto the embankment. Rolls down into the field, torn by the savage leaves and thorns of the aloe plants, till he comes to a halt.

As usual, the investigation remains incomplete. The SDO intervenes. The trigger-happy tough and Amarnath go to jail.

Dhatua does not return.

Dulan ponders, on and on. Finally, he decides to go mad. Because he starts uprooting the aloe and putush from his land at the first Baisakhi showers.

'Where's he gone? In the middle of the afternoon?' his wife asks.

Latua's wife says, 'Father-in-law took the scythe and the shovel and went to the field.'

'Why didn't you stop him?'

'Me? Talk to him?!'

All grief forgotten, his wife rushes out. She climbs the embankment and yells, 'Here, have you gone mad? Why are you trying to clear that jungle?'

'Go home.'

'What do you mean, go home?'

'Go home.'

In tears, his wife goes to the pahaan. The pahaan goes to him. Says, 'Dhatua will come back, Dulan. Don't go crazy in despair over your son. Come, you'll fall ill in the heat of the sun.'

Dulan says, 'Go home, pahaan. Is my son missing or is yours?'

'Yours.'

'Is this my land or yours?'

'Yours.'

'Well, then? I may be mad or I may not. What's it to you? I'll fix that bastard's land!'

'Then get Latua to help you.'

'No, I'll do it all alone.'

Though he doesn't farm, he has green fingers, the pahaan remembers. The pahaan tells Dulan's wife, 'Come let's go home. Let him do what he wants. You have to go to Tohri.'

Dulan's wife and Latua visit Tohri repeatedly to enquire at the thana about Dhatua.

For a few days, Dulan clears the undergrowth. Prepares the land. Then he takes the seeds from his house, telling his wife, 'These seeds are not for eating. I'll sow them.'

'On that land!'

'Yes.'

Scattering the seeds on the land, he chants, like a mantra, 'I won't let you be just aloe and putush. I'll turn you into paddy, Dhatua. I'll turn you into paddy.'

When the seedlings appear, everyone comes to see them. Lachman, Makhan or Ramlagan's fertilizer-fed seedlings are nothing in comparison. These seedlings are as green as they are healthy.

Fallow land, new seedlings. Everyone says so. Dulan, irritated, drives everyone away. He'll do the ploughing and sowing himself, and savour the fresh green by himself.

The pahaan says, 'Lachman Singh would have died of envy if he'd seen this.'

'Who?'

Dulan is indifferent.

'Lachman Singh.'

'Where is he?'

'Gone to Gaya. To his in-laws' place.'

'Oh!'

Then the paddy grows. Tall, strong, healthy plants. A wonderful crop. The paddy ripens. Now Dulan's extreme insanity is revealed.

He says, 'I'm not going to harvest the crop.'

'What? After all the labour of cutting the canal and draining the stagnant water this past monsoon, after staying there day and night, after I wore myself to death carting ghato and water for you each day—you won't reap?'

'No, and no one is to come here. I've work to do.'

'What work? Just sitting?'

'Yes. Just sitting.'

What he was waiting for occurred. Lachman returned for the harvest. The news of Dulan's bumper crop reached him. A year has passed since Dhatua's murder. Lachman is in control of himself again.

Lachman comes to Dulan. Dulan knew he would come. He knew.

'Dulan.'

'Malik, protector?'

'Come here.'

'What's this, you're alone?'

'Don't talk rubbish. What's the meaning of this?'

'What?'

'Why is there paddy on this land?'

'I planted it.'

'What was agreed between us?'

'You tell me.'

'Son of a bitch, didn't I tell you not to farm this land? To leave it as jungle—'

Dulan below, Lachman on horseback. All at once, Dulan grabbed Lachman's foot and pulled hard. Lachman fell. His rifle flew and landed some distance away from him. Then the rifle was in Dulan's hand. Before Lachman could recover his wits, the butt of the rifle slammed into his head. Lachman screamed. Dulan smashed the butt into his collar bone. A snapping sound.

Son of a bitch, bastard... Frightened, Lachman realized that he was crying before Dulan. Tears of agony and terror. He, Lachman Singh, prostrate on the ground, and Dulan Ganju standing erect? He lunged at Dulan's foot and winced because Dulan had hurled a rock at his outstreched hand. It would be a long time before he could use his right hand again.

'Animal! Cur!'

'What was our agreement, malik? That I shouldn't farm. Why not? You'll sow corpses, and I'll guard them. Why? Otherwise you'll burn down the village, kill my family. Very good. But, malik, seven boys—seven. Is it right for only wild, thorny underbrush to grace their graves? So, I sowed paddy, you see. Everyone says I've gone mad. I have, you know. I won't let you go today, malik, I won't let you harvest your crop. Won't let you shoot, burn houses, kill people. You've harvested enough.'

'Do you think the police will let you go?'

'If they don't, they don't. Your henchmen, too will probably go for me. But when haven't they, malik? Has the police ever let up on us? So they'll beat me—if I die, so be it. Everyone dies sometime. Did Dhatua die before his time?'

Knowing that he was helpless, Lachman Singh was filled with the fear of death. But even in the throes of this fear, in southeast Bihar, the Rajput will never beg the lowborn for mercy. Even if he did, the lowborn will not always be able to gift him his life. As Dulan could not.

As Lachman tried his best to stand up, shout, or lift a stone with his left hand, Dulan said, 'What a pity, malik! You had to die by a Ganju's hand!'

He began to smash Lachman's head with a rock. Over and over again. Lachman a professional killer, knew the value of a bullet, so murder was no cause for disturbance. He would have killed Dulan with a single bullet.

Dulan is not used to killing, a rock has no value, this death is the result of years of intense mental turmoil. He continued to smash Lachman's head in till he knew he could stop.

Dulan stood up. There were many things to be done, one by one. He led the horse forward by the reins, brought a stick down on its haunches and drove it off. Let it go where it will. He lashed Lachman, gun and all, with a rope, dragged him away and dumped him in a ditch. Then he rolled stone after stone into it. Stone after stone. Laughter begins to well up inside him. So, malik, protector, you're like the disgusting Oraon Munda? Buried under stones? A stony grave?

No telltale signs were likely to remain on the hard, rocky ground. But he broke off a leafy branch from a nearby putush bush to sweep away any marks of a struggle. Then he climbed onto the machan.

The search for Lachman continued for a few days. Since he never consulted anyone, Lachman had not mentioned that he was going to see Dulan. This was only natural, since his dependence on Dulan had to be kept secret. Those of his henchmen who knew kept their mouths shut. When the malik protector himself goes missing, when his horse is discovered grazing on Daitari Singh's land, why irritate a fresh wound? Lachman's servant said, 'He drank his sweetened milk as usual, and rode off. How do I know where he went?'

A very strange business. Only when the hyenas began to howl did people begin to get suspicious. That too, five days later. For five days, the scavengers, smelling flesh beneath the stones, howled, and with great effort shifted the stones, but managed to devour only the face. The strategic cunning with which the corpse was concealed, plus the presence of the horse in his fields, led to Daitari being suspected. Lachman's son supported this view and, because of an old history of feuds, Daitari was questioned for a few days. Then the police gave up for lack of evidence, though Lachman's son and Daitari continued the old tradition of conflict. At no stage did any suspicion touch Dulan. It was natural not to suspect him. Impossible to imagine Dulan killing Lachman, whatever the circumstances.

∽

On the one hand, Lachman-related investigations continue, on the other, a new, contented Dulan descends from the machan. He speaks to the pahaan, and as a result, all of Kuruda village gathers in the pahaan's courtyard one evening.

Dulan says, 'I've never given anyone anything, ever.'

Everyone is stunned.

'All of you praised my crop. When I didn't harvest it, you said

I was mad. While I was farming, you called me mad. You called this fool a fool. Now listen to what this madman has to say.'

'Go ahead!'

There is a sense of relief after Lachman's death. Right now, no one wants to worry about the son taking on the father's role.

'My paddy is your seed. Take it.'

'You're giving it away?'

'Yes, take it, reap it. There's a long story behind this—did I use fertilizer? Yes I did, very precious fertilizer.' Dulan's voice disappears like the string of a severed kite losing itself in the sky. Then, clearing his throat he says, 'You harvest it. Give me some, as well, I'll sow it again and again.'

After they promise that they will harvest the crop when the time came, Dulan returns to his land. His heart is strangely, wonderfully light today! He stands on the embankment and looks at the paddy.

Karan, Asrafi, Mohar, Bulaki, Mahuban, Paras and Dhatua—what amazing joy there is in the ripe, green paddy nourished on your flesh and bones! Because you will be seed. To be a seed is to stay alive. Slowly, Dulan climbs up to the machan. A tune in his heart. Dhatua made up this song. Dhatua, Dulan's voice trembles as he says the name. Dhatua, I've turned you all into seed.

THE KING'S HARVEST
CHETAN RAJ SHRESTHA

Whenever [a man] loses something, whether valuable or not,
he will console himself, even without consulting a divinity,
that the loss was primarily for the welfare of his own health.
—Norbu Chopel, *Folk Culture of Tibet*

June 2005

The city was built by demons, of that he was sure. Tontem had just
caught his first glimpse of Gangtok as he climbed up the hill in a
giant wheeled rat. Through the pitiless churning of his stomach he
saw the hill honeycombed with cement boxes, all of them bigger than
the monastery and the kothi, the two abodes of his distant childhood.
As they lurched through the unceasing rain, he looked up at the city
again to confront the mirage with repeated prayers. He knew there
was an evil involved, for this strangeness could not have come about
by human effort alone. Then the highest clouds parted, a hundred
thousand windows glittered in the afternoon sun, and Tontem saw the
city for what it was: the worthy citadel of a great king, who, thirty-two
years ago, had entrusted him with the farthest estate in his empire.

'Where have we come? What land is this?' Tontem asked the
driver of the wheeled rat, though he knew the man did not speak
his language. It seemed that nobody did.

His daughter Batti answered. 'You know everything,' she said, 'you
tell us.' She looked faint, her good eye watery with nausea. Turist, her
brother, was asleep next to her, head on her shoulder.

Tontem did not answer her. He pulled down his cap over his pig-like ears and shut his eyes to the moving, colourful and senseless world outside the windows of the groaning rat.

Tontem had undertaken the journey with the reluctance of a man who had never yearned for sights. Lhaizalzed, where he came from, was so far away from the capital that only two people in Gangtok would have heard of it, the king himself—the Chogyal—and his trusted minister, Dandu Kazi. But Tontem's compulsions were irrefutable; the rains were about to pass and the king's share of the harvest had not been collected for three winters now. It was an aberration without precedence, because for twenty-nine years before that, the king's dues had been collected with lunar precision. Tontem had dithered for months, until his mind was finally made up for him by two factors: an unshakeable loyalty which prevented him from appropriating his master's share, and the sorrow of seeing the same share, which he had kept aside in sacred fealty and which came to one thousand and twenty-nine sacks of rice, maize and cardamom, devoured by worms and flies.

As the taxi climbed Gangtok hill, the rain returned and the glittering city retreated behind a liquid curtain. The people beside the road disappeared into their holes. The rain knocked on the metal roof, and to Tontem it sounded like a hundred angry spirits seeking entry into the rat. The driver showed them how to roll the windows up, but then the air inside smelled of steamed vomit and sweat and he cursed and stuck his head out in the rain.

Turist stirred and asked his father, 'Why is it raining in a place without fields?'

Tontem replied, 'The king has heard of our arrival. He's cleaning the city as we enter it.'

The traffic halted, and the taxi stood still. Batti said, 'He should have done it yesterday.'

Tontem shoved his daughter, rude from her first moment of speech. The driver stopped the taxi to open all its windows again and air it. Tontem looked outside; the world was briefly still and he saw that it was a watery cage. He had timed his departure in the wet season, between the seeding of the rice and the harvesting of the second yield of maize. The days were long, the earth as wet as his tongue, and swarms of leeches infested the hills beyond Lhaizalzed like a divine curse, but it was the best time. The journey out of Lhaizalzed had originally been to meet Kaila Sardar at Yeigang, only four hills away. Kaila Sardar was the collector of the king's share of the harvest and in three decades had established a friendship with Tontem far greater than his worth as a collaborator in trade. But he had not been sighted in Lhaizalzed for three years. Tontem had left home only to meet him, and then his journey had turned into a demonic errand, making him travel for three days to Gangtok, a place he had never seen and one that he would be happy to leave.

Tontem spat out a curse, for even after hours of dreaming of death inside the rat, whose noise tortured his ears and whose motions turned his empty stomach, he was not at all certain how the journey would end.

∽

He had gathered his motherless family the evening before his departure—Chyadar, Cimit, Batti and Turist. Chyadar was the eldest, with a strength that came close to matching Tontem's own. He had seen thirty-two winters, and spent the last ten years in a continuous grumble for a wife. Cimit was fifteen winters younger and his elder brother's faithful helper. He caused an annual inconvenience when he disappeared before the rains to shake off the wandering spell that came over him. Batti was at an age when her father inspected the corner she slept in every morning for the crimson evidence of womanhood. And Turist, the youngest, had seen eight winters, enough to know that his brothers were the mightiest people in the world. Tontem's second wife, Wangmo, had died giving birth to Turist on a day when the floor of the forest was strewn with the rusting white flowers of the chilauney trees, an observation that made him remember her with fondness at least once a year.

Dinner was extravagant that evening. They slaughtered their smallest hen and sprinkled the last of their stock of salt on it. As always,

Tontem and Chyadar ate most of the meat, and they passed on the bones with remnants of flesh to Cimit and Batti, and then to Turist who sucked out the marrow from hidden hollows and made whistles out of the leg bones. After dinner, Batti and Turist cleared the hearth blackened by years of soot and whispered to each other about what lay beyond their valley.

Turist asked his father where they were going. Tontem scratched his deformed ears where he experienced a perennial itch and said, 'To Kaila Sardar's house at Yeigang.'

He told them of his decision: he would leave in the morning for Yeigang, four hills away, accompanied by Batti and Turist, all carrying samples of the harvest. They would reach at sundown and there Tontem would find respite from a mystery that had haunted him for six harvests. Why had Kaila Sardar, the king's trusted and punctual collector, and Tontem's only friend, stopped coming to Lhaizalzed from Yeigang to collect the king's share of the harvest? Was he sick, had he left Yeigang, and did he know of the decaying harvest in a damp barn which stank throughout the valley while pests buzzed around it as if it were a giant's corpse? And worse, the harvests this year promised to be the most sumptuous of all that he had raised since he came to Lhaizalzed. Tontem and his children had observed the unusual regularity of the rains and felt the saplings stiffen under their touch.

But even as he explained the need for the journey, Tontem already knew what he would discover at Yeigang. Two days ago, he had seen his friend in a dream wearing new clothes, and he had woken up with the knowledge that Kaila Sardar had already passed from this life to the next. 'We also need some salt. And I think my friend has fallen from this world,' he told his children.

Tontem became reflective then, as he often did after eating meat. He scratched the soles of his feet, to take care of the incessant itch that had nagged him since his dream. The tiny flaps of skin over his ears drooped as he repeated for his children the only story that he knew, the story of his life, and one that, like their salt, had to be consumed a bit at a time and over many seasons.

The tale that Tontem told his children, of his origins and his fortune, is one that cannot be told in his words, for those words are weary and taking their last breaths, spoken now by only a scattered few who cannot find their way to a common house. So it must be recounted in a borrowed tongue, as must the events that followed his departure from Lhaizalzed. These words will be embroidered by imagination, and betrayed by memory, and should be tolerated only because they contain more prophecy than faith, and more faith than fidelity.

∽

Many years ago, when his children were forest animals that had not yet entered the realm of humans, Tontem was a child in Toring village, situated on a red-soiled hill far away towards the setting sun. The houses of the village freckled the hill, and at its centre was the Toring Yabla's estate, where Tontem had been born. And precisely in the middle of the estate was a large two-storied kothi, painted as blue as the Losoong sky and so spacious that fifty people could sleep in it. At its head was the giant-shouldered Yabla who had married the bloodless Chumla for an heir. The Chumla had given him a son after eight years of marriage and then refused to share his bed on the irrefutable grounds that her duty was done and her freedom fairly won.

From Toring the Kanchenjunga range appeared as a distant and majestic rock which began the day as naked as an infant and by midday had settled on a throne of clouds. Between the village and the mountains, there was a hill whose slope resembled the back of a sleeping dragon. On the crest of the dragon's back stood a golden-roofed monastery from which rose occasional plumes of smoke and, on auspicious mornings, the sonorous rhythms of the gyalings, that travelled through the air to reach Tontem's ears as he slept in the servant's hut he shared with his mother. Sometimes Tontem had to sleep alone when the Yabla sent for his mother to prepare a dish whose knowledge was her preserve alone. She told Tontem that it was a heathen confection which took all night to make and had to be eaten in the greatest secrecy. It was the source of the Yabla's strength and wisdom. But he could tell no one, not even Palden, for if word

did get out, there would be a death curse on the cook, his mother.
Tontem never got to see, smell or taste the dish, and he still thought
of it sometimes, almost fifty years later.

Tontem's mother belonged to a clan from the mountains that had
stayed sequestered throughout history and had come down to the hills
only in the last century, attracted by the advantages of agriculture. They
came down first to the lands of the Tibetans, then lower down to
those of the Lepchas, and were gradually beginning a further descent,
this time to the foothills, which the Nepalis had recently made home.
They spoke a language that had evolved in isolation and differed from
the other prevalent ones because it had as many signs as sounds. There
were many of Tontem's kinsmen in the areas around Toring. Some had
converted to Buddhism and worshipped at Dragonback Monastery.
A great many worked in the Toring estate and their language was
common within it, spoken, amongst others, by the Yabla himself, who
had learnt it only to better oversee the workers in his fields.

Tontem's mother told him how she had come to Toring as a
child, and seen her mother die from diseases they had no protection
against. She had grown up in the kothi, and had never married despite
the numerous clansmen who had sworn to look after her. Tontem's
birth had been a miracle, for it had been a fatherless affair. But it
was not this wizardry that got Tontem noticed in the estate. It was
his ears. Instead of the mushroomed folds that everyone possessed, he
had been born with two flaps of cartilage that drooped like winter
leaves over pea-sized holes.

People mocked him on some days and revered him on others, for
they had no way of telling whether his deformity was an auspicious
curse or evidence of a damnable previous life. When Tontem asked
his mother about it, she told him that it was because he had been a
fish in his previous life who had swum the waters of the mountain
lakes, while the other servants had been large-eared dogs scavenging
for shit. Tontem learnt to grow his hair until it covered his ears and
the taunts receded. The solution was partial, though, for while the hair
shielded his ears from sight and ridicule, a slight bump on either side
of his head was always visible. Nevertheless the ruse held for decades

until destiny withdrew the protection and he went bald soon after the birth of his youngest child.

Tontem found respite in the company of Palden, the Yabla's youngest son. He was the only one whose mockery Tontem was spared, because, having one eye smaller than the other, he knew the torments of a deformity. When Tontem was as old as Turist was now, they were together all the time. One day in particular was especially memorable. It was after the Saga Dawa festival, on the fifteenth day of the fourth Buddhist month, which commemorates the birth, enlightenment and parinirvana of the Enlightened Sage. The two friends, who were the same size, nicked Palden's silken festival clothes from the clotheslines in the yard. Tontem wore these clothes and discovered that Palden and he could pass off as brothers. And so they went to the men in the fields and announced their brotherhood. Yes, you are brothers, the men said and laughed to each other. Then they went to the maids in the kitchen and the scullery. Of course, the two of you look alike, they said and laughed. Then they went to the Yabla, who laughed the loudest of all and asked them to tell that to the Chumla, Palden's mother. The Chumla looked at them, sniffed, stripped the silk off Tontem, and sent him naked to his mother, who whipped him so hard that he had to sleep on his stomach for a month.

'Never forget you are a servant unless you want to die eating money,' she said.

By his thirteenth year, Tontem was almost as tall as the Yabla and as broad-shouldered, while the Yabla's own son, Palden, remained slight and pale, a reflection of his mother. As he grew older, Tontem came to resemble the Yabla more visibly, making his mother blush and leaving him secretly happy. He resented his miraculous conception and would have preferred the parentage of the Yabla, so strong that no bears had been seen in Toring since his birth. As the resemblance grew, jealousy twisted the minds of their fellow servants until there came a time when Tontem worked in the fields with men who would not speak to him and his mother worked in the kitchen with women who would not stop talking. She spat on their contempt and asked Tontem to ignore them. The rest were servants because they either had the iron burden of debt on their backs or the stamp of slavery on their souls, while Tontem and his mother were so because the Yabla was taking his time to make up his mind about which house and how many fields to give them for their superior skills.

During Tontem's fifteenth year, after the first maize harvest, word of the secret dish must have escaped from the Yabla's private kitchen for his mother lost the blood from under her fingernails. Two months later the tip of her nose began to sweat, a month later her hearing disappeared, and her exhaled breath turned as cold as the winter wind at midnight. The fever took away her senses of taste and smell, her limbs lost their heat and when a black mark appeared in the centre of her tongue the village shaman was called in to exorcise the curse. He emerged from his trance admiring the ferocious tenacity of the spirit that had possessed her. The blood emanating from her mouth increased from a dribble to a stream, and seven hours after the shaman conceded defeat she vomited out her intestines and went still. When they laid out her corpse, it was as pale as the khadas they had garlanded it with. After her death ceremonies they burnt pine leaves for a week to purify the kothi. Then the Yabla called Tontem and gave him some money and said, 'Your ears are like paper because of your past sins.' To atone for those sins, the Yabla asked him to go to the Dragonback Monastery, whose monks were his clansmen and were expecting him. Tontem was touching money for the first time in his life and his steps staggered under the weight of the three coins. The Yabla also gave him some remnants of old brocades, speckled with green, yellow and red, and from these Tontem fashioned a gown of rags. He walked through the forests looking like a king without dominions and after a day and a night reached the Dragonback Monastery, located between Toring and the mountains and ruled by an Abbot who conversed with the spirits of saints during his daytime meditations and made peace with the wrathful deities in his dreams.

∞

Batti asked her father, 'Where is this village of yours?'

'Far away, but you'll never see it.'

'Why?'

'Because of your stubbornness.'

It was only half an admonition, for the day before, Tontem had watched as she had persevered through the afternoon to light a fire from two witch-stones while it rained outside. Their matches, a beneficent annual gift from Kaila Sardar, were exhausted now and the empty boxes had been made into a garland which hung around the photograph of the king, also gifted by Kaila Sardar.

∽

The Dragonback Monastery was ancient, painted white and red in lime. It had a spire that glistened more than gold and, inside, a great bronze idol of Guru Padmasambhava, the fierce saint who, thirteen centuries ago, had converted the lands of Sikkim, Bhutan and Tibet to the ways of the Buddha. The two-storeyed monastery faced east so that the first rays of the sun lit up the golden faces of the deities. Its walls were as thick as the span of a man's arms, and had been built with mammoth stones carried up from the river valley by men invested with the power of demons and then compacted with a glue extracted by boiling the hides of dead bulls. Within these walls he saw that the gyalings whose sounds had tempered his morning sleep at Toring were as tall as a man and were made from the thigh bones of a long-dead giant. The front of the monastery had a circular court with an obelisk marking its exact centre, and scattered around it were the huts where eighty-seven monks lived.

There were two central figures in the monastery: the Abbot and the Lopen, and they presided over monks orphaned by the world and adopted by the gods. The Abbot was the superior one, the last reincarnation in an illustrious lineage, whose powers as a shaman were equalled only by his reputation as a herbalist. Every winter he retreated for three months into a cave on the northern edge of the monastery's estate. Here he meditated in seclusion and was fed once a day through a hole in the earthen wall. In reality, it was the Lopen, a pumpkin-headed man with the growl of a wolf and a slave-master's reputation, who was in charge. He was the only teacher in the monastery, and all that he knew had been imparted to his students ten times over. He was the one who administered the monastery, taught its students, looked after their food and clothes, whipped them for misdemeanours and expelled them for transgressions that were too grave for forgiveness.

They took Tontem in and soon lamented that he had no aptitude for learning. They gave him the task of cleaning the monastery's surroundings, and after half-a-year he graduated to helping in the kitchen. One day the cook was ill and Tontem was given his charge for the day. That evening Tontem found out the truth behind the Lopen's reputation, when, after the meal was returned even by the starving Abbot inside his cave, the Lopen thrashed him with the explanation that the food they ate was so simple—rice, spinach, squash and potatoes—that it would take more malice than incompetence to spoil it.

Tontem continued to grow taller and stronger. A year after his arrival, he surpassed the Lopen in height. They removed him from the kitchen to fell trees and carry firewood. Once a year, he put on the vestments of the demon in the Chhaam dance. It was during one of these dances, when everyone wore masks and costumes to act out ancient stories, that Tontem had his first taste of chi, extracted from the best millet. He had successive cups of that sweet liquid which confers beauty on coquettes and idiocy on the wise, and then demanded the rest of the dancers sacrifice their share to him, which they did, for his physique, his demon's vestments and his half-intoxicated aggression partnered perfectly in making him appear as an agent of hell. In the second half of the ancient dance, much to the appreciation of the gathered villagers, there was a deviation from the millennial script as the demon refused to be vanquished even when inelegantly wrestled to the ground by the six wrathful deities in ferocious masks. Victory for the forces of good only came when Tontem collapsed under the combined weight of the six deities, four villagers and his own hallucinations.

When he woke up, he found himself tied to a tree near the Abbot's retreat hut. An enquiry had established the reason for the afternoon's laughable misfortune. He was cursed by the Lopen for having ears like horns, which made him a reincarnation of Lang Dharma, the forty-first king of Tibet, evil and horned, who had wasted his life trying to remove Buddhism from his country. Tontem was denied food and drink for four days until the rebellious energy had sapped itself. At the end, famished and vanquished, he was brought back from the nearest of the six heavens by the Abbott who fed him ox soup and told him, 'Never take anything that doesn't belong to you. Theft combines all the three evils at the centre of the wheel of life: ignorance, lust and greed.'

Soon after the incident, the Abbot had a dream in which the monastery was destroyed by a very large yellow mouse with no legs and no ears that came up on a road wider than any they had ever seen. Tontem was then given a windowless hut at the edge of the estate and asked to guard the entry to the monastery, for who better to defend it than its strongest man. He stood guard at the path between the two largest trees and spent his days looking out towards the valley and all around him, letting all men pass, but keeping an eye out for any large rodent.

∽

At this point in his story, Tontem paused for water and Batti asked, 'Did you ever see those demon rats?'

'No.'

'What will you do if you see one?'

'In my younger days I would have killed it with one hand but now, nothing.'

∽

Tontem waited at his post for two years. The only significant event in his tenure as sentinel occurred on his final day at the monastery when, one wet summer's day, Tontem saw a tall stranger with a moustache huff towards him, bow with courtly respect and try four tongues before settling on Tontem's language. There was a sick man on the horse track that skirted the valley, and he was going to die without the attentions of a compassionate hand. Tontem checked him for weapons, asked him if he carried any rats on his person and then gave him directions to the Abbot's quarters. Soon, the Abbot summoned Tontem, and said that he was so old he feared that to leave the monastery was to bid it a final farewell, something he was loath to do, for despite what the scriptures said about detachment, he wanted to die where he had been born. The patient would have to be brought to him and Tontem was going to do it. The Abbot then gave Tontem an arrow to hold while carrying the man uphill.

Tontem rushed down the hill like a bear fleeing wasps. He reached the horse track and saw a group of men beside a humpbacked rock under a leafless tree. They recognized him as the Abbot's emissary. The sick man was lying on the ground and gasping from an unconquerable pain in his stomach. Tontem hauled him onto his shoulder and raced up the hill and as he did so, he felt the man grow fainter. The arrow helped, and with strides that he would have found impossible to match on other days he made rapid progress up the hill. He reached the monastery to find that the Abbot had already prepared a palliative made from pepper. By the time his companions arrived, the sick man had recovered, and was embarrassing the Abbot by offering everything he had in appreciation of the cure for an ailment that had dogged him since childhood and for which the only known cure had been patience.

Tontem had never seen a kinder face than that of the man who thanked the Abbot in a language whose refined cadences made his listeners confront the crudeness of their lives. He was dressed in a dark bakhu whose regality absorbed all light. He wore no jewellery and his head of full black hair was adorned with lightning streaks of grey. And yet the mystery of his identity plagued the Abbot and the Lopen, for the man himself deflected all questions about his origin. Two hours later the visitor's tall moustached companion reached the monastery and announced that their visitor was the Chogyal, the King of Sikkim, the latest in a three-hundred-and-thirty-year lineage, and husband to three queens, one each from the Tibetan provinces of Kham, Amdo and Tsang. The Abbot scolded the tall stranger for concealing the king's identity even when his life seemed doomed. The Chogyal indicated that the order had come from him when he said, 'I'm already half a commoner.'

The Chogyal introduced the tall stranger as Dandu Kazi, his most trusted companion, whose bearing was statelier but who appeared less regal because of his complete deference to his master. The two of them, along with their retainers, were on a survey of the Chogyal's fifty-hill kingdom, set like a ruby on a knuckle between Nepal and Bhutan. This journey would take them from the glacial origins of the Teesta in the alpine north to its tropical confluence with the Rangeet in the south, with diversions at Uttarey in the west where Sikkim bordered Nepal and to Gnathang in the east, bordering Bhutan. He was also going to visit his own estates. They had left Gangtok three days ago, and had travelled against the innumerable stoppages forced by his subjects who wanted to pay obeisance to their sovereign. They were now on their way to Tuminthang, the ancestral seat of Dandu Kazi, before proceeding to Lhaizalzed in the northwest: the furthest, the most bountiful and the most neglected of all the king's inherited estates.

Tontem had never heard of any of these distant places, except Gangtok, which, of course, everyone knew about, for it was the king's home, and he felt proud to be the subject of a master who seemed to rule all the known lands. The Abbot listened with complete attention and then he sniffed in apology for his austere hospitality, but the Chogyal admonished him for his modesty and announced a gift of three cows and seven goats to be delivered from his nearest farm. The Lopen then mentioned how difficult it was for the monks to study, crammed in their small rickety house that had to pass for a sheda. The Chogyal decreed that a school be built in gratitude for his second life.

In return, the Chogyal asked that Tontem be relieved from the monastery's service and allowed to become a member of his royal guard, the praetorian force responsible for his corporeal protection. The Abbot nodded and the Lopen clapped, while the honour's recipient wept at the prospect of being untethered from the people who had shielded him from the world's mockery for three years. The Lopen whacked him on the head with the Abbot's walking stick for his devil-inspired idiocy, and the issue was settled. Shortly before dusk, the Chogyal and the Kazi took their leave of the protesting Abbot and returned to the valley, where a camp had been made, and left Tontem to his final, grieving night at the Dragonback Monastery.

At dawn, before the stars dissolved, Tontem smoothed his hair around his ears and met the Abbot, who pressed three crisp ten-rupee notes into his hand, and the Lopen, who asked him to remain detached from everything in life, for all was transitory. Tontem was eighteen years old, and the possessor of thirty rupees.

When the king's entourage resumed its journey towards Tuminthang, a day's trek away, Tontem rode behind the actual guards, erect and silent on their sombre horses. At the head he could see the Chogyal and Dandu Kazi in deep conversation as they rode abreast, wearing wide-brimmed hats against a drizzle as steady as their paces. The guards had seen Tontem's unsurpassable strength, and now they treated him with an aloof respect and gave no indication that they knew either the language of his clan or his deformity.

The drizzle stayed with them as a constant and inconvenient companion. To avoid steep climbs, they took detours through oily green glades fresh from the rains, beside swift rivers rushing towards their placid destinies in the seas of the south and along narrow ancient tracks that only the most experienced of the king's horsemen could trace under the monsoon's legacy of moss and algae.

It was Tontem's first time on a horse and he soon slipped to the rear where he met the cook, who travelled with the food cart. The cook was cheerful and talkative, born to a yak-herder in the far north, and in his early life of trade he had learnt Tontem's language. He told Tontem that Dandu Kazi's grandfather had been the headman of Tuminthang village when history came looking for him seventy years ago. He was recruited by the British to manage their horses and yaks when they invaded Tibet and marched to Lhasa. He had returned from the trip wise about the limitations of the spirits when it came to modern warfare and had joined the Chogyal's service as an advisor. In return for his unmatched intuition, he was granted Tuminthang, with its priceless cardamom plantations, as a fiefdom. When he died, his son proved that he had inherited the same circumspect wisdom, but he went young, dying of a weak heart three months before the birth of his first son. Thus it was that Dandu Kazi was born in Gangtok and nurtured by the former Chogyal, who raised him with his son, the prince. In time, Dandu Kazi had joined the king's service early, and proved his grasp over matters of state with the same quiet fervour that had won his grandfather such renown.

∽

Cimit interrupted his father to ask, 'How long ago was this?'
'In the year 1973.'
'What does it mean?'
'What do I know? I heard someone say it.'

∽

At sundown they reached the village of Tuminthang, perched on the shoulder of a ravine which overlooked the Tuminchu River as it plunged down a gorge. The village was a mosaic of huts on stilts with thatched roofs, each with garlands of drying corn slung on their eaves and surrounded by idle cattle unimpressed by the visitors, unlike their owners who now lined the muddy street, their faces aglow with reverence for a king who had treated their illustrious kazi as an equal. The party stayed at Dandu Kazi's kothi, which rested on pedestals of stone, had an exterior enriched with carved timber work and which, at forty paces wide and fifty paces long, dwarfed all that Tontem remembered of the Toring Kothi. There was also a timber-latticed balcony on the eastern façade with a hole in the floor for visiting grandee monks from Tibet to shit through while the most reverential amongst the laity fought below for pieces of the sacerdotal excretions.

The quarters for the guards were small and Tontem was asked to find his own bed. He found some space in the store next to the housekeepers' quarters. Inebriated by fatigue and tormented by saddle-burn, Tontem slept soundly on the earthen floor to a symphony of howls in the forest outside.

He woke up startled when he felt a hand slide up his bakhu and ambush his startled piss-pipe. The attacker revealed herself as a clanswoman when she said, 'If you're really as strong as they say you are then chase me out of here.'

He could not see her because the night was as black as the one in which demons misplace their souls. He wanted to fight her but his genitals, which had never asserted themselves before, defected to her side. She won the one-sided wrestling bout, straddled him, and rode him with a lunatic frenzy. Tontem felt his ear-lids flap as they did in moments of preternatural excitement and he knew that not even the most compassionate of deities would ever forgive such joy. She caught his head when she bucked and her hands smelled of soot and cheese. Soon, he felt something thicker than urine push its way through and when it emerged, all the instruments of the monastery clanged in his head, the jackals ceased their rival howls and he touched his ears to feel them erect and stiff.

Immediately, his benefactor left in silence and the next morning a distraught Tontem sniffed the hands of all the maids in the kothi and realized with devastation that all of them smelled of soot and cheese. Through the cook he asked each of the maids if she had been the one to empty his balls and conquer his heart but they only laughed at him. Each one swore that nothing would ever induce her to fuck an earless monster for they had heard about his deformity from the guards. The cruellest amongst them snuck up from behind, raised his hair, exposed his unfortunate ears and showed everyone that the rumour of his accursed body was indeed true.

∽

Now, so many years later, on another earthen floor, Tontem sighed when he remembered the words 'earless monster'. His son Chyadar, insolent with horniness, said, 'At least you had a woman.'

'Quiet, you ungrateful ox. Go to sleep,' Tontem said and threw a stray piece of wood at him.

Chyadar, who was weaker than his father, stretched out beside the hearth and faced away.

∽

They left for the northwestern slopes of Lhaizalzed later that morning.

Tontem's head rang with the insults of the kazi's kitchen women and the sneers of the guards, for the cook had exposed his humiliation and they now banded to ridicule the erotic clarity of his imagination. At sundown they reached the edge of Dandu Kazi's property, brushed with alpine brambles and demarcated by a rivulet identified as the Teesta in its infancy. It was surrounded by fields that were tended by Kaila Sardar, Dandu Kazi's sharecropper and the lone resident of the valley. This was Yeigang and it lay at the forlorn junction of the horse track from Tuminthang, the trail to Lhaizalzed and a cobbled road that came in from the south and led eventually to Gangtok. Dandu Kazi explained that Yeigang took its name from the great rock shaped like an eagle's beak that rose up to its south. The eagle was a creature of legend, a vigilant sentinel now petrified but ready to come alive should anyone disturb the isolated sanctity of the valley. Across the river, they could see Chui Babzer, the snow-dappled range which guarded Lhaizalzed, four hills away.

They trotted towards a house in the centre of the fields and startled its occupant, who had just returned from a day in the fields. Kaila Sardar was a Paharey from Nepal whose forefathers had come to Sikkim three generations ago and assimilated with such earnestness that Kaila Sardar could speak almost every language of his adopted land, including Tontem's, learnt during a mysterious interlude that he never revealed. His face was creased and the long hours of work in that alpine valley had browned his skin to a Tibetan shade. When he saw his masters, he wept in relief for he had begun to think that he was the only human in the world. He offered a pig for slaughter and the party feasted on its roasted meat for dinner. He then offered his hut but the Chogyal declined this imposition and instead commanded his guards to pitch camp. Tontem was kept awake by a new yearning which could be neither understood nor suppressed. His torment did not let him sleep so he watched Dandu Kazi and Kaila Sardar in the hut, settling their accounts for the previous year, long after the camp had gone quiet.

The next day they left through an impenetrable fog and by afternoon reached the foothills of Chui Babzer. It was a sudden depression in the land, with waterfalls that emerged from its escarpments, for the walls surrounding the basin were giant and animate, absorbing and releasing water with cyclical breaths. The Chogyal turned around to say that this was where the gods came to wash themselves after their meals at Lhaizalzed, for a hundred and eight waterfalls, some magnificent and some minute, had been counted on the cliffs. They negotiated a pass through these cliffs and entered the final barrier before Lhaizalzed, a forest of leeches four hills deep which ringed the prized valley.

Now the guards rode ahead of the royal pair, hacking and slashing to clear the path which had long since been swallowed up by the forest. The leeches waiting in the trees with single-minded patience dropped on the party like raindrops and only the Chogyal and Dandu Kazi were protected by their hats. The abdomens and thighs of the horses turned black, but the commander of the guards forbade any cleansing, for a wiped out leech was bound to be replaced by a hungry one. Tontem alone remained untouched by the armies of bloodsuckers that rained down on their way, and speaking to himself, he attributed this luck to his sorrow, for he knew that the blood of a sad man has no taste, and the phrase 'earless monster' still rang in his head, on its way to becoming an eternal echo.

After the first hill, the harassment became intolerable and the camp rested amongst rocks. There, man and beast bathed with salt water and each was given a pouch of tobacco, the only known repellent for leeches. Still, the more aggressive, but less profuse, subspecies continued to torment them as they hacked through the osmotic wall of creepers and undergrowth. The torment abated as they neared the forest's edge. The weather changed from humid to cool, the leeches fell off the horses, the nettle plants thinned out and disappeared completely, and papayas and apples now dangled low on the branches in their path. Then, sometime after dusk, they emerged from the forest to look down on Lhaizalzed by the silver light of the moon.

The Chogyal said, 'We are now in the valley of constant light.'

In the moonlight that gave them clarity without warmth, they looked down on the valley bounded by low hills and saw the glint of a stream on its northern flank which sparkled its way soundlessly through the flat expanse. The valley was the largest Tontem had ever seen. Kaila Sardar whispered that it took a mounted man two hours to ride around it. Closer in the foreground, they could discern a hut without a roof.

The party paused to recover and the Chogyal told them the true history of Lhaizalzed. A long time ago, the god of food came upon this fertile valley and sat down for a feast, pausing only to take water from Chui Babzer. The feast extended for months, for there was nothing that did not grow here, and he ignored the famine that befell the people of Sikkim in his absence. At length, the greater gods came down and persuaded him to leave the valley, and Sikkim was once more prosperous. But Lhaizalzed, so used to attention, was disconsolate. It promised to keep producing until the god of food returned, but for this it set a non-negotiable condition. Every seed, whether it thrived in high altitudes or low, would find fruition here provided it was sown by an incomplete man, for the health of men was what had prompted the disappearance of their favourite god. The last successful caretaker, during the reign of the king's grandfather, had three missing fingers on his right hand. He had died alone and his successors had all failed because they were perfectly formed men unwilling to mutilate themselves.

Lhaizalzed was also the last stretch of habitable land before the Five Deaths Pass, the Chogyal told his entourage. That was the great pass leading to Tibet, so called because of five dangerous crevasses that had killed all but the most skilful of pilgrims and traders in the previous centuries before being bridged by a man called Younghusband on a delirium-inspired invasion of Tibet seventy years ago. Since then, like ants that have found another path, Tibetan caravans passed by Lhaizalzed regularly on their way to Yeigang, where an annual market was held six weeks after the festival of Lhosar. There, hard-nosed Tibetans bartered bricks of tea and salt, turquoise, beads, sacks full of amulets—each of which had been individually blessed by the Dalai Lama himself—for rice and meat. All this had vanished after the Chinese had overrun the Tibetans' homeland fourteen years ago.

The party reached the roofless hut, damp with moss and neglect. This was the hut where Younghusband and Dandu Kazi's grandfather had stayed on their way to Tibet. By firelight, Dandu Kazi guided the Chogyal to parts of the walls where some of the soldiers and sipahis bound for Tibet, terrified that they would die of sorcery or asphyxiation, had etched their own eulogies on the timber.

They camped outside the hut on the glade and set up a fire. And when alcohol had eased the differences between king and commoner, the Chogyal despaired that there was no hope for this valley with its implacable curse. He did not want the riches of the land; merely knowing that it was not barren would console him. Kaila Sardar asked if he could give it a try, he was willing to mutilate himself, cut a finger perhaps, but Dandu Kazi restrained his enthusiasm with a bark: how was he going to manage two fields, a day apart, on his own? When the dilemma was explained to Tontem, he stood up and exposed his ears to the Chogyal—who, although he had not seen them until now, took the sight in with equanimity—and pronounced himself an ideal candidate. Nothing would give him greater contentment than staying here, Tontem said. His ears had turned the world against him and this distant place would shield him from the world.

The Chogyal asked Tontem, 'Why would you renounce a life in the palace for this?'

Tontem did not speak but the cook gave up his soot-and-cheese secret with good cheer. The mists of sorrow lifted from the Chogyal's face and he smiled and said, 'Stay here, nothing cures heartaches like solitude. If only I had your good fortune.'

Tontem said, 'How much should I give you?'

Everyone but the Chogyal and Dandu Kazi laughed and after their laughter subsided, Tontem asked again. The Chogyal replied, 'A tenth from your year's harvest, after next year. Kaila Sardar will collect it from you. And learn to count well because I'm going to be just as honest.'

The Chogyal knew that an essential condition of pride is contempt for unreciprocated generosity. Tontem was a servant, but he was going to be an honourable one. Tontem also had another condition: he wanted a wife who could produce children, for that was the only way to make the valley fertile again. He was not going to farm the entire damn thing on his own. The kitchen women had mocked him but he knew from the sighs of his tormentor that his wife would not be unhappy. Again the guards laughed and this time the king and Dandu Kazi joined them. The cook shouted 'earless monster' from behind the largest guard. The Chogyal nodded at Dandu Kazi, who delegated the responsibility to Kaila Sardar who was going to be Tontem's closest neighbour and the collector of the king's share.

The next morning they could see the Kanchenjunga massif loom close above the valley like a benign guardian. The Chogyal decreed that all the provisions from the food cart be given to Tontem to see him through the winter, for sowing time had already passed. Dandu Kazi instructed Kaila Sardar to spend that winter in Lhaizalzed, helping Tontem prepare his house for habitation and his land for cultivation. Tontem welcomed the order. He also took advantage of a brief unguarded moment to deliver a strategic blow to the cook, which made sure he would have to endure the return journey riding sidesaddle. Kaila Sardar and Tontem watched as the Chogyal and the Kazi moved out of the glade and disappeared into the fog that hovered above the river like vapourized milk. Tontem followed the horses through the waist-high grass, shouting, 'A tenth! A tenth!' The rear horsemen beat him back with their whips and he cursed them for mistaking his joy for desperation.

∽

'How was Lhaizalzed then?' Cimit asked.

'There was nothing. The four of you have it easy.'

'And the spirits?'

'Defeated all but the one which makes you walk around without sense.'

∽

The spirits of Lhaizalzed appreciated Tontem's malformed ear and they left the two men alone, though Kaila Sardar said they had only retreated and were not yet extinct. He was right, and Tontem would quarrel with them later, but now, at the beginning of his stay, his concerns were more material. The land had to be cleared and the house repaired. Kaila Sardar helped him and his skill dovetailed with Tontem's strength as they repaired the house just in time to block out the howling winter. As it grew colder, Kaila Sardar was overcome with worry about his own house at Yeigang, and going against his master's orders he persuaded Tontem to let him go. Kaila Sardar washed his body in salt water and carried a bit of Tontem's blood in a pouch as a safeguard against leeches before departing, a precaution that he used for the next twenty-nine years.

Then the coldest winter Tontem had experienced came in and did its best to freeze the marrow in his bones. He often woke up to find his body stiff and his ears crisp with frost but his body could withstand everything the valley threw at him, and he thought less and less of the night of unrepeatable pleasure and instead spent his days in industry without contemplation. Sometimes it rained so hard that everything around him was drenched and the only dry place in the entire valley was the crack of his arse, which he used to preserve the thirty rupees that the Abbot had given him.

The spirits of the valley and its forests did not make it easier for him. While Tontem was left alone by the larger deities, he was pestered by the tantrums of the lesser spirits. The first months were notable for the war of loud words that he waged against them through the day, and for the fights that he had with the black demon nagas who came disguised as bears to raid his farms at night. These deities were finally propitiated with a week of prayers Tontem conducted just before the first harvest, supplemented by offerings of the first vegetables that had begun to sprout. The bears then took to visiting in the mornings, now manifestations of the medicine nagas, to take the offerings laid out for them, and this arrangement was never again disturbed.

When Kaila Sardar came visiting at the onset of spring with maize seeds, he was astonished to find that Tontem had cleared five acres of land which were now ripe for sowing. Four months later Kaila Sardar visited again and was left speechless by the golden sea of stalks that rippled in the breeze and later, when he visited after the rice harvest, he danced beside the three mounds that awaited him, the smallest one of which was as high as the chamfered eaves of Tontem's house. Even after they had proportioned the Chogyal's share, there was more rice than Tontem could eat over the year. They then established a tradition that was brilliant in its simplicity and promoted their friendship to a righteous pact that held for twenty-nine years. The harvest was divided into three parts: that which Tontem would consume, the king's share and the remainder which Kaila Sardar would purchase at ten rupees per sack. Tontem had earned only thirty rupees in his life so far, so he knew what a generous offer this was. Kaila Sardar also brought some roosters, a goat, and eventually, in a move that signified their deepening friendship, a cow and a bull.

As Tontem's farm expanded, he began to desire a family even more. In the fields he missed not having children to order around. And he missed a wife in the lonely moments before sleep came and in the hour before dawn when the cow mooed to be milked, for that was a woman's duty. Tontem did not lack for human contact, though. Kaila Sardar came by thrice every year: after the maize had ripened, after the rice had been threshed and then once before winter, when he would sell Tontem priceless things such as clothes, salt, kerosene, knives and blankets and adjust their costs from the purchases he made from the harvest. The only gift that Tontem had to refuse was a mirror.

For the first two years, Tontem and Kaila Sardar bundled the king's share and Kaila Sardar's purchases in jute sacks and carried them on their backs for two days until they reached Yeigang. Tontem stayed for a few days in Kaila Sardar's house, as empty as his own. These were the only times he left Lhaizalzed and he wanted to never return to the lonesome valley again, but each time the house he had rebuilt with his hands called to him. If only he had a wife, it might have been easier. His balls were heavy with desire sometimes and they throbbed with an ache that yielded to neither massages nor curses. He would remind Kaila Sardar of the Chogyal's instructions and ask if there was any progress in his quest for a bride for Tontem. Kaila Sardar would point to his own balls and announce his own loneliness. But Tontem reminded him that honour was honour. At that, Kaila Sardar promised to try harder and the men slept, each with his loneliness.

During his third year, on a day thick with rain, Tontem ventured into the forest to forage for wild vegetables. There he saw four wolves and four crows run and chatter together and pass him on some heinous errand. He returned to find that Kaila Sardar had arrived with news. The crown in Sikkim was under threat from a rebellion by the Pahareys in the west, where they wanted to usurp the king's powers in the name of something called democracy, which was people choosing others like themselves to replace kings, which was, they both agreed, an absurd idea. And the Pahareys were supported by the wily Indians, who waited on the outside like a fox after chickens. And some of the kazis like the Toring Yabla too were against the king—actually, the whole lot of Pahareys were led by a kazi, believe it or not. Tontem stood up in anger; if the Chogyal was in danger then Tontem's duty was beside him, even if he had to fight the man in whose mighty shade he had spent his childhood. Yes, he would fight: he had not forgotten that it was as a soldier he had first been chosen. Kaila Sardar then spent the next two days persuading Tontem that his duty remained in Lhaizalzed and that a true servant would not arrive without being called. He promised to get surer word from Gangtok as fast as his legs would allow.

Tontem then prepared his body and spirit for a life of war. But Kaila Sardar took his time and returned three full moons later, in the middle of a seven-day downpour. As the rain hissed outside, he told Tontem about the turn in the king's fortunes. The ant's nest in the west had been smashed and the conspirators had all been banished from the kingdom. The king was firmly on the throne with Dandu Kazi beside him, and his reign was prophesied to continue for thirty years and his lineage was to prosper for eternity. Even India, the great fox in the south, had retreated to the plains where it had come from, for who could mess with the land that had Guru Rinpoche as its protector. In his disappointed happiness, Tontem offered to send the king half his harvest, but Kaila Sardar mocked him for thinking he could make a difference to a man with twelve rooms full of jewels in his palace. Kaila Sardar also showed a letter to Tontem from the royal office, and read it out for him.

The letter assured Tontem of the Chogyal's good health and commanded his loyal subject to stay at Lhaizalzed and tend the fields, for it had become his most valuable estate, and to treat his messages sent through Kaila Sardar as his word. He had also sent Tontem two gifts, a metal statue of Guru Rinpoche that had been blessed by the Karmapa in Tibet, and a photograph of himself. Tontem bowed deeply when he received the gifts, and cleared a corner of his house for an altar where he installed the revered objects.

∞

Cimit waited for a pause in Tontem's story, then asked, 'Did the Chogyal visit again?'

Tontem stared at the floor and answered, 'No.'

Cimit said, 'If Lhaizalzed is so precious, why has the king not visited again?'

Tontem spat on the earthen floor and said, 'You fool! I show you a hundred cows and you ask me where the bull is.'

∞

It was a source of deep sadness for Tontem. Thrice, the king's visit had seemed imminent. As Kaila Sardar measured out the harvest for the fourth year, he mentioned in passing that the Chogyal was considering visiting Lhaizalzed. Tontem instantly began preparations to receive the king and waited with the patience of a tree for his sovereign's visit which Kaila Sardar had said would take place in the spring of the following year. But when Kaila Sardar arrived in spring to collect the year's first maize harvest on a yak, with three more trailing behind him, he was alone. The Chogyal would not be coming. And there was worse news. The Kancha Kumar, the Chogyal's son and the crown prince, had died in an accident. What was an 'accident'? Kaila Sardar didn't know. Tontem wept at his benefactor's misfortune. Their dinner was a solemn one and the next morning Tontem insisted on sending a gift to the king: some mushrooms whose ingestion produced visions that ensured a temporary banishment of grief. Kaila Sardar promised they would be delivered. Kaila Sardar left at the head of a small caravan, the yaks carrying three sacks of maize each; he looked like a Tibetan merchant with his fur-lined hat, and Tontem returned to his hut to mourn the loss of a future master.

But a man whose shoulders bear the burden of a nation must make time for other things besides grief. At the time of the rice harvest just before winter, Kaila Sardar reported that the king had recovered enough to be pleased with the staggering quantity of the harvests, for which man does not like to add to his wealth? The king had sent Tontem a token of appreciation, a medal usually awarded to only two kinds of men: those bravest in battle or those most loyal to the king. Tontem blushed with pride when he bowed his head as Kaila Sardar, in accordance with the king's wishes, garlanded him with the medal.

The king had also sent Tontem something just as priceless and far more useful. Kaila Sardar had come with ten large chyadars or sheets of galvanized corrugated iron, which Tontem had seen only on the roof of the Toring Kothi and the Dragonback Monastery. The Chogyal had sent them all the way from Gangtok, and Tontem was to replace his thatched roof with these, for the sheets did not require upkeep and when the time came to replace them, thirty years later, the Chogyal would send some more.

Tontem would have rewarded himself for his own acumen if he could. The grain that Kaila Sardar purchased from him so enriched him that he now had four hundred rupees to call his own. And every year, for twenty-nine years, he continued to earn ten rupees a sack. Tontem knew it was good money, from a generous man, his only friend. Occasionally, merely for variety's sake, he asked for an increase, and at such times Kaila Sardar had two pertinent observations: Tontem did not have any use for money, and prices in the great world outside were steadily falling for reasons that had their origins in the land of the foreigners. In fact, it was predicted that gold would soon be cheaper than iron, and in such times, Kaila Sardar could not call himself a true friend if he were to lower his prices for Tontem's produce in accordance with their value in the great world outside.

But Tontem did not take Kaila Sardar's protestations of friendship for granted. After the ninth rice harvest, he approached his caretaker with a message. If the Chogyal was indeed pleased with the increasing harvests, then surely he would consent to provide a wife, who would provide children, who would further the cultivable borders of Lhaizalzed. The Chogyal had given his word but maybe he needed to be reminded, Gangtok was only a four-day walk away. Kaila Sardar agreed the argument was flawless, but he also wanted to spare his friend the trials of an unknown journey. As he departed at the head of a six-yak caravan, he promised to visit Gangtok and remind the King of Sikkim and his trusted minister to provide a wife for Tontem.

A few moons later, Kaila Sardar made his only unexpected visit to Lhaizalzed, and he did not come alone. Accompanying him was a frail girl named Duwah. She was to be Tontem's bride and she barely spoke his language, although, said Kaila Sardar, that shouldn't be a problem because the reasons Tontem wanted her had little to do with speech. She had identical crescent birthmarks over her ears and Tontem took this as evidence of their intertwined fates. But when he thanked the kindness of the Chogyal, Kaila Sardar explained that he had not sent her, he was far too busy. Kaila Sardar had found her himself, and he had paid four hundred rupees for her, an amount that Tontem remunerated at once for his lightness of heart triumphed over his disappointment and his ten-winter wait had diluted all impulses of parsimony.

'May she make your seasons pass quicker,' Kaila Sardar told Tontem, and named all the natural aphrodisiacs found in the forests around, the one area where his knowledge of the earth's produce surpassed Tontem's. On their first night together, Duwah wept under the fury of Tontem's deprivation. After the first couple of hours, the heaviness in his balls disappeared, and by morning they had grown so light that he felt himself levitate. Duwah did not express any surprise when he revealed his ears; instead, she furthered his happiness by licking them during their intimate moments, inspiring an arousal that could only be a gift from the gods. They learnt to communicate through signs, and Tontem taught her his words. And though he never forgot the anonymous kindness of the woman at Dandu Kazi's house, he began to see his marriage for what it was: the nourishment of a daily meal against the repletion of a feast.

His bliss died when she revealed herself to be slothful. She did as she was told but no more. While she grew familiar with the cattle, the fowl and the vegetable patches, she was slow and Tontem had to nudge and sometimes beat her. When he complained to Kaila Sardar, he was reminded that a lazy wife was better than no wife at all, the only muscles that he should be bothering himself with were between her legs and in a few years Tontem would have an army working for him in the fields.

In this, too, he was disappointed. Duwah's womb filled twice over the next two years but one child survived for a month and the other for four months. And because they had died in infancy, they were destined to return as malicious spirits, something that terrified Tontem more than the loss of future farmhands. He took the precaution of letting the river take their corpses instead of performing a formal burial. The deaths confirmed Duwah's uselessness and he began to see her as an unshakeable burden with a cursed belly. He tried to sell her back for two hundred rupees to Kaila Sardar, who dissuaded him by revealing that some years ago the king had made it illegal to sell women.

Over the next year, Tontem realized that the children's deaths may have been caused by the absence of physical impairments in their mother. A birthmark wasn't enough. He talked it out with Kaila Sardar the next time he came, and once more the man from Yeigang proved his friendship by endorsing wholeheartedly Tontem's plans to amputate two fingers from Duwah's left hand. On Kaila Sardar's advice, he decided to wait until the full moon. Three days before the full moon, he saw rainbows in the night sky, which he knew portended the death of a king. But the apprehension caused by his pending crime did not let him get to Gangtok to find out, and when he returned home from the fields one day, determined to consummate his stated deed, he found that Duwah had absconded after two years of marriage.

Tontem was so tormented by the loss to his gardens and livestock that he ran all the way to Yeigang, questioning every animal he saw.

Along with Kaila Sardar he pursued her trail as far north as the last green tree and as far south as Dragonback Village. It was only when he remembered that the cows would have fallen sick from neglected udders that he returned. That year Kaila Sardar consoled him with the observation that women and roosters could never walk in a straight line and then gave him a better price for the harvest, eleven rupees per sack, but only for that one year, for he shared his friend's sorrow, and this made Tontem, who now remembered how much Duwah had cost him, weep all the more, for it would be at least two years before he could afford another wife. Kaila Sardar reminded him of the king who had lost a full-grown son but was still wise enough to ignore his sadness. At this Tontem's tears evaporated and he resolved to emulate the unwavering courage of his lord.

Tontem's recovery from Duwah's abandonment was strengthened by a message from the Chogyal in which he promised that his position as a man with fields but no family would soon be corrected. In the meantime, he was to wear this amulet, specially blessed by the high lamas of Chuklakhang, the royal chapel in Gangtok. Tontem kissed the amulet, pressed it to his eyes and promised to follow the instructions that would help him receive a wife and sons who would mature as quickly as bamboo.

Tontem learnt that the Chogyal had recovered from the Kancha Kumar's death and that Sikkim was again prospering within the confines of its high and craggy horizons. But there was also disturbing news: the banished Pahareys had regrouped in Nepal, where they had recruited more men to their cause, with promises of land, women and loot. Tontem stood up and volunteered again for Sikkim's army. He was still young, and had a lot of meat on his bones. Again, Kaila Sardar repeated the Chogyal's words: Tontem was the most valuable soldier he had, for he provided enough grain to feed a hundred soldiers. But alas, more was required. Tontem stood up again and offered to double the king's share. He was producing so much that more could be spared. Kaila Sardar then confessed that not only food but money was also needed to fight the looming battles. He had come with cardamom seeds from the king's plantation in Rabongla and Tontem was to plant them on the slopes around the valley. Cardamom was a 'cash crop' and it would help the king buy some new weapons. A sack of cardamom could be exchanged for a gun, yes, think of the ammunition he would be helping the king buy. Tontem downed his chi and promised that every seed would flower in the next few years and every last cardamom pod would find its way to the king's warehouse in Gangtok. Kaila Sardar then declared Tontem's chi that season as the best he had ever tasted, and the two friends drank to each other's health and the king's eternal reign.

Tontem could afford such bluster, for his estate had grown, and its yield had long surpassed his expectations. The fruit trees he had first planted after arrival were now heavy-branched—mangoes, litchis and papaya in the summer and oranges, pamsis and apples in the winter. Lhaizalzed, the botanical miracle, was blessed with fruits and plants from the lowlands and the highlands. Under his unwavering industry, the number of crops had increased—in addition to rice and maize, he now cultivated millet and barley. His livestock had grown and he could afford meat once a month, though this did not give him much happiness, for he grew aware with each bite that this was the only pleasure open to him without a wife in this valley of plenty.

⁂

'What about my marriage? I'll also have children who can help in the fields.' It was Chyadar again, who had not slept.

'We'll find one for you,' Tontem promised.

Chyadar growled, 'That's what you've been saying for fifteen rice harvests.'

'Unless you wanted to marry a fish. Even I haven't gone and seen the world for thirty-two winters.'

'How did you find our mother, then?'

'She came looking for me, you ox. And you were with her.'

⁂

The Chogyal's amulet proved its worth next spring. As the rhododendrons bloomed on the higher slopes, and Tontem's back ached contemplating the vast fields he now had to prepare for sowing, a woman arrived with a boy too big for his clothes. She said her name was Wangmo and that she was the woman who had assailed him at Dandu Kazi's house in Tuminthang. She explained that she had gone away the next morning for an errand and when she returned Tontem had left with the king. Then her belly had swelled. The child beside her was Tontem's son, the price of that encounter, who had promised to be an extraordinary being because he had talked, cried and laughed when still in her womb. He had been reared as everyone's child, for in that village of happy morals, bastards were as abundant as chickens. But now he was thirteen years old and she could no longer feed him on her own. This had made her follow Tontem's decade-old trail to Lhaizalzed. Tontem did not believe his luck for an instant. A chance encounter could never produce such a wonderful thing: a boy ripe for labour. But he hid his keenness and asked her to prove two things: that it was she who had come to him that night and that the child was his.

She said, 'You have no hair around your balls. And the child has pointed ears.'

She was right on both counts. Tontem's baby-skinned genitals were a secret he had hidden from everyone but the two women he had fornicated with. And the boy did have ears which tapered at the top. Their shape was not as radical as that of Tontem's but it was a respectable deformity. While his own ears were being examined, Chyadar touched Tontem's, accepting for the first time his mother's tales of a pig-eared father. Tontem took them in and deposited the amulet at the Chogyal's shrine for its job was done. The child had a name which Wangmo repeated in his ear but Tontem refuted it and renamed his firstborn Chyadar, after the Chogyal's priceless gift, which protected his house from everything the heavens threw down on him.

That night Tontem let out a cry of joy when he undressed Wangmo to shake the remaining leeches off her body. She had three missing toes on each foot, something he had not noticed that night in Tuminthang fourteen years ago. As they settled into a rhythm around crops and cattle, Tontem discovered the true extent of his fortune. Wangmo's tongue was sweeter than Duwah's and every event, however placid, was for her a reason for joy because it was a misfortune that had been averted. She outdid her husband and son in the fields, pausing only to suckle her newborn, delivered efficiently ten months after she came to Lhaizalzed. And she had a 'fire-hand' which transformed everything she cooked into a feast. Tontem's life then became one of luxury. There were varieties of fruits, and vegetables, and the meats of domesticated cattle and fowl, as well as the animals of the forest: frogs, fish and the occasional boar. In appreciation, Tontem took care to avoid her head whenever he beat her.

Kaila Sardar came by for his quarterly visit and he gifted them an embroidered carpet made from yak's skin, but in truth it was unnecessary because the tidings he bore were gift enough for his greatest friend. He too had found a wife and she was expecting a child very soon. The two friends congratulated each other for making their marks on the world.

In consultation with Kaila Sardar, Tontem began to construct another hut next to the one he lived in, for the walls of the older hut had begun to come apart from the ravages of his habitation. Kaila Sardar made one of his few unscheduled visits in the middle of that year to deliver twenty bags of cement, the most wonderfully plastic and sticky material that Tontem had ever seen. The house he built with it was wondrous, with the paste holding the stones together as if it were the fist of the Guru himself. Tontem was so taken by this gift from the king, wise enough to know exactly what his subjects wanted, that he named his second son, nameless since he was born three months ago, Cimit.

When Cimit was two years old, and just learning to walk, they often found him bending down and looking behind through his legs. They knew what this meant, he was looking to see who was coming after him. And sure enough, when the squash plants had begun to wither on their vines, Wangmo announced that she was again with child. This was to be Tontem's only daughter, who proved the continuance of his good fortune for she was born blind in one eye and named Batti, after the descriptions of electricity that Kaila Sardar brought back from Gangtok, and which Tontem now desired with impatience.

Tontem had to wait five years before Wangmo's steps grew heavy again. He was overjoyed: at last his dream of being at the helm of a large brood of children was coming true. He wanted at least ten to help him stretch his fields until the waterfall, making him rich and the king victorious, for despite twenty years of work he had yet to cover more than half the area of Lhaizalzed. He would then produce every crop, every vegetable and every fruit that the fertile land would allow.

When Wangmo died giving birth to his third son, in the middle of a seven-day shower that Tontem himself had requested from Kanchenjunga for his crop, he could not decide what caused him more grief: the death of a consort, the death of a dream or the burden of two babies. He went to the Chogyal's altar, retrieved the amulet and began to wear it again.

Cimit was nine years old when his mother died, pale and without blemish. Tontem had not forgotten the conditions for fertility in Lhaizalzed, and worried about his second son's perfection, for Cimit was without any bodily defects. But in the second week after his mother's death Cimit showed that his flaws were beyond the simplicity of missing parts. He disappeared on the first of his wanderings and did not return home for eight days and when he did, he only knew that he had been sent to collect firewood. His condition was known to Tontem. Soon after he had joined the Dragonback Monastery, a monk with a reputation for unlicensed wandering had gone missing. During Tontem's final months of sentry duty, the monk had returned after three years with eyes glazed by the death of memory and the Abbot had pronounced him lost.

The monk had died a few days later, suffocated by his tongue which he had tried to swallow. Tontem knew that Cimit was lost to the spirits of Lhaizalzed.

In order to keep his youngest child, who too was pure, Tontem waited till the child was three years old and then cut off the smallest finger of his left hand. It was the best time, for the child was old enough to recover in a week and too young for memory.

While Tontem grieved for his wife and his youngest child remained nameless, Lhaizalzed had an extraordinary visitor. It was in the early days of the rainy season. A man with a large bag upon his back wandered into the valley and collapsed by the river bed where he was found by Chyadar and Cimit. They brought him to their home where they tended his leech wounds. He was a man unlike any other and resembled Kaila Sardar's second-hand descriptions of Englishmen. Pale to the point of whiteness, and with spindly limbs, he communicated enough to say that his name was Turist. They never found out where he came from, or if he had any sisters for Chyadar to marry. The white man stayed with them for a season, and worked with them in the fields. One day in a frenzy that could not be restrained, he decided to walk towards the Five Deaths Pass, from where he never came back. But before going he left them his treasures: a light that showed Batti the origin of her name, photos of the Chogyal with some monks, a box that spoke in his language whenever left out in the sun, slabs of dark sugar and clothes that sustained them for years. So bountiful were the contents of his bag that Tontem named his youngest son after him.

Tontem groomed his children as if they were future soldiers, for whenever Kaila Sardar visited Lhaizalzed around this time, he brought news of the war now being fought by the Chogyal against the Pahareys and of his masterful alliance with Bhutan. The Pahareys had attacked from the west and taken Geyzing, but the army, led by the king, had annihilated their army. And did Tontem know what weapons he had used? The guns bought with his cardamom harvests. There was peace now, though no one knew for how long, for the affairs of high men were always beyond prediction. The Chogyal had sent an exhortation, which Kaila Sardar was now delivering, for production to be speeded up, and Tontem told Kaila Sardar that he was doing his best, but if the Chogyal really wanted the most out of Lhaizalzed, he ought to provide him with a new wife, for he still wanted more children and his balls were heavy again.

∞

'Did you get any more wives after our mother died?' Turist asked.

'No. I've been as alone as this one here,' Tontem said, pointing at Chyadar, now asleep.

'Did our king ever visit Lhaizalzed?' Cimit asked. 'No. He better come soon. He owes me a wife.'

∽

When Turist was two years old, Kaila Sardar came to Lhaizalzed at the head of a twenty-yak caravan, bearing in his hand a medal from the Chogyal commemorating twenty-five years of Tontem's service to the Crown. The Chogyal had also sent gifts for the children, small red rats with wheels. He would visit Lhaizalzed soon, he said, and though Tontem had long given up hope, he kept quiet and conducted the season's business with the medal around his neck. Kaila Sardar's purchases that year came to thirty sacks of maize, nineteen sacks of rice, four sacks of millet, and fourteen sacks of fruits. The price remained sacred and fixed, ten rupees a sack, and at the end of the transaction, Tontem had earned six hundred and seventy rupees from half-a-year's harvest. There were also seventy sacks of cardamom just for the king, Tontem's entire yield, for the 'cash crop' was grown only for the king, but these were not Tontem's to sell or Kaila Sardar's to buy.

In the evening the two friends reminisced about the long years they had known each other, in which time neither had been spared the universal injustices of age. Kaila Sardar was the older of the two, and his skin had sagged and four of his teeth were missing. He talked of keeping a servant and lamented that his daughter had come to him too late in life. Tontem had grown bald, but for a few thin wisps of hair. His ears were now exposed in all their hideous glory but he did not cover them up, for the freedom of isolation was the most precious endowment of Lhaizalzed. He talked again of the entirely practical reasons why he needed a wife. Kaila Sardar left as the first blizzard of the season began and said on parting, 'We'll find someone worthy of the world you have created.'

The blizzard lasted for six days and it blinded the valley with its fury.

After that winter, Kaila Sardar had not visited his friend. There had been three rice harvests since, and an equal number of maize and millet, and they had all been so splendid and fulsome that Tontem had wept while they rotted waiting for Kaila Sardar to transport them to Gangtok. How busy could the king be, he wondered in moments of anguish, that he would forget the most bountiful of all his estates?

In the first year Tontem had built a barn behind his house, close enough to keep watch. But it was full now, and had encouraged daily raids by foxes and bears. Then the animals retreated after it began to rot and the flies swept in, creating a stench that contaminated the whole valley. His livestock had begun to die from diseases that came from the pestilence. Tontem also felt something that he had never experienced before: stabs of possessiveness.

No, he had to leave. He would carry a small section of the harvest, to show its fecundity and also to prove that his honour was still intact. He had thought about it for months, and he knew the best time to visit Yeigang was right now, at the height of the rains, just after the rice had been planted, and before the maize was harvested, and before Cimit set off on his yearly pilgrimage of ghosts.

∽

'Will I find a bride at Yeigang?' Turist asked.

Batti and Cimit were asleep; their limbs had knotted and the girl's breaths were quicker than those of her brother's.

'Not this time. We have to find someone for Chyadar. But your turn will come in a few years.'

'Can I marry my sister, then?'

'If there's no one else.'

∽

Before he left the next morning, with his two youngest children, Tontem prayed at the Chogyal's altar. It now held, amongst other things, a piece of red rope, a cushion cover, four bars of soap, a fistful of metal buttons, a radio without batteries, letters, certificates, medals and three photographs, one each of the Chogyal, the Dalai Lama and Guru Padmasambhava, in identical frames of silver that had been moulded into roses. Of these, he carried the Chogyal's letter and the

medal for his services, just in case he had to prove his credentials. The
evening before the journey, he dug a deep hole in the southeastern
corner of his house and there deposited his entire monetary wealth: six
thousand rupees, the recompense from years of unsurpassable harvests.

When the party of three left for Yeigang, the air was moist enough
to drink. They carried a sack each, Turist carried the smallest one.
In the three sacks of decreasing size, they carried portions of rice,
maize, herbs, pamsis, dalley chillies, garlic, mangoes, papayas, millet and
cardamom—small evidence of the riches that Kaila Sardar had neglected
to collect for the king. They set out and gained speed through a
forest that resounded with cicadas. Their perspiration remained as a
thin film on their skin as they negotiated rocks and slopes with the
agility of animals at one with their terrain. Leeches fell from the trees
and then off their bodies, defeated, for the children had their father's
blood, famously immune to the thirst of leeches. The rain ceased for
an instant when they reached Chui Babzer, whose waterfalls were so
profuse that clouds rose up from the travellers' feet to join their brothers
in the sky. It was the furthest Batti and Turist had been in their lives.

They reached Yeigang in the late afternoon. Tontem was visiting
after many, many years and in his mind's eye Kaila Sardar's estate
still mirrored his own, with its full terraces and pacified forests and
the thatch-roofed stone house in the centre. But what he now saw
in the dwindling light made his eyes grow wide in amazement. The
fields were yellow with neglect, and had disappeared around their
edges where their boundaries battled with the unruly jungle; and a
corral lay at the centre, filled with grazing yaks. But the house itself
was new and almost as large as the Toring Kothi. The thatched roof
had been replaced by chyadars, the ekra walls had been transformed
into impenetrable walls of stone and cement and there was a massive
door of polished wood. From a large window a solitary light shone
and beckoned the three travellers.

They hollered as they approached and were let in. They entered
Kaila Sardar's house and Tontem's ears pricked up in astonishment when
he saw that the woman who let them in was his first wife, Duwah,
the no-good woman who had abandoned him eighteen winters ago.

She had aged, and the decline in her skin's tautness mirrored Tontem's own experiences. His surprise was instantly supplanted by rage for the futile season he had spent hunting for her. After he was done beating her, he resumed his language of simple words and elaborate signs with her and asked her for an explanation.

She told him, 'You wanted to cut off my fingers while I slept. What did you expect?'

She had run away from Lhaizalzed after Kaila Sardar, a true Buddhist who could not bear bringing hurt on other beings, told her about Tontem's plans. She had taken a week to find Yeigang, and Kaila Sardar had hidden her in a hut in the jungle for the entire wet season, where she'd had nothing but leeches and blood clots for company. Then he had brought her home and she had stayed with him and, in time, given him a daughter. She had also helped him handle the huge amount of grain and fruit now coming out of Lhaizalzed. He had taught her to read and write and keep accounts, for even when he was away trading in distant towns and in Gangtok, people had started to come to his house for grain and fruit. So much had changed, she told Tontem. Yeigang was going to become a big town. She took them to the window and pointed in the darkness towards the road being built over the old path.

Tontem's admiration increased for Kaila Sardar, for the man had saved him from the sin of mutilation or murder and spared him the burden of a lazy wife. He asked, 'What happened to my only friend?'

Kaila Sardar had survived the blizzard but had passed away later that year of an inexplicable disease that caused his arsehole to burn for seven days before spreading its fire to the rest of his body. Tontem's grief was immediate and primal. He wept through the evening, for he had lost a prudent friend, a priceless customer and an irreplaceable link to the Chogyal. He wept as he ate and asked how long Kaila Sardar's fields had remained fallow and Duwah replied that they had been thus since she came to Yeigang, eighteen years ago. Tontem's tears sprang up and flowed afresh and mingled with his food as he realized that his friend had sacrificed the joys of farming to handle Tontem's own produce. His health, too, must have deteriorated during the trips between Lhaizalzed and Gangtok, merely to help Tontem keep his vow, and then he had died, exhausted by brokering and the misfortune of keeping a woman who let his fields go to ruin.

When he finished eating and when his tears had dried, Tontem noticed another girl in the room. She was Kaila Sardar's daughter, whom he had named Saraswati. She was a little older than Cimit, and was now introducing Batti and Turist to electricity as they examined the lit bulb that hung in the centre of the room.

Tontem knew now that the journey to Gangtok to visit the Chogyal, one that he both feared and dreamed about, was a certainty. Kaila Sardar's replacement would have to be found. The Chogyal and Dandu Kazi had erred so far in not sending a replacement and it was his duty to tell them. He asked Duwah if her deceased husband had mentioned the king. She remembered one sentence.

'Sikkim will always have a king,' he had said.

Tontem began to plan his journey. Gangtok was a four-day trek from Yeigang. They could take shelter at the Dragonback Monastery tomorrow and at Toring Yabla's house the day after. He would meet Dandu Kazi in Gangtok and tell him that his overseer had died. He would test the limits of his fortune and request an audience with the Chogyal, and thank him for the letter, the medal, for life itself. The Chogyal would be shown the contents of the sacks to demonstrate the fecundity of his estate, and told that his share of the previous three harvests now emitted a stench strong enough to earn a reprimand from the gods. With his plans finalized, Tontem put his children to sleep in the kitchen and returned to the same room as Duwah, put down his bedding away from her and turned towards the wall.

∽

Tontem woke up at midnight with a strange feeling in his trousers. It was Duwah's hand. Tontem brushed it away.

He said, 'You don't deserve anything.'

'It's for you, not for me,' she said.

They rekindled their marriage and Tontem went to sleep with a light heart knowing Kaila Sardar's spirit was at ease, for his child was going to be provided for and his widow's unhappiness banished by a faithful friend.

∞

Tontem shoved Duwah out of bed at dawn, and she prepared food for them, and packed enough rice, beaten maize, salt and matches for the two days they would spend on their feet. She also gifted Tontem one of Kaila Sardar's caps, deep enough to cover his ears. It was a moist morning and the sun came through like a diffused beacon. The fog contracted their world and made their journey more forbidding. At mid-morning, they made their way around the hill south of Yeigang and entered another river basin, and Tontem spotted Dragonback Hill when the clouds thinned for an instant. The children kept pace, for their loads were light, and with their lithe limbs they skipped over rocks and mud paths. When they rested, Tontem scolded them for squandering their energy. Turist's compliant mischief contrasted with his sister's sullen obduracy; her father had long ago identified her as the reincarnation of a mule. On this day, however, her stubbornness was tempered by her continual surprise as they travelled through the dense, unfamiliar and sticky forests.

They reached the base of Dragonback Hill at midday. Here they washed themselves in the river, Tontem caught some fish, which they smoked in banana leaves and added to their lunch. They looked up at the hill and it was so large that its summit couldn't be seen. As they ascended the hillside, they came to a wide road with a strange black top. Tontem broke off a piece and chewed it: it tasted nothing like mud. He saw a large humpbacked rock which looked familiar and beside it the gigantic leafless tree. With a cry of joy Tontem pointed out to his children the spot where he had rescued the Chogyal so many winters ago; he began to tell them the story again but they moved away in protest. When they had walked a little distance they found the upward stone path that led to the monastery.

As they approached the ridge, Tontem experienced a terrifying mixture of fear, inspired by his eternal fear of the Lopen, and happiness, for the Abbot would surely appreciate it when Tontem presented his children as evidence that he had made his way in the world. Then he saw what had earlier been hidden by the foliage and his distress forced him to drop his load and run the last leg of his journey.

The monastery had been stripped of everything that had given it glory: its red-and-white walls, its ancient thangkas, its gilded finial, the masks of demons, the scriptures and the embryonic soot of the butter-lamps. All that remained were the broad walls, and these too were being slowly picked apart by four labourers who worked with the grace of vultures. Tontem shouted at them to lead him to the Abbot or the Lopen but they only laughed at the strange tongue he spoke in. It was then that Tontem realized that there was going to be a profound hindrance in his quest for an audience with the king, for the only language he knew, that of his clan, was no longer understood. Tontem tried to communicate through signs, but the men laughed louder than before, and then Tontem, wise enough to know he was being mocked, picked up the nearest one by his neck and held him up until his eyes went white. When he was dropped the man led his team away in a mad scamper towards the valley and the visitors found themselves alone. They stayed the night amidst the ruins and Tontem slapped his children into silence when they asked him about his childhood.

The next morning Tontem looked around in the monastery's estate for any monk who could explain its collapse. He could find no one, for the place was as deserted as a yogi's mind. He walked towards the cave which the Abbot used for his yearly retreats. It was empty as well, though he could hear some chants coming in from further off. He and his two children followed the chants and reached a clearing in the forest that had been set up as a home without a roof by an old man in rags, infinitely wrinkled, whom Tontem recognized as the Abbot in the final stages of his life. He was still strong, and he stood to welcome them, though it was apparent that his spirit was abandoning its worldly shell in dribbles. Tontem prostrated himself three times before the Abbot and made his children do the same. He then sought explanations from the Abbot but there was only an uncomprehending contempt on the Abbot's face as he took his frail body away from Tontem's presence and began swaying to a silent song. Tontem waited beside the Abbot for a while but learnt nothing, for the Abbot was on his way to becoming a Bodhisattva. He was halfway poised between the sentient world and the realm of the Buddhas, his wisdom apparent to no one but himself. He would look back only after he reached the blessed realms.

Tontem set eastward for Toring, beyond two river-valleys and a hill, shielded by a cover of opaque clouds. Just above the river, the three wayfarers encountered another road. Tontem recognized from afar the labourers who had run away yesterday and he saw that they were building another monastery, which was being fed by the giant wheeled rats that the Abbot had spoken of three decades ago.

The large rats were surrounded by maroon-robed monks. At the centre of this crowd, Tontem recognized another great figure from his childhood. The Lopen had greyed but the shape of his pumpkin head had not altered. He stood between the monks and some men in stiff clothes and looked animated. Tontem approached him with trepidation, for his memories had not receded.

'What do you want?' the Lopen said, after removing the shiny black discs covering his eyes to look at Tontem more closely.

'I used to be the strongest man in the Dragonback Monastery,' Tontem said.

The words in a language almost dead darkened the Lopen's face. His expression settled into one of contemptuous recognition and he began to shout at Tontem for wasting his time on such an important day when the ministers were due to visit and check on the progress of works at the new Dragonback Monastery, for the 'CM' would be visiting soon. The monks around the Lopen snarled, ready to bite at his command. Tontem lifted his hat, exposed his ears and they sloped away. Tontem grew ready to rebel for the first time in his life. His ears stiffened, his eyes bulged and the Lopen softened at the sight. He grew peaceable and explained that he was doing all that he could for the greater good of their clan, which was disappearing with rapidity, and of the Abbot, who needed a glorious monument to commemorate his imminent Buddhahood.

Tontem accepted this explanation, his former reverence returned and he bowed three times before the Lopen, and put his strength at the tireless man's disposal, despite being in a hurry to meet the king and Dandu Kazi. The Lopen told him that he would best serve the faith by going ahead with his plan, for who better to serve as an emissary of their clan than Tontem himself, chosen from amongst so many by their beloved Chogyal, who was also the spiritual and temporal overlord of all Sikkim.

Tontem bowed again before the Lopen and took his leave with a heavy heart, for though he had much to share with the great disciplinarian who had shaped him in his formative years, he knew better than to interfere with such purpose of mind. He then wiped his moist eyes and taking his children moved out of Dragonback Hill. They crossed the river over a great bridge made of cement and began to climb the hill between Dragonback Hill and Toring. The sky had darkened by the time they climbed it. They stood at the ridge and Tontem pointed out the village of his childhood located halfway up the hill, and in its centre, the magnificent Toring Kothi with its stone chimney. Tontem even saw smoke curling out from it but Batti accused him of propagating a mirage.

He walked towards Toring with the leaden steps of a traitor, knowing the Chogyal would disapprove of his decision to visit someone who had joined the rebellion against him, but he longed to meet the man whom he had wanted as a father and hear his resonant laugh again. His stratagem was simple: he would visit the Yabla but not mention the Chogyal, and he would be equally circumspect at Gangtok. He tutored his children on the ruse and invented a story for their mission: they were going to get cardamom seeds from Gangtok.

They ate their meagre lunches and rested for a while, for Batti's leg had begun to hurt. Then, when she felt better, they walked downhill and arrived at another road on which a variety of the same giant rats, some so big that they reminded him of buffaloes, ran around, farting like demons to warn each other; the rider of one even popped his head out and yelled at him in greeting. Tontem knew that all these wheeled animals belonged to the Chogyal, the only man in Sikkim with enough money to own them and waved back out of respect for their common master.

Through a drizzle so fine that droplets settled like frost on their hair, they meandered through Toring with their loads on their backs. The village of his childhood had grown unrecognizable. In the place of timber houses with leaky roofs were gigantic boxes of cement with harsh windows. The road was wider and topped with the same tasteless black cake, the shops no longer sold just rice and oil and had shiny bags in colours that hurt the eyes. The only landmarks that had survived were the hills around Toring. Turist shrank back against his father when taunted by the children dressed in trousers made of material that looked like rough blue sand; but Batti responded by forcing one of them to eat dust. Tontem tugged at his children, moved on and soon reached the kothi to find that it was as busy as it had been on the day of his departure, so many years ago.

It bustled with people in spotless clothes and Tontem felt ashamed of looking like a forest dweller despite the fortune of six thousand rupees he had in his name. He drew stares without even uncovering his ears, the one act which would have obtained him instant recognition. Aromas of meat and soup assailed his nostrils, the kinds of which he had not smelled since encountering the Chogyal's entourage, and he warned his children not to follow their noses. He then searched for the one person whom he would recognize despite the passage of years and his quest ended when he saw a greying man with asymmetrical eyes. Tontem tapped his shoulder and offered him a glimpse of his ears. Palden's face creased in alarm; he took Tontem aside and with a low voice asked him his business at the kothi after all these years. Tontem confessed his purpose: he was on his way to Gangtok to sell his cardamom harvest. Palden's face cleared and then he told Tontem that he had come too late, for Toring Yabla had died three days ago.

Tontem's tears were instant and mingled with the rain. His regret at leaving Lhaizalzed was complete. Palden led Tontem and his children to an upstairs room, strewn with khadas and khabseys and here Tontem wept with unrestrained groans while his childhood friend comforted him. They were guided to the servant's hut where Tontem had spent his early years with his mother. Here, Batti and Turist were gifted some children's clothes, and Tontem also received some from Palden's wardrobe. Palden warned them not to re-emerge until they had cleaned themselves, and left their sacks in the rooms. The hut had changed: the walls were still of mud but now painted, the wood on the floor wasn't half-rotten and did not creak, the electric light flattened everything and the toilet was in the room itself, with taps Tontem could not trust so he led his children to the brook and coaxed away the dirt that clung to their bodies like second skins. The clothes that he now wore were colourful, they itched in awkward places and he felt his toes fight against their sudden confinement. But he was proud that he now resembled the people in the crowd below, as long as he wore a cap, of course. He could feel his children beginning to re-evaluate him for having had such a fortunate childhood.

∽

'Why didn't you stay here until you grew old?' Batti asked as they moved through the kothi.

'The king wanted me for other things,' Tontem replied.

'You should have stayed. Then they wouldn't be laughing at us right now,' she said.

∽

The three of them were guided to the tent behind the main house, where the guests ate. A riot of dishes assaulted their senses: meats, nettle, spinach, cheeses and countless others which had yet to find a name. They considered their lifelong diets which put survival before taste and gulped in astonishment. Turist held on to Batti, who held on to her father, who thanked the Chogyal's reign for such prosperity. And, fortified by an unstated wish to taste everything, they exited the line with mountains on their plates. As the genteel people around them looked askance, the mountains disappeared into their bellies and they licked their plates clean to make it easier for the dishwashers who made a racket behind the tent. They suppressed the astonishment in their bellies and wandered in a daze in the dying daylight as Tontem searched for his childhood recesses and shouted when the suspended bulbs exploded with light as if by a wizard's decree.

He found his way to the lhakhang. The prayer room had changed from the sooty alcove to a large rainbow of a hall lined with monks in parallel seats, to whose sonorous chants an army of sleepwalkers could have marched. At its end was an iridescent timber altar before which Tontem prostrated himself thrice. He did the same before the Yabla, now confined in a wooden pyramid, his corpse inside moulded into the seated lotus pose, the only one in which a mortal could ascend to the heavens. Tontem touched the shell with his forehead, and remembered the giant whom he had worked so hard to emulate, who had yearned for his mother's dishes, and who had set him on the one fortuitous journey of his life.

As they followed Palden back to Tontem's childhood quarters, they passed a yellow room and Palden asked Tontem to glance inside. There were seven men brooding around a table lamp, all of whom had a marked deformity—a nose which hung like frozen snot, eyes without eyelids, a mouth without lips, a hive of goitres instead of a neck, cheeks without bones, skin like moss, and hair the colour of shit. There was a knock on the door, their heads moved and their hideousness assailed Tontem. He fled from the window, his mouth clamped shut lest his heart emerge from it.

In the old servant's hut, the fatigued children slept while Tontem conversed with Palden in the language of their childhood. He learnt that the Yabla had died from a disease of the pancreas, an organ he had never heard of. He had left behind three sons, two daughters and seven known bastards, whom Tontem had just seen through the window. They had all arrived after the Yabla's death to claim their inheritance, and now they were being dissuaded from attending the funeral which was going to be held the day after. Palden asked him to stay for it and Tontem began to make his excuse.

He longed to talk about and hear of his beloved king, of whom he had had no news for three years, and wanted to know how the war was going. He tried to elicit information without revealing his own association with it. 'What war?' Palden said, looking puzzled, but then he stopped. 'My father asked us never to talk about the Chogyal again, and he's still in the house.' They settled on their common childhood, but were soon defeated, for the air between them was contaminated by their unequal destinies. They quarantined their thoughts and speech, and stopped trying to regain the mud-soaked candour of their shared childhood.

They talked of cardamom instead. Tontem was sick with anxiety for his harvest, rotting in the humid sun. Palden touched Tontem's arm and told him of the Department of Agriculture in the capital, he could arrange a taxi to take them there in the morning, since they were going to Gangtok anyway. He sighed as he mentioned the Toring Kothi's cardamom fields, dying from a blight that pervaded the land, and cursed the thumbless government officials whose remedies were massacring the few that remained. Harvests in Sikkim had failed for ten years in a row. And at a time when farmers wept during their harvests, Tontem's isolation was indeed fortuitous, for his crop would be worth its weight in gold.

That night Tontem dreamt without sleeping of the diseased apparitions from the yellow room. He shook his children awake in the hour before dawn, and restrained his daughter heading to the cowshed out of habit. There was a flicker of early sunlight, a cloud moved outside their window and soon there was the steady patter of morning rain on the roofs. Tontem decided to leave the smallest sack, which contained some fruits and samples of cardamom from his fields, with Palden, who embraced his departing friend. And Tontem's knees shook when he saw that they were to travel to Gangtok in a wheeled rat, of the kind that had excited the children, and terrified him.

∽

Batti was happy she did not have to walk today, and Turist asked questions about everything and Tontem clarified all his doubts.

'What is that, Father?' Turist asked, pointing at the steering wheel. 'That is the ear of the deformed rat. That man pinches and pulls it to let it know which way to turn,' Tontem replied.

'And that?' Turist asked, pointing at the gear stick. 'It is a male rat,' his father replied.

∽

On the road, the drizzle turned into an insolent torrent. Tontem missed the rain in Lhaizalzed which came only when summoned. The driver said something that they did not understand. He stopped the taxi, leaned back and rolled up the windows, and they gasped from the sticky air inside. Tontem wiped the windows to look outside for signs of war. But the people looked placid and their movements were not urgent. The driver tried to converse with Tontem, but gave up when he realized he needed his hands for the steering wheel. The journey turned memorable for the driver when the three passengers regurgitated every undigested morsel from their two meals at the Yabla's house all over his seats. He had to stop at a stream and wash down his car, which stank like the end of the world, while his dazed passengers squatted beside the road, recovering from their sickness. He let them in only after they demonstrated with forceful retches that they had nothing left in their stomachs to soil his jeep with.

When the journey recommenced, Tontem's doubts about the state of war were confirmed. Ahead of them was a convoy of green trucks loaded with soldiers who stared with vacant eyes at the jeep following them. They looked Indian, if the descriptions of Kaila Sardar had any truth, and he also knew they were allied to the Pahareys. He withheld himself from anger, for it was unsoldierly to fight without proper orders. But he took the precaution of telling Batti and Turist that they would have to travel back to Lhaizalzed alone, a declaration they bore with equanimity before falling asleep.

As they climbed towards Gangtok from Ranipool, Tontem took in the city that had spread like a cloud on the hillside, the crowd of tall and ugly houses, the innumerable wheeled rats on the roads, the people on the pavements and the outrageous clothes they wore. He wanted to turn back to the security of Lhaizalzed, where everything had a name. He saw himself being lost, separated from his children and again his heart contracted. He resolved to tie his children to himself as he navigated his way to the palace. The city was a wet and busy giant, and he realized that his presumption that its king should make time for him was a misplaced and absurd one.

∽

The children woke up and their father's terror bypassed them. They had not outgrown their capacity for surprise, everything was new and the world's wonders were infinite.

'Does the king own all this?' they asked.

'Of course he does.'

'And will he remember you?'

'Of course he will.'

∽

The driver stopped his taxi outside the Department of Agriculture, halfway into Gangtok, according to Palden's instructions. There he let out his passengers, and sped away without a farewell. Tontem waited until the jeep had passed out of sight before accosting everyone and repeating the one foreign word he knew would lead him to the Chogyal: 'Palace'. He knew it from years of talking with Kaila Sardar. It was an effective strategy, for everyone knew the palace and pointed to the summit of the third visible hill. They picked up their sacks and began to walk. Turist offered to carry Batti's sack since his had been left for their father's friend in Toring. She laughed and hit him on the head.

The Chogyal was all that mattered and Tontem ignored everything on the way. His children were less constrained. They paused, they dallied, they were awed and they slowed him down. He stopped every once in a while to plead with them, for the decorum of the king's city did not permit him an outright assault. Near the taxi stand, there were three men in blue uniforms who stopped him, and when he did not understand their words, conveyed through signs that they would hit him with their sticks if he continued to make the girl carry such a load. Batti was forced to drop her sack and Tontem made to carry it as well. The children now danced around their father who promised to skin them alive once they were out of public view.

Every time they came to a division in the road, which was often, they asked for the palace. At Deorali, where the road to Namnang diverges, they were directed to Hotel Palace. They went into the opulent lobby of the hotel and squatted in front of the reception desk, causing a commotion and eliciting surprised and angry noises from the staff. The floors shone, the lights twinkled, and each object looked as if it would be sullied by their touch: it was the grandest space they had ever been in and Tontem knew for certain that he had reached the Chogyal's home. Batti utilized a word she had learnt since yesterday—'Raja'—and the painted woman standing behind the large table seemed to soften and nod in understanding. She guided them to an open, smaller room, where they sipped on water and waited for the king.

When the king arrived, Tontem cried in surprise for his worst suspicions were confirmed. The Chogyal had been overthrown. This king was dark, hairy, with the eyes of a drunkard, a belly that indicated perennial laziness, and he could not converse with Tontem in the language of his land. Tontem seized the pretender's soiled shirt and prepared to avenge his master's dethronement. Soon, the hotel's workers rushed in from the lobby and restrained Tontem, who wept in loud sobs for the dark days that had befallen Sikkim.

A boy stepped forward and said in Tontem's tongue, 'What are you doing so far from your fields?' His name was Buru, his hair fell on his face, and he had the features of their tribe. He explained that the dark and hairy man had not usurped the throne of the Chogyal of Sikkim. He was the head cook of the hotel and his name was Raja. Tontem sighed in relief and asked Buru,

'Is our king in good health?'

'He was healthy the last time I saw him. He waved at me,' Buru assured him.

Relieved, Tontem asked his clansman how they could get to the palace and if he would marry his daughter, despite her bedevilled tongue. Buru declined the proposal with grace, for he was already married to a woman from the plains. Then he pointed to the Namnang road and explained the simplest way to get to the top: Tontem was to follow the road and wherever he met a junction, he was to take the steeper road.

The rain was now a downpour, and the roads abandoned their purpose and worked as streams. The three of them walked up the Namnang road. There were no people, only wheeled rats passed them by, throwing water on them. Tontem again transferred the sack to his daughter. Batti walked beside her father, cursing, angry with him for the rain, the hunger in her stomach, and for the deep shame that came from carrying a sack through the city. Tontem held her when a taxi passed, she pulled away and he struck her. She dropped her sack and sat down on the road, resisting Tontem's commands to stand up. Her mulishness had returned, she stared at him until her good eye welled with anger and he could not even beat her.

But Tontem was less concerned with the vagaries of her behaviour than he was with the imminent realization of his dream. He beckoned Turist, who refused to leave his sister. Tontem abandoned his children there, picked up the two sacks and began to walk uphill. The slope, the rain, the city's cacophony and the nearness of his destination made his journey seem interminable. Soon he reached Namnang, and without knowing it, walked up the bend that had seen the Chogyal's son die from a speeding accident in March 1978, around the same time that Kaila Sardar had come to Lhaizalzed with the news and the two men had wept over a forlorn dinner. Soon there was a diversion, and just as Buru had instructed, Tontem took the steeper one. It curved around a giant white disc of a building, the State Assembly Hall. A soldier with a gun lifted his hand and stopped Tontem, who did not argue when the man shoved him with urgency into the sentry box. He admired the gun in the guard's hands with a stakeholder's pride, for his cardamom had helped pay for it. From the sentry box he heard the wail of a giant cat and he stuck out his head. An open vehicle with armed soldiers glided in, followed by a cavalcade of vehicles with black glasses from which smiling, polite men emerged. Tontem guessed the reason: the Chogyal was gravely ill, his powers had been usurped by his ministers, and for some reason, the war had been suspended though both sides were preparing.

The smiling men disappeared through a large ornamented door. The guard let Tontem out and he continued with the sacks, his thoughts converging on the king's illness. He walked up Kazi Road with freedom because of the blinding rain which dissuaded even the wheeled rats from plying on the roads. Drenched to his bones, his sweat overpowered by the rain and his ears twitching in moist discomfort underneath his cap, he reached Bhanu Path, the road which circled the crest of the hill where the palace was located. He could see the ridge, the crest of the chopped hill that had given Gangtok its name, and where, a hundred years ago, the eastern part had been flattened for a palace for the Chogyals. Tontem found himself in front of the palace gates, proportioned like the gates to paradise he had seen painted long ago on a mural at the Dragonback Monastery, and manned by two unarmed sentries. Their only mandate was to tell tourists to use the other entry, at the estate's rear, to visit the palace monastery, but Tontem had no way of knowing this and was angry when they failed to understand the urgency of his purpose and continued to shake their heads, speak loud gibberish and bar his way. Tontem resisted the urge to bash their heads in, for the king would not like it, and he did not want to be met as a common supplicant but for what he was, the custodian of the king's most prized estate. He then repeated the two words he had often heard Kaila Sardar speak, and which he knew would lead him to Dandu Kazi: 'Tuminthang Kothi.'

The sentries pointed to a road on the other side of the ridge. Tontem picked up his sacks and moved on. He soon reached a large house with sloping roofs but Tontem had seen so many large homes in the course of a single day that he was unmoved. At the gate, there was a large dog with a polished coat which barked when he entered the gate but went quiet when he bent over and revealed his ears. Here, liberated from the constraints of etiquette which had ensured his silence at the palace gates, Tontem wailed. Soon Dandu Kazi emerged, carrying a dotted umbrella, wearing common clothes, with only his air of unassailable solemnity to show that he was an aristocrat of the highest order, servant only to the gods and the king of the land.

Dandu Kazi stood astonished while Tontem prostrated himself on the ground, further soiling his wet clothes. He had to repeat the most important words of his life—Yeigang, Lhaizalzed and Kaila Sardar—before the Kazi's ageing face lit with recognition and he instructed his servant to open the gates.

Tontem disburdened himself of the heavy sacks under the eaves of the house. He then extracted the irrevocable proofs of his position: the Imperial Certificate of Appreciation and the Medal for Loyal Service. A shadow passed over Dandu Kazi's kind face and his eyes were both happy and sad as he put a hand on Tontem's shoulder. Tontem's heart expanded with happiness, for he could see that the great Kazi was proud of him, the most loyal and able of the king's subjects, and also sorry for the neglect he had had to suffer for three long years.

He could not know, however, that the Kazi's pity was in fact boundless. He had not refused to acknowledge Tontem, nor had he turned him away, though he recognized and remembered well the paper and the piece of metal he had sent two decades ago through Kaila Sardar, his ally for twenty-seven years. The Imperial Certificate of Appreciation he now held in his hands was a one-page report, printed on the letterhead of the Animal Husbandry Department of the State Government of Sikkim, on a census of livestock around Tashiding in West Sikkim. And the medal, its metallic edges still intact, belonged to the winners of the annual debate at St Joseph's College in 1968, when Dandu Kazi was studying in Darjeeling with the Chogyal as his friend and adjunct.

Dandu Kazi said to Tontem in a voice soft with compassion, 'You should have told me you were coming,' and led him into the house.

Inside, Tontem squatted beside the door in the time-honoured way of the visiting poor, but Dandu Kazi admonished him into sitting on a stool, before disappearing into another room. The room Tontem sat in was the most colourful that he had ever seen. There were books, a carpet, paintings on the walls showing the Kazi in distant lands with strange-looking people who reminded Tontem of the tourist. There was also a large cupboard with pictures of the Chogyal and the Dalai Lama, and one of Guru Padmasambhava in a silver frame that was a

twin of the one the Chogyal had sent him two decades ago. Then the
Kazi emerged from the inner room, dressed in the magnificent regalia
of his position, his bearing made worthier for the noble clothes he
now wore. Tontem prostrated himself before the Kazi again. Dandu
Kazi lifted him up and broke his heart by saying, 'The Chogyal is ill.
And he has gone away for treatment.'

Tontem wept copious tears. The departures of Kaila Sardar and
Toring Yabla, and the madness of the Abbot, had exhausted his fortitude,
and he had no strength left in his heart. He wept for himself, for he
knew now with the certainty of instinct that he would never again see
the Chogyal, who was finishing his time on earth. The king was old,
he was already greying when Tontem saw him last and he had aged
thirty-two years since then. Dandu Kazi soothed him with better news.
The doctors were saying it was just a small operation. The Chogyal
was away in a great country, but he had already heard of Tontem's
arrival in the capital and had sent his warm blessings.

Tontem was pacified by this news and Dandu Kazi asked him if
he had been good friends with Kaila Sardar. The best, Tontem said,
and summarized the story of their friendship, from the time they
had been left together in Lhaizalzed. Tontem recalled that but for
his unwavering friend, he would not have known about the turmoil
in the state, the rebellion from the west, and the long war with
India. He described his last memory of Kaila Sardar, at the head of a
twenty-yak caravan. This was followed by the epilogue of the rotting
harvest. Here he paused to allow his tears free passage down his face.
Dandu Kazi nodded through it all, his face grave, and his expression
inscrutable. How much had Kaila Sardar taken away on his last visit,
Dandu Kazi asked, and how much did the three years of uncollected
harvests add up to?

Tontem narrated a series of figures from memory which began
with three hundred sacks of rice, three hundred and twelve sacks of
maize, four hundred and seventeen sacks of cardamom, and ended
with three jackfruits. He tore open the sacks of samples that he had
carried with him as proof of his word. Dandu Kazi stroked his beard
and said the figure tallied with the Chogyal's receipts, except for the

jackfruits. He apologized to Tontem for his dereliction in not sending a replacement for Kaila Sardar, he had three hundred estates under his watch. It was very difficult. The Kazi looked defeated when he turned to Tontem and said with a sadness tinged with humiliation, 'It isn't the same as before.' Tontem shared his sorrow. He had seen the arrogance of the drivers, the bad temper on the roads, the laughter he had endured when asking for directions. This, he deduced, was what happened to kingdoms when their kings grew old.

Then he voiced a thought that was surely on every subject's mind: 'What happens after the king?'

There was a new crown prince, he was told—the Chogyal's youngest son, now eleven years old, born of the Chogyal's youngest wife from Kham. He was being groomed to take over and Dandu Kazi himself was responsible for his tutelage. The chief monks had already prophesied a fifty-year reign. The only thing that he needed was the continued loyalty of subjects like Tontem. And things had changed in the last three years. Tontem would have made a fine soldier but there really was no need for battles. There was peace in the land. The Pahareys had finally been subdued and the Indians had learnt not to interfere in the affairs of a land protected by the gods. The soldiers that Tontem had seen on the road to Gangtok were those given by India, now a large-hearted friend, for protection against China, that great and constant enemy beyond the mountains.

All was well with their land. 'Sikkim will always have a king,' Dandu Kazi said, reminding Tontem of something he had heard before.

Some food came for Tontem. The Kazi enquired if anyone else knew of Tontem's journey. Tontem now remembered Batti and Turist and surrendered to panic. He fretted for his children, condemned by his thoughtlessness. He thought of their hunger, for the food was in the sacks that he carried, and he refused to eat. Dandu Kazi, who recognized the tears of a grieving parent, pressed him for details. When Tontem told him about the children, the unflustered Kazi extracted a dark stone from his pocket and spoke into it in Nepali. When he had finished, he assured Tontem that someone had indeed gone to check up on the welfare of Batti and Turist.

Tontem, whose curiosity exceeded his servant's restraint and his father's sorrow, asked about the strange stone in Dandu Kazi's hands and was told that it was a phone, which enabled people to speak to each other without actually meeting. This sounded like pure laziness to Tontem but he held his opinion. Dandu Kazi then told him that Sikkim had advanced a great deal since they had last met. There were roads going everywhere, large buildings that were built by the government under the king's guidance, electricity and running water in all homes. White-skinned foreigners were coming to Sikkim to learn from the Chogyal, who had become the first monarch in history to put the happiness of his people above all else, despite the claims of the King of Bhutan to the contrary.

Yes, there were some bad changes as well. The blood in Sikkimese veins was growing less pure, people were marrying each other without research and without shame. And the prosperity that the king had brought was being misused, beggary was being mistaken for employment, but all this would soon change with the formal installation of the crown prince on the throne, an occasion for which Tontem would be sent a special invitation.

The drizzle continued outside, the thick cover of mist thinned, and the sunlight broke through like gold dust scattered by the gods on their favoured land. Dandu Kazi comforted Tontem with questions. He was interested in the rivers around Yeigang and Lhaizalzed, particularly Chui Babzer. How large were they, and at what points were the gorges closest to each other, and how stable were the hills around them? How swiftly did the rivers flow?

Tontem gave routine answers. He could think of little else beyond his children. He dreaded the four-day walk back home alone, with the ghosts of his disappeared children. He pleaded with Dandu Kazi again and the good man assured him that they were on their way. Soon enough, two uniformed men arrived, and they had Batti and Turist with them. Tontem snatched his children from them and embraced them long and hard before proceeding to implement his promise of skinning them alive. The Kazi and the two men were so inconvenienced by the children's wails that they persuaded Tontem to defer this ritual until later. It turned out that one of the uniformed men was a native of Tuminthang—Dandu Kazi had procured him his job years ago—and Tontem could understand a bit of his dialect.

The constable asked, 'Why does the girl keep talking about meeting the king? Where has she been living? Everyone knows he's...'

'He's ill, and we all know that,' Dandu Kazi said. 'They've only come to meet him.'

'I thought...' the constable said.

'You think too much,' Dandu Kazi cut in. 'Tell us how you found the children.'

∽

The constable explained that he was on his beat at Tadong when the Kazi's phone call came through. But he had dared not move from his post, because the chief minister—the king's chief minister, Dandu Kazi said, and the constable corrected himself—the king's chief minister was about to pass, and the constable's salute was indispensable for his safe journey. The king's chief minister, as everyone knew, was leaving on a secret trip to New Delhi, where his third mistress was about to deliver their second child. After the king's chief minister passed, the constable had hurried to Namnang where he found Batti and Turist at the Deorali police station where they had been delivered as lost waifs.

Now Tontem agreed to eat the dinner prepared for him and despite the Kazi's entreaties, would not eat at the table, out of grave respect, and mistrust of the chair's slender legs. After dinner, master and servant reminisced about their days together thirty-two years ago. At the end of the conversation, Tontem summoned all the courage within him and said:

'I won't return to Lhaizalzed without meeting him.'

Dandu Kazi explained that the king was away in a foreign land, to which it would be difficult for Tontem to travel. However, he would arrange for a phone call, and they could speak to each other tomorrow. Tontem accepted this compromise. Dandu Kazi also offered to take them on a tour of the palace tomorrow, vacant because the entire royal family was beside the ailing king. Then they could leave for Lhaizalzed. The next morning Tontem was summoned to the living room where Dandu Kazi sat with two dark men who wore crisp clothes, spoke with gentle voices and sipped their tea like women. Dandu Kazi demanded that Tontem sit beside him, and his stern expression compelled Tontem to follow his directive. He asked Tontem the same questions about the rivers that he had asked yesterday and translated his answers for the crisp men. They had questions of their own: how swift were the rivers in the different seasons? How high was their fall? How wide was their reach? After they left, Dandu Kazi explained that the men were coming into Sikkim to build walls of cement across the rivers to bring electricity and then tourists. Tontem, who heard three of his children invoked in a single sentence, nodded with reverence for the king, who knew how beneficial all this would be for his kingdom. There was already one wall of cement being made at Tuminthang, and Dandu Kazi had donated all the land for it in the name of progress. He had not taken a single rupee, so great was his concern for Sikkim. They were thinking of building one at Chui Babzer too, for the land to the south had one of the narrowest gorges, and Tontem could help them with this. Tontem's face creased with apprehension. He had taken three decades to negotiate with and eventually subdue the forest deities and devils. The thought of repeating the fight hurt his bones, for some of them were prettier and gentler than people and did not deserve bad fortune.

Dandu Kazi noted this and said, 'Of course we are all worried about the feelings of the forest deities, and the trees and the fishes, but one must never put sentiment before fortune.'

Tontem thought about the bounties he had accumulated at Lhaizalzed over the years by following the same philosophy and agreed. He was far keener to visit the palace, the abode of his absent lord. They spent the morning calculating harvests and yields and in the early afternoon Batti and Turist followed their father and Dandu Kazi to the palace. They entered through the rear gate and the short road brought them in front of the royal chapel. All of Tontem's notions about his king's grandness were confirmed when he saw Tsuklakhang, the royal monastery. It was greater than the Dragonback Monastery, and was freshly painted, and the men and women coming to pray were respectable and nobly clothed and there were also white-skinned foreigners among them. They walked away from the monastery and a short while later reached the palace, a two-storeyed building—in the sahib's style, the Kazi told them, built by the king's grandfather after visiting a faraway country called England. Tontem's awe dimmed a little because the palace was smaller than the monastery. But Dandu Kazi explained that it was unimposing because the Chogyals disliked grandeur, and wanted nothing that would put them at any remove from their subjects. Austerity was the greatest Buddhist virtue, and the Chogyal's predecessors had baulked at building anything larger than the monasteries, abodes of their gods.

A guard on his rounds recognized Dandu Kazi and saluted him. There was a concrete pedestal in front of the palace. Dandu Kazi identified it as the spot from which, many years ago, the Chogyal had acknowledged Tontem's agricultural contribution with the letter of appreciation, and much later, the medal of honour. Tontem knelt and with his head he touched the spot where the king's feet had rested, his ears drooping with sadness.

Dandu Kazi did what he could to assuage Tontem's dejection. In the evening, as Batti and Turist continued their unceasing feast in the kitchen, interrupted only by the sighs and admonitions of the cook, he received a phone call from the Chogyal and, after pleasantries and deep wishes for the king's recovery on behalf of Tuminthang and the kingdom, he offered the instrument to Tontem.

His monarch whispered his greetings in the same regal language Tontem had heard so many years ago, whose sonorous delivery and immaculate words had shamed everyone at the Dragonback Monastery. The voice had gone raspy with age, and it had changed a little, but that was natural with the passing of so many years. Tontem understood that. And so it was that Tontem was mesmerized once again by the voice of the man whose memory had bound him in happy loyalty for three decades. The voice thanked Tontem for all he had done. The yields from Lhaizalzed were yearly odes to fertility that sustained the palace kitchen for one week a year when the royal family would eat nothing but that had been grown in the garden of the gods. He then apologized for his infirmity; he said the doctors' feared that he would soon pass from this realm, which was something he prayed for as he could feel an incurable fatigue deep in his bones. Tontem was to return and tend his priceless land, it would soon be his in name and deed. Although the sovereign and the subject would not meet again in this life, they would surely cross paths in one of the six regions of rebirth. Then the stone went silent and Tontem handed it back to the kazi and walked outside, his ears down, his heart heavy, but unaware how blessed he was, for only the most fortunate among men have their illusions protected by a conspiracy of the fates.

∽

He was to leave at dawn the next morning. In the evening, Dandu Kazi called him aside and told him, 'Leave your daughter with me. She'll stay in my house, eat with us, and marry well in some years. She won't have to work anymore than at Lhaizalzed. And I will have the Chogyal's personal doctor treat her eyes so that she can be whole again.'

The request was in conformance with Tontem's wishes. He had begun to despair of ever finding a husband for his knife-tongued daughter.

He asked Batti, 'You want to stay in Gangtok?'

Batti nodded, because the city attracted her. Dandu Kazi had already talked to her but she did not show her thrill, lest her father be disappointed.

'He'll find a husband for you,' Tontem said.

'I'll scratch his eyes out,' she said.

∽

Tontem woke up Turist three hours before dawn, intending to leave without disturbing Batti, who awoke because of Turist's wailing. Father and daughter wasted time assuaging the child with assurances that his sister would return to be his bride when he was of a marriageable age.

Dandu Kazi also arose, his old bones gave him no rest, he said.

He presented Tontem with a dagger in a jewelled sheath on behalf of the crown and promised to send Kaila Sardar's replacement by the time of the rice harvest. He also promised to visit next year to have a look at the rivers.

Tontem had already descended the hill from Pangthang to Gangtok's north by the time it was dawn. He carried Turist on his shoulder and as he walked he plotted for the future. The world was large. At Yeigang he would take Kaila Sardar's wife, as a gesture of gratitude for the good man's worth. Her daughter could marry Chyadar and maybe lessen his surliness. At the end, there would be a village of people in Lhaizalzed, each deformed in a small way, and Tontem would sit at the head whenever everyone gathered, and become the founding father of a new clan. He would be as wise as the Abbot, as clear-sighted as the Lopen, as rich as the Yabla and as honourable as Dandu Kazi. He walked with steady steps, for he planned to reach Yeigang by next evening.

SIGNS

NIRMAL VERMA

Translated from the Hindi by Pratik Kanjilal

The way he took the stairs, you wouldn't know that he was at least sixty or sixty-five. People silently made way for him. At the reception counter, he always showed his library membership card. There was really no need—everyone knew him.

He would turn to the reference section. Polished wooden almirahs crammed with encyclopedias, dictionaries, film and theatre journals. He browsed through one, then another. Then he would sit down in his favourite corner at an empty table. Out of the window, he could see the branches of an ancient peepul tree swaying in the wind.

Like he did every day, he would put down on a table the newspapers and magazines that he had picked up from another section. It was against library rules, of course—you were not supposed to take material from one section into another. But no one said anything to Amar Babu. He was an old member, and more significantly, he was hard of hearing. You had to speak so loudly to him that to prevent him from breaking one rule, you would have to break another yourself. There was a notice on every wall: *Please speak softly in the library.*

So Amar Babu was left to deport himself according to his own rules. His was the loneliest corner in the library—the heap of reference volumes and journals completely concealed him. From afar, no one could make out who lay hidden behind those battlements of books. When he tired of reading, he would put his head down on a thick encyclopedia and doze off. This was the other advantage of sitting in the reference section—there were thick, leather-bound pillows ready at hand.

But something unexpected happened that day. He set the magazines aside and wiped the glass top of the table with a handkerchief. Then he took a letter out of his pocket, unfolded it slowly and began to read.

He was reading this letter for the fifth time. He had read it three times at home and once on the bus. He closed his eyes. The breath trapped in his chest by the climb up the stairs was now whistling slowly out of the minute airways of the lungs. He sat there, immobile. His name in green ink on the envelope, Amrish Ray 'Amar', regarded him with as much surprise as he regarded that inscription.

The letter had arrived in the morning. Not really a letter, just a mimeograph on pale, flimsy paper. A mimeograph in which a magazine editor had said, in impersonal typescript, that they were putting together a special issue on the Delhi of the Partition years. They would be happy to publish whatever he could write for them. Not less than a thousand words, and if he happened to write too much, he mustn't worry about it—they would cut it down to size. And he was to rest assured that no one would tamper with the sense...

He stopped reading. Why me? Where did they get my address? They must have taken it from an old journal...but how did they guess my age? Lots of people from that time come to the library. Someone could have seen me here. But finally, why? His eye ran down the lines of black typewritten characters to the end, to the one line written by hand...the only sign of life in the whole letter: I hope you will not disappoint us. And below it, the editor's signature, as flamboyant as a missile in flight.

He folded up the letter neatly and put it back in the envelope. Then he took out the notebook he always brought to the library. If he came across interesting information, or just happened to like a writer's style, he always made a little note of it. But today, he opened the notebook on a fresh page. He wrote his name at the top and the date at the bottom of the sheet. Then he began to compose a reply to the letter. For the first time he was using the notebook to write a letter.

Dear Sir,

> I have received your letter and am surprised at your request. I
> am grateful to you, but I should inform you that I have not
> written for the press for quite a long time. Perhaps you have
> seen me in the library and concluded that I still write. But I
> now come to the library merely to pass the time, not to gather
> material as I used to...

He paused. His pen stood poised above the paper. And then he started
a new paragraph.

> Sir, even if I were to agree to your request, I am not sure that I
> shall be able to do justice to your chosen subject—Delhi during
> the days of the Partition. True, I was here at the time—I was
> in school, and have lived here ever since—but my memory is
> failing. It was never particularly sharp anyway. At my age, it is
> difficult to recall anything in any sort of order. And events that
> I do recall... I am never certain if they are true to history, or
> the fruit of my imagination...

Amar Babu sat gazing blankly at the page. He felt tired. It was a long
time since he had written so much all at once. He had a daughter
in Kanpur, and another was in California, with her husband. He did
his duty by the one in Kanpur, sending her a couple of lines on a
postcard once in a while. The one in California always called on his
birthday. He had become a stranger to the art of writing. He yawned,
put the fountain pen down by the notebook, put his head down on
the table and closed his eyes.

This is his happiest hour—seated here, his head down, behind a
wall of weighty tomes, volumes ranged all about him. An observer
would never know what he was doing—was he pondering something,
or merely asleep? People passed by on tiptoe, reluctant to disturb his
meditations. And among the piles of books on the table, he always
left a gap so that he could catch a glimpse of the peepul tree through
the window. It swayed in the breeze, as did Amar Babu on the deep
surge of sleep. Wide, clean avenues, the lanes of Barakhamba, flights of

parakeets in the thick foliage above Connaught Place...this is what he remembers when he thinks of the Delhi of that time. So many years on, the mists of age have parted and from the window of a speeding bus, swimming in heat and air, he sees Majnu ka Tila, the shops of Daryaganj, Irwin Hospital, Minto Bridge and the tall white pillars of Connaught Place. He was so naïve that he believed Barakhamba Road was named after those pillars. That's where he used to live.

That was the very school bus in which he had dozed all the way home after the final examinations. He couldn't have been more than fifteen or sixteen. Back home, he had slept all day and all night.

The slumber of youth, and after a gruelling examination! Amar Babu woke with a start, as though he had seen deep sleep billowing like sunshine outside the window. April sunshine, when the bougainvillea flowered on the bungalow walls. His father had been allotted the bungalow in the last years of his government service. A big lawn, jamun and simul trees, wide verandas. Delhi this side of Minto Road lived in bungalows like this. On the far side were Daryaganj, the Red Fort, Dariba Kalan, Kashmere Gate...where the very shadows were tinted by history.

If there was a partition at all, it was between the old and new cities, which you had to cross in a bus or tonga. Even in his dreams, he could never have guessed that some day, someone would ask him to write on any other partition.

Amar Babu raised his eyes from the encyclopedia and gazed out of the window. The leaves of the peepul flashed in the sunlight. He smiled. He had been given the bicycle later, he remembered. When the higher secondary results were out, his father had told his mother to ask him what he wanted for a reward. His mother had told him—skates.

∽

Father looked at Mother in surprise. I was summoned to the other room. I said what I wanted again, and he exploded: 'What will you do with skates? Do you see any ice hereabouts?'

I laughed. No, I had not been talking about ice skates. These skates...you could run them anywhere, on the bare floor at home, on the streets.

To keep Mother happy, Father agreed, on one condition—I was not to skate on the streets. I was to skate only on the veranda and the driveway. And only after Father had left for work. The roar of rollerskate wheels was not to grate upon his ears.

I had anticipated that. Actually, I had mentioned the home only to reassure Father. I was quite aware of the fact that I had picked up this lust for skates in another place altogether. In the narrow lane behind Plaza Cinema.

∽

It was called Plaza even in those days. The uproar, the screams of joy, the bubbling laughter that flowed from the lane dragged his feet to a standstill whenever he passed that way. A fierce exultation coursed through his very being. Then his feet would move on, leaving his heart behind. Years later, Amar Babu could still hear those voices echoing in his ears.

It was so strange. If it was not for that impersonal letter he had received, perhaps he would have never recalled that skating rink, which had now broken the calm surface of the deep of memory. It was Zahir Bhai who had first taken him there.

∽

Zahir Bhai was not exactly a friend—he was always with Bhai Sahib, my older brother. When he visited, Bhai Sahib would take him straight to his room, where they would sit for hours, chatting. Once, I had crept up to the window and peeked in through the glass. The sight had shaken my heart—the two sat on either side of a carrom board, smoking. I ran back to my chair on the lawn.

A while later, I saw Zahir Bhai walking towards me from between the trees. I became totally absorbed in my book, as though oblivious to all else.

'What are you reading?'

His voice was oddly mature, serious, but with a streak of good humour. I had never caught that note in Bhai Sahib's voice. I showed him the cover—Dumas's *The Three Musketeers*.

'Like it?'

I nodded.

'Are you dumb? Why don't you speak?'

I reddened. My cheeks burned and I giggled.

'Like to come with me?'

This time. I had to speak: 'Where to?'

'Let's go, mister.' He picked me up from the chair. 'You want to know everything right here?'

In a short while, I saw Bhai Sahib coming out of the bungalow. He had changed into a khaki shirt. The collar was open, and the hair on his chest showed.

'He's coming with us.'

Bhai Sahib looked at me suspiciously. He could not believe that this stay-at-home could go anywhere except to school.

'I'll get ready!' I glanced at Bhai Sahib for permission.

'Don't bother, it isn't a fancy-dress parade. Just put on your shoes. They won't let you in in sandals.'

∽

With a start, Amar Babu woke up. Delhi in the days of the Partition?

∽

Quiet, empty streets, bungalow gates shaded by flame of the forest red as a bride, wide lawns and me, perched behind Zahir Bhai as he rode his bicycle under the jamun trees. Bhai Sahib and he cycled along, whistling. If there was a policeman at the traffic lights, Zahir Bhai would hop off and wheel the cycle along, with me still sitting on it. When we were out of eyeshot, he would hop on again. And so we wended our way to this place that I had not even known of before.

A great, whirling hall—really whirling. It was an illusion, of course, set in motion by the crowd of boys and girls circling the floor on skates. The skating rink was lined by iron railings; behind them were ranks of green benches for the spectators, which were almost as thickly peopled as the rink. Music blared from loudspeakers at all corners of the spinning hall. A gentle nudge brought me back to reality.

'Look, we'll be sitting over there. Don't get lost...'

Bhai Sahib headed for an empty bench in the corner. Zahir Bhai seemed to be nowhere. Then I saw him, coming up with three ice cream cones in his hand. He handed me one. 'Eat this first, then you can skate.'

I looked at him in embarrassment. 'I can't skate.'

Zahir Bhai was surprised. 'What do you mean, you can't skate?'

Two girls skated up, grabbed Zahir Bhai from behind and pulled at him. He turned around.

'You're crazy! Could have fallen.'

He was talking about the ice cream cones, of course. There was no danger of the girls tipping over. They watched him eat his cone. A hint of a smile played upon the older girl's lips, but the younger one just stared, dead serious.

'Won't you skate?' the older girl asked.

It was the first time anyone had addressed me with the formal pronoun, 'aap'. I felt older.

'That's why I've brought him along,' said Zahir Bhai.

'This young man needs to be liberated from his books. You'll have to teach him to skate, though.'

The younger girl seemed to shed some of her gloom. Maybe she felt sorry for me.

'Do you want my skates?' she asked. 'I'm through.'

'Oh, no, not right now,' I said. 'I'll come back another day.'

They stood for a while, clutching the iron railings as they chatted with Zahir Bhai and Bhai Sahib. And then they were lost in the swirling crowd in the rink.

Later on, I learned that they were Zahir Bhai's sisters. Let alone introducing me, he had not even told me their names. It would have been awkward to ask them their names afterwards, when I already knew them. So I called them Bari and Chhoti—'Big' and 'Little'—and before I could get to know their names, I...

A veil dropped before Amar Babu's eyes. We forget the names of so many people. It's water under the bridge. We halt in mid-stride, remember, look down and suddenly, in the river of forgetfulness, we see their faces.

There they are, we think, but they are whirled away by the current. We walk on.

∽

I now remember that the higher secondary exam results were announced right after that day at the rink. By the grace of a few numbers, I had made it to the first division. I was quite amazed and, for Father, this was completely unexpected. He rarely looked at my school reports, and even when he did, he could spare only a cursory glance before he signed on the dotted line like the nawabs of old. But this time, he was all eyes. He had never thought much of me, but then, surely my name had not been published in all the English newspapers in error. So when he asked me what I wanted—or Mother asked, for he never asked me anything directly, preferring to use her as a middle-woman—he found Mother primed and ready. He tried to evade the issue, but she was firm and he had to agree.

But Bhai Sahib was irritated: 'You had said that you would ask for a complete set of Sherlock Holmes if you passed. What's happened now?'

'I can always get that from the college library.'

'Why didn't that occur to you earlier?'

I could not explain to him that, at my age, even Sherlock Holmes could not possibly keep track of the ideas that strike you.

I was not sure of Bhai Sahib, given the mood he was in, and decided to go with Zahir Bhai to buy my skates.

When we came out of the shop, Zahir Bhai seemed to be even happier than me. He had decided to carry the skates himself, and was striding energetically in the direction of the rink. He was tall, rangy and fair skinned. Everywhere, the sun seemed to shine on him alone.

His younger sister resembled him, while the older one actually looked younger. When they were whirling in the rink, it was impossible to tell which of them was older, unless you looked closely.

Zahir Bhai halted abruptly. He smiled and put his hand on my shoulder. 'Don't let them see, all right? It'll be a surprise—when you go onto the rink.' My heart sank.

'Don't worry, they'll teach you in a couple of days.'

'Can't you teach me, Zahir Bhai?'

'You're a caution, friend,' he laughed.

∽

I took heart as we walked up the stairs to the rink. It wasn't as crowded as it had been on my first visit. There were just some schoolboys, as unschooled in skating as I was.

Zahir Bhai bought my ticket. He took me into a corner, expertly tied on my skates and drew me towards the rink, like a lamb to the slaughter.

I grabbed hold of the railings and drew myself along on the skates. I felt more confident. Zahir Bhai waved from the distance, urging me on. And then I felt a gentle hand on my shoulder. I turned. Chhoti's wide eyes, and her sister, smiling. Suddenly, I lost my balance and fell. There, in the brightly illuminated rink, I learned how it is possible to see stars in the daytime. And they...

They were nowhere, I was aware only of their hands, helping me up, back to my feet.

∽

Amar Babu started and glanced around him. No, in the drowsy afternoon hour, no one was staring at him. Not too many people about, anyway. Just a few pensioners like him scattered about the tables, and a few young men, obviously unemployed. They were idly turning the pages of their newspapers and magazines. Through the tall windows, he could see the peepul shining through the November mist, the branches casting the lengthening shade of afternoon. He had been looking at this tree for years...in the long summer afternoons, the chiaroscuro of the monsoon and now, the brilliant sheen of early autumn.

His eyes drifted to the letter he had been writing. 'My memory is failing...' Was it just an excuse not to remember? An excuse to forget? We forget much, but never our shame. Tossing in a sleepless bed, crossing the street or dozing in the library, it appears to us with no warning and it feels as though we are still as we were years ago, sensitive, callow, cowardly... Our age is just the surface of the pool and the noose of shame still lies coiled in the depths below, immune to time.

He is still sprawled over, and Bari is lifting him up, and Chhoti is dusting off the seat of his pants with the end of her chunni.

'You'll learn fast now. Everyone falls over in the beginning,' Bari smiled. 'Remember how you used to keep falling over?' she asked her sister.

'And you?'

They were both laughing—not at him, but at each other, so that he could forget the whole episode.

∽

Perhaps that's why he couldn't remember. In the days that followed, he forgot not only himself, but also the very world, in which so much was happening at the time.

∽

When Bhai Sahib and Zahir Bhai came to the rink a few days later, they were amazed. Bhai Sahib had always put me down for a bookworm, and now the worm had turned. In fact, it had stepped out of the covers and was whirling like a windmill's sails on the shining floor of the rink. 'You could get a job in the circus now,' he said. 'Haven't been falling over, have you?'

I shook my head, though under my trouser legs, I was mottled with bruises.

'Your college admission papers have arrived. You'll have to fill them out and send them off. You're hardly ever home these days.' His tone was half proud, half accusing. I had got admission to a college which had refused him.

Chhoti skated up and dragged me off by the hand. 'Please excuse him. He's left our game to talk to you.'

To her, I was a thing of wonder. Not a day passed without her teaching me a new trick. And I learned that life on wheels could be as magical and exciting as that of the creatures of the deep. I had been drawing angles and triangles in my geometry schoolbook, ignorant of the bewitching shapes that could be drawn with a set of wheels. Chhoti took me by the hand and whirled me about, her breath hot. Finally, tired out, I would slip out of the rink when she wasn't looking.

Often, Bari was out there, sitting on a bench, her skates off. She would smile: 'Out early today?'

'Not really, it's been over an hour,' I would say, sitting down beside her and glancing at the cheap watch that Mother had bought me with her own money, without letting Father know. 'Didn't see you at all today.'

'I tire easily these days. I prefer to watch, anyway—you're wonderful.'

୶

The word was laced with a bit of laughter and irony, and a touch of praise. Even today, when Amar Babu hears that word from the mouth of another he feels an ache he can't put a finger on. Her face swims before his eyes, the chunni flung about her throat like a muffler, beads of perspiration on her broad forehead, the red heat of her cheeks. And a strange emptiness in the eyes that he had first seen when she was helping him up from the floor of the rink. And for the first time, he had become aware of the blood thudding in his veins—all unknown to him, blood shaking his heart.

୶

'Chhoti keeps talking about you... You're different—not like the rest of Zahir Bhai's friends.'

'What do you mean, different? Maybe I'm the stupidest of them.'

'Oh, no,' she laughed.

'No, really,' I said. 'That's what she used to call me, Stupid, when she was teaching me to skate.'

'She has names for everyone. Know what she calls me? Bundle.'

'Why?'

'Because I just sit there, she says. No sign of getting up and leaving.'

Chhoti came after a while, quickly took her skates off and dragged her sister to her feet.

'We're late—hurry up or Zahir Bhai will be here with an official summons.'

The stairs led down to the lane behind Plaza Cinema, which still looks the same, and the cycle stand. They would look back after they had climbed onto their bicycles, and I waited, watching them melt away into the evening mist.

Sometimes, Amar Babu fancies that he is still standing there in that lane. He watches the parakeets whirling among the trees of Connaught Place in flocks as thick as dust-devils.

∽

Back home, he went straight to his room. He did not switch on the lights; no one knew he was home. Without bothering to change, he stretched out on the bed. There were many doors within, he thought. If one opened, he heard the creak of another's hinges. Chhoti opens the door, and Bari stands on the threshold; he speaks with one, and he feels the other's eyes boring into his back. It's amazing, you speak with me and listen to someone else—stupid people are like that even when they are grown up. You learned to skate from me and you go sit with Bari.

Perhaps it was all in his mind; perhaps he had actually heard these words. And now, when he was alone, he saw them. He had always found it strange—when you are alone, you can actually see the words you spoke with others. And most of all with Bari, whose silence deepened with every meeting.

∽

I was taken aback that day when I walked up to her bench. Instead of a salwar-kameez, she was in a long skirt and had covered her head with a veil.

'Won't you skate?'

'No,' she shook her head. 'Today, I've come to watch.'

'Aren't you well?' I sat down by her on the bench.

She was silent.

Chhoti glided across the rink. She looked at us once, and then she was lost in the crowd.

'Hasn't Zahir Bhai come?' I asked.

She shook her head. 'He's at home. He needs to pack.' She glanced at me. For the first time, I saw a smile on her pale, tired face. 'You've started going to college, haven't you?'

'Not yet—I've just got admission. The college doesn't open for another week. Are you going somewhere? You didn't tell me anything.'

She was silent, and then she shook her head in a way which could mean anything.

'I've heard you read a lot.'

I laughed in embarrassment. 'Says who?'

'Zahir Bhai,' she laughed. 'He brought you here to free you from the clutches of your books.'

She was looking for something in her bag.

'I brought this for you.' Something gift-wrapped.

'May I open it?'

'Not now. Open it when you get home.'

I looked up, Chhoti stood before me.

Bari looked at her, her eyes far away. She was smiling over the secret of the gift.

∽

When the three of them took the stairs that evening and went their separate ways, there was nothing to rouse his suspicions, and like always, the girls turned back to wave as they rode away on their bicycles. Everyday events always seem unremarkable; the shadow of ill omen that falls across them is invisible. But long after, he remembers Bari's silence, the gift-wrapped book, how Chhoti had left them alone together on the bench. Ordinary, everyday events bring so many signs swaddled in their folds. We understand what they mean long after they are history. Only an unnamed sadness remains, which steals upon you unawares.

∽

Going home in the bus, I felt that the gift wrapped in coloured paper was a sign. If I opened the package, everything that we keep concealed from ourselves would come tumbling out—love, happiness, pain, remorse. All from this little bundle that she had left behind.

Bundle—that's what Chhoti used to call her. Who would just sit there, would not leave. And once she left, would be lost to sight forever.

∽

The lights of the library were being switched on. Outside the window, the peepul was lost in the twilight. Amar Babu picked up the books that surrounded him and set them aside—the Oxford Dictionary, the Encyclopaedia Britannica, reference titles on Hollywood, all the weighty volumes in whose cover he spent his afternoons. His gaze drifted to the letter he had received that day: 'You were in Delhi in the days of the Partition; could you write about it for us?'

Amar Babu stood up. Slowly, very slowly, he walked down the stairs of the library.

PERIOD OF MOURNING

BOLWAR MAHAMAD KUNHI

Translated from the Kannada by Keerti Ramachandra

1

If any of you die
And leave widows behind;
They shall wait concerning themselves
Four months and ten days
When they have fulfilled their term there is no blame
On you if they dispose
Of themselves in a just
And reasonable manner.
And Allah is well acquainted
With what ye do.

—Quran, Surah Al-Baqarah 234

Mehrunissa's calculation was right. When this night passes into day, the iddath, the period of mourning, will come to an end. Abbah! It's gone so quickly. Seems like it all happened yesterday.

How do I look now? 'You must not look into the mirror during iddath,' Chikkamma, her stepmother, had said. But the other day she had caught her reflection in the copper water pot while bathing. She was startled. Earlobes bare, without the alikhat, every piece of jewellery locked away in a trunk. No one had seen her peep at herself but the All-knowing, All-seeing Allah had. He holds all the strings. He rewards those who live by the rules. He would have heard my tauba of repentance when I looked at myself. He will definitely forgive me.

> *You alone can pardon my sins, Allah!*
> *Show me mercy.*
> *For diligently reading the Holy Quran every day for these past weeks,*
> *Show mercy to me.*
> *Allah, grant that by reading the Quran*
> *I will remember that which I have forgotten.*
> *Lord of the Universe, grant that this Book*
> *Will be my life's anchor. Ameen.*

Mehrunissa finished her prayer, raised the book to her lips, wrapped it in green cloth and placed it on the table. She then pressed her hands to her eyes.

Just one more night. Tomorrow she would be free to warm herself on the washing stone near the well. It would not be a sin to sit on the armchair in the veranda and listen to songs on the radio. She could comb her hair in front of the mirrored cupboard in Samad's room, and Kaijamma would not scold her.

How must Samad be now? It seemed like years since she had seen him. His banter, as he talked to Kaijamma, had forced his way into her room despite her resistance. They used to laugh at him, but he continued to say, 'Let all that be, I am here, aren't I?' So much has happened in these two years! Like a dream, all of it. Anything is possible if Allah so desires it. He is the great magician.

Mehrunissa had never imagined that she would be the mistress of such a large house. In her impoverished dreams even a palace would have a thatched roof.

When Mehrunissa was about fifteen, two monsoons before her wedding, her father had been admitted to the government hospital. A week later, he came home on a bier. Mehrunissa's tears would have drowned the whole village that day. She had rushed into the courtyard where her father's body was being washed and fallen on the ground, wailing. Someone had picked her up as if she were a bird and taken her indoors.

Why had I wept so much? Because my father had died? Or

because I was afraid for myself, my own fate? Would I have grieved like this if my mother had been alive? Was Chikkamma, my stepmother, the reason? And yet this same Chikkamma had made her the mistress of this mansion. Who would not have given his daughter to such a wealthy merchant!

On the first night itself Puttaba Sahukar had sat his bride on the bed and explained, 'You are the mistress of this household. You will not want for anything. Allah has given me enough. You will never have to hold out your hands to anyone for anything.' Even if she did, who was there to see it? That was not true. There were two others who cared about her.

Thirty years ago Puttaba had walked the streets of Muthupady with a basket of dried fish on his head. Soon he was riding a bicycle selling fresh fish. In no time at all he gave up the fish trade and opened a provision shop near the panchayat office and before long, had built this huge house. Behind the transformation of Puttaba the fish seller to Puttaba Sahukar was the story of years of hard work.

Puttaba Sahukar, who had passed away four months and ten days ago, had not been old enough to die. Only forty or forty-five and not afflicted by any serious ailment. Is it possible to explain what or why things happen in Allah's game?

Puttaba had an imposing personality. When customers saw him with a turban on his head, seated behind the counter, they instinctively addressed him as 'sahukar'. If he raised his voice he could be heard a hundred yards away. A few streaks of grey had appeared in his hair, but his bushy eyebrows were still coal black. Six months before his wedding, the dentist had replaced the bad teeth in his mouth with six false ones, but no one could tell. Though his belly had gone out of shape, he was stronger than most young men.

This man, who stood out in a crowd, had married Sakina before a hundred witnesses. But after barely three months, Sakina had run out into the courtyard in the middle of the night and despite Puttaba's entreaties, had thrown herself into the well. For four days Puttaba had burned with fever. He had clung to young Samad, the boy he had hired to help in the shop, and sobbed inconsolably. People felt sorry for him. Samad, on the threshold of fifteen, was frightened by his master's behaviour.

Vowing never to bring another woman into the house, Puttaba Sahukar sent for Kaijamma, a distant cousin, to manage his household. After twelve years, one month before the monsoon season last year, he had suddenly decided to remarry and brought Mehrunissa, twenty-five years younger than himself, into the house. And Samad smiled from under his newly sprouted moustache.

'You don't need to veil yourself in Samad's presence. He is an orphan. He has been with me for many years. There is no distinction between him and me in this house,' said Puttaba Sahukar, as he introduced Samad. Oozing virility, Samad had offered Mehrunissa a bouquet of flowers with respectful affection.

The nubile eighteen year-old-girl, seeing such a bright face for the first time, broke into a sweat.

Puttaba Sahukar did not come home for lunch. Samad would arrive as the afternoon call to prayer sounded, to pick up the Sahukar's lunch box. The tinkle of Samad's cycle bell as she waited by the window, her face pressed to the bars, gave Mehrunissa much pleasure.

Everything her husband had told her that first night was true. She lacked for nothing. Who but a princess would eat chicken curry twice a week? She only had to mention it and a juicy chicken leg would appear by her side as she sat twiddling the knobs of the radio. Even her own mother could not have given her so much love.

Mehrunissa had no recollection of her mother. She had died when Mehrunissa was just a year old. That the woman in the house was not her mother, Mehrunissa had realized very early. Her three stepsisters were born in quick succession and when a son's cries filled the house, the responsibility for the girls fell on Mehrunissa's young shoulders.

By the time Mehrunissa was twelve she held the record for rolling a thousand beedis a day in the Muthupady beedi factory. That record is still unbroken. Besides rolling beedis, Mehrunissa had to bathe, dress, and feed her younger sisters. Her day began before sunrise, when she had to fill the clay pot with water to heat it for a bath. Chikkamma suffered from severe back pain and a steaming hot bath provided some relief. In between the other chores, Mehrunissa would do the cooking. After lunch Chikkamma would sleep till four, wake up, nag Mehrunissa, then go off to the neighbour's to gossip. She would remember to come home only when dusk had fallen. Mehrunissa's father, a coolie in Kini's godown near the bus stand, would leave in the morning and return at night. It wasn't as if he was unaware of the 'badar yuddha', the great war (a key battle in the early days of Islam) going on at home. He had had a word with his wife about it, but immediately after that her back pain would intensify and Mehrunissa would have to sit up all night massaging her back. Her father could do nothing to prevent Mehrunissa from being ill-treated. But the day before he went into the hospital, he told his wife, 'Don't be unkind to Mehrunissa. Allah won't like it.'

Chikkamma had heeded her husband's last words. Within two years of being widowed she arranged a nikah between Puttaba Sahukar, the provision merchant, and Mehrunissa—something she was sure Allah would approve of. Mehrunissa may have been radiant with the glow of youth but would getting her married off be easy? Where would the ten sovereigns of gold and three thousand rupees come from? Allah didn't shower gold and cash from the sky, did he?

Puttaba Sahukar had gold. He had wealth. What he did not have, Mehrunissa had in plenty. As soon as he saw her, he agreed to the match and thanked Allah for creating this lovely girl exclusively for him.

And yet when Sahukar extended his hands during the nikah ceremony, his hands shook. Samad noticed this, and often joked about it. 'Your women are like your fields. Approach them as you wish.'

When the bride was about to depart for Puttaba Sahukar's house, Chikkamma embraced her and wept. Mehrunissa was taken aback. Even when they had prepared to carry her father's body away she had not sobbed like this. 'You are going into a big house, Unissa... don't forget your Chikkamma's children once you are there,' she cried.

Even if Mehrunissa wanted to, Chikkamma would not let her forget. Every other week she turned up to ask after Mehrunissa's welfare. She brought an empty sack with her and Kaijamma filled it with rice and coconuts before she left. For whom was her brother accumulating wealth anyway? And Chikkamma's children were not such distant relatives after all.

Mehrunissa could not understand Kaijamma's behaviour. She had never had a confrontation with Mehrunissa. Mehrunissa had sometimes spoken rudely to her. Kaijamma had laughed it off. 'You don't know anything, you silly girl. You have not bathed in as much water as I have drunk in my lifetime,' she'd said.

Mehrunissa got out of bed, crossed the kitchen and opened the back door leading to the bathing room. A pile of dry wood lay in a corner, waiting to be put under the boiler outside so the smoke didn't enter the house. Whenever Mehrunissa had felt low she would lock herself in this room and weep her heart out. If crying could give her relief she would have bawled so loudly that the paddy mudis stacked in the loft would have come tumbling down. Her pain might have eased a little if she could share it with someone. But how could she tell anyone that her saintly husband, much older than her father, had fallen at her feet on their wedding night and wept like a woman? What use would that have been? Tauba, tauba! How could I even think such wicked thoughts!

She poured lotas of water on herself in her attempt to forget the image dancing before her eyes—of Samad, bathing by the well, emptying the large copper pot over himself in one fluid movement, his strong male body shivering under a cascade of cold water. Every time she watched him through the crack in the kitchen window she would say tauba and pray that she would be spared punishment by lashes.

2

Not much longer now. The clock in the veranda had struck twelve a long time back. Even when Sahukar was alive it had been Samad's job to wind the clock once a week. He must be fast asleep now, spread-eagled like a frog.

Soon the chickens in the backyard would start clucking. There were many more chickens in the coop then. Twice a week a meal of chicken saaru and akki roti meant that Samad would grab two birds from the coop, and take them to the nearby mosque to be slaughtered according to the rules. He would buy two more chickens and bring them home, dangling upside down from the handlebar of his cycle. To this day, Mehrunissa had not seen a single chicken escape Samad's grasp.

Everything Samad did was perfect. Always enthusiastic, never indifferent. Ask for anything and he'd say, 'Leave it to me, I'm there, aren't I?' Hair pins, tins of kajal, perfumed oil...all delivered the very same evening. Puttaba Sahukar was too embarrassed to go looking for plastic bangles or hair clips! Samad had as much authority in the house as Puttaba, and enjoyed free access to the cash box in the shop, as well as to the pickle jars in the kitchen.

But the keys to the shop were always at Puttaba Sahukar's waist. The bunch hung from a specially made thick leather belt and Puttaba would insist on opening the shop every morning and shutting it at night. It was a strange obsession. Samad had never touched the shop keys. Nor had he ever wanted to. His mischievous smile needed no doors or keys to enter.

The only time seriousness and anxiety had appeared on Samad's broad face, it had lasted for exactly eight days. During that time the big brass lock remained on the wooden door of Puttaba Sahukar's provision shop.

One evening, barely a month after Ramzan, Puttaba Sahukar came home earlier than usual, refused his dinner and lay down, complaining of mild chest pain. Immediately Mehrunissa thought of her father. While she sat by her husband's side, massaging his chest she could hear Samad's voice talking to Kaijamma in the room with the mirrored cupboard. He had come to the door of the bedroom a couple of times and asked, 'Shall I get the doctor?' Puttaba had waved him away.

The following morning, when Puttaba Sahukar showed no signs of getting up, Samad looked grim—something Mehrunissa had not expected—and said, 'He who can decide whether to call the doctor or not does not lie in bed like this. Leave it to me. I am here, aren't I?' Like a gust of wind he went out. Mehrunissa couldn't believe it. This worried look did not sit well on the face that broke into a mischievous smile so readily.

Puttaba had a heart like wax. It melted at the mention of sorrow or pain. But he wasn't stupid, and did not fail to notice the admiring glances Mehrunissa threw Samad's way.

Making poor light an excuse, Puttaba had had his bed moved to the outer room with the mirrored cupboard. He had not wanted the doctor or Samad barging into his bedroom ten times a day. Mehrunissa never stepped into that room when Samad was in the house.

In the days before her husband fell ill, it had been Mehrunissa's habit to stand before the full-length mirror, stroking her golden, smooth as silk stomach and sigh, after Puttaba and Samad had left the house.

One day, as he lay on his sick bed, Puttaba's attention was caught by his wife's long dark hair, flowing serpent-like down her back, reflected in the mirror. He said, 'I have done you great injustice. Who will be there for you now?'

'Don't worry about that. I am there, aren't I?' said Samad, 'I am not one to give up so easily. The doctor refused to come at night. But I grabbed his bag and ran. You please go inside, now,' he said to Mehrunissa and summoned the doctor. Her husband's last words had faded away before they were uttered.

Puttaba suffered for only four days. On Thursday night he seemed slightly better, but on Friday morning he did not open his eyes.

✆

All night Samad had remained awake but had dozed off early in the morning. When he woke up, crows were circling about the courtyard.

> *Oh peaceful soul, return to your God.*
> *You will be happy there*
> *He too will be satisfied with you.*
> *Join those in my service*
> *And enter now my heaven.*

From the courtyard came sounds of voices, footsteps, wailing, consoling. In the bedroom, Mehrunissa sat alone, her face on her knees. 'Let no one talk to her. Let the young girl cry herself out,' she heard Kaijamma tell someone. Boobamma and her daughters, Saramma and Radhakka, were all there. How had the news spread so quickly? Chikkamma had dragged her two youngest ones along with her and was demanding to be the chief mourner. Even Kaijamma found her wailing 'What will become of you now, Unissa?'—intolerable.

When Mehrunissa had thrown herself on her husband's wooden body, Kaijamma had taken hold of her and led her into her room. 'You will not come out of here now, child. There is no use grieving so much. You have to face what has happened. Besides, what has happened? One less person to talk to, that's all, isn't it?'

Hmmm. How does Kaijamma know everything? Within four months of becoming the mistress of the house Mehrunissa had discovered that nothing could be hidden from the old woman.

One day, just after Samad had left with Puttaba's lunch box, Kaijamma had said to Mehrunissa, holding her by the arm, 'Look, my child, I too was once young like you. This Puttaba is very tender-hearted. He cannot harm even an ant. You know what he is. Whether you put him in water or immerse him in milk, it is entirely up to you.' Mehrunissa had fallen at Kaijamma's feet and sobbed bitterly. Kaijamma's eyes too had filled. Kaijamma never had to speak to her like that again. Mehrunissa's behaviour had not warranted it.

∽

Samad knew hundreds of stories. Some he had heard, some he made up. When Mehrunissa and Kaijamma sat by the well plucking a chicken, Samad would join them and talk to them about brave princes and beautiful princesses. The prince would enter the seven-walled fort in the guise of a guard. The soldiers would try to capture him. He would mount his white Arab steed and fly off into the sky. Or, the prince would set off to fetch the pearl necklace the princess wanted. He would mount his magic horse and cross the seven seas and reach the demon's cave. When the demon assumed the form of a pig the prince would turn tail and run away. Samad's stories had humour too! Both women would forget the chicken and lose themselves in the adventure. When the story ended, Samad would clap his hands and laugh loudly, bringing them back to reality. Embarrassed, Kaijamma would scold him, 'Now, will you get out of here or shall I tell Puttaba to stitch up your tongue?'

Even after Samad had gone back to the shop Mehrunissa would wander around the seven-walled fort with the prince until Kaijamma brought her out of her reverie. And each time Mehrunissa would bite her lip and admit her guilt. But the day her husband died, the prince who pushed into the seven-walled fort and reached for the throne startled Mehrunissa.

After the ritual bathing of the body, prayers were recited in the courtyard. Soon they will carry his body away. And then there will be no man in this whole house. Mehrunissa trembled with fear. Just then she heard footsteps. She looked up and saw Samad leaning against the door. Quickly she stood up, cowering against the wall, her heart thudding. Samad must have heard it too.

'I need the keys to the shop.'

Mehrunissa's blood ran cold. Her lips began to tremble, her mouth went dry.

'Have to buy agarbattis. Also require some cash.'

Her legs wobbled. She felt faint but steadied herself and sat down on the bed. Her right hand reached for the keys that were always kept under the pillow.

Puttaba Sahukar had insisted on having his beloved keys under his pillow. He had told Mehrunissa, 'You see these keys? They are mine. Only I have the right over them. My elders left me nothing. I have worked hard and earned all this. Not by breaking anyone's head. You must keep these keys safely.'

Mehrunissa had fulfilled her duty diligently. When Puttaba returned from the shop he would unhook the key bunch from his belt and hand it to Mehrunissa. She would tuck it under his pillow every night and hand it to him the next morning before he left for the shop. This had been the practice for the last two years. Even Kaijamma had not touched the keys. But the day Puttaba had been moved to the outer room with a mirror, the keys had remained under the pillow in the bedroom.

'It's getting late. Where are the keys?' This time it was not a request. It was a demand.

...Lord of the universe, Allah,
If You wish it, You grant authority,
If You so wish You snatch it away.
You reward those who You please,
You are capable of executing all things,
If my thoughts are wrong, forgive me.

Biting her lip Mehrunissa stood up, reached for the keys under the pillow, and held them out to Samad.

3

Even as a child Mehrunissa had learnt that crows start cawing before sunrise. In an hour daylight would nudge its way into the room. Mehrunissa had got used to waking up for the morning namaz because of Chikkamma. No one would question her if she woke up at ten o'clock in Puttaba's house. Kaijamma could manage all the work herself, but Mehrunissa would say her morning prayers and finish the work in the kitchen before Kaijamma could protest.

However, when Mehrunissa sat for iddath Kaijamma had to do everything. Mehrunissa was not to step out of the room, except to go to the bathroom. No male eye was to fall on her. If she had children, then it would have been different.

Surprisingly, she had no difficulty adjusting to the new routine. It was not very different from her life with Chikkamma. Except for the visit to the government hospital when ill or the annual Muthupady fair she never stepped out of the house.

What with looking after her sisters and rolling beedis, she had had no desire to meet strange men. Yet when she heard Chikkamma making plans for her marriage she must have had some vague dreams about it. As for the man she would marry, she had no idea. So she was more or less happy to be Puttaba Sahukar's wife. Who would not like getting three good meals a day without having to roll beedis?

The main change in her routine after iddath was not entering the room with the mirrored cupboard and the veranda. She used to visit Maimoona sometimes to play with her child. But she did not miss that. Those visits were more humiliation than happiness.

Thirteen days after Puttaba Sahukar's death the fatiha prayer for the dead was conducted. The following day Kaijamma said with some hesitation, 'The shop has been closed for almost a month. The provisions in the house won't last forever. What should we do?' Kaijamma left the decision entirely to Mehrunissa.

It was not difficult for Mehrunissa to answer her question. Puttaba had been telling her everything about the business—how much profit he had made, what to do if the price of coconuts fell suddenly— 'Make coconut chutney and plaster it on our heads, that's all,' he would say, and doze off. Mehrunissa would lie there staring at the ceiling, coaxing sleep to come.

Kaijamma waited for Mehrunissa's answer.

Then she said, 'I've told Samad I will speak to him in the evening. Nothing wrong if he asks what is to be done. He is a man. He must know what there is for him. We can easily tell him to leave. But who else do we have? Think it over till evening.' Kaijamma walked away.

The key bunch still lay under the pillow. Samad had taken it the day her husband died and returned it through Kaijamma the same evening.

Mehrunissa tried to read the Quran but a hundred thoughts kept running through her mind. Which other man can take charge of this house? Had Kaijamma been suggesting something this morning? Would Samad walk away if they told him to go? He may not be a blood relation, but he came to this house before I did. He too has a share in this property. He is a man, what if he tells Kaijamma and me to get out and takes possession of the house? Mehrunissa shuddered. Would Samad send me away? Chee! He is not like that. I will remain the mistress here.

So what did Kaijamma have in mind? Tauba, tauba! Mehrunissa rubbed her eyes and focussed on the lines of the Quran:

During the period of iddath
Discussing remarriage with the widows or considering it
Is not wrong. Allah knows everything.
However, until the period of mourning is over
Do not take a decision about marriage.
Allah would be aware of it.
Hence be fearful of Him.
He is compassionate and merciful.

When Kaijamma brought Mehrunissa's lunch into the room that afternoon, Mehrunissa held out the keys to her. Kaijamma took them without a word. She did not like chatting with anyone in iddath. She was saddled with another job now—taking the keys every morning and bringing them back at night. She did not refer to the shop nor did she mention Samad. Mehrunissa did not ask. Reading the Quran all day and spending the night in restless sleep—that's how four months and ten days had gone by. But when Kaijamma came for the keys and when she returned them, Mehrunissa's mind galloped out of control.

Samad did not come home for lunch. Kaijamma had casually mentioned that he had employed a small boy to take his food to the shop. Mehrunissa had not reacted.

Allah, who controls the movement of Sun and Moon
Save me from the torment of hell.
Keep the doors of heaven open for me.
For those who have feared Allah, two heavenly gardens are available.
Gardens with spreading green trees
Each one bearing two kinds of fruit
Within one's reach. Reclining under them,
On silken cushions, honourable women. Not just beautiful
Chaste, virtuous,
Untouched by man or devil.
He who fears the Lord will be bound in matrimony
With a beautiful, large-eyed woman.

A shiver went through Mehrunissa as she finished her namaz. The words thrilled her. She prayed that her husband would receive all these pleasures. And for herself? Being born a woman is a grave sin. So where's the question of reward?

She saw daylight creeping in through the window. In a few minutes everything would be bright. She heard sounds from the kitchen. Must be Kaijamma. Samad woke up late.

She had often seen his reflection as he lay by the window, legs spread wide, the sunlight making a halo around him. Was he sprawled like that today, too? It was four months and ten days since she had seen his face.

Kaijamma called out from the kitchen, 'Are you awake, child?'

She had been asking the same question every day during the iddath and Mehrunissa had not bothered to answer. But today she felt like replying. It was not a sin to go out now. But go where? To the kitchen? What will Kaijamma say? Let her come and call me. Putting away the Quran, touching her fingertips to her eyes, Mehrunissa lay down on the bed. She had waited so long, what was a few minutes more?

She heard Samad talking to Kaijamma in the veranda. It was not yet time to go to the shop. She waited eagerly for Kaijamma to come and take the keys. But she didn't come. The front door opened, then closed. Mehrunissa was surprised. Where could Samad have gone?

When Kaijamma came in with her breakfast, Mehrunissa was confused. Had she miscalculated? She used to mark the pages of the Quran every day. Kaijamma had told her only yesterday that she did not have much longer to wait. Why didn't she call me to the kitchen, then? Swallowing the question that was rising in her throat she reached for the plate.

'Puttaba couldn't stand menthe dosai,' Kaijamma said. 'Samad loves them. Asked me to make them yesterday.'

Mehrunissa suspected something. She peered at Kaijamma's face but there was no deceit in her eyes.

'Samad is not going to the shop today. He is going to Kasargod,' Kaijamma said casually.

'To Kasargod? Why?'

Picking up the empty plate and glass Kaijamma said, 'He made me swear not to tell you till the iddath was over. The Kasargod party has been after him. He told them, in my presence, that only when *you* go and approve of the girl will it be possible for them to take things forward. He has gone to inform them that the girl viewing will be next Thursday or Friday.' She paused. 'My time too is limited. You must like the girl who will be your daughter-in-law. Samad has agreed. If you say yes, he will marry her—even if she is blind or lame. One must have done some good deeds to get a boy like Samad, no?'

Mehrunissa did not faint. In a daze, she prayed:

Oh Allah!
Let fall the red, scalded sun on a sinner like me
Make me tread boiling water
Pour molten copper over me.

BULBULS

HABIB KAMRAN

Translated from the Kashmiri by Neerja Mattoo

1

It was the last fortnight of April, that time of year when one loves to sit in the sun. That is what I was doing, sitting in my garden right opposite the rose bush which is entangled with the branches of another tree next to the wall. I was just a few metres away from the wall and saw a bulbul fly right into its centre. Another bulbul kept watch on the wall. The first one came out and the second went in. For the rest of the day, I saw the pair taking turns bringing twigs, blades of grass, bits of string, some long, some thick, in their beaks and taking them into the rose bush.

One day I peeped into the bush and saw that the bulbuls had woven a nest. It had been fashioned with twigs on the outside, secured tightly with the inner branches of the rose bush. The inside of the nest was soft, woven with linen-like fibres of god-knows-what tree. It looked so downy inside, smooth and tender. It was the size of a large china cup on the outside, while the inside was smaller. What surprised me, however, was that it had room to accommodate just one bulbul. I had always imagined that, like human beings, birds too had homes in which the adult pair and their children could live. In the case of bulbuls, at least, I was proved wrong. It was obvious that only one, the female, could stay in the nest, while the male spent the night outside.

A few days later, I peeped into the nest and found three tiny eggs in it. They were the size of little marbles, but not perfectly

120

round. They were oval in shape. So far, I had only seen white eggs, but these had black spots and streaks over the white surface. I picked one up. It felt warm. I kept looking at it. It really was a pretty little thing. Suddenly, there was a loud twittering. I looked up and saw the pair of bulbuls in a highly disturbed state, making a commotion from where they were perched on the wall. They appeared to be glaring at me. I felt like someone who had been caught trespassing. It was almost as if I had put my hand into someone's pocket and had my wrist gripped hard by him. The egg had been in my palm for barely a few seconds, yet the agitation of the bulbuls was extreme. I hastily put back the egg in the nest.

The next morning I was again drawn to the rose bush and took a look inside. The eggs were hidden, under the bulbul's protective warmth. Whenever I looked into the nest afterwards, I always found the bulbul in it. I wondered when it went out to find food. So far the only eggs I had seen being hatched were pigeon's eggs. And there both the male and female took turns sitting on them. But here it was not possible for me to tell whether a similar practice was being followed or only the mother bird at the job. As far as I could see, there was this one bulbul, always there, on duty, steadfast and constant.

A few days later when I went to take a look, I found the bulbul not in the nest, but perched on its edge, looking intently at something in the nest. After a while it flew away, giving me an opportunity to look inside. There were tiny baby bulbuls in place of the eggs. They were very small, each hardly the size of a tiny tadpole. Two little twigs for wings, two more thin ones for legs, no sign of a beak. Two small dots suggested the eyes. Now I understood the meaning of the Kashmiri phrase used to describe someone of very tender age as 'one whose very eyes are not yet fashioned!' They were extremely delicate looking things even more fragile than a newborn baby, just little lumps of frail flesh, with not even a trace of down on them. The neck was just a bit of thick thread; one of them stretched its neck and something like a beak opened at the end of it, as if begging for food. But the next moment it fell back among its siblings, and once again all three lay huddled together, resting on one another, necks intertwined. The tiny faces of the chicks were still undefined by any features. All three birds put together were no longer than the yolk of a hen's egg. I must have observed them for hardly ten or fifteen seconds—it is taking longer to describe it—when I was startled by loud twittering. Once again the pair of bulbuls were highly agitated, fluttering their wings restlessly, perched on the wall, their eyes on me and the nest. Somewhat nervous, I withdrew quickly. Instantly, one of the adult birds flew into the nest and sheltered the chicks. It was afternoon at that time. Till the light faded, I kept peeping into the nest through the tracery of the rose branches, and always found the babies hidden under the mother's wings.

The next morning I went out again, curious to see what the bulbuls were feeding their young ones. For most of the day, I noticed one bulbul constantly in the nest, the babies under its wing. Its mate came in with something in its beak. It looked like a slender bit of peel. God knows whether it was plant matter or perhaps the wing of a dead moth, but it was certainly something soft. The bulbul bringing the food would land on a rose branch near the nest and the one in the nest would fly away, as if to give the other one room to feed the chicks what it had fetched. After the babies were fed, it too would fly away. From then onwards, the two would take turns foraging for food, bringing in something or the other in their beaks and feeding the babies. I noticed, however, that the interval between meal times seemed to progressively lengthen. Perhaps they did not want to overfeed those delicate stomachs.

As a matter of routine, I would leave grains of rice or crumbs of bread for the bulbuls on my veranda. As soon as the bulbuls saw them, they would fly down from wherever they were—swinging from an electric cable or the branch of a tree—and begin pecking at the food. On the day I observed the babies being fed for the first time, I scattered some rice as usual. The adult bulbuls arrived and began to eat. I wondered why they did not pick any for their babies, perhaps it was too hard and not the right kind of food for the tiny ones.

∽

Two days later, clouds began to gather in the afternoon and by evening it was raining. During the night it turned into a regular downpour. I couldn't keep my thoughts away from the bulbuls and their little ones in the nest in the rose bush, unprotected from the pelting rain. The next morning I went out very early to take a look and found one of the bulbuls in the nest, guarding its treasure under its wing. Meanwhile, the cloud cover thickened further and soon there was thunder and lightning. The fury of the storm increased very quickly and the rain came down in a deluge. The wind was so powerful that it bent the tallest willow, forcing it to touch the earth. The rose bush shook violently. Suddenly it was so cold that people were forced to hug their kangris in the month of May! Even through the raging storm, I stepped out from time to time and always found the bulbul at its post, sheltering the babies from the onslaught of the elements. Drenched to the bone, and seemingly shrunk by the intense cold it held on, bearing the brunt of the piercing wind and water, while shielding the fledglings, and giving them the warmth of its own body.

⌇

That day I never saw the bulbul leave its nest to look for food. Apparently, what was necessary was to save the babies from the rain and cold, the question of satisfying its own hunger did not arise.

By afternoon the rain had stopped and the bulbul emerged, quickly foraged for food and, putting a few grains in its mouth, picked up something for the babies and fed them. Soon it was joined by the other bulbul and the two fed them as fast as they could, obviously the famished babies needed quick nourishment.

Today, the fourth day, was bright and sunny and warmer. Now it was continuous hard work for the bulbuls; they took it in turns to find food for the babies and to shelter them under their wings.

The next day, I threw some rice on the veranda floor. The bulbuls came and pecked at the food as usual. But today they carried some grains in their beaks to the nest and fed them to the little ones. Within four days then, the fledglings graduated to what had been deemed too tough for them to eat at birth. But I also noticed that for the adult bulbuls, rice was not as important as worms. They would forage among branches of trees and plants intently, their quick, sharp eyes searching for insects and other tiny living things that they would grab at with lightning speed. The main focus of their search was flowering plants, because these were the haunts of bees, butterflies and other insects. Throughout the day, with no rest at all, they would flit from plant to nest and back again.

⁂

Suddenly I wanted to see how much the little birds had grown. I waited for both the bulbuls to fly away to a distance, before taking a peep into the nest. The baby birds had grown beyond my expectations. They even had tiny, soft feathers covering their heads and backs. I had hardly looked at them for a few seconds when I was startled by a loud flapping of wings above my head. It was one of the adult bulbuls, trying to frighten me away from the nest.

I retreated obediently.

⁂

For the next three or four days, I would sit in the sunny garden, reading the newspaper or a book, keeping an eye on the comings and goings of the bulbuls, but not approaching the nest too often.

The baby bulbuls had hatched eight days ago. Now the parents were busy throughout the day, gathering caterpillars and other tiny creatures to feed the babies. They did not seem to rest at all. They no longer hid their young under their wings. Their main preoccupation was to feed them as much as possible. The babies seemed to have become insatiable. One of the parents just had to approach the nest for them to stretch their necks and start twittering, trying to push each other away to snatch every morsel.

Again I was seized by the desire to take a look inside the nest to see how much they had grown since I had last checked on them. I waited for the parents to leave on their mission and peeped in. How they had grown in eight days! The feathers on their head and neck were quite thick. They even had little wings now. The beaks looked bigger and they could open their eyes too. The pace at which they had grown quite justified the amount of food they seemed to need. No wonder they were always hungry! This time too I was startled by one of the parents agitatedly flapping its wings next to my ear. I did not know how it had rushed back so quickly, barely a few seconds after I had peered into the nest. Its flight, so close to me was no ordinary flight, it rushed at me like a bullet and if I had been hit I would certainly have been injured, even knocked unconscious. It was not the fear of me that had kept it from striking me, it was fear for its own safety. Its life and safety were precious for the sake of its offspring. Hence the bulbul's explosive flight, so close to my ear, had missed me on purpose; its intention had been to move me away from the nest by startling me.

The next afternoon, as I was sitting in the sun as usual, a cat appeared and climbed the wall against which the rose bush containing the bulbul nest leaned. The cat leapt down and began to pace the yard, sniffing as she went. Then she saw the nest in the bush. Eyes riveted on the nest, she advanced slowly towards it. I could see that the cat posed grave danger to the nest so I got up and shooed her away. But now I began to worry, I could not guard the nest all the time, who knew when the cat might strike again? What would happen to the vulnerable nest? I wondered how I could keep the fledglings safe. Supposing I lifted the nest, along with the baby bulbuls, and settled it in a wooden crate, leaving just a small hole for the parent bulbul to enter? But would it be wise to shift the nest? I wondered. They say that birds are suspicious by nature, they might refuse to go into the crate. What would happen then? Wouldn't it do the babies even greater harm? The only thing to do was to pull the portion of the bush that we had trained to climb the wall away from it and wrap it, thorns and all, around the branches on which the nest had been constructed. Soon enough, I was able to make a thorny fortification around it. I was satisfied that no cat could penetrate the defensive wall I had built, the long, pointed thorns would be excellent deterrents.

As the wall itself might give the predator a foothold, I fortified the nest on that side of the wall by barricading it with thorny robinia branches and brambles. Now I was satisfied that the nest was secure from the cat.

∾

One outcome of my elaborate security arrangements was that I myself could no longer reach the nest to peek inside. All I could see from a distance was the baby bulbuls, stretching out their necks with beaks open, begging for food. Their growth never ceased to amaze me. Each passing day saw more and more of their bodies covered with thicker and ever thicker feathers. But whenever I lingered near the nest for a while, I would find the parent bulbuls flying in agitatedly, setting off a loud clamour, hovering uncomfortably close to my head, as if warning me to stay off their territory, causing me to move back hastily.

I noticed something odd in the way they fed their babies. Whenever they flew in with something in their beaks—a worm, or insect, they would not rush to the nest straightaway. First, they would perch for a while on a robinia or willow branch, then fly to the flower bush adjacent to the rose bush with the nest in it and wait for a few minutes more. Only then would they go into the nest and feed the babies. Leaving the nest for more food, they would go through the same motions: the flowering tree, the wall, the wire, the robinia. I cannot tell whether they behaved this way always or only when they found me watching them. Perhaps they did not want to be followed to the nest by the watchful eyes of a stranger, man or animal.

∾

One day when I was, as usual, deeply absorbed in their activity, I thought I could hear one of the bulbuls, 'Do you have nothing else to do? Why are you so fascinated by us that you cannot keep your eyes off us, following all our movements like a spy? Do you think we are some kind of performers or jugglers, putting on a show to entertain you? We are just feeding and bringing up our young ones, don't you humans do the same with your children? Does someone watch you like this too? Or was it a mistake to build our nest under your eye, hatch our eggs within your sight? Is that why you are constantly bothering us?'

Had the bulbuls been really endowed with the power of speech, they would certainly have spoken like this. We humans dislike being watched by others. That a stranger should be spying on us all the time would certainly be a torment.

❧

It was the twenty-first of May, exactly two weeks since the hatching. The rose bush was in full bloom, laden from top to bottom with flowers, with hardly a leaf in sight. They were blazing red roses, as though the whole bush was a burning brand. Or perhaps a bride in crimson robes. The nest could no longer be seen.

But still the bulbuls and their family continued to be the focus of my attention. I saw the male bulbul fly in with a caterpillar dangling from his beak. As usual he flew around for a while, perched on a branch of a tree, a wire, the wall and finally the rose bush. But strangely enough, I did not see him go into the nest, nor did I see the caterpillar in his beak a little later.

Did he eat it all by himself or lose it in flight? I wondered. I bowed my head low and tried to look inside the nest, but I could not see it, hidden as it was behind the blooming roses. What I did see, however, were two baby bulbuls, perched on a branch of the flowering tree adjacent to the rose bush. 'Oh, so they have come out for their first stroll,' I said aloud to myself. I had not imagined at all that within such a short time they would be strong enough to leave the security of the nest. That explains why the bulbul did not need to go inside the nest to feed them.

The little bulbuls were perched contentedly on the branch of the tree. They were now completely covered with little feathers and the wings too could be seen, tiny, of course. But the feathers were short, not having grown to their full length yet. The tail too was still short, though the beak had acquired respectable dimensions. There was just a hint of a plume on the heads. But there were only two baby bulbuls.

What happened to their sibling? I wondered. My query was soon answered when I saw the other bulbul fly in and rush into the bush with something in its beak. After a while it emerged, and following its movements, I looked in and saw the third little bulbul, not in the nest, but nicely esconced on a branch of the rose bush. The bulbuls kept coming in and leaving after feeding all three baby bulbuls.

The tiny bulbuls sat still on the branch, eyes closed, heads joined together. Their stillness was almost like that of a yogi in meditation or a Sufi brooding on eternal truths. Only when a parent came with something for them would they open their eyes briefly, flutter their wings, stretch their necks and open their mouths to receive nourishment, twittering loudly, competing with the others. The feeding session over, they would again close their eyes, as if to get back to meditating upon issues of grave concern. From time to time, one of them would plunge its beak into its feathers, scratching its chest and abdomen, or pecking under its wings. They would do this to each other too, opening their eyes briefly for the purpose.

The baby bulbuls looked as pretty and cute as little boys decked out for a ceremony. I could well imagine the satisfaction and pride a mother feels when she takes her children for an outing, all washed, groomed and dressed up for the occasion. The bulbul couple were perhaps experiencing a similar sense of elation and satisfaction, at a job well done. What an effort it had taken to make it possible for their babies to not only be able to leave the nest but also to swing so confidently from the branch of a tree! I could not take my eyes off the scene for quite some time. Then I went up the steps of the veranda to go in for tea, but suddenly retraced my steps and went back to my chair in the garden and began to watch the baby bulbuls again. The thought that had brought me back, foregoing my tea, was that the branch occupied by the little bulbuls was barely a foot or so from the cat's take-off point. In a single leap they would become a morsel in her mouth. The perch they had chosen had no thorny branch or bramble to protect it. In my mind, I went over the whole painful process of how the bulbuls had woven their nest, laid eggs in it, hatched them, shielded the young ones from thunder and lightning,

kept them warm under their wings and spared no effort to feed and
to nurture them, day and night, until they were capable of leaving the
nest and perching on the branch of a flowering tree all by themselves.
Did they go through all these travails only to have the cat finish them
off in a couple of minutes? I had to prevent it. I decided to stay on
and keep watch. In the evening they might go back to the nest and
then I would be free from my vigil.

⁂

It was almost sunset and I was still at my self-appointed post. Once
I went very close to the little ones. I brought my head almost next
to them. I noticed that their eyes were open, but they did not stir.
I should say that, in fact, they took no notice of me at all, it was
as if they did not see me. Maybe they did see me but had not yet
acquired the sense to distinguish friend from foe, or to know fear. I
remembered that a couple of years ago I had found a baby mynah
under a tree in my own garden and waited to see if any adult mynah
would come looking for it, but none came. I thought it was some
child's doing, throwing it here after plucking it out of its nest. The
little thing could only flutter its wings; it could not fly. When I held
my hand out to it, it stretched its neck and opened its beak wide as
though hoping to be fed. I put a few grains of rice into it and the
nestling quickly swallowed them. This led me to believe—wrongly,
as it turned out—that baby birds do not recognize their parents, any
approaching shadow will make them stretch their necks out and open
their beaks for food.

⁂

The memory of that incident with the baby mynah gave rise to an
unusual desire in me—I wanted to put something with my own fingers
into mouths of the baby bulbuls. This wave of desire rose with such
a compelling surge that I was swept along and found myself standing
right next to the baby bulbuls. But still they took no notice of me.
I held out my hand with a few grains of rice in it in the belief that
as soon as the shadow fell upon their field of vision, their beaks

would open to receive my offering. But that did not happen, in fact quite the opposite—the approaching shadow made one little bird hop away to the other side of the wall, towards the alley. This was most unexpected. I had never thought the nestling was capable of proper flight. In fact only a short while ago I had found it stretching its little wings and there were not even regular feathers on them yet. I panicked, almost certain that the nestling must have fallen into the alley to be consumed within moments by a street dog or an alley cat, or picked up by a child, to get crushed in his fist. I rushed out into the street to save it and put it back in the nest, but it was nowhere to be seen. I scanned the whole street, even went into my neighbouring compound to look, with no luck. Then I happened to glance at my neighbour's wall and found the baby bulbul comfortably perched there. I went into my house and climbed the stairs to the next floor, from where I could get a better view of what the baby bulbul would do next. I was still a bit apprehensive of it losing its way. The little bird took flight again and landed on a branch of a willow tree in a corner of my compound. After a while, another flight, and it was almost on the top of a tree outside. Now it was no longer possible to see this creature, hardly the size of a walnut, through the thick foliage. I saw a bulbul approaching with something in its beak, sitting for a while under the tree on which the baby bulbuls had been perched earlier. Then it suddenly flew directly to the tree to which the baby bulbul had flown. How could the parent see its offspring through that thick screen of leaves? I was amazed that the parent could so easily spot the tiny thing. No, it could not be their eyesight, the little birds certainly had an innate sense that enabled them to locate their young ones, I was sure.

         ∽

Meanwhile, the fledgling from the interior of the rose bush emerged and flew to the ground. It did not fly high but hopped around a bit, keeping low. There were a number of flowering shrubs and plants close to where I was seated in my chair, their branches all entangled together. They grew all haphazardy, a dense growth rather than a wild plantation. So there was a huge heap of leaves underneath, almost a metre in height and equally wide. It was so densely packed that it was almost impenetrable. The little bird from the rose bush went towards this very leaf dump and before I knew it, it had disappeared into the dump. I went close to the dump, tried to probe it, but could see nothing. The other parent flew in with food. It, too, went to the same dump, flying around it. It seemed as if it had spotted the little bulbul going into the dump. After a while it too disappeared from view. God knows how it had found its way through the tightly packed mound of dead leaves. Soon it was out again, perched on the wall.

∞

Shortly after, the little bird followed. I did not move from my chair—I did not want to frighten it back into the dump and lose it. The other parent flew in and joined its mate on the wall, both watching their baby. It seemed to me that they were trying to suggest something to it. The baby apparently took the hint and began to try to fly up with the aid of its tiny wings to where the parents were. It rose to half the height of the wall, wavered a little and then clung to it, frozen, unable to fly either up or down, watched agitatedly by its parents from above. But they made no move to come to its aid. I was again driven by the desire to do something for the baby in distress—why should I not help it? I could easily pick it up and put it back into its nest in the rose bush. That seemed to be the only way to rescue it. Otherwise it might be forced to fall back and seek refuge in the leaf dump. I rose and rushed to it. The baby made no movement at all, which confirmed my belief that these baby bulbuls had not yet learnt to fly properly. I picked it up and it set up a huge clamour, a loud twitter. As I moved away, both parents threw themselves on the ground near my feet. I took one step and they too moved and again they were before my feet, on the ground. This was no pleading and falling on my feet—they were trying to block my way, afraid that I was trying to snatch the baby away from them. But I managed to somehow place the nestling on the rose bush and came away. But what surprised me now was that instead of going to the baby now back in the rose bush, they both went to the crown of the tree, where the first baby had flown to. Why did they not go to the rescued baby? I looked into the rose bush again, but I could not see the baby anywhere, I had no idea where it could have gone. And what happened to the third baby whom I had not seen leaving the rose bush? Why were the parents not worried about him being fed? Why were they not going to him? I wanted to find answers to all these questions. The biggest mystery was why the parents were not going to the rose bush at all. After all, their nest was still there and so were two of their nestlings. I just could not accept that the parents would not carry food for them—it was impossible. I inspected the bush again but neither baby bulbul was visible. I went around the whole clump, the flowering tree and all around, I even turned the branches and shoots this way and that way, scanning the whole area, stood on my toes and looked behind the wall, crawled under the bush and searched through the tangle of branches, but there was no sign of a bird. Obviously they were no longer there. The only thing there was the nest, now empty. I had been there all the time, not moved away even for a second, how did they give me the slip? Now I knew why the parents did not go to the rose bush—there was no need. But what I still did not know was how they knew the babies were not there without going to the nest. I sat down in my chair, despondent. I was deeply remorseful, holding myself responsible for breaking up this family of bulbuls.

❦

Suddenly, from the leaf dump emerged a bulbul, advancing slowly, with a strange gait, its wings spread out, as if wanting to fly but unable to do so. Is that what is meant by 'broken knees', or rather 'broken wings', I wondered. The bulbul hopped and went into another grassy growth opposite the rose bush. I consoled myself that this was one of the two babies that had disappeared earlier and waited for it to re-emerge from the dump—I no longer dared to go close. After a while the bulbul did re-emerge and I saw it from close quarters: it had a tall crest, long tail, it was the size of a full grown adult bulbul—it was not a baby bulbul but one of the parents. Again it advanced with slow, hesitant steps, wings spread out, as if dragging its dead weight along. It came very close to me and began to do something which I have no words to describe. It was a dance of agony, a painful writhing, an attempt to annihilate itself. Before my very eyes the bulbul seemed to assume a human face. It was sorrow in an excruciating form, a mourning and an appeal. But it was not a loud human wail, it was a silent weeping. Birds of the air can only be articulate in joy, sorrow makes them dumb. To anyone who can read it, the message in the eyes of all creatures in pain is loud and clear. I saw its mate arrive and come close to it, as if offering solace and support. The bulbul seemed to somewhat compose itself. Then they both flew to the tree to where the first baby had flown.

∽

For a long time after, I could not bring myself to leave the place. I waited for as long as there was light, for any member of the family to return to the nest. But my hope was in vain—none of them came back.

I spent a restless night, worrying about the fate of the bulbuls and their young ones. Where could they have spent the night? In what plight? I had never wished them any harm, and now my guilt was overpowering, the thought that it was my hand that was responsible for this state. It was I who had destroyed their home and hearth, how could I forgive myself? Man considers himself wise and capable and tries to intervene, hoping to do good to creatures so much smaller than him, forgetting that the wisdom and ability required for their good is inherent in the very nature of these creatures, big and small. An intervening human hand ultimately only does damage.

∽

As soon as it was light, I went to the nest. It was still empty. No bird had returned to it. I stood there for a long time, looking around, hoping. After a couple of hours I saw a bulbul foraging among the branches of a tree. Finally, finding something, I saw it flying with its laden beak to the same tree to which that first baby bulbul had flown the previous day.

I did not see either the parents or a baby bulbul for the next few days. It was the last day of May when I saw one of the bulbuls flying to a tree in my yard with food in its beak. I looked hard and noticed two baby bulbuls perched on a branch of the tree. I did not see the third sibling. The babies I saw were now quite capable of flying from one branch of a tree to another with their parents.

I would still glance occasionally at the empty nest. I was hoping that the bulbuls would hatch two batches of eggs in a season. Something that I had understood very well by now was that as parents, the birds were extremely responsible, not leaving their offspring till the time they were capable of finding their food. They continued to feed them till a certain time and after that they forced them to find their own nourishment. I thought that sooner or later it would be time for the bulbuls to lay eggs again and then they would need this nest in the rose bush. That is why I was determined to keep it safe, so that one day the pair would return to it.

∽

One day when I went to the bush as usual, the nest had disappeared. Where was it? Could the bulbuls have taken it away? But that was unbelievable. So what had happened? The mystery was solved when I found it ensconced in a showcase in my own home. It contained two white pigeon-egg-like forms. Someone from the household had torn the nest from the bush, put two white elliptical objects in it to turn it into a decoration piece, and put it on display in the showcase. I lifted it out and threw away the two pebbles. Carefully, I attached it to the branch from where it had been plucked, securing it with wires. I believed that the bulbuls would certainly need it again.

But that never happened—the bulbuls did not return to their old nest, which they had left that day when the rose bush was rich with blooms. They did not come back because their offspring had left it for some unknown place.

2

It's now been a year since the incident I've narrated earlier. The windows of my bedroom face the Anchar Lake, which lies to the west of my house. It is spring, time to get the rooms painted, for which my room was stripped bare. Since it would take a day or two, I shifted to the room above, which faced my own yard. It was that season of the year when the days are warm but the nights cold. So the windows were kept closed at night. When I woke up the next morning, it was almost dawn. In fact, something had woken me up. It was the loud and clear chirruping of a bulbul, coming from somewhere very close, perhaps just outside the closed window. I got out of bed, threw the windows open and went downstairs.

The same thing happened the next morning. I was woken up by birdsong—the loud, clear, persistent chirruping of a bulbul. I sat up in my bed and listened to the regular, intermittent chirp. It was so close, but how could the bulbul be here, in this room with the windows still shut? I looked around and was amazed to see a bulbul on the floor, almost next to my pillow. I couldn't tell out how it had come in through the closed windows. The door was still bolted. Obviously the bird had come in the previous evening and spent the night in my bedroom. But why did it give no hint of its presence last evening or throughout the night? It was only when it felt the need to go out in the morning that it had actually called out to me so that I would get up and open the window for it. I got up, and threw the window open and it flew away.

That day, as my daughter came out of the room after making my bed, she said that every day, just before dusk, a bulbul had been flying into the room and apparently spending the night perched on the base of the electric light on the wall. I went up to look and saw it there. My entry into the room or even the fact that I went so close to it did not seem to disturb it at all. Perhaps it had accepted that there was someone else to share the comfort of the room with it. The next morning I got up before the bulbul called me and opened the window for it.

The bulbul was alone. My belief that a bulbul builds a nest only to lay eggs, hatch them and nurture its fledgings was now confirmed. The nest is not a home in the human sense. Since it was early spring, this bird had not yet thought of building a nest, perhaps it didn't even have a mate yet.

∽

A few days later, a TV set was set up in the room and in the evening the whole family gathered there to watch television. The set had been placed opposite the light fixture where the bulbul would perch. At sunset, the bulbul came in as usual and sat on a windowsill for a while, shifted to another, and finally to the light fixture on the ceiling. Here, its perch was precarious, so it moved again and went towards its own perch, but seeing figures moving on the TV screen and people sitting before it, it was distracted and moved back to a windowsill. Then it flew away, god knows where. It never came back to the room to spend the night.

3

Another year had passed.

There is a willow tree in a corner of my yard towards the west. It is a young tree, not full grown yet, its trunk just about the size of a large pestle. We had pruned it drastically last winter, and left it standing barely two metres tall. The adjacent wall is only about a metre high. The pruning had left three thick horns at the base where the branches had been. When spring came, they burst into tiny shoots which began to grow into branches. By early May, there was a luxuriant coppice of willow branches on the crest. As was my habit, I was sitting in the chair in my garden, basking in the spring sunshine. There was still a nip in the air. Towards afternoon I caught sight of a bulbul carrying a blade of grass in its beak and flying into the dense thicket of the willow. It was followed by its mate, which also carried a bit of grass in its beak. It was obvious that they were building their nest, but this time I did not interest myself in their activity. The experience of the past two years had taught me that I should not interfere in the affairs of birds or other animals, neither try to help nor harm them through any of my actions. I would go nowhere near their nest. What it contained was none of my business.

There is a bathroom near the willow in the yard, infrequently used. One day when I went to the tree, I saw a nest. There was a bulbul, brooding in it. About a week later, I saw the pair taking turns foraging for insects and worms, bringing them in their beaks and disappearing into the willow branches. From my seat neither the nest nor its inhabitants were visible, but their purposeful comings and goings left no doubt that they had their little ones in the interior of the thick willow branches.

∽

A couple of days later, I was at my usual place basking in the sun when I happened to glance at the ground under my feet and my heart missed a beat—there was a dead bird lying there, a very small bird. I shuddered at the sight. It wasn't easy to identify it—though in size and colouring it looked like a bulbul, its head was hidden. I picked up a twig and began to turn the body over. I was horror struck to see that it had no head, it had apparently been chopped off. I gave it another turn and saw the yellow of its bottom. It was a bulbul. I had to know whether it was one of the pair from the nest in the willow. I went to take a look at the nestlings and noticed bulbul feathers scattered all around the tree. There were some feathers near the nest too. There was no doubt now that the dead bulbul was one from the nest.

From a distance, I kept watch to see if someone would come to feed the babies. Soon a bulbul flew in, a caterpillar in its beak, fed it to its babies and flew away. It made similar trips with something or the other as grub, one after the other. Now it was alone at the job. At noon, I saw a cat striding across the wall, and I understood the whole scenario: the bulbul shielding its young under its wings, and the cat pouncing upon it so easily in one leap from the wall. After all, there was just a metre between the top of the wall and the nest. But why had the predator consumed only the bird's head? A closer examination of the location of the nest revealed that the willow branches must have facilitated the cat's job, providing convenient footholds. The sight got rid of my vows of non-interference, how could I watch and not do anything to help? I tore away the branches from the side of the wall, but then realized that I had made a mistake by removing a screen from that side and laid the nest bare for everyone to see. But the screen when still standing had provided no protection from a predator either, I thought. Would the bulbul have met this fate, its head eaten and the body cast to the ground, if it had been effective?

∽

Now there was only one bulbul trying to do the job of two, so the nestlings had to wait longer for their feed. Earlier, taking turns had resulted in shorter sorties. Another thought that bothered me now was whether the dead bird was male or female. It is not easy to determine the sex of bulbuls as in the case of poultry or sparrows, because the male and female bulbuls are the same in colour and appearance. Perhaps, one way to distinguish gender was the size. I think that, like in all species, the female is slightly smaller in frame. But there was a problem here—there was no other bulbul to compare it with. I gave the problem much thought. I remembered that two years ago I would see one of the pair go into the nest from time to time and give the warmth of its body to the babies. This bulbul was not doing that, it could barely manage to feed them, the question of brooding did not arise. Perhaps that was a female's job. Maybe when the cat climbed the tree, the bulbul was aware of what was coming—birds and animals are supposed to have a sharper sense of danger. It would have had the option of flying away to save itself. But this bulbul must not have done so for that would have left the babies unprotected; it had chosen to sacrifice itself to the cat rather than let harm come to the little ones. Such sacrifice only a mother can make, generally. All this made me feel that the dead one must have been female, though nothing could be said with a degree of certainty.

∽

Now I began to worry about the safety of the babies. I noticed two sheets of galvanized iron lying in the yard. I lifted them one by one and placed them near the wall against the willow. They stood a good metre above the top of the willow. Now there was no way the cat could get at the nest from the wall. I took my seat and watched out for the bulbul to come with food for its young ones. It came and occupied its place on a branch; after a while it flew to the wall, where it stayed for a while. But when it tried to approach the nest, the metal sheets blocked its way. Every time it tried to fly into the nest, the sight of black rusted sheets seemed to frighten it, making it turn back. Defeated, it went back to its perch on the branch with the food still in its beak. I could see that it was feeling quite disoriented with the altered position of the nest, no longer sure whether it was safe to go in. Assessing the situation, I got up and flung away the sheets. The bulbul flew to the wall, then into the nest. It came out after a while, the worm in its beak gone—the babies had been fed.

∽

My observation two years ago had shown that as dusk began to fall, the bulbul would come and cover the babies in the nest under its breast. Throughout the night it would maintain its position, its underbelly serving as an incubator to give the fragile ones warmth, its wings spread over them as a protective umbrella. Once, out of curiosity, I had shone a torch inside, but the beam of light shining on its head did not make the bulbul shift its position. It calmly sat on, shielding its young. So I waited for this bulbul too to come to its post before night fell. But it did not come. I waited till it was quite dark. By this time all the feathered creatures had returned to their nests. The bulbul still did not come. I was in a dilemma—should I put up the sheets or not? Supposing the bulbul returned at some time in the night and the sheets held it back? But even if it went to its duty in the nest, without the protection of the sheets, it would only suffer the same fate as its mate. My mind was made up—I would put up the sheets, I must, if the bulbul family was to be saved from the cat. I went ahead and put the sheets back in place. After some time I took a look at the nest, but the bulbul was not back. God knows where it had decided to spend the night. Now I was even more sure that the dead bird was a female. I prodded the nest with a stick and a little bird stretched its neck to see. I thought there must be a couple of other babies in it.

∽

The next morning I was up at dawn. I went out and dragged a stool to the willow. This would be my first close look at the nest. I had to check on the babies to see whether they had weathered the cold of the night or were frozen to death. I saw that there were three of them, covered with fine, tiny feathers. The wings had just begun to grow. But they seemed to be stuck to one another, almost bundled together; their heads seemed to have fallen upon each others' backs, as if their necks had been broken. I could hear a painful wheeze emanating from the little ones rather like a death rattle. I prodded one with a pencil, but there was no response. The same with another. No lifting of the head or any other movement to suggest that they were alive except for the fact that they were breathing. I waited for the parent bird to come. How would it deal with the situation? Whom would he feed the morsels he brought? These ones were certainly not in any position to accept them. When the adult bulbul arrived, it peered into the nest, as if to examine its contents. There was no food in its beak. Then it just flew away.

∽

About half an hour later, when the sun shone upon the nest directly, the bulbul was back. This time he had something in his beak. He flew in and dropped what he had brought into the nest. He made another trip and again almost threw the food in. Apparently the babies were accepting the food, because the bulbul continued to make one sortie after another. Why the bulbul had waited to feed them only after the sun had been hitting the nest for quite some time became clear to me. The cold had rendered the babies nearly unconscious and quite unable to feed. It was only when the warmth of the sun breathed new life into them that the bulbul understood that now was the time to feed them, and proceeded to do so, making regular sorties thereafter. It seemed to me that the trips were occurring with greater frequency, as though the whole purpose of his life was to feed his babies.

∽

Something new appeared on the scene now—something quite unexpected which lent a totally different dimension to the situation: as the bulbul flew in with food, it was accompanied by another bulbul. When he perched on a branch, the other one did the same. If he landed on a wire, sure enough the other one followed. The same pattern was followed as the bulbul went to the wall, but when he went to the nest to his babies, the other one would hold back, finding a perch on another branch. It just wouldn't go anywhere near the nest itself, but kept its eyes on the bulbul in the nest all the time. As soon as the babies had been fed and the bulbul flew down searching for grains on the ground, the other bulbul would take its place next to him, either doing the same or waiting for it to finish. Wherever the bulbul from the nest went, he was trailed by the other. I wondered where the newcomer had come from. There had been no sign of another bulbul yesterday, so where had it sprung from? Why was it clinging to the other like a shadow?

There could be only one explanation—the other one was probably a loner too, it had no mate, hence its decision to attach itself to the former. I still wanted to know who, between the two, was the female. I had already decided that the dead bird was the babies' mother. Besides, I knew that birds are not homosexual and their mate is always of the opposite sex. This was the season for the female of the species to build a nest and lay eggs, hence her need to find a mate. That is why she was constantly at his side, trying to woo him. However, he seemed completely uninterested, showing no inclination at all for building a relationship with her. The question of raising another family until the nestlings were ready to fend for themselves did not arise.

∽

One attribute of the feathered species is that they move in pairs, with no room for a third. Neither of the couple can be wooed away by an interloper of another sex. In fact, no bird tries to do so. If at all an attempt is made, the intruder is soon driven away, pecked at mercilessly by the others, till it disappears from the scene. But here the case was slightly different. Though the male was paying no heed to the new female's overtures he was not trying to chase or push her away either. Apparently, while burdened with the responsibility of the babies, he had to stay aloof, but was not keen to antagonize her by an aggressively hostile stance. After all, he was mateless and would soon need one. Strangely enough, even while she was so enamoured of him, the female made no attempt to associate herself with the nest and its inmates.

I watched the whole drama till noon. It was time for my tea—a cup of tea is all I have for lunch. I rose to go in, but not before carefully scanning the surrounding area to satisfy myself that no predator lay in wait. I came back immediately after finishing my tea, hardly taking ten minutes or so. I dragged a stool to the willow and climbed on it to take a look inside the nest. The earth seemed to fall from under my feet when I saw that there were just two fledglings in the nest. Where was the third sibling? It was impossible that it could have flown away from the nest, or fallen from it. The babies had no wings at all, just some tiny feathers, so how could it fly. I looked in every direction, but there was no sign of a cat anywhere. I should not have moved, I should have kept watch, I blamed myself, but what was the use?

∾

The bulbul flew in with food, trailed by the female. Once he had fed the young ones, he perched on a branch. The female, who had kept her gaze on him all the time while he was feeding his brood, flew very close to him, almost sticking to him. By now the male seemed to have softened towards her; he allowed her to touch him and sit so close that the two bodies seemed to be one. They stayed like that for a while and then flew away together. It was quite some time before he returned with food. Now the intervals between feeds grew longer and longer and with each departure, it was a longer wait for the babies, even though with their rapid growth, the need for food was more pressing. At one time, when the food-bearing

male came, accompanied as usual by the female, the babies had had
to wait a really long time. After feeding them, he flew down and sat
on the lawn. The female followed, and drew very close to him and
began to flutter her wings provocatively. Then she flew around him
in progressively smaller circles till her body touched his again. Finally
she gave him a caress with her beak, planting what looked like a kiss
on his neck and the two flew away together in a different direction.

∽

Suddenly an idea struck me. Why not check my watch for the time
he would take to come back this time, I thought. Ten minutes passed,
then fifteen, half an hour, an hour and a quarter, but there was still no
sign of his coming. Finally, after about an hour and a half, they both
turned up, the male sat on the wall and the female on a stretched rope.
I glanced up and found that the male bulbul's beak was empty—no
worm, insect or grain of food for the nestlings. He went to the nest
and sat on a willow branch, and then he seemed to examine the nest
and the babies in it carefully. But he did not go into the nest, nor
did he drop any morsel of food into it. Then he went to the same
branch where the female was and perched on it. He had arrived after
such a long interval of time but with nothing for the babies, made no
attempt to feed them, in fact suddenly he had become distant—had
he lost all interest in them? Consumed by this anxiety, and in order
to check, again I drew the stool to the willow and looked into the
nest, holding out my hand. The female was unconcerned, but the male
raised a huge clamour, displaying tremendous unease. He seemed to
be in agony, flitting from one branch to another in a panic until I
withdrew. Only then did the two of them fly away, while it was now
my turn to wait restlessly for his return, glancing at my watch every
minute. When would he bring food for the little ones—I couldn't
rid myself of this worry. I looked in every direction—somehow I did
not want to believe that he would abandon them thus. Half an hour
or so later, the pair returned and the first thing I looked at was the
male's beak, and my dismay was deep to see it empty. This time, too,
he had brought no food for them. Even though this was not the first

time that he had come empty-beaked, yet he would go to the nest and seemed to be keen to ascertain the welfare of his brood, but this time there was no such gesture. Now he was as unconcerned and untouched by feeling towards the nest and its contents as his new mate was. And I was plagued by the worry of who would care for the little ones or feed them now.

∽

Meanwhile, a visitor arrived. Since I was in the garden he let himself in. I had no choice but to get up, greet him and take him inside the house. I did ask for tea to be brought to my guest, but apart from some formal small talk I had no desire to really converse with him. I was afraid that the conversation might drag on, and my thoughts were actually on the bulbul babies. I did not want them to come to any harm. My lack of conversation soon bored the guest and he rose to leave. Seeing him off, I returned to my usual place in the garden. I had been away for slightly over twenty minutes. Once again I stood on the stool, peeping into the nest. My breath stopped when I saw that there was only one baby bulbul in it. There was no sign of the second one anywhere, neither was there any evidence of the presence of a cat in the vicinity. So who could have taken the little thing away from its nest? It did not seem likely that the cat had made its appearance in my brief absence from the scene, killed the baby bulbul and made such a clean getaway. I had never seen it trying to approach the nest from my side or withdraw at my sight. The fact, however, was that now there was only one baby bulbul left. I no longer nourished any hope that he would be fed by anyone, he would certainly die of hunger or the cold at night, I was sure. I was also convinced, more than ever before, that the dead bulbul had been a female. If the male had died instead of her, would she have abandoned her babies, no matter how hard another male might have tried to woo her? Even if she did build another relationship, I was sure the babies would have been her first priority. In fact she would have made the new male in her life join in and help her raise them. All this was my feeling, there was no way that I could prove this with a scientific experiment. But my observation of human behaviour told me that I was right. Of course it could well be said that no judgement on birds could be based on a study of the behaviour of humans—but how am I to explain?

I plunged into gloom over the fate of the poor lone bulbul baby. Even though I had lost all hope, something kept me glued to my place in the garden, hoping against hope that a glimmer of paternal love might grow into a blazing light and bring the bulbul back to his offspring. It was almost evening by now, but there was still enough light. Suddenly my heart leapt to see the pair of bulbuls swim into my field of vision. Again I looked at the bulbul's beak, but it was empty. He flew to the willow and took his place on a branch, making no attempt to go and look inside the nest. Then he went back to the other tree, where his new mate was. The two then went into an elaborate courtship ritual beak to beak. The female buried her beak in the male's feathers and began to stroke his head, neck, breast, belly and back. The male who seemed to have surrendered himself completely to her attentions, appeared to relax, totally at peace with everything, content. The female flew down to the ground, picked up a blade of grass in her beak and threw it away. Perhaps the preparations for a new home were afoot, I told myself.

౷

The two flew away, leaving me to worry about the lone baby bulbul in the nest. It was nearly dark and again I stood on my stool. The baby did not seem to be doing too badly, considering it had had nothing to eat for almost three hours. It held its head high and peered this way and that. I climbed down from the stool and picked up a few grains from the ground, held them out on my palm to its beak. My plan was to see if it would accept food from me. In that case, I could take it inside the house, nest and all and save it from hunger and cold. But no matter how hard I tried, it would not open its mouth. Nothing could persuade it to budge. I just could not offer it any nourishment. Defeated, I climbed down. Soon it would be time for me to go in, have my cup of evening kahwa, what was the use of lingering here, I thought. But I had one problem to solve before I retired for the night—I had to decide whether to put up the shield of sheets against the wall or not. Would it be all right to continue to protect this baby from the cat or not? Supposing I did nothing, the cat would finish it off in no time at all. It might thus find a quick death and be released from the agony of a sure but slow death by starvation. Last night, the three of them had been hugging each other for warmth; they had been in a pathetic state in the morning, but at least they had been alive. Tonight, the baby bulbul was all by itself. How cruelly the cold put an end to its life. Even if it survived it somehow, what torture it would be to wait for food that would never come. No one to pay heed to its open beak and a creeping death... I would be abominably cruel to leave it to such a fate. I just could not make up my mind.

Which way would it be best for the bulbul chick to die—to be devoured by the cat or a slow, lingering, more painful death caused by the chill and starvation? That was the question I kept asking myself.

As I took sips of my kahwa, hope began to rise in my heart. I thought the sun might breathe new life into it. The male bulbul might show affection again by coming back and feeding it... The tender thing might be saved after all... So many possibilities pressed upon my mind. I decided to go and look into the nest first. I stood on the stool and peered in. The little birdling was gone and the nest was empty.

It remained empty, but the bulbul did not bring his new bride into it. Perhaps she did not want to lay her eggs or hatch them in someone else's home. As winter approached, we again pruned the willow. Along with the cut branches, down came the nest and, mingling with the heap of rubbish, it vanished.

THE DEEPEST BLUE

K. R. MEERA

Translated from the Malayalam by J. Devika

The experience of love that I'm going to describe is the strangest you'll have ever encountered. So here's advance warning: chaste wives (in the satisavitri mould) and strictly monogamous men (in the maryaadaapurushottam mould) are advised against reading this account. I will not be responsible for whatever breaches of morality that may result from reading it. This thing called 'chastity' is so desecrated these days. The days of flawless devotion to husbands are over. What wives do these days, through email, the cell phone, and the landline, when their husbands aren't around the house! The Sreeramachandras, the ones who know no doe-eyed damsel other than their wives, and the Jewels of Feminine Virtue, alas, have all disappeared, root, branch and all, from the face of this earth. I, too, am quite saddened by all this. I'm sincerely fired by the desire to write stories that salute the few well-born, homely women of virtue (so rare are they—so scarce) who walk with assured gait and firm step upon the tightrope of morality, even as this world is going all topsy-turvy. But then, fiction isn't life, ah, a fact that renders one so powerless! A life—that's easier to end as we please. Not even a mangy dog would be curious about its denouement. But when it comes to a story, the game is entirely different. The story's movement upon paper is like a serpent's movement upon a rock. An unpredictable slithering. If it goes wrong, that's it. Readers will pull out daggers. And every other wayfaring Marykutty will step in, to perform a critique. So then, why bother with all the nonsense? For that reason, there's no story on offer. In its place, a bit of life, a burning sliver of experience.

This is experience, and must therefore be honestly recounted. Wherever honesty thrives, morality must decline. So, before proceeding any further—caution! There's still time. You can stop reading right now. It's the readers' responsibility to hold tight to their chastity and peace of mind so that these don't fall in a heap on the floor. Reading ahead may adversely affect children, pregnant women, heart patients, and my husband: they are advised against venturing any further.

Only the firm-hearted are advised to proceed.

1

I've already told you. A sliver of experience—of love. That too, a burning speck. I loved him. The name will remain a secret. If it doesn't remain a secret, my husband will leave me. My children will grow up suffering their stepmother's taunts. Friends and relatives will hate me. My husband may even finish me off with poison. I'm not worried about all this. Death doesn't look like a problem to me. If this life ends, the next one will begin. That's all there is to it. But no, not when I remember him. A terrible weakness overpowers me then. He, poor soul, someone who's suffered much pain in this birth, and perhaps in former births too. Someone upon whom life weighed so heavily that he became a hermit. Should I drag such a man into all this? Should I throw him to the sharks? No. Therefore, be so kind as to forgive me for not identifying him. After all, what's in a name?

Let me tell you of our love. Make no mistake; this is not my first love. I have been in love perpetually. Before marriage and after. My love is a languid serpent, an utterly venomous one. For a long time it lay still, coiled upon its own body, biding its time, lying in wait. For someone. Who, one didn't know. Someone. Who wouldn't die of my fangs? Who was deep blue by birth. The three-eyed one. Never saw him. Ever. Those whom I met, were all false Vasudevas. Ones whose bluish tinge vanished under a tight kiss. Each time it was a mistake I made. I moulted; I left each one of them behind. To those who tried to hold fast, I gave my decaying, old scaly skin. No one saw me, no one really touched me. They measured the length and breadth of the skin, heaved huge sighs of relief—what a huge poisonous snake, how lucky that it slid away—and were consoled. The silver spots upon my sloughed off skins glistened in the daylight as they lay in the backyards of their lives.

Let that be. I will speak about us. We met late. He'd become a hermit by then. And I, married, and a mother of two. People who had gone a long way down opposite paths. We'd have to walk back, start all over again together. If that's possible, that is. But that isn't possible. If that was, human beings would have tried. What distance would they not walk back, if it was possible?

I will speak of how we found each other. The partitioning of the family property brought me some money. I insisted to my husband that we buy an old naalukettu house. One like the house I was born and raised in. A house with doors so low that one could enter only with head bowed, with a ceiling so low that it could be touched by merely raising your arm. My house was like that—a cool, breezy house. The wind from the river used to rush in through the south window and whirl about, flustered at not finding a way out. That house doesn't exist any more. It was wiped out by lightning. As the flames leapt up from one side, my mother, sisters and I, picked up all that we could and ran out. That was the month of the November rains. It was raining so hard, a drop would have filled a pot. But the house didn't stop burning. It fought against the downpour and went down blazing, reduced to ashes. My father burned to death inside. The place where it stood became a void. In my father's place was another void, a greater one.

I wanted a house like that one. We advertised in the newspapers many times. Several sellers wrote back to us. We would go to see each house on offer.

'Why not buy this one?'

Each time, my husband would be enthused.

'No...' I replied, each time. 'This isn't what I have in my mind...'

'That's going to be only in your mind.' His tone turned accusing after a while. 'It's only a fantasy.'

That house is real; it stands somewhere. Of that I am sure. The same house that I have in my mind. The one with the serpent grove on its south side and the kili tree on its east, upon which lush tangles of wild jasmine thrive. Where the sleepy murmur of birds and the hot sighs of the snakes enter, if the southside window is opened at night. Funny, but I also knew that he'd be there. Yes, I knew all that well before. All of it. He's the one who didn't know. Poor man. He lived in the lightness of his ignorance, detached. All alone, in that naalukettu house, with its many windows. I sought him out there, asked him to name a price for the house, but he didn't recognize me.

We had gone to those parts to look at another house. I didn't like it. So on the way back, the broker suggested, 'There's another house nearby... It's something that might appeal to you, madam...but the owner is a sannyasi...what a pity, he won't sell.'

'Let's go over,' I insisted, 'maybe he will sell?'

My husband decided to try. He turned into the road the broker had pointed out to us. The car stopped in front of the tile-roofed gateway. A thrill ran through my pores at the very first sight of the house. This was it, I knew. The tile-roofed gateway built of sandstone blocks. The curving doorway. The rough, gravelly village road. Paddy fields opening out on the other side. The water channel running by the road in which tiny fish swam.

From the fields rose a clay-scented breeze. There must be a path north of the yard, I mused, and that must lead to the river. A kaitha bush growing in the river, one that tumbled onto the riverbank in riotous abandon. There must be waterfowls that tiptoed out when no one was around. The kaitha must be in full bloom now. I could catch a whiff of its scent, though the kaitha hadn't bloomed yet. My nerves tingled.

We entered the gateway. The garden was full of trees and cool languor. Dusk was falling. A greenish dark hovered about. Birds cooed, hurrying to roost. In the dim light, I saw him sitting on a floor mat in the distant veranda. There was a harmonium before him, and ten little children gathered around him. It was a music class. He turned towards us, his left hand still on the harmonium. My husband and the broker went up to the veranda to speak with him. I didn't. I stood inside the gateway, near the kili tree upon which the wild jasmine grew. The jasmine burst into bloom, as if from a sudden thrill. A forest-caller flew up suddenly, calling out loud and long, flashing its bright tail feathers.

He stood up. He was clad in an ochre dhoti; an ochre towel covered his shoulders. His beard reached his chest; a long mane of hair fell to his shoulders. I didn't look at his face. The blood in my body raced through its tiny rivulets. I stepped out of the gateway hurriedly. I got into the car, panting. Nearly weeping. A terrible bitterness welled up within me.

My husband and the broker returned.

'He is not selling. He's giving it away to some ashram...'

I made no answer. My husband had liked him, he said so. He's a scholar, a gentleman, well-off. But an ascetic. How radiant his face! What deep calm in his voice! No ordinary ascetic, this.

'Let's go,' I said, sickened. 'I have a headache.'

My husband started the car. I closed my eyes tight. The pain was real. But it wasn't in my head. It throbbed in my chest and loins. Piercing pain. Not pain, really. Piercing, stabbing desire. Desire smouldering, like specks of flame eating slowly, slowly, into raw flesh. I want to bear a child in my womb. I want to give birth. To a son. His son. I meditated. His face. His form. What would he look like? How would he be? The hermit's sperm; the slut's ovum. Renunciation and desire, in equal measure.

You've got it, I suppose? I'm terribly decadent.

2

The unmarried have keener eyesight. Once you're married, it diminishes. When he was my lover, my husband wrote four or five whole essays about a small birthmark I have on the little finger of my right hand. That trivial birthmark was indeed exalted! Subject to much unnecessary coddling, it turned into a Movement. But the moment the thali—the marriage pendant—was tied around my neck like a noose, it reverted to being a humble birthmark. He never saw it again.

I've already told you. Marriage weakens the eyesight. He forgot the birthmark, the flowery words he'd uttered about it, and our romance itself. Marriage weakens the memory, too.

It's thirteen years now since we got married. You can imagine the state of his eyesight. He's shortsighted. Never notices my face or its expressions. I was uneasy, like a snake stifled in a wicker basket. The music of the makuti came to me, loud and clear. I had to escape. I need to slither out to the place from where the sound rose. But how? I squirmed, uneasy within the four walls of the house. I scolded both my daughters; accused them of lacking discipline; reminded them that chastity was their greatest wealth. Then I shut myself in my bedroom and tossed about in bed.

I wanted to see him. But how? There was a day's gap between us. The distance of a long journey. He's not selling the house. It was being given away to some ashram. What excuse could I possible fashion to go over? Clouds of smoke smothered my brain.

'What are you thinking about?' my husband asked.

'That was a lovely house.'

'Oh, so you haven't forgotten it?'

I shut my eyes tightly. No. Not yet. How could I? Exuberant wild jasmine springs into sight whenever I shut my eyes. I see the veranda. A luxuriant crown of tangled hair.

'The ascetic won't sell it. And even if he does, let's not buy it. He's the last heir; no child has been born in that house since him...'

My eyes opened. My womb throbbed.

'Let's go there once more, let's try again...'

'Don't I have anything better to do?' He was angry. I slid closer to him on the bed and wrapped my arms around him.

'Please...'

'You are too much. Enough!'

'If he isn't selling, let it be. Let's just go and see the house... We could build one like it...'

He agreed. I knew he would. There was no other way. Because this is not fiction. This is life. What one writes after experience—that's fiction.

Experiencing what's written—that's life. That's the inconvenience of life. And the freedom of fiction.

∽

Let that be. He came with me. We went there again. The same house. The tile-roofed gateway, the kili tree, the wild jasmine. A hundred flowers with no one to pluck them. Another world inside the gateway. The retreating sunlight outside. The languid dusk inside. Outside, the clamour of folk returning from the market. Inside, the silence of roosting birds.

He walked ahead. I followed him, slowly. In the courtyard, a sacred basil stood, as tall as a man. On the half-wall, delicate white mandaaram flowers, plucked. The parijatham bloomed in the front yard. Their fragrance borne upon by the breeze. My heart beat hard. My stomach ached as if from terrible hunger.

My husband pressed a finger to the doorbell. He came to the door. A huge man. Ochre dhoti, ochre towel, sacred ash smeared on the forehead and chest. The long hair, the long beard, silver starting to streak it.

'You?'

He smiled. My husband folded his hands, saluting.

'Come...do have a seat...'

'You remember me, I hope?' my husband asked.

'Yes...'

I gazed intently at him. Nothing new to the eye. This wooden house. Him. The luminous smile. The meditative eyes. The shoulder covered with fine hair, under the ochre towel. The stooping posture—he was very tall. All this, I've long known.

'You aren't selling the house, isn't that so?' my husband said with a smile.

'My wife liked it a lot. Could we look around?'

'Why not? Do come in.'

He led the way inside. 'Most of it is shut up. It's swept only once or twice a month, so there'll be a lot of dust.'

My husband tripped on one of the wooden steps.

'Be careful,' he said, 'the house is really old. Don't hit your head.'

I ignored the comment haughtily. Don't you teach me. I know. After the sitting room comes the central room. Step into the veranda of the central room, and you reach the central courtyard. The platform in the middle on which the sacred basil grew. In the rain, the tinkling of rainwater upon the bronze metal-leaf on the roof-edge. I know. I've known.

My husband asked him something about the carvings on the wooden door. He turned to respond. I walked ahead, not needing a guide. The northern door beyond the kitchen and the central room where the mortar and pestle are kept. I placed a hand on the bolt. He suddenly inclined his head, looking at me.

'That won't open, it can't be opened.'

He walked up to me.

'I want to see the river,' I said.

He looked at me more closely. For a second. I too saw in his eyes a female form clad in a shimmering sari of green silk, her hair coiled behind. That was it. He looked away.

'Go around through the front door...that's easier,' he said. I felt annoyed suddenly, as if he had shrunk me! He wasn't even trying to open the door. I put my hand on the door and tried to loosen the bolt, hitting the wooden planks with my elbow.

'Don't open it. It can't be closed again if you do.' He tried to stop me.

But before he had even finished speaking, how wonderful, the bolt loosened. The door opened. He looked a bit startled. And then, his detached air reappeared, and he smiled.

'Oh...so it opened?'

'It did...' I stood there, triumphant.

'It's been years. The bottom must have rotted...'

I did not reply; I stepped out into the yard. Darkness amidst the dense foliage of kilichundan mango trees. Beyond that, another tree, the poovarasu; and further on, a bramble fence, then the river. The kaitha bushes stood at the edge of the property. They were in bloom. The river breeze wafted by, delicate and fragrant as a flower. I became free as if all my bonds had been loosened. Where is the serpent grove? Where is the njaaval tree?

I reached the sacred grove, a verdant umbrella open to the sky. Mildly swaying vines glided down from the naagadanti. I wanted to creep under its branches. How cool it was! The wet leaves. The moist soil. How would it feel to lie on the ground, on the bare ground? The grasshoppers would leap up from the greenery below. Onto my head first. Then onto my forehead. And then onto my breasts. A little snake might hatch from its egg, pressing upon the warmth of my belly. A dark-skinned one. I tried to imagine its face. Its forked tongue flicking in a relaxed manner from its mouth. Pretty little milk teeth. The next thing I knew I was bitten by a snake. You won't believe it when I tell you. I can't believe it either. That's the difference between fiction and life. Life, that's fiction written at some unknown time. I was bitten on the left leg, exactly where I used to wear an anklet as a child. I think it was a cobra. I didn't see. Two little teeth had sunk in. That's all that happened. I stood where I was. I broke into a heavy sweat, as if I'd run a long way. The spot where I had been bitten felt as though an oilwick had been lit on it. I was in flames even as the sweat streamed down my body.

Quite like how my house had blazed in the rain.

3

Later, I realized. Every love affair needs a go-between. The beloved's medium, that which reveals her heart to her lover. The snake was revealing my message.

I was lying on his veranda when I came to. When I opened my eyes his face was close to mine. The depth of his eyes, the proud outline of his nose. The ascetic detachment. The sage-like calm. He was tying a tourniquet above the bite mark. He lowered his face on to the wound, sucked out the poison and spat it out. I was in pain and I rejoiced in it. I saw everything as if through a prism. The ascetic's face at my feet. My blood on his lips. A strange sight. Strange indeed. I told you, love is like that. Strange, from top to toe. Astonishingly so.

'Geeta... Geeta...' my husband was calling out to me, worried.

'She's opened her eyes...now there's nothing to be concerned about,' he said.

'The venom hasn't moved up her body. That was fortunate...take her to the doctor quickly...'

He gave the keys of the north gate to my husband so he could bring the car into the front yard. My husband went off. I came awake from my stupor. I lay there, watching him wash my blood from his mouth, pour water on his face, sprinkle it on his head, as if to purify himself. A cool breeze wafted in, redolent with the fragrance of wild jasmine and gandharajan. His eyes were on the garden path. I looked at him intently. He was magnetic. His face was radiant. What did he feel when he pressed his lips on my wound? What sensation did my blood evoke on his tongue? I ached badly, from head to toe. My heart screamed. I groaned. He turned and looked at me. With compassionate eyes.

'Yes, what is it?'

I moved my lips.

'Water?'

I stretched out my arm.

He picked up the water jar and came up to where I lay on the floor. He sat down next to me, knees folded as if in a funeral rite. Light lay scattered within those eyes. Eyes rapt in contemplation. Eyes that did not look at me. I warned you early on. I'm shameless. The mother of two girls. The wife of a forty-year-old man. Impossibly bold. Immeasurably assertive. I was in a hurry. My husband could return any minute. My arms curved around his neck. My teeth sunk into his lips as I pulled his face down towards me. Two of my best venom teeth. Believe it or not, he turned completely blue.

4

The many lives I have traversed, shedding many outer skins. I crawl on. From one to another. Over prickly cacti, rough boulders. Above mountains and trees. Over wet, fallen leaves, wilted flowers. One life at a time. He is present in each one of them. Always of the same colour. The deepest blue.

While convalescing after being bitten by the snake, these things passed through my mind. I was amused by them. Two beings wandering through space and time searching for the other. Who finally met, but did not recognize each other. The secrets of life are strange. I thought of him whenever my husband and children appeared before me. His eyes. His eyes, deep enough for me to dip into and rise again.

'Why did you have to go there at that time, my dear?' my husband asked. Whenever he was free, he would sit beside me, stroking my forehead. I held fast to his hands.

'Did I bother you?'

'It's not that...it hurts to see you like this, so weak...'

'Anyway let's not think of buying a house again... Let's give it up. If we put the money in the bank, there'll be peace of mind at least...'

I didn't reply. Why did I need a house any more? I didn't seek the house, I sought the owner. Selling or buying a house wasn't an issue any more! There was just one issue: him. The distance between us. The distance of years, ages. How was I going to get him back? Each time I shut my eyes, his face appeared—the face in which the bluish tinge keeps spreading, slowly, slowly. Right before me, close enough to touch. I stretched out my hands and touched him again and again. True. And strange.

I looked closely at myself in the mirror. What did I see? A female form. A woman who has lived some three decades and a half. My mother bore me in her womb, gave birth to me, nursed me at her breast. I crawled on my knees; sat up; stood up; walked; ate; slept; grew; reproduced. And now I draw close to old age and death.

My form made me laugh. Who is this? A woman, with her hair tied up or down; clad in a sari or a mundu; lining her eyes with kohl, and touching herself up with face powder. A woman who sautéed cabbage thoran for lunch; who sprayed perfume on her husband's handkerchiefs and folded them neatly; who combed out the lice from the girls' hair, braiding them nicely; who never failed to give her husband his daily dose of high blood pressure drugs on time. What is this woman? Why was she born? Why is she living? This forty-year-old man with his slightly greying hair and these girls aged ten and twelve, who are they to her? She herself, who is she, really?

Who am I? What am I? These questions vexed me. So, the first opportunity I got, I went to see him again, without my husband's knowledge. I went there alone. As usual, it was evening when I reached the house. The languorous dusk. The sky stretched above, bluish, as if consumed by venom.

He was preparing for evening worship. I entered through the open front door without waiting for permission.

He started, seeing me. The memory of the bite still stung. Inside was a large image of Goddess Tripurasundari, almost as tall as a human being. The goddess sat astride a roaring lion, bedecked with jewels. A garland of white mandaaram flowers hung around her neck. The ceremonial dish was full of camphor cubes. The lamps were filled with oil and decked with oil wicks.

He got up slowly. He looked extraordinarily imposing. Extraordinarily powerful. Someone beyond the reach of simple touch.

'Come...' he said.

He walked over to a sofa in the sitting room and sat down. His fingers strummed the veena kept on the teapoy next to the sofa. It emitted an awesome sound. I was amused. This is someone who would not be defeated.

'Take a seat... Did you come alone?'

'Yes...'

I sat down on the sofa opposite him. I kept looking at him. He never looked at me. The seconds flew between us.

'This house is not for sale...' he said quickly.

I laughed. He suddenly looked straight into my eyes, unwaveringly.

'Do you think you are rich enough to quote a price for this house?'

I laughed out aloud.

'Tell me the truth, what is on your mind? Why have you come here again?'

What a thing to ask. Why have I come, indeed? I felt dispirited. Well, is there a man in this world who doesn't disappoint? Ask how

I came to be here, I whispered in my mind. It took a lot of trouble. A lot of lies. Many obstacles had to be overcome. Many concessions had to be given; many compromises had to be made. Just think of it. That moment. That house. That desolation. That dusk. The two of us. Two beings who had grown weary in their search for each other, across many lives. The moment in which we came face to face. Intense, ardent, volatile. But what happened, really? He did not remember a thing. Did not recognize anything. I alone knew. He ought to have been the one to know. He should have come in search of me. He should have removed my outer skins; he should have received my venom in his palms. But what did he do? He ran away to Tripurasundari. He worshipped her, adored her. Devoted his whole life to her. And me? I sought him through many lives. Like a serpent which had lost the gem it guarded, I lurched and staggered. Well, is there a woman in this world who has been loved fairly?

I tried to say something. I don't remember the words. Surely, they were about love. And about this life. He spoke about asceticism. He warned me about the soul, about sacred vows. I challenged him; ridiculed him, asking, where does asceticism lie, in the body or the soul? I don't know what he made of that. He may or may not have understood. I kissed him forcibly. It had been easier to open the old wooden door! But even that opened in the end. I challenged him again to rise above the body. He accepted it and kissed me. To speak of his kiss, well—it wasn't spectacular. I forgave him for that. Men should kiss with their souls, not with their lips. I had taught him that, in each of our lives. Poor thing, he forgot all of it. I must remind him again. I will make the ascetic separate himself from his body. I'll make him an unadorned soul. I broke into laughter as I held him. No change at all. Aeons have passed, life after life has withered and drooped, but nothing has changed. His hands, his neck, his chest. It's the same as before.

I've already told you. This love story is a strange one. I sought him madly. And finally I found him. But he didn't remember me. How was I to remind him? I had no ring to stir the memory, no jewel, no gift retained from our past that could remind him. I had only my desire for him; my ancient memory of him. Would that be enough to rouse the ascetic from his trance? And that too, this man. This powerful, undefeated man. He who reduced the God of Love to a pile of ashes. It is not easy to lead a man into physical love. Especially this one, who was Tripurasundari's slave. But, I've told you, he is my other half; he has only half my strength. I led him as far as the bedroom; as far as nakedness.

'Thirty years...thirty years since the vows...' he panted. That was just before our bodies were to join. The very moment he'd gone beyond his body. The moment in which I awaited his embrace, upon the wooden cot. A moment in which but a finger's distance separated us. One single moment.

He woke up, suddenly.

'No...' he said, decisively. 'I can't do it...the Devi's image in my mind...'

He dressed without looking at me and went out. That moment. Just think. The dusk before the November rain fell. The sky smitten by venom. A cage with wooden walls. A woman lies waiting, all her outer skins discarded. For him. For his touch, his tenderness. His surrender. I lay there, sapped, like a snake with a broken spine. The darkness built its lair around me. A fruitless life.

The wind blew hard. The leaves of the money-vine clinging to the mango tree fluttered feebly in the garden.

The rain must have come and gone; the fireflies must have flitted about; the midnight bird must have trilled aloud. I did not know.

At dawn, I dressed and returned to my husband and children.

5

I've told you. This love is not only strange, but also painful. Anyway, what is love without pain? It must ache as if your bosom has been cleaved apart. The gnawing pain from jealousy's sharp-toothed saw. The scorching pain of the embers of loss. I will tear out my wings and fly to him. The blood will flow from my torn wings. His white mandaaram blossoms will turn red from my blood. I will defeat him with blood and pain.

I was jealous of Tripurasundari. She stole my man. He's mesmerized by her image. He calls her by her thousand names, yet his mind is not full. She is but a feeling. Nothing but his imagination. When I remembered that, I burned. Frustration fuelled my rage; my rage fuelled my revenge. My feet ached when I walked; my fingers ached when I ate my food. Every pore of my body ached. He is mine. His soft fingers, his immaculate feet, his radiant eyes. I own all of this, I alone. I have no knowledge of black magic. If I had, I would have turned him into a bird and locked him in a cage. I would have made him into a nail, hammered deep into my forehead. I would have turned him into an embryo and carried in my womb. I would not have left him to worship any Tripurasundari; I would have distilled him into a terrible poison and died drinking it.

I wrote to him:

I dream of your death. One night I will arrive at your house with a sharp dagger. I will plunge it right into your heart as you sleep peacefully. I will drink your blood. I will eat your liver raw. That way I will blend you, burn you, into my blood and flesh.

His reply, written in an impeccable hand, arrived in a few days:

I am anguished, too. Would like to see you.

I set off immediately. I don't remember all the lies I told my husband. I've been open with you. I don't care for honesty when love and this ascetic are involved. I'll betray everyone—my children, my husband, my family, you, this whole world... I'll be cruelly disloyal.

Just as I was setting out, my younger daughter cried for something. I paid no heed. My older daughter fretted. That too escaped my attention. My husband looked gloomy. I didn't bother about that. I'm helpless. I cannot but go. All these folk, they are the business of this birth alone. He isn't like that. He's the ceaseless flow that links births past and forthcoming. My taproot.

I reached his house in the evening. It was a full moon night. The dusk lay all around me tranquil, silent. The moonlight fell upon his garden. Everywhere you looked, flowers were in bloom, white-clad and scented.

He had lit an oil lamp on the veranda and was reading something in its light. I pushed open the tile-roofed door. He looked up, anxious, hearing it creak. He saw me and set his reading aside. He stood up, leaning on the wall. He stood there gazing at me, arms behind his head.

That night I bathed in the river. He stood guard on the bank, with a lit lantern. The river was clear and cool. He picked the kaitha flowers for me. I lined my eyes with kohl for him. I braided my hair. We walked through the fields upon which the moonlight lay scattered. We sat on the path, in the middle of the fields, dipping our legs in the water. The moon shone bright upon the tangled tresses of the sky. The frogs croaked aloud. The green ones, memories from our past births. We listened carefully, silent. I was hurting inside and outside, a hard pain. My legs gave way when we began walking back. He held me.

We lit lamps in the serpent grove. We sat brushing against each other beneath the njaaval tree, looking at the lit lamps, at the swaying vines, at the birds drifting into slumber. Njaaval fruit fell like rain in the breeze. Then we talked.

He talked of his childhood. About his deceased parents, friends, romance in college, the early rigours of the ascetic life. I told him of my house. About my south-facing window, my river, my room, the breeze I trapped in it, of how I danced to the breeze clad in my silken skirt, the one with the golden brocade border. I kept eating the njaaval berries. My lips turned a dusky blue. He lifted my face to the moonlight. He kissed me. His lips turned dusky blue too.

The moonlight, the njaaval tree, the wet withered leaves. The terrible pain. The pain of desire. This is the most painful part of this love. The touch-me-not clumps on the ground. Thorns fallen off a thorny tree. The sharp stones. The harder we embraced, the harder the ache. The njaaval berries were bruised, crushed. Their juice smeared my wound; it ached again.

'I remember now,' he said... 'For some time we were both bluebirds. You had a yellow spot on your beak.'

'And afterwards, for a long while we were fish. You had red spots on your tail...' I said.

'Weren't we sandal trees once? Didn't my roots entwine with yours under the soil?'

'After that we were stars...'

'And what are we now?'

He was sad.

Snakes, I consoled him. Snakes whose mouths and tongues had turned dusky blue from njaaval berries. We looked at each other vengefully. We hissed aloud. Fought with our venomous fangs. We struck each other with our tails and heads.

At dawn, beneath the tree, the njaaval berries lay crushed. Both of us turned deep blue, a dusky hue. He became mine. Defeated. Weak. But a slave. I found the answer to my question—Who am I? His owner. His mistress. His soul. He was completely mine. His eyes existed upon my image. His long curly tresses existed for me to run my fingers through. His long beard, to graze my breasts. His fingers, to caress me. His chest, for me to rest my head upon. His neck, for me to bite, again and again. His life, for me to wound. His birth, to give me pleasure. I was half of him, the man in me. He was half of me, the woman in me. Two souls, intertwined. Two beings who'd sought each other through many births.

We were in ecstasy. I dug my nails into him. Bit and tore at his body. He received me tenderly and with pleasure. We laughed the whole night. In the morning we made rice gruel and chutney and ate from the same bowl. The ascetic told little jokes and light tales; he sang love songs. He spoke of my tresses, the colours that suited me. Of the son I might bear him. We delighted together in his frolic. We took pride in the quickness of his mind. Hoped that he reposed now in my womb, his tiny spine as delicate as a silken thread, his little brain, the size of a mustard seed. He pressed his face to my womb and gave our son a name. We laughed. I kissed him till he was exhausted.

It was now time for me to leave. We sagged. Our smiles faded. The pain rushed back. That moment, when I looked into his eyes to bid goodbye. His eyes. His deep eyes. Pain, tenderness, desire. Terrible loss. That's how I'll remember him on my deathbed. He too will remember my face from that moment. Maybe for many births. You do not know how we embraced at the parting moment. Surely, no woman has ever embraced a man like that. I didn't embrace him with my body. I held him with my soul. He replied with his soul. Our bones were crushed; our flesh was bruised. We melted into each other. Never can we embrace like this again. For, we will never meet again. Never will we hold each other. Never will we spend the night together like this.

We will meet again, perhaps, in our next birth. Then too, I will slither like this. Over trees, and hills, over leaves and rocks. I'll seek him, slithering. Find him.

Then too, he will resist me, like now. He will try to push me away, to hate me. In the end, he will collapse from my bite.

Then too we will mate like now. And part, our hearts torn asunder. Even if we part, my blood will long to blend with his.

6

I can't bear it. I am worn out. Body and soul, both are wounded. Memories. I've loved, loved, my blood vessels are clogged. I'm ageing fast. I'm becoming an old woman. My heart beats heavy each time, strained and worn. Each time, his name booms out. Each time, my eyes blink in pain. I see his face. Truly, I can't bear it. I'm worn out, trying to stop the immense Ganga in mid-air from falling. The river Ganga has to fall upon the earth. My eyes smart, not seeing him. My ears tingle, missing his voice. My fingers, my lips, this whole body, my blood, my heart, brain...without him, I writhe in smouldering pain.

I told you. Life experience needs honesty. Honesty has no need for morality. At night when my husband approaches me all aroused, I turn away, pretending I have a migraine. I sit transfixed, forgetting myself, as I prepare to sew a button on my older daughter's dress. As I sit beside my younger daughter's sickbed tending to her feverish body, I remember the wound on my left leg where he touched me first.

'What are you thinking about?' my husband asks me, sometimes.

'Nothing...' I say, with an attempt at a smile.

I dress in silk saris for my husband. Wear jasmine in my hair. Darken my eyes with kohl. Put colour on my lips. We go together to dinner parties and on vacations. We discuss the girls' future. On more settled nights, when he comes close, I may even let him do it.

My husband, my children, my house, my servants, my marble floors, my orchids, my anthurium...my outer skins growing tight. I stifle and gasp, for him.

I have never gone to that house afterwards. He wasn't there anyway. He was sent to some ashram in Kashi or Haridwar. We never wrote to each other. I do not know where he is. I don't want to know, either. My love was a languid serpent of tremendous venom. It lay in wait for him, biding its time. He came. He trod on its hood. Made it into Takshaka, Kaliya, Anantha. He received it, and left. I will imagine him as a mendicant. In countries I do not know, traversing paths I'm ignorant of. Mountain passes clad in the white of snow. Paths paved with red sand. His feet reddened by the long walks. My form in his eyes. My love in his neck. In his arms, our son, who mirrors his face.

I can't take more. I can't say or write any more. Why, I've told you. This is not fiction, this is experience. An honest burning sliver of experience. If it were fiction I could have turned it around. Could have said that he gave up asceticism, and I gave up a familial existence, and eloped. Or, I could have said that I apologized to my husband and remained a chaste wife for the rest of my days. But I'm helpless, this just happens to be a bit of life experience. A smouldering bit of life that can't be rewritten or denied. My love is like the house freshly on fire. Even in the downpour of separation, it blazes bright. Tongues of flame raise their hoods to the sky. This birth falls apart, seared, baked. Soon, another birth. The ascetic will come again. We will find each other again.

Once again, my deadly fangs will turn him blue—the deepest blue.

JUMMAN

SHRIPAD NARAYAN PENDSE

Translated from the Marathi by Shanta Gokhale

Just behind the temple of Mhasoba lies an extensive bit of flat land which they call 'Jotya's backyard'. In the old days, this place was known as 'Dankhni's backyard'. Dankhni is the Devil. There is another place in the village connected to Jotya. As you come to the end of Maharwada you notice a ramshackle porch to your right. This is where Jotya's house stood. The bit of land behind the porch was where Jotya grew his coconuts and vegetables. Pointing to the left of the porch villagers say, 'That was the frontyard. That is where Jotya used to tie Jumman.'

Even today, innumerable legends cling to Jotya's name. Challenges are thrown out, 'Let's see you enter Mhasoba's temple on new moon night,' the villagers say. 'We'll eat our heads, if Jotya doesn't come up to you, all sweaty and wild-eyed, demanding his Jumman back.' So vehement are their voices that no one feels inclined to take up the challenge. Instead, they grow absorbed in the fascinating story of Jumman.

Jotya drew his last breath crying out for Jumman; yet he had never been destined to love a human being. It wasn't that he didn't have family. He did have kids, and a wife, and he earned enough for all of them to eat well and live happily. But such are the quirks of fate, that all the love and devotion he was capable of were lavished on an animal.

If truth be told, it was only after Jumman entered Jotya's life, that it acquired some purpose and meaning. Otherwise nobody would have known or cared even if Jotya had suddenly fallen dead one day.

What was his earlier life like? It had been one long procession of carcasses that had to be skinned and a wife who had to be beaten. Mhasoba had actually been kind to him. He had given him many children. But Jotya never once caressed them. The word 'love' didn't figure in his vocabulary.

His was a life of unremitting toil, but he never stopped to ask himself why. He worked himself to the bone, but nobody had a kind word for him. How could they, when he had never said a polite word to anybody in his life?

When he came home tired from the day's work, his wife and children would look fearful. Others waited impatiently for their men to return, but in Jotya's house it was different, like everything else. As soon as he stepped inside the house, all hell would break loose. He was destined never to hear words of solicitude from members of his family. It was not even as if he drank too much. No. The fault lay in his nature.

If he found there was no curry with his bhakri, he would begin to fling obscenities at his wife. It didn't matter if his children had no curry with their bhakri, as long as he got it. As for his wife and kids, a satisfied belch from him was enough to half-fill their stomachs.

The same story was repeated outside the house. At village meetings, Jotya would sit in a corner. All of a sudden he'd start talking loudly and belligerently. Of course people never paid any attention to him. On the contrary, such was the ill will they bore him on account of his strange and eccentric ways, that a word from him was considered a universal signal for hostilities to begin. Whatever he said, whether it was right or wrong, was promptly squashed. It was generally assumed that he never said anything remotely acceptable.

Perhaps it was his profession that lay at the root of his peculiarities. His work was skinning dead cattle. He had a hereditary right over all the cattle that died in his village and in the neighbouring villages. He had a bit of land, too, but he never tended it. That was women's work according to him. Had he worked on the land, perhaps some of its softness might have entered his heart. But that was not to be!

Jotya was approaching his fifties when death touched his house. He never quite understood what took his wife. The poor wretch would scream about a lump in her stomach. Jotya decided that this was a pretext to avoid work. So the minute she started screaming he would beat her. 'Are you the only one who feels pain?' he would shout. 'How is it that we never feel any?' Because of this, even when she could barely stand, she would still come out into the yard to clean the skins. Flies would be buzzing around. She would begin to retch. When the retching began, Jotya would yell, 'So that's the new trick eh? You think you can fool me by vomiting, do you? But you can't.'

He could not be fooled. So she died. She dropped dead in the midst of the skins and vomit. At first Jotya thought she was faking her own death. 'She's putting it on,' he said. It was only when the villagers had got all the funeral things ready that he seemed to wake up to reality. Jotya cremated her and came home to find his children weeping disconsolately. For the first time in his life something moved inside his guts, and he wept. But that was that. The children, however, went on and on with their grief. At this, his anger blazed forth. According to him, there was a limit to grief. Two days was enough.

Cholera broke out in the village the following year. Though the entire village suffered, no one was as crushed by the disease as Jotya's family. By the end of the epidemic, the only one alive in that entire house, which had once hummed with human voices, was a spectral Jotya.

At night Jotya would hear the sounds of crying. He would get up, search the house and then return to his bed, disappointed. There was a gaping void in his life which he struggled to fill.

It wasn't an easy thing to do. When he woke up in the morning he would sit still for a long time. There was nobody he could shout at and curse now. He would sit there, then slowly lift the palm of his hand up to his eyes, with the vacant gaze of one demented. His hand seemed to tell him long-forgotten tales. It told of fingers that had slapped and fingers that had pinched. And even now, he could feel those fingers tingle with the memory. Remember, said the hand, remember how you pinched your children's ears between this very thumb and forefinger? Remember their screams? Look at us. We are

the five Pandavas. We beat your wife with sticks. The hand seemed
to sprout teeth and grin mockingly at him. The fingers seemed to
push hard at his pupils. He saw his wife once again as she had been,
limping and moaning in agony.

If he went near the hearth, the pots, pans and ladles would start
talking to him. Their voices were quiet, but Jotya felt they were hurling
themselves at him in fury.

His work came to a halt. What was he to do with the skins he
brought home? Who was there to be bullied into scraping off the
gobs of flesh that clung to them? And whose maw was he going
to fill with the money he made breaking his back over these skins?

Life was a void into which came old memories, crowding and
jostling. Jotya had never asked himself the meaning of life, but he was
now convinced that his life had lost all meaning. He wouldn't eat
for two days at a time, and then, when his head swam with hunger
pangs, he would scrape the ashes out of the hearth and light a fire.
He would sit over the dough, brooding, and then return to kneading
it. As he bit into his bhakri, he would ask himself, 'What does it all
mean? This eating and drinking and walking and laughing and talking?'
He found all his actions incomprehensible. When he walked he would
mutter to himself, 'Now, what is this I'm doing? I'm walking. What
exactly does that mean? I place one foot forward, like this. Then?
Then I put the other one forward. Really? How fascinating. But
why be so fascinating? Why not just stand in one place?' He would
open his mouth to yawn and immediately mutter to himself, 'Now
why did I do that?'

For days he hovered on the brink of insanity.

Strangely enough, even in this state, there was one thing which
hurt him deeply. There he was, the lone survivor of the holocaust, and
yet not a soul from the village had come to enquire after him. Yet
every time one of his family had died, he had plied his neighbours
with liquor, and done everything else that custom required of him.

He felt disproportionately dejected over this show of callousness.
But actually, Maharwada was behaving with him exactly as it had
always done. It was he who had changed. He had now begun to

think about things which had never occured to him before. In the old days, he had never had the time for such thoughts. All his time had been taken up by cursing and beating. Now there was nothing to do. So he began noticing all kinds of trivial matters.

At last, tired of being alone, he started visiting people himself. If people don't talk to me, he thought, there's no reason why I can't talk to them. People responded immediately. He discovered later that they had felt very deeply sorry for him in his misfortune. The more he saw of them, the more he blamed himself for having doubted them.

He began spending a great deal of his time away from home. At the end of the day's work, he would drop in at some neighbour's house, and sit chewing tobacco and lime and exchanging news. People said, 'Jotya has changed. But too late. His wife and kids weren't meant to enjoy this happiness.'

Jotya had really changed. Babies were no longer afraid of cuddling up to him. When they learned to stand by holding on to his shoulders, he would ache with remorse and guilt. 'Were my kids hungry for this kind of love? Did Mhasoba take them away from me because I wouldn't give it to them?' He trembled with fear at this thought. He mustn't spurn these little ones now, or Mhasoba might take them away too. Then he would hold the babies close and kiss them. Once in a while, an infant would smile at him, and he would feel exhilarated. God must have created babies to bring some happiness into human life, he thought. Children began to play happily around the old man and with him too. Jotya had certainly changed.

It was around this time that Jumman entered his life. How they met would seem an irrelevant question in the light of what happened. The important thing is that they met.

Jotya's transformation received its finishing touch with Jumman. Jumman turned him into a ball of butter, ready to melt at the slightest hint of heat. He continued to go out for work as he had always done. But now with Jumman in tow. Many were the occasions when Jotya would plead with him, 'My pet, why do you come after me? I am out till the sun comes overhead. You are too young. How can you possibly bear the heat? Won't you feel hungry, thirsty?' But Jumman paid no heed to him. The minute Jotya stepped out of the house Jumman would be right behind. Sometimes Jotya would play around with him. He would push him back onto the porch and scold him with mock severity, 'Now stop being naughty.' And when Jumman popped right out again, he would laugh and say, 'You were never one for obeying. Come on, then.' As he passed through Maharwada with Jumman on his shoulders, the entire neighbourhood would come out to watch the pair. They would say, 'Jotya, you had children, but you didn't want them. And now you pamper Jumman.' Once in a while Jotya would hear these remarks, and pain would tear through his heart. He would imagine his children running ahead of him crying, 'Baba, let us come with you. If you can take Jumman, why not us?' There was a time when such thoughts would have driven him berserk. But now he had Jumman to give him courage and fortitude.

When such thoughts assailed him, he would lower Jumman to the ground and rub his grizzled face against the little goat's over and over again. This chased all inauspicious thoughts out of his mind, and he would resume his journey with his usual energy. As soon as he came to his place of work, he would set Jumman down. Jumman would gambol away while Jotya got down to work. He would call out to Jumman when it was time to go home; Jumman would come frisking back and rub himself against Jotya's legs. Jotya would once again hoist him on to his shoulders, and thus father and son...

Often Jotya would trick Jumman and leave the hut without being noticed. People would ask, 'Where's the little one today, Jotya?' and he would reply, 'He is a real pest. I've left him behind.' Their reunion after three or four hours of separation was a touching sight. Jumman would rub himself against Jotya again and again. Then Jotya would lift him onto his lap and caress him. Ever since Jumman had come into his house, Jotya had not eaten alone. At dinner, he would make Jumman sit beside him. He would feed him a piece of bhakri first and then have some himself. That is the way all their meals went.

Jumman was growing up. He began to figure out how things worked. He grew horns. He began to find his way around alone. He began visiting the neighbours' houses. The children loved him. As soon as they saw him, they would start chasing him, shouting, 'Jumman, Jumman.' Right away, a game of catch-catch would begin. Jumman would dodge away and disappear. The whole of Maharwada would then ring with shouts. The children would set up a chant:

> *There goes the thief, catch him quick.*
> *Silly old Jumman, we know your trick.*

Jumman would run helter-skelter. With the greatest effort, the children would surround him. They would then tie him up and drag him around the village. Jumman bore the rough handling without any complaint, in fact he rather enjoyed it.

When these games were being played, a worried looking Jotya would suddenly appear. He would scold the children and take Jumman away by the ear. On the way home, Jumman too would come in for his share of scolding. Jotya would say, 'It's no use looking at me like that. You're just as bad as they are.'

There was something about Jumman which won the people over. The kids adored him, and so did the grown-ups. He had managed to soften their hearts too. When the kids became rough with Jumman, Jotya wasn't the only one to give them a scolding. Whoever happened to be nearby would run to Jumman's aid. The women would give him leftovers. If they had put papads and other stuff out to dry, he would come and sniff at the food; but nobody minded him. Instead, they would playfully pinch him and say, 'Aren't you going to leave anything for us to eat, you little rascal?'

With all this pampering, Jumman grew fat and sleek. His body began to attract many glances. He now possessed a pair of haughty horns.

And then one day, he suddenly began to behave in the strangest manner. Never before had he disobeyed Jotya. His word had always been the law. But now he paid no heed to Jotya. When Jotya caressed him and tried to kiss him as usual, Jumman butted him with all his might.

Then he set off at great speed. The children chanted:

> *There goes the thief, catch him quick.*

But Jumman was in a strange mood. When the children tried to stop him, he butted them too and slipped away. The children knew at once that this was not his usual playful butting. They ran back to Maharwada and told their amazing tale to everybody.

The villagers joined Jotya in the chase. They could see Jumman in the distance. He had bleated himself hoarse. Jotya ran towards him, and as soon as he was within earshot, he called out, 'Jumman, Jumman! Aren't you tired? Come back.'

Jumman turned around. As soon as he saw the exhausted Jotya coming up behind him, he broke into a run again. He was too tired now either to run or bleat, but he kept on running. The villagers were right behind Jotya. The chase continued. Jumman dodged all of them. If anyone came too near, he would rise up on his haunches, fix him with surly eyes and go full tilt for him.

Finally they managed, somehow, to hem him in. He was exhausted after all the running. Jumman, who had so far stood firmly on his hind legs at every assault, now lost his balance and came crashing down. He lay on the ground, helpless. Panting like a pair of bellows, Jotya threw himself upon Jumman. He called out in a piteous voice, 'What came over you, Jumman? Why did you run away like that? I shall not let you go anywhere now.' Jotya began to hoist him on to his shoulders. Somebody shouted, 'Jotya, he's not a kid any more. Give him a couple of hard slaps, and let him walk. He's given you enough trouble today.'

'Oh please, don't say that. Look at the state he's in. Yes, he's been wicked today, but has he ever been like this before?' So saying, Jotya picked him up. His knees quaked under the weight of that huge body. He looked as if he would collapse any moment but he somehow made it home.

Everybody gathered at Jotya's house, curious to know what had come over Jumman. They examined him thoroughly, but found nothing wrong. Only his eyes looked bloodshot. Somebody fetched an onion from the woods. It was cut in two and the pieces placed on Jumman's eyes. There was nothing wrong with his eyes, of course, but some old man had suggested an onion be pressed into service, and someone had run off to find one. Somebody else suggested that it was all due to the evil eye. The idea was so appealing that everyone agreed with it. There was nothing more natural than that someone should have cast an evil eye on Jumman. You just had to see his sleek body, and his haughty carriage to know he was a rare beast. Someone said just then that he had seen Jumman going towards Black Madhwa's house a couple of days ago. Madhwa had noticed him. He must have cast an evil eye on him. There was no doubt in anybody's mind. Curd and rice were brought out. Jotya waved the mixture in circles around Jumman's head. Jumman watched with stupid eyes.

Jumman now lay motionless. His stomach was hollow with hunger. Jotya brought him something to eat and drink. Soon Jumman fell asleep.

But Jotya didn't sleep at all that night. He remembered how his children had suddenly left him one day. He would start up from his mat, go to Jumman and stroke him all over. Jumman slept peacefully till the morning.

No sooner did the cock crow than he began once again to bleat loudly. It was the same wild call of the previous day. It drove Jotya crazy with worry. He called out to Jumman from where he lay, 'Jumman, my pet, what has happened to you? Why are you doing this? All these days you've been a companion to me. Are you now going to betray me?' There were tears in Jotya's eyes.

Jotya got up and went to Jumman who was straining at the rope that held him, while he continued to scream and cry. The neighbours woke up. They called out, 'Are you awake, Jotya? Jumman is crying.' Jotya answered from his house, 'Please come, somebody. I need your help, Jumman is acting strange.' Jotya tried to cover Jumman's mouth with his hand. Jumman lowered his head menacingly. Jotya mustered his courage and caught hold of Jumman's proud horns in his tight fists. Fortunately, he was on his guard, for the next moment Jumman charged. Jotya kept his grip on his horns, and, in the scuffle that followed, Jumman lost his balance. Before Jotya could do anything, Jumman had crashed to the ground. On the verge of tears, Jotya shouted, 'Oh, why don't you listen? You've fallen now, and you've hurt yourself badly, haven't you?' He bent over to check if Jumman was hurt, but the goat was already up and ready to charge.

Jotya gave up then. 'To hell with you,' he muttered and lay down on his rough mat. But that did not solve the problem. Jumman continued his weird bleating. A little while later, a thought flashed into Jotya's mind. 'Maybe he's hungry, that's all.' He got up instantly, went out and plucked a basketful of green leaves. He called out soothingly to Jumman. 'Jumma, Jumma,' he said, holding the basket before him. Jumman had just been waiting for something to butt. He flung himself at the basket, making it fly in the air like straw. Jotya sat with his hand pressed against his head. Then he got up again. He drew fresh water from the well and placed it before Jumman. Jumman might have butted that too, but this time Jotya was ready. Guessing his mood from his stance, he removed the bucket before the goat could overturn it.

Jotya didn't know what to do now. He hadn't eaten a morsel since the previous evening. Jumman had killed any interest he might have had in food and drink.

By this time dawn had brightened into day. Jotya left the house. Everybody enquired after Jumman. Jotya merely shook his head, unable to speak. People wanted to help. They made various suggestions. Someone said, 'Maybe, he is rabid.'

'What do you mean he is rabid?' Jotya asked.

'Rabid, like a dog goes rabid.'

Jotya was incensed by the idea. He felt that if this kind of talk spread, they wouldn't think twice before killing Jumman.

'Dogs go rabid. But whoever heard of a goat going rabid? Don't talk like a fool.' Jumman had not gone rabid, but Jotya was certainly on the verge of doing so. He consulted the village elders. None of them knew what to make of Jumman's malady. Jotya asked them in despair, 'Please tell me. What should I be doing?'

'Jotya, why have you left Jumman alone at home and come away? He'll strain at the rope too hard and break his neck, or something. Run home this minute…'

'I am scared to go home alone. Will someone come with me?'

Jotya returned home, accompanied by a few people, Jumman was still struggling and screaming.

'This is how it's been since morning. What shall I do? Tell me, please?'

'Jotya, let him go,' an old man said.

'How will that help? He'll run away.'

'Let him.'

'Let him?'

'Yes. Let him run away. Let him go where he wants to. We'll know what he wants then.'

'And if he falls down and breaks his bones?'

'We'll be right behind. Only we won't try to stop him.'

As soon as he was released, Jumman set off at tremendous speed. There was nobody to hold him now. Jotya and the villagers followed at a distance. Jumman twisted and turned. After some time, his followers realized where he was going. He was off to Black Madhwa's place. As soon as he got there, he walked into the midst of the herd of she-goats, his head held high, and his pulse back to normal. There was no sign of the frenzy that had been driving him crazy.

'Jotya, oh Jotya, your Jumman's come of age, that's all. He needs a wife. Nothing we can do for him. Let's go home.'

Jumman became a permanent guest at Black Madhwa's place. Jotya would make a daily trip to Madhwa's and return home with a crestfallen face. Trying to bring Jumman home was futile.

One day he forcibly brought him home. The children began to dance around him singing, 'Jumman's back. Jumman's back.' Jumman too seemed happy. All the villagers came to see him. Jotya felt as if a stone had been lifted off his chest. But the relief didn't last long. Within a few days, Jumman suffered a relapse of the old malady. Quietly, Jotya set him free. Jumman pranced away to his new home. Jotya sat forlornly, muttering, 'Jumman, how can you be so ungrateful? I saved you from the knife when you were but two months old. I felt sorry for you then. I knew those scoundrels were feeding you and looking after you only to make a good bit of mutton two years later. You endeared yourself to me, and now, suddenly you've become independent. You've grown horns. It's not right to run after women so much; to forsake the man who saved you, reared you like a child, often gave you his food when there wasn't enough for two. Does a wife mean so much? Who do I have now to care for in my old age? My children left me; maybe that was my fault. But where did I go wrong with you? I never let you suffer, did I?'

He couldn't sleep, food had lost its savour. The only thing he could see was a vision of Jumman standing before him. 'The little idiot is at Madhwa's. They'll torture him there, I know,' he would say to himself. He knew Madhwa only too well. There wasn't much to choose between him and the butcher, though he might not wield the knife himself. His way of life had always shocked Jotya. To be able to rear little lambs, feed them till they grew nice and fat, and then sell them off for slaughter was incomprehensible to him. It was sheer barbarity. Madhwa was a shrewd man whose fields and spacious house had all received sustenance from the blood of countless goats. Others could have made their pile too in similar fashion. All you needed was four she-goats. Within a year they would breed you a decent herd. But people didn't want such tainted money. The very idea used to repel Jotya. Whenever he met Madhwa on the road, he would remember this about him and avert his eyes.

Jotya was in a dreadful state now. All these days the villagers had been sympathetic, but now even they had given up. How long could they continue to show concern? They were slowly forgetting Jumman. They said, 'There's no need to worry about Jumman now. He's done well for himself.' The cause of the malady had been discovered, the cure found, the patient had recovered, and so people forgot him. They thought Jotya's love for Jumman exaggerated. Whenever Jotya visited them now, they grew nervous. Jotya would always ask the same question, 'How long do you think Jumman will be like this?'

'Till he dies,' they would answer, annoyed. Jotya would gape at them and say, 'Please don't say that. I've seen too much death. I'm tired now. I'd rather you killed me...' When Jotya talked like this, the speaker would feel sorry. He would remember what Jotya had been through. Then he would hasten to reassure Jotya, 'He'll be back one of these days. He's not been away too long. Why are you in such a hurry?'

'He won't come. If I go there, he doesn't even look at me. He's grown so strange. Wine and women, they are equally bad. He has become an addict. He'll never come back.'

What could anybody say to this? The listener would escape under the pretext of having to drive away a cow from his yard.

Jotya would return home. He was alone in that deserted house. He could not concentrate on his work. Then, to add to his troubles, he quarreled with Madhwa. Jotya would go to Madhwa's place at all hours. If the goats were out grazing, he would run after them. He would start cleaning Jumman. Jumman would run away. Then the she-goats would become restive. This would make the goatherd angry. He would shout at Jotya. Jotya would plead with him, try to pacify him. One day the goatherd blew up. If Jumman was such a wonderful creature, let him be admired in his own village, the goatherd didn't give a damn. At last he complained to Madhwa. Madhwa said, 'Don't ever come here again.'

'Give me back my Jumman. Then I won't.'

'Give you back what I didn't take? I've got two dozen Jummans like yours.'

'You have taken my Jumman from me.'

'I took him? Am I on the streets begging to want your Jumman?'

Jotya stood with his head bowed. He realized how foolishly he had spoken. After some time Madhwa said to him, 'If you take Jumman away within two days, well and good. If not, he's mine by the law of trespass. If you ever come this way after that, I'll break your leg. Just remember that. There he comes. Now take him away, and keep him...'

Jotya tried all sorts of tricks, but Jumman would not go with him. He tried to lift him, but Jumman was stronger and heavier than before and he had grown weak. Even then he managed to lift up Jumman. He lowered Jumman's belly across his shoulders and grasped hold of the goat's legs. As Jotya staggered off with the goat his legs trembled under the strain, and out of sheer fear. If Jumman didn't go with him he would have to give up his right on him. The thought petrified him. Jumman was bleating harshly. Jotya blubbered, 'Jumma, please don't cry. My legs are trembling.'

He hadn't gone more than ten paces when he collapsed under Jumman's weight, bringing Jumman down with him. Jumman promptly shook himself free and made off.

'Jumman, Jumman, Jumman,' Jotya called after him, but the arrogant lecher was nowhere in sight. Jotya stood up with a great effort. His knees were bruised. He rubbed some mud on them, and went back to Madhwa's house.

The goats were tied in the yard. He spotted Jumman in the corner. He went to him, stroked his back, made sure he wasn't hurt, and then settled down to wait for Madhwa.

Madhwa came out to the yard. Jotya's state made him laugh.

'Have you gone mad, Jotya?' he asked.

'Not yet, but I shall very soon. What did you say a while ago? That I could take Jumman in the next two days, didn't you?'

'Yes. By day after tomorrow. I'll give you two more days if you like. I don't want your goat. But I can't have you nosing around here every day. That's why I made up my mind. Otherwise he doesn't bother me. I've got forty. One more makes no difference. But you'd better take him. I'll give you four days. Or make it eight. But I don't want to see you here after that.'

Jotya felt weighed down with gratitude. He wouldn't have imagined Madhwa could be so soft. Eight days! Enough time to tie Jumman up and take him home if need be. He went home happy.

And...

On the ninth day Jumman became Madhwa's property.

∽

The terrible news spread throughout the village the minute Madhwa claimed Jumman. Many had predicted this would happen. And yet, though they'd been fully prepared for the dreadful eventuality, they were shocked when it actually came about. People whispered in subdued voices. Someone said, 'Is the news true in the first place? I don't want to waste my tears.' The speaker's untimely wit was not appreciated. But he had expressed a valid doubt. So a few elders left hurriedly to make sure.

They discovered that every bit of the news was true.

How was Jotya to be told of this ghastly development? The villagers sat brooding over the problem. Jotya would start weeping the minute he heard the news. But there was no time to waste. If they acted quickly, there was still some chance that Jumman might be saved.

Four village elders got together and started for Jotya's house. Jotya was lying on his mat. He had lost his grip on himself since Jumman had become Madhwa's. He spent most of his time lying flat on his mat. He got up, or slept, as his mood took him. There was nothing left to eat in the house now, except for a measure of flour.

Jotya saw the elders approaching while they were still some distance away. When he saw them turning towards his house, he was surprised. People had gradually stopped coming to see him after Jumman had left. It had been different when Jumman...

Whenever he thought of this, he felt sad. He was sad now. When Jumman had been with him, there had been joy in the house. Children used to turn up, morning, noon and night. They would tease Jumman. They would complain to Jotya about him. Then Jotya would scold him. He would explain to the children, 'He's still young. That's why he's naughty. I'll scold him, don't worry. We'll punish him.'

The children would protest, 'No, no. Don't punish him. We don't mind if he plays pranks on us. We'll do the same to him. Please don't worry.'

When the adults passed by his house they would say, 'Jotya, how is Jumman today? Is he at home, or is he out visiting?'

Jotya would say, 'Oh, I've given up. He's too much for me.'

Then they would say, 'That's because you've spoilt him. What he needs is a good spanking.'

That was the way it used to be all through the day. And now, not a soul came his way. They were too scared to come. They weren't prepared to listen to Jotya talk about Jumman. It was always the same. Old stories, memories, and then inevitably, the tears. It was the same with the children as with the grown-ups. Nobody had the patience to console him every day. There's not much you can say to console people, and once all that could be said was said, people stopped coming.

The house now looked sepulchral. It was the second time Jotya was going through this kind of experience. The first time, he hadn't known what was happening. It took him many days to understand. But in those days he had been strong, not old and frail as he was now. This time he had known what was coming. And yet, when the expected happened, it took half his life from him.

Jotya cheered up when he saw that people were still concerned about him. And right on the heels of this thought came another, sweeter thought. 'Perhaps they have come with some good news about Jumman.' So far all news had been bad. Who knows...

But a single glance at their faces dashed all his hopes, and now he trembled with fear.

The elders sat down beside him and said, 'How are you feeling, Jotya?'

Jotya remained silent. 'Why don't you speak, Jotya?' they asked again.

By now Jotya, observing their long, solemn faces, was making the most ghastly conjectures about the object of their visit. He said angrily, 'Look here. Why don't you just tell me what you've come to tell me? I don't like the way you look. I know it's something terrible...'

'Where's Jumman?'

'Dead. Didn't you know? Or at least he's at Madhwa's. But that's as good as dead to me. It's two days since he died...'

'He's really going to die. If you hurry, you might save him.'

'H...he's...w...w...w...' However hard he tried, not a single word would form.

'Jotya, Jotya, don't worry. Jumman isn't dead...yet.'

Jotya gaped at them without understanding. He slapped his forehead with his hand, meaning to say that he was suffering the results of his own doings. He was born to bring sorrow upon me... But not a single word emerged from his mouth. He couldn't speak. The visitors tried to reassure him. They had decided to break the news to him gently to lessen the shock of it. But Jotya had got into such a bad state merely imagining what had happened that they were baffled. They didn't know how to deal with him. The end that faced Jumman was not unavoidable. It was true that he was on the road to death, but he could still be saved. Yet what could they do if Jotya suddenly fainted when they finally told him the news? Looking at him now they realized one thing for sure. If Jumman died, whenever that happened, Jotya would be his companion on the funeral pyre.

'Jotya, Jumman is not dead. But if you insist on behaving as though he his, then he might have to die. So don't waste any more time. Put on your shirt and come with us.'

'He's at Madhwa's, isn't he?'

'Don't ask questions. Just come.'

'I can't go alone...'

'You're not going alone. We're going with you.'

'But Jumman won't come with me.'

'We'll see about that. Just come with us.'

'Please don't shout at me. I said that only because he's grown woman-mad these days.'

'That madness has got him into bad trouble. The butcher isn't going to spare him for his women.'

'And then...'

'And then nothing. Are you coming with us or not? Or, do you just want to go and die with your Jumman?'

'Please don't be like that.'

'Be like what? You've become impossible. Things were better without Jumman around here.'

'But you care all the same, don't you?' Jotya said, putting on his shirt.

'That's the whole trouble. Ready? Got your money?'

'Will we need money?'

'Won't we? Or do you think the butcher values your tears the way we do? You can cry as much as you like and nobody there will even notice. Now hurry up. Get your money, and come.'

'How much?'

'At least ten rupees.'

'Ten?' said Jotya, and promptly sat down.

'How much do you have?'

'I might be able to scrape together a couple of rupees...'

'That's just great. Then you might as well keep sitting here. Bloody pauper.'

Jotya remained sitting, his hand pressed to his forehead.

'Aren't you coming?'

'But the money? Where can I get that much from? You'd better go.'

'Go? And what about Jumman?'

'Let him die.'

'Let Jumman die?'

'What else? Why did he have to choose a pauper for a master? He'll die out there and I'll die here. Will my hide help?'

'Human hide fetches nothing. And yours isn't even healthy, with all those scars and wrinkles…'

Jotya didn't respond. The visitors left, and Jotya lay down once again, thinking… Something had got hold of Jumman. They were dragging him off somewhere. He couldn't even walk, they were dragging him so mercilessly. He was casting pathetic glances at Jotya. Jotya was in despair. Jumman was saying, 'I'll never do it again. It was all my fault. Take me back. Please take me back. These people are going to slaughter me. Please take me home…'

Jotya hurriedly looked through all his pockets. There wasn't a paisa in them. Jumman's cries asking to be taken back grew fainter and fainter, and then faded away. Soon after he heard a 'baaaaaa'. That was the last bleat Jumman was destined to utter. Then there was a sound of gulping and Jotya saw a struggling body…

Crazy with fear, Jotya flung himself down on his mat. He remained that way for a long time, listening to Jumman's heart-rending bleating.

An hour later the elders of the village returned. One of them said roughly, 'Come on, get up. We're going.'

'Where?' asked Jotya, starting up.

'Now stop being a fool, just come.'

'But the money?'

'We've seen to that.'

'Which good person did you meet?'

'The whole village. We went begging to every house, collecting twenty-five paise here and fifty paise there. Your Jumman is a nuisance…'

'And yet you love him.'

'That's why he's a nuisance. He's made everybody mad.'

But Jotya remained sitting where he was. When he seemed to be making no signs of moving, someone said, 'What are you thinking of now, Jotya?'

'How can I return the money? I don't even remember to eat these days. I've grown weak. I can't work the way I used to.'

'You don't have to return the money.'

'But then...' Jotya wasn't sure at all whether he should say what was in his mind. They might not like it. He was trying to make up his mind...

'What's the "but" now for? Here we are, running around for you, and you decide to act like a bashful bridegroom.'

'I'll tell you if you promise not to get annoyed...'

'We've had enough of that, Jotya, goodbye.' The villagers rose to go.

'Please don't go,' Jotya pleaded, on the verge of tears. 'I'm coming.'

∽

The place reeked with a stench that even Jotya found difficult to endure. Ten of twelve fattened goats stood in a corner. Among them was Jumman, cowering against the wall. His once proud head was now lowered. Every minute brought to his ears the screams of his brethren. He had finally understood where he had been brought. His milk-white body now bore a red mark. His eyes brimmed with fear. Every sound, every human voice, made him look around fearfully. His eyes met Jotya's and he let out a terrified bleat of appeal to him. Jotya's heart melted to water.

'Oh, Jumman. Is this what you were destined for?'

Tears flowed from Jotya's eyes. He rushed to Jumman's side. Jumman instantly recognized his love-filled caress, so familiar to him from infancy. He allowed his head to rest on Jotya's hand.

∽

When Jotya arrived on the outskirts of the village with Jumman, the whole village turned out to welcome this unlikely pair of father and son. It was the return of the runaway son. Children hung garlands around his neck, and stuck nosegays in his graceful horns. The red footprints of Death had been washed off his body. The villagers followed the pair into the village crying, 'Jumman's back, Jumman's back.'

The village collected another fund and handed it over to Jotya.

'Jotya, you must use this for a Satyanarayan puja. With bhajans.'

This puja became a much talked about event, even in the surrounding villages.

Jotya's house came alive once again. The children began to flock there. Once again there was shouting, noisy games, quarrels and scoldings. Jotya began working again and earning money. When he had saved ten rupees, he went from house to house; but no one wanted their money back. People told him not to be a fool.

'Jotya, do you think you're the only one who loves Jumman? We love him too. He has brought us joy. If we take your money, our children will be ashamed of us.'

Till then Jumman was known only within the village. But soon he began to be talked of in all the neighbouring villages. There was obviously something very unusual about an animal for whose redemption a whole village had raised money. The way the villagers had bought him from the butcher, welcomed him with garlands and nosegays, performed a Satyanarayan puja in celebration—these strange events gripped people's imagination. Every man had his own opinion to express on the Jumman episode. One said, 'The whole village must be mad. Whoever heard of a goat being given a name! Jumman! And the fund. And the puja. The whole thing is crazy.' They silenced the man saying, 'People don't go around wasting time on a goat unless there's a very special reason!' The man immediately realized his mistake.

Of course the surrounding villages made these events out to be much more astonishing and miraculous than they had actually been. What was this Jumman actually like, for whose salvation an entire village had pooled its resources and for whom a Satyanarayan puja had been performed? How did he walk? How did he talk? What did he eat? What did he drink?

Someone started the rumour that he only ate food which was

generally eaten on fast days; that he never touched leftovers; that he granted boons; that he licked the ailing, and believe it or not, cured them of their ailments.

Another man made an unexpected discovery. Since Jumman's arrival in the area, the annual scourge of cholera had not made an appearance. The discovery was verified. It was quite true. There hadn't been an outbreak of cholera in the last two years. It didn't take long after this for Jumman, the goat to become Jumman, the local deity.

Jotya knew nothing about these developments. One fine morning somebody came to visit Jotya's child. Then a second came, and a third. There seemed to be no end to the visitors that morning. Jotya was completely baffled. Everybody who came would stand before Jumman reverently, inspect him from head to foot and then go away with the sublime conviction that they had been in the presence of some kind of divine phenomenon. They swore that Jumman was different from other goats as earth is from sky. Each person would return saying, 'When I went in I was sure this was some tall story that some joker had put about. But, god help me; it's not so at all. You've got to see it to believe it. He's obviously got something in him. Did you notice his eyes? Oh you didn't? You must observe the shape. They are like conchshells. And the pupils are like whorls. Yes. Both the pupils. That is what I found so strange. Forgive my doubts, Lord Jumman. I never meant to doubt you.' Saying this, the speaker would slap himself across the face and bow reverently before Lord Jumman.

The number of devotes increased from day to day. The yard where Jumman was tied up was spruced up. The corner where Jumman actually sat was plastered smooth with cowdung. Framed pictures of gods and saints were hung up. The roof was covered with bundles of grass to prevent the sun from troubling Jumman.

To begin with, nobody actually folded their hands before Jumman. They didn't have the courage to. They would worship him without any outward sign. Then they began doing furtive namaskars. One devotee noticed these surreptitious signs of worship; he folded his hands openly, in full view of the people. This made namaskars an accepted ritual in Jumman worship. This was followed by the burning of camphor and incense sticks, and the offering of fruits and flowers. The devotees would begin to crowd in even before the sun rose. Some of them would come to ask for boons, some to offer thanks for boons granted. There seemed to be no end to those asking Jumman for boons. He was adorned every day with garlands and nosegays. Bright new clothes were made for him. Jumman no longer needed to go searching for succulent green leaves in the hot sun. His devotees came to him with flowers in one hand and a branch of foliage in the other.

Jumman now took to blessing his devotees with divine revelations. He appeared to one man in a dream. The man broadcast the news. Another felt, 'It might happen to me too.' And it did, regularly. Every small movement that Jumman made now acquired portentous significance. When he shook his head sideways, it meant 'No'. When he moved it up and down, it meant 'Yes'. Everybody came to recognize these signs. They would ask him a question and then sit staring at his head for an answer. Even his ears, feet, and body revealed important answers to people. The hopes, ambitions, and desires of many depended on the movements of these organs. 'Our boy says he wants to work on daily wages in Bombay. Should he go or not?' A young man's parents would ask Jumman. And so it went.

Jotya no longer needed to worry about food, or anything else. In fact, he found it difficult to cope with all the rice, fruits, garlands, money and coconuts that had to be collected at the end of the day. The village children came to help him. He would distribute the offerings amongst them. In the old days they had gone to Jotya's place to visit Jumman. Now the offerings became an added attraction, and one which was, perhaps, stronger than Jumman. By nine o'clock at night, the devotees would disperse and the children would come hurrying in. The slower ones were encouraged, with clouts from their parents, to go and collect their share from Jotya. Of course, what the parents said was, 'You little wretch. Do you want poor Jotya to die of all that work? Go help him. Go.' When the child returned there was always the satisfying clink of coins in his pocket, and some rice and a couple of coconuts in his hands. Jumman had become a sort of cornucopia for the entire village.

When the whole place had been put back into order, Jotya would drag Jumman indoors, tear the garlands and clothes off his body, and demand angrily, 'Look here, you bastard, what tricks are you up to? Where's this god of yours, just show me. A few lunkheads decide to start worshipping you, and you sit back and take it, do you? All you had to do was to butt that first dimwit good and proper, and he would have chased all the others away. But you're just lapping it all up. Aren't you? Go on, own up. I'm asking you a question like one of those foolish devotees. Tell me, yes or no?'

Jumman shook his head sideways. Jotya roared, 'No? No? Then why don't you butt them? All your show of might is reserved for your old man? Isn't that right? Don't gape at me like a halfwit. Just tell me if I'm right or wrong...'

Jumman moved his head up and down. Jotya laughed and said, 'Then why don't you show them how you feel about it? Did I save you from the slaughterhouse so you could start these monkey tricks? You know Jumma, this is really strange. I twist your ears, I curse you, but your god doesn't seem to mind. Where's he run off to? Doesn't he want to punish me? Oh the fools, the dolts...' Then Jotya would pinch Jumman's cheeks, fondle him and make him sleep beside him.

The first crowing of the cock would give Jotya nervous palpitations. Now the monsters will start pouring in. They will torture Jumman in a hundred ways. I won't get a minute with him till nightfall. What is to be done with these fools...

At last Jotya decided he had had enough. 'This foolishness must end. Here's an ordinary goat, and they make him into a god. If he was god, why did I have to run around so much to save him from the knife? I've just about had enough. From tomorrow nobody comes here. We'll live on anything, Jumman and I—even on air. That's our problem.'

The next day Jotya got up and left the house with Jumman in tow as in the old days. The whole village was stunned. They said, 'Where are you off to?'

'Where do you think? To work.'

'But why do you want to take god with you?'

'God? What god are you talking about? This is my Jumman, and I'm taking him out to graze.'

'Jotya, you've got too smart for your boots. Watch out.'

'What did I do?'

'You are offending god.'

Jotya went on without heeding them. Further on, Jotya began to meet Jumman's devotees. Jotya was dragging Jumman along. That terrible sight rent their hearts. Such an outrage was not to be allowed to continue. The devotees stopped Jotya.

'Where are you going, Jotya?'

'Where? To work, of course. Get out of my way.'

'Why do you need to work?'

'Why do *you*?'

'You've not been starving all these days have you, you ungrateful man?'

'Watch what you are saying. I can't help it if people choose to pour stuff into my house.'

'So, what did we say? It was just a remark... Look. You brought up Jumman with such love. Do you know how much merit that has brought you? You have every right to sit back and be fed.'

'I don't want to sit back and be fed. I don't want dead food.'

'How could you call offerings to Jumman dead food? You are blaspheming.'

'Offerings for a goat! You've all gone mad and you're trying to make a fool of me.'

'We're mad, are we? We'll forgive you only on account of that one merit of yours. What do you take Jumman for?'

'A goat with the usual horns, beard and four legs.'

'Dear god, block our ears against such evil. Jotya will bring disaster upon us if he talks this way. The cholera will return. Jotya, you're asking for a beating.'

'Do garlands and flowers make a god out of goat? How can you be so foolish? Some idiot started talking nonsense and you started running after a goat. I can't even fondle him when I want to with you people around. I won't stand for it. Get out of my way.'

'Let Jumman go, then we'll let you go wherever you want to.'

'What do you mean? Do you think Jumman belongs to you?'

'If you don't hand him over quietly, we'll have to take him by force.'

'You will not get Jumman. And you will stop coming to my house from now on. I don't want your money or anything else. I'll work as I've always done, and earn my bit of bhakri. My Jumman will graze and fill his stomach.'

'Your Jumman? Who gave him to you?'

'Who gave him to me? It's a very old story. I'll tell you if you want to know.'

'But who saved Jumman? Who paid the money?'

'I offered it to you. You wouldn't take it. That's not my fault.'

'Just tell us whether we paid the money or not.'

Jotya did not answer. Somebody repeated in a louder voice, 'Jotya, is it true or false that we paid the money?'

'False. Absolutely false.'

'False? Say that again.'

'Of course, it's false. Why didn't you take the money when I offered to return it to you? I had a suspicion then that you might stake a claim on Jumman. I should have made things clearer... I was a fool not to.'

'Then you must bear the consequences. But why are you behaving like this, Jotya? There's nothing you don't have!'

'Oh no? I can't even get near Jumman. The yard is always choked with people. He's just a common goat, but you have made him into a god. What do I have left then to call my own? You'll get your Jumman on one condition.'

'Just say it. We can't do a thing unless you tell us what you want.'

'Give me a poison which will kill me in five minutes. You can then have Jumman. Nothing will matter once I'm dead.'

'Jotya, you were never one to talk straight. Come on folks. Get hold of Jumman.'

'Hey, don't. What are you...'

'There's no "hey don't" now.'

'Don't treat him roughly. No. I won't let him go. You watch it.

I will...the bastards...'

A short struggle and then Jumman was in the hands of the villagers. Jotya stood looking at the fools for some time. Then he retraced his steps sadly homewards. He felt forsaken once again just as he had been that first time that his life had been ruined. He came home reluctantly. Seeing him, somebody shouted, 'Jotya has come.' But Jotya paid no attention to him. He went inside the house with his head bent. Jumman was already looking ugly. That night was as disturbed as the previous night. Jotya twisted and turned, thinking. He had heard whispered remarks that Jumman would be removed from his yard. He made up his mind that he would never let that happen.

∽

He woke up early the next morning and went to Jumman. Jumman was already awake. Jotya stroked him and said, 'Jumma, we'll have to leave, don't you agree? Don't look so sad. Come. Where? Silly Billy. Wherever the road takes us. We'll first go to Dankhni's yard, and do our namaskar to Mhasoba. Then we'll go into the hills. The Katkaris live there. They are an illiterate tribe, but not half as illiterate as these fools. Let us spend the rest of our lives there. If I die first, you must kill yourself. If you die first, I'll kill myself.'

So saying, he untied Jumman, and the two of them started off. They emerged from Maharwada and entered Dankhni's yard. Jotya did a namaskar to Mhasoba, and they took the hill road.

The morning had grown bright by the time they reached the jungle path. Just then...Jotya thought he heard a kind of buzzing sound. He pricked up his ears but couldn't identify it. He walked a few paces more, and soon there was no doubt left at all. The buzzing sound was quite clear now.

From far away a black cloud seemed to be moving over the sea shorewards, at great speed. Jotya's legs gave way. He pulled Jumman towards him and pointed out the weird phenomenon to him. At one point Jotya was convinced that the cloud was coming straight at him. But when he looked closer he thought otherwise. The buzzing was continuous. Jotya tried to gauge the dimensions of this quivering cloud but soon gave up the attempt. Seeing its immensity, Jotya trembled with fear. Where was this cloud, stretching across the entire horizon, travelling to? It swung from side to side making it difficult to tell where it was going. Jotya forgot all about going to live with the Katkaris in the hills as he sat watching the apparition. Jumman gradually moved away in search of leaves.

The buzzing continued. Jotya realized that the cloud was unmistakably moving towards him. Suddenly he remembered the words of the villagers, 'You will bring disaster upon the village.'

Could this be that disaster? The thought struck fear into his heart. He began to sweat profusely. The strength drained out of his limbs. He sank to the ground. He held his head between his hands to stop the hammering inside, he looked around for Jumman. The buzzing was growing louder.

He stood up, petrified, calling out, 'Jumman, Jumman.' But Jumman was nowhere around. The terrifying buzzing that continued to come from across the sea, the villagers' words, Jumman's disappearance were the three fears that chased Jotya with malevolent ferocity. He wondered, 'Was I wrong to bring Jumman away? Suppose some calamity does strike the village?'

Bzz, bzz. The sound grew louder and louder. Jotya racked his brains. 'What shall I do, what shall I do?'

Bzz, bzz, bzzzzz...

'Oh my god! I don't want to live in this jungle! What a terrible prediction!!! Where's Jumman?'

Bzzzz, bzzzz, bzzzz...

Jotya was drowning in a whirlpool of turbulent thoughts.

'Jumman, Jumman, Jumman.' Jotya called out in a voice cracked with fear. Jotya began to run. He couldn't afford to stop, as the buzzing grew louder, and yet louder.

Were the villagers' words going to come true after all?

It was true then that Jumman *was* a divine animal.

He still couldn't believe it.

The sound grew louder, it was on the verge of swallowing him up.

There was still no sign of Jumman.

Jotya mustered all his strength, pressed his hands against his stomach and screamed, 'Jumman. Don't try my patience. Please come. As you are. We'll go home. I can't bear this, really I can't.'

From somewhere far away came the sound of Jumman's bleating. Soon he was by Jotya's side. 'Thank god, you've come. Let's go. We will go home. Forget what I told you. I don't like what I'm seeing. Do you see that, in the west?'

Jotya glanced in the direction he was pointing out to Jumman. The cloud, which had been black all this while, was now glowing bright red. It was like witchcraft. Had god sent a cloud of fire upon the village for Jotya's sin?

Jotya couldn't bear to look at it. He took hold of Jumman, and beating his head with his hand, he hastened home.

∽

They reached Dankhni's yard once again, and Jotya couldn't believe what he saw. Every tree within sight was glowing bright red like live ember. Whole plantations of coconut and betel were alight with the same red glow.

He set off for the village at tremendous speed, but had to stop soon to call out to Jumman, 'Jumma, Jumma, hurry. What is happening? Do you really have divine powers? Do you belong to god? Not to me? I was wrong. Forgive me.' He bowed before Jumman with profound devotion. 'I'm a fool. I'm a villain. I'm a swine. Please forgive me. Will you? I give up my claim on you. But we'll have to hurry. The day's no longer ours. It belongs to the enemy.' Jotya walked faster.

Every tree in the village had turned red. All of a sudden Jotya shouted, 'Locusts! A locust invasion. That's the end of the village. We're ruined.'

Whatever courage Jotya had left, now drained away. Something within him seemed to be heaving up in waves, and, with every wave, his mouth began to taste rancid. He felt feverish. It seemed as though his eyes were being sucked into his body. His old body seemed to be getting smaller every moment. But there was one thing he had to do before his body caved in. He must tie Jumman in the yard, garland him and do a namaskar to him. But if he collapsed before that, where would Jumman go? And what would happen to the village? He was sure that what he intended doing was the only way of saving the village from this awful visitation.

The locusts were everywhere. They were ahead of him, behind him, and all around him. Masses of locusts. Not a single tree had been spared. Many trees were already ruined. They looked like beautiful women shaved of their luxuriant locks. It was a terrifying sight.

Jotya reached his house. Someone from a neighbouring house shouted, 'Jotya, where have you been? Run in, and don't kill a single locust.'

Jotya pulled Jumman in, and stared out with dead eyes. He didn't have the courage to go into the backyard. Everything was bright red, and the obscene sound of nibbling echoed through the air. Everything was being destroyed. Palm fronds were turning in an instant into bare ribs. Jotya couldn't bear to sit indoors. He came out into the backyard. Jumman came after him, but he pushed him back in.

'What do you want? Are you hungry? There's not a single green leaf for you. You'll have to make do with dry grass now, if you can get it.'

He locked Jumman in, and came out. The ground was covered with a thick layer of something black. Now what was this? Jotya bent down. Showers of something that was red and black came pelting down from above. He picked up a bit of the substance from the ground, and shouted, 'Shit, it's shit. That's right, you bastards. Eat, and shit, and spread havoc.' He picked up a stone. He was about to fling it into the air when he remembered the warning, 'Don't kill the locusts.'

'And why not?' Jotya demanded enraged. 'Are these locusts also creatures of god like Jumman?' The thought sapped him of all his strength. The stone fell from his hand. His trees were being rapidly shaved.

Tick, tick, tick, they nibbled.

Zzzzzzzzzzz, they buzzed.

Pitter patter, they shat.

Jotya couldn't bear to stand there. He turned into the house with his hand pressed to his head. How was it all going to end? Why doesn't anybody stop these creatures? What's happened to the village? What kind of spell is it under? And who had cast that spell? How could the village calmly watch death approaching it?

But that was the way it was. Not a single person was willing to come out of his house. Jotya was sure that if everybody made a din, if they beat drums and old tins, hurled stones, and made fires, the locusts would go back the way they had come. But some of them would die, and the villagers had said that they must not be killed. Why? Nobody had the answer to that. And what if the entire village became destitute? What if? It already was.

All that was left in the gardens and plantations were stumps and shit. The place was one big graveyard. The entire coastal strip had been reduced to ashes by the locusts.

∾

Soon after this, a meeting was held in Jotya's village. The villagers pondered the problem deeply. How were they to recover from such a loss? With whose help? It was obviously not possible for man alone to solve the problem so they prostrated themselves before Mhasoba. They asked for a boon in return for which they made a promise. They prayed to Mhasoba to help them make up this year's losses within the coming year. Jotya vehemently opposed the idea. But he stood alone against the entire village. All he could hope for now was that Mhasoba would not let him down, and it was on the strength of this hope that he finally consented to this inhuman solution.

His feet dragged heavily as he returned home. As soon as he stepped into the yard, Jumman came racing towards him. Jumman always eased Jotya's sorrow during times of trial. So he pulled Jumman towards him and kissed him over and over again.

He was ravenously hungry, yet he did not feel like eating. Every now and again he would glance at Jumman and suddenly hug him. Then he'd console himself, saying Mhasoba will never grant them the boon. It was simply not possible to make good the loss of an entire year's crop within a year. He felt he was worrying unnecessarily about something which would never take place. He would smile confidently and stroke Jumman's back, then take him out.

The villagers began, once again, to shower Jumman with love. True, there were no more flowers and garlands, but Jumman knew again that he was something special. He carried himself with the hauteur of a bull who was dedicated to the gods. He could go where he liked, graze where he liked, and return home only when he was full. Jumman, who had grown thin for a while, now fattened up again. He wandered around with his head held high while children followed him, calling out, 'Jumman, Jumman.'

Jotya, however, was being corroded with doubt from within. What if the villagers were granted the boon they had asked of Mhasoba? He had no desire to eat, or sleep or live.

He lived merely because he breathed.

He stopped visiting people. He stopped talking to people. People asked him, 'Jotya, what's come over you all of a sudden? Why do you let the famine get you down so much? You've neither wife nor kids. The famine hardly affects you.' Jotya would look at them uncomprehendingly.

He would hang around the house for hours on end. And when Jumman came near him he would burn with shame. After all he had raised him like a son...

The village had now begun to feel the effects of the locust invasion. Because people had reserve stocks of rice, they didn't actually starve but money became scarce. There were no betel nuts, and no coconuts. There was no money to buy spices. Falling ill became a luxury, because nobody could afford medicines. People went around with pinched faces.

And yet they didn't give way to despair.

As soon as the first showers came, they got down to work with every ounce of energy they could muster. Every yard was cleared of the layers of excreta that had gathered there and then thoroughly cleaned.

The palm trees, shorn of their foliage, were cut down. It was a terrible sight. Trees which had pulsated with the sap of life but a few days ago were now being torn down and stacked up for firewood. The village performed the last rites of the dead yards with tears in their eyes; the womenfolk worked with tears in their eyes; and when children brought out bhakris to their parents, they too were weeping.

The tasks were done, all the same, with the heartlessness of butchers. The heaps of excreta that had been collected were flung into the fields. The yards were clean. Now the rains would come, and planting would begin.

Everybody had the greatest faith in Mhasoba. How could he not grant them the boon they had asked for? Their faith was indestructible, their hope strong. This saw them through the famine.

Jotya was watching everything.

The fields were ploughed.

They were sown.

And, exactly on the expected day, the rains came.

There was jubilation all around.

The rains did not let them down a single time throughout the season.

The incessant showers made Jotya fearful.

He sent up a silent prayer to Mhasoba.

But the rains continued unabated. Never before had Jotya seen such a perfect monsoon.

Navratra ended. Dussehra came.

Jotya said to Jumman, 'Jumman, Jumman, what have I done? What will I do if something dreadful happens? Nothing will wash away my sins.'

The reaping began.

A weight descended on Jotya's heart with every sheaf of corn he saw, bursting with ripened grain.

The whole village danced in ecstatic joy.

Even the palms planted in the backyards came thrusting out of the soil to welcome this splendid harvest. People were stunned to see the height and grace of the saplings. Such things had never before occurred in the memory of even the oldest inhabitants of the village.

The day for measuring the paddy came. People called out to Jotya on their way to the threshing floor.

'Jotya, Jotya, god has been merciful. Mhasoba has blessed us. Come out to the threshing floor. We bring the paddy home today.'

Jotya neither moved nor spoke.

They shook him. He said after a time, 'Go on without me.'

'And have you complain later on? No thanks.'

'I can't make it. I've lost all my strength. You go along.'

'How can you lose your strength in one day? You managed to walk by yourself to the threshing floor yesterday all right.'

So they brought a cart and tried to lift Jotya into it. Jotya protested, 'You monsters, what are you doing? I don't want to come.'

Nobody paid any attention to his blabbering. One took hold of his head, another supported his back, a third turned to his legs, and a fourth cried, 'Heave ho!' And the next minute Jotya found himself being gently placed inside the cart.

The cart moved.

Jotya could see neither houses nor people. When he was being put in the cart, Jumman had looked on curiously. Jotya glanced at Jumman once and he could no longer control his tears.

The measuring began.

'One, two...'

The pile of grain grew rapidly higher. The measuring ended. The villagers danced. The pile stood before them, and yet they could not believe their eyes. The harvest had increased threefold. Whose doing was it?

Mhasoba's.

Who else?

Nobody knew where Jotya found the strength to do it, but he jumped out of the cart shouting, 'That's not true. Not true. Mhasoba has not granted the boon.'

'Jotya, stop drivelling.'

'I am not drivelling. Mhasoba had nothing to do with it.'

'Then maybe it was your father who gave us this harvest.'

'I don't know about that, but Mhasoba didn't.'

'Jotya's being too clever for his own good. He needs to be thrashed so he stops this foolishness. Else, we'll have the locusts back again.'

'Let him have his say. Now, Jotya, you say that this isn't Mhasoba's doing.'

'It isn't.'

'Then how do you account for this bumper harvest? None of the other villages have had one.'

'You worked hard. You threw the excreta into the fields...'

People guffawed loudly at this.

'Jotya, being old doesn't give you the right to talk nonsense.'

'I'm not talking nonsense. Just use your heads. If you ask the people in the other villages, they'll tell you that they threw the excreta into the sea. That's why they lost their crop. Our fields got readymade manure; it's simply a question of coincidence.'

'You're right. It is a coincidence. And why was this coincidence beneficial to us and not to others? Why are you silent now? Don't you understand, you fool, that it is the boon that has worked for us. Not shit manure!'

Jotya found no answer to this.

* confused*

The next day a meeting was held. When was the promise made to Mhasoba to be fulfilled? Jotya had decided not to attend the meeting, but as on the previous day, people went to his house. They carried him bodily to the meeting. Their behaviour seemed to make Jumman nervous and he bleated in a strange voice.

When Jotya returned after the meeting, Jumman was even more astonished. Jotya was actually sobbing as he walked home. As he entered the house, the sound of his helpless sobbing filled the air.

'Jumman, Jumman,' Jotya cried, flinging his arms around him, and laying his trembling head on his shoulders. 'Jumman, what have I done!'

This continued all through the night. And, as usual, the night hurried on to make way for a new day. But it seemed to Jotya that people were walking on their heads instead of their legs, that birds were sobbing in agony instead of singing, that the village was on fire, that a disaster worse than the locust invasion had struck the village, and that the flames from this immense conflagration were leaping up towards the sky.

The villagers came to Jotya's house even before the sun had risen. They came with flowers and garlands and incense.

They called out, 'Jotya, it's time to go.'

Jotya did not say a word.

They entered the house.

Jotya was nowhere to be seen.

They searched the whole house.

Then they began looking for Jumman.

Even Jumman seemed to have disappeared.

The house was empty.

Where were they?

The villagers hurried out.

The auspicious time must not be missed. What if they couldn't find them before sunrise?

The thought put fear into them, and they ran around looking for the man and his goat. Their suspicions were right.

Jotya and Jumman were running as fast as they could through Dankhni's yard.

Jotya glanced around, and shouted, 'Jumman, we're done for. Run faster. Run.'

Jumman loitered on the way. He found the green leaves too tempting. Jotya shouted, 'What kind of a famine have you come out of? Don't you understand how important every second is?'

Saying this, Jotya picked up Jumman and tried running carrying him. But a few paces later, he put him down again, panting heavily. He couldn't understand why his strength had suddenly deserted him. Beside himself with fury, he whacked Jumman hard and shouted, 'Trot. Run. Walking's not going to get us anywhere.'

Jumman started running with Jotya following. Not far behind them were the pursuing villagers.

As the pair was trying to cut through Dankhni's yard someone should have told them how futile it was to flee. But who was to tell them? They were frothing at the mouth, and dripping with sweat, but they continued to run, foolishly.

The distance between them and the villagers had closed to almost nothing. The villagers were shouting again and again, 'Jotya, you can't get away. How far will you run? Look at the state you're in!'

Jotya ran past the Mhasoba temple and began climbing the hill.

And then, the villagers were upon him. 'Jotya, why are you being such a fool?'

'Who's being a fool, you swine? You're the fools. You worshipped Jumman first as a god and now...' He couldn't bear to complete the sentence. Mhasoba was just behind. He silently called upon his help. But even before his prayer was out, the villagers had got hold of Jumman. It wasn't very long now to sunrise. They tied Jumman's limbs. Jotya winced to see how roughly they handled him. 'Please be gentle, at least,' he pleaded.

'We're being gentle, Jotya. You are not the only one who loved Jumman.'

'Oh, you bastards. Is this your love?'

They began to take Jumman away. Jotya's legs were barely holding him up. Jumman was somewhere in the middle of the crowd of villagers. Jotya followed the crowd. The distance between Jumman and Jotya was growing wider. Jotya could not bear to see the way Jumman was being handled. 'Don't drag him like that. He's tired. Can't you understand? How can I make you understand?'

The villagers crowded around Mhasoba's temple. Jotya stood a great distance away. They worshipped Jumman, adorning him with flowers and garlands. Then somebody shouted, 'Call Jotya. Otherwise he'll complain that he wasn't allowed to see him before the end.'

Some people went to call Jotya. His eyes were alight with flames of fire. He stood there without a word. His lips were dry, his body drenched with sweat; his tongue felt as if it was being pulled inwards and the ground below his feet seemed to be shifting.

The scent of burning incense wafted through the air.

A moment later...

As Jotya watched from a distance...

Somebody pressed Jumman's chest. The jet of blood that spurted out of his body drenched the idol of Mhasoba.

THE WITCH

KAMALAKANTA MOHAPATRA

Translated from the Odia by Leelawati
Mohapatra & Paul St. Pierre

1

We were out on the hostel terrace the evening following the full moon night of Dola, drinking a bottle of local rotgut about as safe as rat poison. We did have a pitcher of water, but preferred our drinks neat. The oil-soaked paper bags were empty: omelettes, diced onions, spicy gram and fried chips had all been eaten. There was only a finger of drink left in the bottle. We lit a cigarette—just one, so we could pass it around.

Ramesh finished his story with the burp of satisfaction rustics reserve for a hearty meal. 'So there,' he said. 'Big pricks and tiny pricks, can someone please sum up the moral of the story?'

Before anyone could speak up, he added, 'The moral of the story, if there's one, is this: don't trust the police any more than you would thieves, or even less. Although several years have passed since the incident, my arse hots up when I think of it. Therefore, ladies and ledas, eunuchs and double-pricks, the finger of rotgut in the bottle is rightfully mine—something to cool my scorched arse with; nobody else has a stronger claim, let me tell you. And in the meanwhile the morning is a long way off.'

When the half-smoked cigarette reached me, I held it up against the moon. 'Who the hell sucked on it as if his life depended on it?

The damn stick's almost down to the filter before even one full round. Go easy, boys. There aren't many left. This is the last but one, and when we've had the last there'll be nothing left to smoke but your pricks. And what baby prick Ramesh said about the police is really true—they bugger you so hard the pain lasts for seven generations.'

'You too had some experience, huh?' Siva said, tenderly cradling the bottle against his breast as if it were a baby.

I could have shot back something smart-alecky but didn't.

'Listen, Sasank,' Siva continued. 'I don't know where you'll get it, but you have to find me fifteen rupees tomorrow morning. I've got to go home. A second letter from my mother arrived two days ago, but I didn't breathe a word to anyone 'cause I didn't want to miss out on the binge tonight.'

'What did she have to say? How come you've sat on it for two days without letting us know? If this is how you behave, what should we expect from outsiders and strangers?' we teased in unison.

'Quit joking, boys,' Siva said with a long sigh. 'It's bloody serious business. Ma writes that for the last fortnight my younger brother seems to be possessed by a witch. He's fine during the day—plays about, eats, screams and fights like any young child—but come evening he starts bawling for no earthly reason. It goes on and on for hours on end until he drops off to sleep, tired out and hungry. Ma says he's become as thin as a stick, you can see all his ribs. He's been seen by local doctors and quacks of all kinds, but to no avail. Then somebody told Ma it could be the evil eye, and an exorcist was roped in. He did his bit but nothing's helped. Then somebody told Ma that it couldn't be a simple case of possession by a witch, but that it must be a virgin witch who's just reached puberty. In such cases, it seems, even the witch herself doesn't realize she has someone in her thrall. Dangerous witches, these; if they even look at you sideways they can wreak havoc. The only cure is a consecrated wood-apple leaf from the temple of Lord Lingaraj. That's what I'll do tomorrow morning— collect a leaf and catch the first bus home. Though how I'll identify the new witch among all the pubescent girls in the village remains to be seen. Anyway, that's not my problem. So give me fifteen rupees, someone, and I give you my solemn word: once I finish college and find a job, the first thing I'll do is repay the loan, even if it takes ten years or fifteen.'

'Wait, wait,' said Gandharb. 'I'm dying to pee. Don't say another word, anyone, until I'm done. Meanwhile, anyone up for a gulp of hot water?' He walked to the edge of the terrace and peed on the peepul tree growing out of a crack in the parapet. 'The tree must be wondering why hot rain is falling from a cloudless, clear sky.'

'Move away from the peepul, you dimwit,' I warned him. 'It's a nesting place for witches and spirits—attracts them in droves, like iron to a magnet.'

A round-bellied moon hung perilously in the sky. The stray clouds looked anaemic. A covey of birds flew by overhead, their wings almost motionless, like an aeroplane's.

'Ghosts and witches!' guffawed Ramesh, getting to his feet to pee. 'Tall tales.'

'Tall tales, you say,' I retorted, munching on a peanut which the dew had turned soggy. 'You mean ghosts and witches don't exist. Is that what you're implying? Ah, you little bugger, you've lived all your life in a town, so what would you know about witches? They don't crowd towns, mind you. They don't like din and bustle, well-lit roads and markets, fast moving cars and trucks, arid and treeless spaces. Why, towns don't even have a decent cremation ground. The little patch that passes for one is so tiny that pyres have to be lit on top of each other. No mango or polang groves, of course, not even a big, wide field with a few trees for taking a shit outdoors. Besides...' My voice was sounding like my father's—deep, heavy and thick from chewing paan, '...you city slickers, you don't have the pure, unadulterated blood witches love to suck. Flies, mosquitoes, bedbugs, disease, politics and corruption have turned your blood so black and bitter that if a witch sucks your blood she'll die before you do.'

'Shut up, Sasank Mishra,' said Ramesh. 'It's not for nothing you're known as foolish prick. Spare us, for heaven's sake. Spare us a lecture on the wonders of village life and the crooked ways of the town. We've heard it all before. And let me tell you: last year I went to my uncle's village after a long time, hoping to see some lusty-busty village belles, who, as literature would have us believe, grow like wild flowers in such an idyllic environment, their beautiful breasts bared for all the world to marvel at. My bloody prick, I didn't come across a single girl who wasn't wearing a goddamn blouse. So much for your idyll of rural innocence! And now you're telling us villages are teeming with witches.'

'How dare you run down villages,' I said, warming up. 'Wait a sec. Let me wet the wall and then I'll ask all you poor little city pricks to open your stuffed arses and ears wide and listen to what I have to say. It's a two-in-one tale. You'll have the police and the witch in a single story.'

A dog howled in the distance. A train whistled. Someone farted. We covered our heads with our handkerchiefs to protect ourselves from the dew. Someone filled the rum bottle with water and our glasses were replenished for one last round. A quarrel sprang up between Arun and Gandharb over the empty bottle, but we all scolded Gandharb. It was always up to Arun to rub the empty bottle against his thigh to warm it up. He was always the one to strike a match and drop it into the bottle. The thin blue ribbon of light that swirled out with a sigh was a sacred ritual of our drinking binges. Ramesh collected the cigarette butts lying around and said, 'See why I insist on cigarettes without filters? Then there'd be something to fall back on!'

We opened the dinner packets—bread, baked potatoes and boiled eggs wrapped in large thick lotus leaves, but none of us had much of an appetite.

'Get on with your story,' Siva said, turning to me.

'Yes, start,' said the rest. 'But don't go overboard.'

'Not a single word is an exaggeration, let me tell you,' I assured them. 'Here goes.'

2

I sat on the cement bench at the police station cooling my arse. It was past eight in the morning, and there was no policeman in sight.

Two deodars and a few mango trees, their branches hacked off, stood like sad, servile sentries. Not a whiff of a breeze, but there was a chill in the air. The dew was still on the grass. The red-pebbled road from the doorsteps of the police station to the canal bank lay like a line of dried blood. There were just two people ahead of me, but the crowd thickened afterwards. And we all waited. Occasional coughing, betel-spitting, throat-clearing, arse-shifting, but mostly silence.

Around ten, along came the inspector, bare-bodied, a blue silk lungi knotted around his bulging waist. People who knew him sprang to their feet. He swept a smiling glance over us all, spat a thick jet of blood-red betel juice down the veranda and shouted: 'Eh! Where are you—Pitambar, Nityanand, Nabaghan, et cetera, et cetera? Have you all died and gone to the cremation ground? Bring me water, someone. Quick. A bird's chosen to drop its precious shit on my bald head. What is that—good or bad? Who knows how the day will go!' He looked around at us, his captive audience. 'Ladies and gents, what do the shastras, scriptures, holy books have to say about this? Is having a bird shit on your head on your way to the office a good omen?'

A sleepy constable came out with a bucket of water. The inspector became even more theatrical. 'Why, Agani! My dear man, you're still here? I thought you'd hurried off after last night. Did you know the fish you brought me last evening was so bitter I couldn't eat it? The bile sac must have burst as the fish was being chopped to pieces. Did you get it for free? Or did you discover the fish was bad and decide you'd better palm it off on the son of a bitch of an inspector so he'd drop dead the moment he ate it?'

I was watching the dark-skinned squat balding man standing beside me. A fat pink ant was crawling about on the collar of his sweat-stained off-white shirt. The way the ant was scurrying about from one end of the collar to the other made me doubt its sanity; I was just waiting to see if it'd bite the poor man on the neck. All I had to do was just raise a finger and flick the ant away, but I had lost any inclination to be a good scout since early morning.

The inspector splashed water on his scalp and removed the flecks of bird shit. He washed his face and rinsed his mouth. Every jet of water he sprayed down the veranda produced a fleeting little rainbow. I took a good look at him: middle-aged, maybe around fifty, tall, full-bodied, dark-skinned, a flat nose, small ears glued to the sides of the head, a thick moustache with flecks of grey, thick lips red from betel chewing. 'All right, no ladies, all gents,' he began solemnly. 'Now rattle off your precious complaints. Anyone here whose village is being ravaged by tigers, bears, snakes, frogs, grasshoppers, thieves, dacoits, thugs, burglars, house-breakers, tunnel-diggers, spirits or demons? Anyone with a missing cow or goat or wife or daughter, or the same raped, assaulted, molested, obscenely gestured at? Anyone whose fish pond has been emptied? Anyone who's had a cucumber stolen from his patch of green? Now, my good folks, make it snappy. Tell you what, let me chant aloud the sections of the Indian Penal Code and you stop me at whichever one applies. Good god, what miserable times we're living in! People think nothing of rushing to the police station if they step on a thorn, or if a monkey bares its teeth at them; people enjoy reporting their neighbours for a coconut frond blown by the wind. Everyone's so eager to file an FIR these days. And they want us to write down every damn word that drops from their eager lips. They treat the police station like their uncle's home! In the good old days, when the whites ruled over us, even flies and mosquitoes, not to mention human beings, would think twice before venturing anywhere near!'

We all remained silent. This was the inspector's show.

'Agani!' he hollered. 'Where're you, you son of a police stick? Bring out the paraphernalia—chair, table, register, pen, ink bottle and whatever else. We'll have an outdoors office today. Surely our friends here can't have a problem with that?'

Something seemed to hold Agani back.

'Are you dead, Agani, you bastard?' the inspector screamed. 'Gone for a shit or what? Got the runs from eating bitter fish last night?'

Another constable, thin as a stick and as brittle, hauled out a chair. The inspector sat down, and eyed the constable quizzically. 'By god, Nityanand, you seem to have put on weight overnight! What did you have for dinner last night, man? Never mind. Have you asked this grand gathering here whether anyone has come not to file a complaint but to invite us to a feast? Isn't anyone celebrating a son's or a daughter's wedding? No one's holding his son's sacred thread ceremony? When did we last get an invitation? No wonder you're so thin, Nityanand!'

Nityanand dragged out a table. Its top looked like the map of a hitherto unknown territory, stained as it was with ink and blotches of unknown antiquity. On it he placed a register, a pen and a ruler.

'Now then,' the inspector barked. 'Enough horseplay. Let's get down to business. Tell me who's at the head of the queue.'

The two men in front of me looked at each other.

'File your complaint,' said the first to the second. 'Mine will take time.'

'You're first in line,' protested the second man. 'File yours first.'

The inspector guffawed good-humouredly. 'Listen here, keep one thing in mind: at the police station and the doctor's it's the same. The moment you go there you have to jump the queue.'

Silence.

'Will either of you begin, or shall I call the third fellow?' The inspector was enjoying himself.

'My complaint's a trifle,' said the first man.

'If it's a trifle why are you here? Is the police station your uncle's home or what?'

Silence.

'What's your name?'

'Arjun.'

'Arjun what?'

'Arjun Das.'

'Your village?'

'Khandipara.'

'Hey, how's Madan Santra? How's he doing? Tell him I remember him. And what shape's his fish pond in? No one has been poisoning the water to kill off the fish, I hope! All right, tell me what brings you here.'

'How can I, sir, in the presence of so many people? I came with the hope of whispering into sir's ears.'

'Anything embarrassing?'

'Oh no, nothing of the sort.'

Pretending to be annoyed, the inspector rolled his eyes as he got up and walked into his chamber.

The first man and the inspector remained closeted for ten to fifteen minutes. When they came out, both looked cheerful and satisfied. The inspector said, 'Don't worry. Go back home. I'm sending some constables right away. See how precarious my position is! Such a huge area to police and so few constables. From river Devi in the east to Balikuda in the west, from Nanigaon in the south to Goddess Sarala's temple at Jhankad in the north—it's unmanageable. So huge. Listen, Das, don't go and shout from the rooftops you've filed a police complaint. Another thing: everyone talks highly of the bananas from Khandipara. Send us along a big bunch, will you? The test of the pudding is in the eating, they say, don't they, eh, Das?'

The first man, whose name we all now knew, bowed down from his waist and took leave of the inspector, walking backwards. The whole thing was so theatrical and absurd, it took a great effort not to laugh.

Before the second man's turn, there was a tea break. A little imp of a boy from the nearby tea stall turned up with a moss-green glass of tea in a wire-tray. His loose, flapping khaki shorts, crisscrossed with patches, reached his heels. They were obviously a gift from a kindly constable. A thread from the hem of a sari fastened them at the waist.

'How dare you come to the police station in a state of partial undress, boy!' said the inspector. 'What for—to show off your impressive physique? One of these days I'm going to put you in jail. That'll teach you.'

The boy laughed, his bright white eyes shining. He was obviously used to the banter.

The inspector raised the glass to his lips and stopped. 'Hey, there's a dead ant floating in the tea.'

'You expected an elephant?' replied the boy, jumping off the veranda.

The audience tittered. The inspector roared with laughter. I waited for the hot tea to splash from his shaking glass and stain his lungi.

But nothing of the sort happened, and the fellow put the glass on the table. He threw back his head and laughed for a long time.

'What do you want to be when you grow up?' the inspector asked the boy.

'Police.'

'So you can have free fish?'

'And also free oil to fry it.'

'Wait until I catch you. I'll have the hide off your back.'

'I'll file a complaint with the police.'

'Oh, my god, in that case I'll invite you to play dice.'

There was a familiar, practised ring to the exchange. Had I heard it before?

The inspector raised his ruler and made as if to fling it at the boy. The little scamp took to his heels.

'The little devil!' the inspector said. 'He's so quick. Not even the governor can match him when it comes to repartee.' He swept an imperious glance over us. 'Back to business. Hurry up! The sun's getting hotter. Very soon I'll be thirsty. A new fresh fruit juice shop has opened in Balikuda. Who's going to stand us the first drink of the day?'

The second man had his complaint recorded. It turned out to be a case of a missing cow. The poor little beast had been gone four days, and he had looked for her everywhere. A black cow that had calved only twice so far. She gave a litre of thick, sweet, creamy milk twice daily, and had a white spot the shape of a crescent moon on her head. She was extremely gentle—didn't even shake her horns or swish her tail to whisk off a fly.

The inspector joked with the complainant even as he jotted down the details. 'What's today—Tuesday? Isn't today the Jagatsinghpur cattle market day? My hunch is you'll find your black cow there. If I bring back your cow, will you send me a litre of milk and paneer every other Sunday for a year?'

Then it was my turn. The inspector fixed me with a detective-like stare. Maybe he thought he was Sherlock goddamn Holmes or something. 'My guess is you're in college,' he said.

'What else?' I retorted in a devil-may-care way.

He gave me a hard look. Then he burst into a guffaw. 'You've been holding your pee for a long time.'

'Really?'

'Oh, yes! Why else would a young man like you sit tucking his legs in like a woman?'

Truth be told, I badly wanted to pee. 'Go on.'

'No, you go on. Out with your name and address. For the record state your father's name. Make it quick, we don't have all day. Keep the long queue in mind. Oh god, what am I to do—sit here and take down first information reports or go and make on-the-spot enquiries? The station writer's on long leave and I, the inspector, have to do both!'

After I mentioned my father's name, the inspector put his pen down and stood up. 'Our former magistrate's son? Guess what. From the moment I saw you I've been trying to think where I have seen this face before, why it look so familiar? Dear boy, I'm truly angry with you. Why didn't you tell me who you were the moment I arrived? You didn't have to sit here on this chipped cement bench waiting for me! My residence is right behind the office, not some six or seven miles away, and you could've gone straight there. Who told you to wait here?'

He wiped his face with the corner of his lungi and hollered: 'Agani, Nityanand, where are you bastards? Bring another chair. Quick. This is our former magistrate's son!' He looked at me. 'The eldest or the middle? I can't believe that any of our ex-magistrate's sons has grown so big.'

A constable dragged out a chair with a broken arm.

'So, does the sahib come home sometimes?' the inspector continued. 'Or does he stick to his office in Koraput? I've never seen anyone so keen about his job, and I've seen quite a few in my time, mind you. Certainly, no other magistrate with so little vanity! Whenever he saw me he'd pat me on the back and ask after my children.' He turned to the constable. 'Nabaghan, run along to the tea shop and bring our guest a glass of tea. Make it special tea. And ask the chap to add cardamom and ginger. And yes, if there're any freshly fried potato chops, pick up half a dozen or more. Hurry.'

I was beginning to feel uncomfortable with this fuss. It was all going too far; I didn't want to be entertained like a cherished guest or something. All I wanted was have my complaint recorded and return home and sleep.

'Someone's stealing our firewood regularly,' I began.

'Stealing firewood? What thief could be that petty?'

'It's been going on for quite some time. When the pile started going down fast, we decided to keep watch. Last night...'

'Did you catch the thief red-handed?'

'No. Yes.'

'A man or a woman?'

'A woman most likely.'

'Could you place her?'

'She ran away before I could reach her.'

'Of course she'd run away. What did you expect—wait for you to catch her so she could put her arms around you and thank you?' The inspector gave a croak of a laugh and bit his tongue. 'This tongue of mine is my own worst enemy. Always quick with the wisecracks. Someday it'll land me in deep shit. Won't be surprised if I say something outrageous in the presence of a superior and he takes my job away. Never mind, continue with your complaint. Where were we? Yes, you saw the thief from a distance. Where were you when you saw the thief?'

'I was on the veranda covered in a blanket. Our garden is huge and the cowshed is some hundred yards from the gate. Late in the night—I'm not sure about the exact time—a woman opened the gate and entered the garden. The cowshed is never locked—just a bamboo trellis door. She pushed it open and went inside. After a while she came out with a bunch of firewood on her head.'

'And you saw it all?'

'Yes. I'd forgotten to keep a stick handy.'

'A stick to beat the thief with? Go on.'

'When she was in the middle of the garden I ran towards her, flailing my upraised arms. She threw the firewood on the ground the moment she saw me and broke into a run. But instead of heading for the front gate she made for our backyard.'

'And you chased her?'

'I did. But I was scared too.'

'Go on.'

'She stumbled and fell. Perhaps she tore her sari; perhaps she broke one or two bangles. But before I could pounce on her she leaped up and bolted away.'

'If only you had laid a finger on her when she was down. She'd have remained curled up like a centipede until eternity and a day. What a missed chance! Did you collect bits of her broken bangles? Or a bit of her torn sari? Very necessary for identification.'

I shook my head. 'I was shaking all over.'

'Naturally.'

'I was frightened out of my wits.'

'Frightened, why? You knew the thief was a woman. Never mind, tell me, did you see her face?'

Just as I was wondering what to say and how much to reveal, someone got off his bicycle and salaamed the inspector. I looked at him. A thin, unsteady man, with a sunken face and protruding cheekbones, bloodshot eyes, grey stubble that seemed like a coat of ash on the face. The red police turban sat askew on his head and his khaki uniform was wrinkled like crumpled paper.

'Bholi!' the inspector bawled. 'Bloody Bholi, son of a gun, Guntayat! Where were you?'

Bholi Guntayat leaned his bicycle against the veranda and freed something wrapped in straw from the carrier.

'First, tell me who was buggering you and where. Imagine a constable missing from the station for two whole days and the inspector none the wiser.'

Bholi unwrapped the straw and took out a fish. A big fish, a rohu.

'Fuck the fish,' the inspector screamed. 'Don't show me the tail of a fish as if you've brought me a whale. I'm sure this rohu weighs less than three kilos. Bholi, you can shove it up your arse. No self-respecting police inspector would touch a fish this size with the long end of his baton.'

'Sir!' Bholi hung his head down, drawing lines on the ground with the tip of his worn boots. 'Sir, the thing is, sir...how do I put it, sir...forget it, sir, I have never been in worse trouble, sir, see sir, I'm boxing my ears and taking a vow in your presence, sir...I'm ready for whatever punishment you hand me...'

'Enough sir-siring. Don't think I don't see through your trick. Are you taking me for the son of a donkey? I'm going to put the screws on you one of these days. Unless I do, you won't remember that my name's Haradhan Pradhan, son of late Somnath Pradhan, grandson of late Sanatan Pradhan. Go. Take the fish to my residence and then run along with this young gentleman here to his village, Nuagaon. Make full enquiries about the theft and get back here before sundown. Make sure you bring the thief in tow, too. I don't care if it's a man or a woman or a bird or a frog or a ghost—I want to see the culprit handcuffed, with a rope around the waist.'

The inspector looked at me and beamed. 'I'm sending this man with you. All you've got to do is point out the suspect to him, that's all. The rest is his job. Most of my constables might be thin, but they're efficient. At least none is scared of a woman. How could anyone be scared of a woman?'

3

As I waited for Bholi Guntayat I mulled over the inspector's last words. The incident of the previous night was still vivid in my mind.

The fat pot-bellied moon had climbed up to the middle of the sky, surrounded by a halo of white haze. Fluffy clouds, as white as soap bubbles, were scattered about the heavens. The moonlight made everything seem magical and mysterious: the spindly one-legged coconut palms, their drooping fronds flapping like dogs' ears; the tamarind tree with its dark impenetrable foliage, brooding like a temperamental child; the chakundarain tree, free and frivolous, its leaves folded for the night; flocks of night birds criss-crossing the sky, their wings not disturbing the stillness of the night. Far away, a wakeful dog howled. The night suddenly seemed to have many voices: the sound of something slithering over a bed of dry leaves; the keening of bamboos brushing against one another; the sharp, agitated call of a solitary bird separated from its flock.

A blanket over my head, I took in the magical night. I began to get aroused as I thought of girls. What would they be doing now? Fast asleep, lips and eyes shut tight, or getting aroused thinking of boys? Their breasts swollen like the earth after rain and their skins glowing. I once ran full tilt into a girl just as she was hurrying out of her class; the sensation of softness lingered for seven days. And because of the teasing of my friends I continued to blush for two whole days. My friend Ghana said, 'Sasank, you're damn timid; had I been in your place I'd have hugged and kissed that little thing no matter what the consequences.' Gazing into the heart of the thick moonlight I began to blame god for not making me as daring as Ghana. Why had he made me as someone whose throat went dry, who stammered, whose heart thudded violently and who broke into a sweat at the sight of a girl?

I must have dozed off. The creaking of the bamboo door of the cowshed jolted me awake and I thought I saw a yellow ball rolling into its cavernous darkness. I started; my heart began to beat wildly. Throwing aside the blanket, I rubbed my eyes. I could not make out whether the cowshed door was open or shut. The moon had ducked behind a cloud. As if sucked into the vortex of a great silence, the world seemed to stand still. I felt light and bodiless—as when in the throes of great joy a moment seems like an aeon, or an aeon like a moment. Only when a trickle of steaming perspiration slid down my neck did I come up for air, breathless and chilled to the bone.

I stood up, listening intently.

Not a sound.

I climbed down from the veranda and headed for the cowshed. Halfway there, I saw someone coming out carrying a head-load of firewood. Obviously a woman, in a yellow sari, but I couldn't make out her face.

With a weak cough I pressed on, despite my fear.

The moon came out from behind the cloud. The woman's bare

arms twined around the load seemed to burn like molten gold.

The thief stopped short the moment she heard me. Instead of running away she stood still. What did she think—that she'd become invisible or could blend into the landscape like a chameleon?

A whiff of breeze would have felled me. I was light in the head, my legs wobbled; I couldn't take a step forward or back. My body was drenched but my throat was so dry it hurt to swallow.

'Who're you?' I asked, my voice breaking. It came out like gibberish, which even I couldn't make out.

She lowered the load of firewood and stood covering her arms.

'Tell me,' I croaked. 'Who're you?' This time I spoke slowly and clearly.

No answer.

I took a step forward.

A breeze sprang up. The end of her sari twirled up like an elephant's trunk. She raised her right hand. I thought she was going to brush it aside and reveal her face. Instead, she undraped the garment from her shoulders.

I began to tremble with fear, excitement and god knows what else. This was the first time I was seeing a young woman's breasts up close. Not in broad daylight, true, but the full moon had never been brighter than on that night. It was bright enough to read.

'Who?' I asked again, but my voice was so weak I couldn't hear it myself. Or maybe, I hadn't spoken at all but simply imagined it. Who knew?

She ran a hand across her breasts.

I took another step.

Her breasts seemed to stare at me like the lidless round eyes of Lord Jagannath.

'Answer me while I'm still being polite,' I said in a hoarse whisper.

In reply, she covered her breasts and pulled up the hem of her sari to her belly.

It was dark and dangerous where her thighs met. Moonlight fell between her legs.

'Are you a human or a ghost?' I had already noticed she cast a shadow. 'Answer me or I'll scream.'

'Scream,' she said, stepping up to me, uncovering her face. Her eyes gleamed like red-hot embers.

I flinched.

She took another step towards me.

'You!' I couldn't believe my eyes.

Koili was grinning, her white teeth shining. I stared at her like a drowning dimwit.

Let me tell you who or what Koili was, otherwise you won't understand why I was so startled.

Five or six houses down from ours is the village weaver Pahala's house. He was by no means well off. Four days a week he didn't work his loom. Handwoven towels were costlier than mill-made ones, their colours not fast enough, and so his clientele had fallen. He had very few customers. Poor chap, he was forced to resort to a bit of stealing. A wrinkled old fellow, at fifty-five he looked eighty, with thin arms and thinner legs and poor eyesight. But barely six months after his first wife's death he had married again, this time to a very young thing. She was as thin as a stick when she first came to the village, but the wedding waters did wonders for her and in just a couple of months she metamorphosed into a beauty who made people stop and stare. Once she had put on the right amount of weight in the right places, she looked like a ripe, juicy mango, ready to be plucked. Although the regrettable fashion of young women wearing blouses had caught on in the village, not every young woman, from eight to eighty, sported that stupid piece of attire. So, many people in the village had a chance to glimpse Koili's back or breasts, particularly when she leaned over the mouth of a well to draw water. These sightings only drove them even madder with lust. How could the shrivelled old weaver satisfy a young wench like her, was what boys and young men asked each other. Although I never took part in these discussions and treated them with a show of utter indifference, I was probably more heated up than the rest. In that state, I'd have sooner than later gone and grabbed her breasts or buttocks or done something as shameful. Mercifully, a rumour began to spread that Koili was a witch. After dark her light blue eyes became like the burning eyes of a wild cat. The colour of her tongue, pink during the day but pitch black at night, was like a snake coiled up inside her mouth. She went out in the dead of night to gorge on shit. Three or four villagers swore to having seen her at it. Apparently, she would take off all her clothes on the canal bank and walk upside down, head to the ground, feet in the air, and slurp up slop like a pig. Grass withered where she peed, and a hole would open up that reached down to the navel of the earth. Three young children had perished since she came to the village and a fourth was hovering between life and death. The well she drew water from had dried up earlier than others, or else its water turned bitter. Her husband aged twenty years in six months; she must have sucked his blood through a straw. She was an ugly duckling when she married but had become, in just six months' time, a striking beauty who could fell even a confirmed misogynist. No ordinary witch, this one. She could suck anyone's life out with just a sideways glance. If you met her face-to-face on a moonless night, you'd perish in an instant; on a full moon night she'd make love to you so fiercely that she'd steal all your semen and have you run around her like an impotent dog for the rest of your life—which wouldn't be more than a week, anyway.

That was the woman who now stood smiling at me in the moonlight. She began to run her long, tapered witch-fingers across her breasts. I shivered so uncontrollably that I feared I'd fall into a swoon. Strange things were happening to me. One moment I wished I were dead, the next I felt I was roasting over a cold fire of sexual excitement I didn't want to ever end.

'How can you be sure I'm a ghost or a human unless you touch me?' Koili said in a breathy whisper.

She loosened the knot of her sari at the waist. My eyes were riveted on her breasts.

With a smile she started walking towards our back garden, her sari trailing behind her. The dust, stones and dew on the grass were of no consequence to her.

I followed her like a mesmerized sheep. She stopped in the middle of the garden, turned and faced the moon and me. I stopped two or three steps from her. She dropped her sari; all she had on was the black thread around her waist, her glass bangles and a dot of vermilion the size of a quarter-rupee on her forehead.

The moon overhead became fierce, casting its white light on the garden. The place seemed to catch fire. The breeze became warmer. I started to sweat again.

She moved towards me.

I stood as if turned to stone.

Our bodies touched. The heat from her body seemed to singe me. My sweat turned to blue smoke and clouds floated up into the sky. Her breasts were round and firm like chitou cakes; and the nipples, jutting out like spikes, pricked me.

Her icy left hand caressed my thighs and I shivered like a patient in the grip of malarial fever. She placed her right hand on my shoulder and lifted my dead left hand and placed it on her left breast. I don't think I had ever touched anything as soft and as spongy. As I leaned against her, trembling like a leaf in a storm, she undid the buttons of my damp shirt; her nails seemed to scratch and draw blood from my chest.

The bamboo clumps started swaying even though there was no breeze. A crow began to caw. Blood rushed to my brain and my head felt so heavy that I thought my neck would break. Koili's scent overwhelmed my senses: her body seemed to give off several odours and fragrances all at once, a unique blend of sweat, unwashed clothes, sun-baked earth, coconut oil, overripe jackfruit, yellow kaniar flowers—sharp, fruity, intimate, fleshy—a smell that would make the lame scale mountains, the wingless fly, non-swimmers cross the seven seas. It suddenly struck me that if I made love to her I'd be burnt to cinders, and that I'd explode if I didn't; one moment I was a ball of fire, the next, a block of ice.

The moon went behind a cloud again. Koili did not seem human.

'Are you really a witch?' I asked.

She smiled silently, but I felt the earth shake. Perhaps like bat's her voice was too high-pitched to be heard by humans. The world went oddly silent as I watched her smile widen.

'I eat people alive,' she whispered. 'Tell me which part I should start with.'

She held me so tight I thought she had become part of me. I was choking with desire. 'Witch, witch, witch,' I repeated like a dull student trying to learn a difficult word.

'I'm going to chew you up and you're going to enjoy it too.'

And I was ready for it.

She folded her sari in four and spread it on the ground between the dew-drenched grass and the moon. It was as if a gossamer yellow bed was floating in the void. Pressing a finger against my chest, she lowered me to the magic bed. The sky seemed so blue that it hurt my eyes. There were just a few popcorn stars scattered here and there. Koili's long black tresses were outlined in the moonlight. Her shadow fell on me, covering my entire body, as if swallowing me whole. I fought not to faint.

Just as she was lowering herself onto me I sat up suddenly. For no reason the bamboos began beating against each other, as if a school of monkeys were jumping about in the clump. Birds of all kinds began calling. A tomcat started mewling. A thick dark cloud blotted out the moon and in the dim light hundreds of snakes—of all colours, shapes and sizes—slithered out of their holes entwined around each other. Some coiled around Koili and their hoods swayed, coming out from her hands, breasts and thighs. Was this all a dream? Some kind of furry animal—difficult to say what, mouse or puppy—brushed past me.

Someone started coughing and couldn't stop. Doors and windows started banging. The snakes sneaked off to their lairs, the bamboo clump became still, the birds suddenly fell silent. Koili pulled her sari out from under me, her face split in a grin that was more a grimace, her teeth gleaming blood red in the moonlight. She seemed to have fangs, her canine teeth appeared needle-sharp, her long tongue twirled out and swayed, like a snake's split in two—wet, red, ravenous. And before she ran off she spoke under her breath: 'You're damn lucky, you Brahmin boy. Damn lucky. Another moment and you'd have been my dog for life. But don't worry, you won't escape me. I'll come again under the pretext of stealing firewood from your cowshed. I'll come soon. Be ready.'

A strong beam of light dazzled my eyes and I felt I was hurtling down from a great height. I screamed—an endless, silent, blood-soaked scream of fright, longing and loathing.

Someone splashed cool water on my face. When I came to I found myself surrounded by my mother and younger brothers. They were armed to the teeth—stick, knife, axe and sickle. I was making a weird guttural sound and had wet my pants. To this day, I don't know whether I had come in my pants or just peed.

I was carried to the veranda. My mother went to inspect the cowshed. When she came back she asked, 'Were you not able to recognize the thief?'

I nodded my head: Yes, no, yes, no...

'Who was it?'

I continued to nod my head.

'A man or a woman?'

'Don't know,' I croaked, my voice hoarse.

4

'So you didn't know!' Constable Bholi Guntayat mocked.

Bholi had wormed out of me what I had kept from everyone— from my mother, my brothers, the police inspector. But I tried to throw him off: the thief simply resembled Koili, it could easily have been someone else, my suspicion was entirely unfounded, my eyes could have played a trick on me.

We weren't more than a mile from the police station when Bholi's bicycle had a flat tyre—it exploded like a firecracker. Leaving it in the custody of a roadside grocer he sat on the crossbar of my cycle. He wanted to sit on the carrier at the back, but I told him I wouldn't be able to keep control over the two-wheeler. He said the crossbar would eat into his bum, which would ache for a fortnight and need hot mustard oil with salt rubbed into the sore spot. Every fifteen minutes he wanted me to stop so he could get down to ease his pain. I made faces at his red turban and deposited droplets of spit on its crest.

'So how's this Koili of yours to look at—an eyeful?' Bholi suddenly asked.

'What do you mean?'

'Is she dark or fair, short or tall, slim or fat, sweet or sour? You get my point?'

'No, I don't.'

Bholi turned his head a hundred and eighty degrees and gave me a broad wink. 'What are you trying to keep from me?'

'Look, I don't suspect her at all. Her name simply slipped from my lips.'

'All right, this bitch Koili isn't a thief. Fair enough. But tell me, what does she look like?'

'Like any other witch.'

'Thick black lips, protruding teeth, black tongue, large forehead, spiky hair, duck feet, thick thighs jutting from a slim waist, breasts as big as pumpkins?'

'Didn't care to note all that.'

Bholi dragged his left foot along the ground and forced me to stop. He patted his sore bottom and lit a beedi. 'Sir,' he said. 'I can't conduct this enquiry. I'm scared shitless of witches. If someone tells me there's a witch in some village, I skirt past it. To tell you the truth, I'm scared to go to my own village, Nadeigarh, east of Sahdevpur. People make fun of the name. Until a year ago there was a witch in this village. She's since been neutralized, unmasked. Fisherman Madhua's daughter-in-law, she came to our village when she was sixteen, maybe seventeen. She had two miscarriages in the first two years of marriage. That was when an ugly rumour raised its head that this beautiful young thing—Nitei was her name—was sucking her father-in-law's blood. Madhua was around fifty-five, broad as a sal tree from casting the fishing net, his arms thick as maces and as hard, his skin light, with a shock of curly black hair hanging down over his eyes. He played the part of Lakshman in the village Ram Navami performances. He was handsome enough to appear as Ram—look here, don't mind my saying this because you're a Brahmin—but the whore-fucking Brahmins

of our village would never let a fisherman play that role. So Dharmu
Rath, that stick of a mean Brahmin bastard played the part of Ram,
but the women in the audience only had eyes for Lakshman. When
Madhua began shrivelling up, with a malady of an unknown kind,
naturally people started talking. His son was a peon at the government
printing press in Cuttack, and over and above his regular salary he
made a fair amount on the side by selling stolen paper and ink. Plus
he had free meals at his boss's place, where he doubled up as a cook.
He didn't have to spend a rupee on himself and was rolling in money,
as you can imagine. He took his father to the town hospital and
showed him to the best doctors. Madhua returned to the village with
a big bundle of medicines, but his health continued to deteriorate. He
began to avoid company, took to hiding from everybody. By day he
didn't stir out. He would only take a pee or a shit long after nightfall,
rushing through them like a newly married young woman. That bull
of a man shrank to a twig in just a few months. Some said he came
face to face with the water goddess, others said his hopeless condition
was brought on by eating the liver of some poisonous fish. When
medicines failed, quacks and witch doctors were called in. He was
treated for the evil eye. Nothing worked. One day a sadhu arrived in
the village. Six and a feet tall and as much in width, skin like liquid
gold, his white beard reaching his navel. He had a pair of brass tongs
that weighed not less than seven kilograms. The villagers came to him
with their problems. In the end they mentioned Madhua's plight. The
sadhu asked them several questions and finally wanted to see the man.
As soon as he reached Madhua's house he began to bellow: "Arre salaa
behenchod, this is the den of a blood-sucking witch!" The villagers
couldn't believe their ears. The news crackled around the village that
a witch was sucking Madhua's blood and that she was none other
than his own daughter-in-law, his own son's wife. The sadhu asked
her to come out, but she wouldn't. "Bitch," screamed the sadhu. "I'm
going to break your poison tooth today." After many a threat she
shuffled out. A tall, strapping female, in full bloom—you know what
I mean? All high hills and deep valleys. An undulating landscape. And
her complexion? Ripe wheat. Nobody would ever have suspected she

was a witch—just didn't look like one, you know. Not to ordinary eyes, not to yours or mine. But the sadhu's were something else. He could sniff out a witch from a mile away. He asked Nitei to stick out her tongue. After much hesitation she did. It was pink like everybody else's, but the sadhu noticed six black spots. He asked her to show him her nails and when she did they seemed no different than ours, but the sadhu said he found horizontal cracks and black spots on them too. He asked to see her feet. To us they looked all right—five toes and all in front, and not too crooked either—not webbed like a duck's. But the sadhu let out blood-curdling screams: "The bitch has mastered the art of covering her tracks. We have to see her hidden parts." Madhua sat in a stupor throughout all this. The sadhu pulled him to his feet and herded him and his daughter-in-law into a room he locked from inside. They stayed there almost an hour and when they emerged the daughter-in-law, tears streaming down her cheeks, admitted to sucking her father-in-law's blood.'

∽

'You know what,' said Gandharb, rolling the empty bottle across the terrace.

I stopped.

We were silent for a while.

'Sucking the father-in-law's blood is all bunkum,' Gandharb continued. 'The young woman was sleeping with him. It was an acute sense of guilt that was doing the man in.'

'Don't think this didn't occur to me while Bholi Guntayat was telling the story,' I said. 'Brother, I learnt the ins and outs of sex three seconds after I was born, if not earlier, and have been chasing girls ever since. I told Bholi the same thing but he wouldn't buy it. He said he had suspected that too. But in his village attractive young girls were not exactly in short supply and where Madhua was concerned any young thing would gladly have parted her legs for a handsome hunk like him. So he had no good reason for bedding his daughter-in-law.'

Then Bholi told me another story: 'There was another witch in the neighbouring village. I've forgotten her name. She was already very old when we were children. She was so dark we called her Night. And what a vocabulary of swear words she had. Sometimes we'd provoke her just to hear them. She didn't spare her own husband and sucked his blood. The poor man suddenly began to lose weight and shrivel up without any kind of visible ailment. "What's wrong with me?" he wondered. "Why am I drying up for no reason?" The more concerned he became the less he slept well. One night he lay sleepless, eyes shut, when he heard his wife stirring restlessly. He opened his eyes a crack to see what was the matter and would you believe what he saw? The woman took a piece of straw from under her pillow, stuck one end between her lips and the other to his neck and began to suck his blood. The man got the shock of his life. He pretended to thrash about in his sleep and gave the woman a mighty push, sending her sprawling. Then he sprang up and pinned her down, sitting on her chest. The night passed and when the morning came he drove her out of the house. She went mad. Shortly afterwards he married a young thing. Some people said the crummy old bastard wanted to marry a second time so he turned the old woman out, branding her a witch. Who knows the truth! Truth is the hardest thing in this world to know. I sometimes think there's nothing called absolute truth.'

5

'Wait a sec,' Ramesh said. 'I'm dying to pee.'

'I've got a bad taste in the mouth,' complained Arun, 'from not having a smoke in a long time.'

We laughed.

A meteor streaked across the night sky. Before I could alert the others it was gone.

Gandharb began to sing an old Hindi film song, which we all loved to death, and his voice was suddenly so tremulous that Siva said, 'Be careful. You might wake up the young girls in the neighbourhood, and they'll come rushing here.'

The breeze dropped. Swarms of mosquitoes descended on us.

Siva put a brick under his head. 'A hard pillow heightens one's wisdom.'

Ramesh leaned over the terrace parapet and peed.

'Be careful,' Siva warned. 'Piss like a bull—in spurts, so no witch can climb up the line of your pee.'

'Don't worry,' Ramesh reassured him. 'I'll stop when she's just a hand away. She'll crash to her death. I love peeing from heights, that's what I always do. You remember how I peed on the policemen when there was a strike on campus last summer?'

I picked up a small stone and threw it at him, missing, of course.

'If you look up at the moon while peeing,' Gandharb commented gravely, 'you lose your power.'

'What power?'

'Your sexual power.'

Arun sighed deeply. 'I badly need a couple of beautiful young witches to drain mine. I have so much I might burst.'

'Spill your seed thrice a week. That'll help you until the witches take pity on you.'

Siva took a crooked cigarette from his shirt pocket; it had no fewer than eight bends. He looked for the matchbox, and we all searched our pockets. Finally we found it under a leaf plate, but there were no sticks. We got very upset with Arun for having wasted seven or eight matchsticks.

'Don't worry,' he said. 'I'll sing Raga Deepak and invoke fire.'

Ramesh came back and lay down. 'Go ahead, Sasank.'

'Where was I?'

'On the canal bank road. You and Bholi Guntayat were on your way to your village.'

6

Oh yes. Bholi Guntayat, that snake of a constable. Don't underestimate him, he was a policeman to the marrow of his bones: he had managed to extract from me every bit of information about Koili—her age, looks, husband's age and profession, their relationship with the villagers. Twice, he made me stop on the way and treat him to tea. After all, he was coming to conduct an enquiry into our case, so he had to be kept in good humour. He continued to prattle on. He had lots of problems: last year's cyclone had completely destroyed his crops; his eldest boy became a failure because of his mother's pampering—he had flunked class eight three times already; his wife never felt she had enough jewellery and was always demanding more. Police inspector Haradhan Pradhan might talk and act like a clown but was an ace investigator, the only problem with such a competent boss being that he'd pocket everything himself and leave the constables only the crumbs. A young superintendent who was honest to the bone had been posted to the district and came on inspection twice a month. He suspended two inspectors and four constables for dereliction of duty. The police force was the butt of jokes; no one was prepared to accept that policemen were ordinary human beings underneath their khaki uniforms and red turbans.

From time to time he'd assure me: 'Wait until I lay my hands on that Koili. I'll make her sorry she's a witch. I'm going to put a rope around her waist and drag her all the way to the police station. If I don't rid her of her witchcraft I'll change my name and ask you to name your pet dog Bholi Guntayat! Just you wait, you bloody witch. I'm coming to straighten out every bend in your body. Choose what you want to be—a witch or a thief. You can't be both. I'm going to take the sari off your arse and horsewhip you.'

Our village was just half a kilometre away when he got off the bicycle. 'It won't look good if we reach the spot together. Jump on your bicycle and be off. I'll follow you on foot. Look here, sir, I'm dying of hunger. Tell your mother to give me some lunch right away. Hot rice with dal and vegetables will be enough. I shouldn't expect fish at short notice. Don't worry, I'll find my way to your house. It must be the only two-storey building in the whole village.'

It was half past one by the time I reached home. My tummy was growling with hunger, my throat was dry, my mouth stank like dank mud and my body was caked with sweat and dust. My younger brothers were overcome with excitement; avid readers of the detective novels churned out by Kanduri Das and Yogendra Mohanty, they wanted to follow the police investigation up close.

After Bholi Guntayat reached our place the villagers gathered there too. Bholi, however, shooed them off: 'Get a move on, go run your errands for now, I'll call and question you one by one once I've had a moment to myself to catch my breath. I'll ask each one all sorts of questions, but all in my own sweet time. Anyone who disturbs or distracts me or doesn't cooperate with me will have the bloodthirsty Haradhan Pradhan to contend with. Is that clear? Now, off with you.'

I took a bath and kept Bholi company at lunch. He ate like it was his last meal, praising Ma's prawn curry with spinach to the heavens. Then he took a nap.

I was so tired my eyes closed before lunch was over. I slept so soundly and so long that when I woke up it was twilight, and I couldn't make out whether it was day or night. I looked for a twig to brush my teeth, and my younger brothers tittered. The youngest was whining: Bholi Guntayat had made off with his magnifying glass—he had borrowed it and conveniently forgotten to return it. Ma was angry with him: 'Serves you right. Who asked you to lend it to that monkey face of a constable? One look at him and I knew he'd be the last person to catch the thief.'

I washed my face and decided to take a walk to the bazaar. On the way I saw Koili come out of her house with a lighted wick, which she placed at the foot of the sacred basil plant in front of her house with a deep bow. Our eyes met and her mouth widened in a grin that set the three worlds quivering.

'Did she brush her sari off her shoulder and show you her breasts again?' Gandharb asked. Before I could answer, he added, 'If I'd been you I'd have grabbed her the way a male frog grabs a female, even if it landed me in the clink!'

'Don't brag,' said Siva. 'Save it for strangers. We know you through and through.'

A white cloud sailed by. 'What if it rains wine now?' asked Ramesh.

'I'll keep my mouth wide open,' I answered.

'Then you'd better finish your story before it rains.'

'I don't think I will. You people have interrupted me once too often.' I was tired, my mouth dry.

So my friends begged me to continue, showering me with outlandish promises they had no intention of keeping if only I would finish—ten movie shows, five dinners in the city's best restaurants, a trip to Puri, virgins from Kashmir and what not.

I groaned, I farted, I sighed. With a great show of reluctance I told them the rest of my tale.

7

I didn't find out the details about the investigation—how it got underway, whom Bholi Guntayat questioned, whom he threatened, whose homes and barns he inspected—because early next morning I went to my uncle's place, where I promptly fell ill and was bedridden for two weeks. Only on the last two days of my convalescence did I feel cheerful enough to sit up and play cards in the afternoon. A sweet young thing, my uncle's neighbour's daughter, dropped in on both afternoons but I could make no great headway with her. Only once did I brush my hand against her left breast. The results of the matriculation exams were out and I had to apply for a college seat. Naturally, I had forgotten all about Bholi Guntayat. Besides, firewood no longer went missing from our cowshed. At least for the time being. I was after Ma to buy me a pair of terry-cotton trousers and bush shirts, but my brother played the spoilsport, demanding the same treat. Father hadn't sent money home for the last three months, and Ma stayed away from spending like a monkey from water.

A couple of days later I went to the bazaar to drink tea and have a smoke on the sly. It was then that I ran into Bholi Guntayat. He seemed to be in a tearing hurry, the way he was pushing on the pedals of his bicycle. I called out to him. 'Hello, there! Where're you headed this evening?'

'Oh!' Bholi stopped when he saw me. 'So?'

'So?'

'How are you?'

'How are you? What happened to the enquiry?'

'Going on.'

'How long will it go on?'

'Let's see.'

'And how are *you*?'

Bholi looked up at me. For some inexplicable reason I gave him a broad wink.

Bholi leaned his bicycle on a slender custard apple tree by the roadside; the sapling bent backwards. Bholi couldn't have cared less. He gripped my arm and dragged me to the tea shop, ordering special tea with a lot of cream on top.

'Want a cigarette?' he asked. 'Have you started smoking?'

When I turned down his offer, he took a beedi from his breast pocket. 'In that case let me make do with a khaki cigarette,' he said with a croak of a laugh. With a pair of tongs he picked an ember out of the fire and lit his beedi. He took two hefty drags and, linking his fingers in mine, gently dragged me out of earshot.

'So what's new?' he asked.

'You tell me.'

'What's there to tell! I'm swamped with work and haven't a moment to breathe in peace. Crime seems to be multiplying faster than human beings: a theft here, a murder there, and a rape somewhere else—no end in sight. What can the police do? We're too few and completely stretched. But don't think I won't figure out the case of the mysterious theft of firewood from your cowshed. I'm determined to catch the thief.'

'We heard the police had already reached an understanding with the culprit!' It was a shot in the dark, but it seemed to hit home. Bholi Guntayat winced.

'Is that the talk in the village?'

'Of course!'

'Who can stop people from talking? Every time there's a little delay in an investigation, this is what they come out with.'

'Yes, professional hazard.'

'You said it.'

'So you don't suspect Koili any longer?'

Bholi winced again. An inch of ash fell from his beedi straight into his bulging breast pocket.

I stared at him, surprised.

'Who's Koili?' he stammered.

So Bholi had forgotten about Koili, I thought with delight. Good.

'Oh, are you talking about the old weaver's young wife? You were absolutely right when you insisted she wasn't the one who stole firewood from your cowshed. You know something, I scared the daylights out of her. I told her I'd drag her to jail and keep her there for seven days without a drop of water or a morsel of food, but her behaviour didn't give me the slightest cause to suspect her. You know, you can't fool us police fellows. We catch on to a twitch, a batting of an eyelid, a puckering of the lips—nothing escapes our notice; we can sniff out a criminal from five miles away. The job has given us some kind of a sixth sense. But don't think I didn't keep my eyes on that girl! I did, but the more I saw her the more I was inclined to agree with you. She was simply incapable of stealing even a piece of straw, let alone firewood. But that doesn't mean I've cleared her entirely. I'm still investigating her. I still make surprise visits and inspections. We policemen have our methods.'

I smiled.

God knows why it rattled him, he began to babble. 'You know something, sir. She might not be a thief but she's no saint either. She's full of crap.'

'How did you find out?'

'Like I said, we can sniff.'

'Her shit?'

'The woman.'

'You sniffed her?'

'Just an expression, sir. Are you thinking I buried my nose into her or something?'

He looked around and fished out another beedi from his pocket. His hands trembled when he lit the match; the horse head label stuck on the matchbox wobbled. He took off his red turban. Without it he looked helpless and vulnerable.

'You ill or something?' I asked.

'No, why?'

'You seem run down.'

'Do I?' He looked around as if afraid someone might be eavesdropping. 'The thing is...' His voice trailed off. He puffed at his beedi thoughtfully. 'The thing is...'

The smoke stung my eyes and I stepped back. A swarm of insects descended on us, and I waved my arms frantically to fight them off.

'The thing is,' Bholi tried again, his voice a hoarse whisper. 'Is this what the villagers are gossiping about?'

'About what?'

'The police enquiry and all, and my frequent visits to the village.'

'I don't know. I've been away from the village for over a fortnight. Returned only recently.'

'Good you were gone from the village.'

His face looked different, unlike his own. He sounded so unlike himself too.

'Tell me, do you believe in witches and spells and all that mumbo-jumbo?'

'Why bring that up?'

Bholi started a third time. Clutching his head, he sighed. 'My brain's completely addled. Conducting enquiries and investigations day in and day out has done me in. I'm going completely mad. If Haradhan Pradhan hears of this he'll twist my neck. There's a rumour he might be transferred. I hope to god he will, and soon.'

'By the way, did you take my brother's magnifying glass by mistake?' I asked, suddenly remembering.

'Magnifying glass? Whatever's that?'

Bholi Guntayat seemed to have regained his composure. He was back to playing the insensitive buffoon. He wouldn't let me pay for the tea. He promised to wrap up the investigation within eight days, nab the thief, and drag him to the police station, a rope around his neck.

I reminded him the thief was a woman.

'Thieves dress up as females to mislead the police,' he said.

'What do female thieves dress up as—males?'

'Fairies.' Bholi Guntayat laughed as he took his bicycle.

I returned home.

The following night a stack of firewood was stolen from our cowshed.

'It's started again,' Ma said.

'Don't ask me to go to the police station a second time,' I said. 'I'm off to Bhubaneswar this afternoon to collect college admission forms.' *An Evening in Paris* was showing at Ravi Talkies, and word had it that the heroine wore a bikini and flaunted a goodly amount of her golden skin.

'What will I do when there's no more firewood left—shove my legs into the oven and burn them?' Ma wanted to know. I kept quiet. A wisecrack would have been disastrous. Ma would have slapped me, and if I got away she'd have slapped herself, which would have been worse.

'Ma,' I said. 'Last evening, I ran into Bholi Guntayat. He said he'd complete his investigation in the next eight days and arrest the thief.'

'To hell with Bholi Guntayat.'

I had never heard Ma swear before.

'Don't ever mention his name in my presence,' she fumed.

'Why, Ma? What's the matter? What can he do? He's trying his best.'

'Trying his best, my foot.'

'How can you say he isn't trying? He said he's been coming to our village every two or three days.'

'That's just it! Why does he come every two or three days? What does he do here? Who is he investigating?'

'So what is it he does here?'

'What do I know?'

'Tell me, Ma. You seem to be keeping something from me.'

'Forget it.' Ma walked off.

8

Gandharb yawned, cracking his knuckles. Arun seemed to have fallen asleep. Ramesh and Siva, covered from head to foot to keep away the mosquitoes, were quiet, difficult to say if they were still awake. The night too seemed asleep. Not a sound.

I looked up at the sky. An aeroplane seemed to be flying at a great height, its red tail light blinking. A night bird flew by. Who was it looking for—parents, children, wife, husband, lover, mistress, witch, who?

'You never met Bholi Guntayat again?" Siva asked suddenly, his voice hoarse with phlegm.

That startled me; my heart gave a lurch. I spat on my chest to calm myself down.

'So it was constable Bholi Guntayat's great good fortune,' said Ramesh, 'to enjoy that delicious witch of yours!'

'God knows who enjoyed whom—the constable the witch, or vice versa.' I said. 'Do you guys remember a piece of news in the papers around four years ago? A small news item in a box: Constable Missing. That was just about a week before my college admission. The news crackled around the village that Koili the witch had vanished. Her old husband looked for her everywhere—in the bushes of the cremation ground, in the waters of the village wells, in ponds, ditches and rivers, everywhere. That went on for five days and only afterwards did he go to the police station to file a report. It was there that he learnt that constable Bholi Guntayat too was missing. The man had left behind his red turban, his tiffin box and his bicycle. Why a middle-aged man with a wife and children and landed property had chosen to disappear nobody could say, nor with whom.'

THE FOURTH DIRECTION

WARYAM SINGH SANDHU

Translated from the Punjabi by Nirupama Dutt

My heart was keeping pace with the sunset. Just as the orange ball of light in the far west sank beyond the tall trees, my heart too thudded and began to descend.

My thoughts raced sometimes to the ticking of my watch, sometimes to the driver and the slow speed of the bus, and other times to the dusk spreading outside. I glanced at my friend, Jugal Kishore seated next to me, to see if there were signs of fear and worry on his face but he laughed and said, 'This driver is a slowcoach if ever there was one. He slows down the moment he sees just about any vehicle approaching. It's as though he is saying, "Sir, you go first, please. If you want, I will stop by the side." Wretched son of a motherless goat!'

He shook his head in irritation.

Instead of continuing the conversation, I started counting the heads in the bus to see how many were turbaned and how many short-haired. To my dismay the turbaned heads outnumbered the others two to one. I wondered if I had messed up in my haste. So I started counting all over again. This time the two kinds of passengers were equal in number. Heaving a sigh of relief, I relaxed and taking out a small pocket comb, ran it through my hair.

I put the comb back in my pocket and looked out of the window. The momentary relief I had experienced was inked out by the darkness outside. Travelling in a bus in this place after sunset was like walking with death—and the direction we were heading in, which took us deeper into this terrible place, made things even more frightening.

Last week my cousin, my father's sister's son, wrote to me declining an invitation to a family wedding in Amritsar saying, 'I really want to attend Sheela's wedding but, my brother, the truth is that I feel scared to visit Punjab and more so Amritsar. I am reminded of the story our nani used to tell us of taking 'The Fourth Direction'. You surely remember because she was your granny too although a dadi. Do you recall how many times we must have heard it together sitting on her bed, wrapped in the warmth of her quilt as well as her words? I was in fourth standard and staying with all of you in Amritsar for three months. I had a constant low fever and when I recovered Nani took me to the Golden Temple to give thanks for my recovery. She bathed me in the pool and we then bowed our heads to the Dukhbhanjni Beri. Tending to me all day she would keep muttering praises to the glory of Guru Ramdas, the fourth Sikh Guru who had founded the city of Amritsar. I would so like to see her pious face again for she is frail and may soon be gone. However, nothing but fear keeps me away. I am sending you a draft for rupees five hundred, do buy our dear sister a gift from me. Do ask my mama and mami to forgive me for being not able to make it for this auspicious occasion. No matter how old one may be it is always a joy to visit one's maternal home, but...'

This letter reminded me of the story of a prince or a rajkumar that our grandmother used to tell us. Once, at a crossroads, a prince was told that he was free to take three routes but was forbidden the fourth direction because it was perilous and he might face danger and not return alive. But the curiosity and courage of the prince took him in the fourth direction.

Battling grave dangers, not only did he return safely home but brought back with him something priceless—what it was, whether wealth or wisdom, or something that gave him joy or in courage is anybody's guess.

Well I, too, could claim to be a prince of sorts for I was named Rajkumar. But in no manner was I the prince of the story. I was a mere clerk in a remote government school close to the Indo-Pak border in Amritsar district who rushed every evening to Jalandhar to catch the last train to Amritsar on working days. What should I know of courage?

Well, in the time I am speaking of, it did require courage to go and work in villages if one was clean-shaven and short-haired. What use was courage anyway when an anonymous bullet might fly from the left or the right and kill just about anyone? No one knew the enemy's true capability, his intent or the time the bullet would be fired. Really—no one knew anything.

Just then the bulb right above my seat lit up and I read the notice written by its side: *Passengers will be responsible for their luggage.*

I read the line and repeated it to Jugal with a smile saying, 'They should also write that passengers will be responsible for their own lives.'

At this Jugal laughed and pointed to another line on the side that said: *Do not put your head or arm out of the window.* Then he pretended to be a gunman and said menacingly, 'Don't bother to put your head or arm out of the window for we will be at your service right inside the bus.'

We tried to laugh at our own dark humour but a streak of dread accompanied our laughter.

Jugal had some work to take care of at the office of the Director of Public Instruction at Chandigarh and I had gone along with him. After we had finished our work we hastened to the bus stand only to see the last bus to Amritsar speeding away. The departure of the last bus placed people like us in danger for there were few safe places to stay in the city.

It was necessary indeed to reach Amritsar by nightfall. We had assured our families that we would be home on time. If we didn't get back two families would spend the entire night in fear as though hung on the cross of anxiety. But for marriages or mourning, I rarely think of going out at night. At sunset one enters the house and firmly shuts the doors and windows. Another reason I was anxious to get back was because my colleague, Master Harcharan's daughter was getting married in the morning. Harcharan was a good man and had lent me ten thousand rupees at the time of my sister Sheela's wedding. I still owed him that money. I would also borrow oil, basmati rice, molasses and sugarcane from him as and when I needed them. I too did not go into clerical details with him. I would get it done and that too without charging a fee. If I was unable to reach the wedding ceremony he would have wondered what it was all about. I was keen to go and bless his daughter with a small gift. On top of all these reasons to get back to Amritsar, where did clerks like us have the resources to stay in a safe hotel in Chandigrah?

'Raju! Do you recall those days when we would come to Chandigarh on work and after we had finished have a drink, watch a film and then take a late-night bus from Chandigarh and reach Amritsar in the morning. We would take a short nap and then get ready to go for work.'

As I listened to Jugal I felt that the Punjab he was reminiscing about an era long past. We had left it far behind.

∽

After having missed the last bus to Amritsar, as we were trying to figure out what to do, someone had suggested that we take the bus to Jalandhar that was just about to leave; from there we could catch a train to Amritsar. That was how we came to be sitting on this bus. As we drove along my heart beat faster even than the speed of the bus. I kept looking at my watch, trying to calculate whether we would make it on time to Jalandhar to catch the last train to Amritsar. The bus seemed to be arriving at each of the towns en route—Kharar, Ropar, Nawanshahr, Banga, Phagwara—behind schedule. I felt the distance between me and the last train increasing with each passing minute. I grew more and more uneasy as I thought about what would happen if we didn't get to Jalandhar on time.

Then I told myself that instead of worrying if we would reach Jalandhar on time, I should be more concerned about reaching it safely. It seemed to me that any moment someone would hold a gun to the driver's head and ask him to divert the bus to a side road leading to some village while at the same moment the turbaned sardar seated behind me would open his score for the evening by shooting me dead.

Jugal once again started mourning the days gone by. It seems unimaginable that there were times when if someone missed a bus, he would put his arm under his head and sleep by the roadside. How different things were then?'

I kept nodding. Then something he said set off questions in my mind. 'What have they done?' I found myself wondering 'Who had changed Punjab so much?' My thoughts were interrupted by the loud voice of the very pious Sikh physical education instructor of my school. He was saying, 'The Brahmans, who else?' He would never say Hindu but Brahman, a word that he ground angrily beneath his teeth before uttering it. Then he would say, 'A treacherous, blood-sucking community that can never be relied upon...first, they asked us to stay with them...let us gain freedom, they said, and then we will share its bounties...but what was our share—burning tyres flung around our necks? And now they wish to compromise...and when the Sikhs ask for freedom they make such a din...the entire country goes on high alert.'

The truth, however, is that we Brahmans never fought back, we would meekly agree with whatever was being said. None of the staff members stood up to the insults of the PE teacher. Everyone chose to ignore his words because to speak out would be to call out death. One of the boys from our school had joined the other side. Only four months ago he, along with two others, had marched into a neighbouring village and killed three schoolteachers in broad daylight.

∞

The bus halted with a jolt. We had reached Jalandhar cantonment. We decided to get down there as there would be less of a rush and we could save time by boarding the train there. We rushed up the stairs into the station but were told by a bystander that the train had already departed. He said, 'Why don't you take a three-wheeler to the main station and catch the train that has just left?'

Cursing the slowcoach of a bus driver, we hurriedly caught a three-wheeler and reached the main Jalandhar Railway Station only to find that the train had departed from there too.

I slapped my head in disappointment.

'What now?'

I had not real answer to Jugal's frightened question.

'All that can be done now is to get some magic carpet out of a fairy tale or charter a plane and reach Amritsar by air.'

Sitting on a wooden bench on the platform, I felt that my reply had a tinge of irritation to it. Instead of saying anything to me, Jugal started cursing the government for first stopping late-night buses and then late-night trains to Amritsar. After sometime a train from Ludhiana arrived and halted at the platform. I got up from the bench hopefully. Passengers were getting off the train. Before I could do anything, Jugal asked one of them, 'Is this train going to Amritsar?'

'No, I think Jalandhar is the last halt,' the passenger said, extinguishing the last ray of hope in our hearts. Soon all the passengers left the station. We were the only ones remaining on the platform disappointed, sad and anxious.

Some security personnel, including members of the Railway Police and the Central Reserve Police got onto the train and began checking it for stowaways. They were also shutting the doors and windows of the train.

A middle-aged Sikh carrying a suitcase came up to us and asked, 'Do you have to go to Amritsar?' He had heard us enquiring about a train to Amritsar.

I looked the man up and down. The truth is that I was suspicious of him. But soon I realized that he was just another passenger like us.

'I too have to go to Amritsar but I am late. Actually this train is going to Amritsar. But it does not take passengers. If we were to plead our case to them, they might take us.'

He was a Sikh, a man from the other side but our shared helplessness made us allies in the moment.

'Whom should we ask?' I said.

'Let's ask one of the policemen in the accompanying coach. Who knows—some kind man may agree,' he said.

Outside one of the coaches of the stationary train stood a havaldar of the Punjab Police. He was shouting orders to a constable inside, 'Come on, young man, look under and above the seats carefully.'

We decided to talk to the havaldar. Jugal and I trailed two steps behind as we'd decided it would be better for a Sikh to speak to the policeman.

'Sardar Bahadur, the three of us have to get to Amritsar. Do help us. We will give what we can in return.'

I felt that the Sardar had couched his request correctly but I was wrong.

'No, my brother,' said the havaldar, 'the Punjab Police has already acquired a bad reputation...now people will say we take money and carry passengers illegally.' Then taking his eyes off us he asked the constable who was alighting from the train, 'Everything in order inside?'

'It is, sir, all is F-I-T FIT,' joked the younger man and laughing they moved on to talk to another constable standing some distance away.

The three of us just stood there looking at each other not knowing what to do next.

'I will go and find out...' Jugal said and made his way to a Railway Police official. He returned laughing and said in his usual colourful way, 'Pimps all of them, not one of them gave any sign of hope.'

The havaldar came up to us and this time I pleaded with him, 'Sardarji, please help us out.' He seemed a bit irritated but as he was moving away, he turned and said, 'Check with the guard and see...'

Filled with hope, we started walking towards the guard's coach. He was standing outside talking to someone. We stood a few steps away waiting for him to be free but the conversation he was having seemed to go on and on. We were anxious that while we were waiting the train might leave.

'Why don't you talk to the guard?' our Sikh companion said to me, perhaps because the guard was clean-shaven too.

I approached the guard hesitantly, 'Sir! We are stranded. We took a bus from Chandigarh to Jalandhar in the hope of catching the last train to Amritsar from here but we missed it. We would be very grateful if you could get us to Amritsar. Who else can we ask for help? We will travel standing in your coach.'

From his looks, the guard seemed to be a gentle person I thought he would say yes.

'Mister, have you no idea of the times we are going through. Allowing unauthorized people into the guard's compartment would put my job in danger. It could even put my life in danger. How can one trust anyone these days? If all was well why would we be operating an empty train? There must have been some reason for the authorities to have made these new rules. I understand your predicament and I sympathize with you but I cannot take the responsibility of taking you along...it is all because of the times we are passing through, I am really sorry.' Having said this, the guard boarded the train.

'Wretched spokesmen of the times!' Jugal said laughing and then started talking like Pandit Ram Chand, who lived down our lane, and could be heard complaining all the time about the wretched times we were living in. 'The times we are passing through are very hard... Anything can happen anytime. It is difficult for a thinking person to live through all this. Gone are the days when people would embrace one another like brothers and be ready to help if required. These politicians hungry for power have poisoned society. No one trusts anyone else. Everything has changed.'

The people had nicknamed him the 'Pandit of Hard Times' and would tease him: 'Pandit Hard Times-ji, when will things change?'

Jugal said, 'Now where has this "Guard of Hard Times" come from?'

The havaldar came up to the guard and announced, 'Okay, sir... we're ready!'

'Have all your people boarded?'

'Yes-yes,' the havaldar replied raising his hand in a customary salute.

The guard gave the green signal from the window of his compartment, the whistle blew and the train jerked forward.

What was to be done now?

I quickly put my hand on the window. The guard said, 'What are you doing? Please step back.'

I walked two steps beside the moving train and pleaded with him,' Sir, please...we are your Hindu brothers...if you will not help us then who will...have mercy on us?'

I noticed that he had softened a bit. I put my foot on the step of the guard's compartment and climbed in. The guard spoke to Jugal who had followed me in. 'What are you two doing...have some sense and get down at once.'

The train continued to move slowly forward. The middle-aged Sikh with us had folded his hands and was begging the guard to let him in too. The guard had blocked the door.

'Nothing doing, Sardarji!'

'I beg you in the name of god...the train can easily accommodate me... May the Almighty bless your children with a long life.'

I was quiet fearing that the guard might ask us to get down too but then my heart went out to the Sardarji who had befriended us.

'Please let him in, he is known to us', I said. I felt that now that I was on the train it gave me some right to intercede on his behalf.

'If you have so much sympathy for him then why don't you two also get down,' said the guard angrily.

By then the Sardarji had ducked under the arm with which the guard was blocking the entryway and had entered the compartment. Helpless, the guard mumbled, 'Really this is too much... This is no way to behave. What on earth are you trying to do?'

By now the train had left the platform.

'The best thing for me to do would be to stop the train at a station like Butari and throw you three out. You seem to have no concern for yourselves or others. I allowed one and two more climbed in. There is no point in being kind to anyone. Let me see what needs to be done.'

The words, 'Let me see what needs to be done', filled us with dread. I thought for a moment that he might stop the train by the Beas River and throw us out into the wilderness on the banks of the river, a notorious hideout for terrorists. There were many stories of terrorists escaping from the police on the pretext of relieving themselves, only to vanish into the rushes that fringed the river.

'Don't fret, brother, all will be well,' Jugal said touching the knees of the guard.

The guard shook his head despairingly.

As the tension slowly receded, and I began to feel a bit more relaxed, I glanced around the small compartment. There were four other persons inside. Two were crouching on the luggage carrier and two were seated on a wooden crate. Not one of them had spoken during the entire exchange between the guard and us. Perhaps they were in the same predicament as us but their silence seemed to amount to indifference.

Although I was rather less tense now, my mind was still numb with all the fear and pain I had been experiencing. I looked carefully at those travelling with us. The two Hindus seated on the luggage rack with their heads down seemed to be railway employees. This was evident from their exchanges with the guard. A little further away, on the wooden crate, two Sikh men were sitting close to each other. The slim boy had just sprouted hair on his chin. He had on a smart a maroon turban wound in a style popular with college students. The other one seemed five or seven years older. He was well built and wore a blue turban and had a thick flowing beard. They sat quietly.

To me their silence seemed conspiratorial. Such silent operators waited tensely like a tiger and pounced on their prey at the right moment. The older one looked like the physical education instructor of our school. He was glaring at me. At least it seemed so to me.

A glance at his expression and I braced myself for the familiar tone and words I expected to hear: 'So now we have captured the progeny of Gangu Brahmin, who betrayed our tenth Guru. Now there is no getting away for you...the words heard at Harmandar were still troubling my soul... "*No one can win a battle against the Sikhs...*"'

For a moment I shivered when the same man whom I was dreading began to speak to me, 'Listen...'

I meekly raised my head like a child being addressed by an authority figure.

'One of you can come and sit with us. We will manage somehow. The journey will take over an hour. You will get tired standing all the way. The other two can sit on the trunk next to you,' he said.

I felt ashamed of my suspicion. It was my own fear that was making me so insecure. However, I still did not feel like sitting next to him. I asked the middle-aged Sikh to go and sit with them.

'May you live long...may your live long...thanks,' the Sikh, said patting the young man's back.

I signalled to Jugal to sit on the trunk next us and he in turn pointed to the guard who was staring out the window at the deepening darkness and some lights flickering in the distance. Giving Jugal a reassuring wink both of us sat down on the trunk. Just then when one of the railway employees spoke up, 'Be careful that you don't break with trunk with your weight.'

The trunk seemed quite sturdy. There was little chance of it breaking. The man probably just wanted to needle us because we had pushed our way in. The guard turned to look at us and said, 'Break it...break it...You are up to no good.'

Just as students stand up on being reprimanded by an angry teacher, I too got up from where I was sitting with alacrity.

'Oh, sit down...sit down now,' the guard muttered and I sat down once again on the trunk like a trained pet. I felt like a wound-up toy, I seemed to have no will of my own.

∞

Till now I had seen few nights as frightening as the one we were travelling through. The only uncertain night that I was able to recall from about ten years ago when I had accompanied my wife and son to her home in Rampur on the occasion of her sister's wedding. It was pay-day and I had gone with the headmaster to withdraw money. Disbursing it among the staff, took a long time. By the time I reached home, picked up my wife and young son, Neetu and got into the bus, the winter sun was already setting. Those times were not as bad as now. When we got off at the bus stand it was dark. The road to Rampur was a mile away ahead and wound its way through another village. The other route we could take passed through the fields of this village—after walking some distance we could then take the dust track to Rampur. Since the second option was shorter I picked up Neetu and asked my wife to follow and started walking through the fields.

It was a dark night. Somehow finding our way through the dust we walked on. My wife was grumbling about the delay in setting off. She was wearing her jewellery and I was carrying money with me. If we ran into the wrong sort of person, it could be dangerous. I reassured her by saying I could see a light; the dirt track to the village was just beyond the light.

But, when we reached the light, I found that I was mistaken. I had expected to find the light shining from a house but there was no house just a tubewell shed. I had lost my way. I could hear people talking inside. In the dim light of the bulb, I could see clouds of grey smoke. The smell of country-brewed liquor was in the air. What had I done? I was unarmed, had my wife and son with me and here I was in the dead of the night in the midst of a group of drunken louts. Anything could happen. I trembled in fear.

I put my finger on my wife's lips. I could see two lights at some distance. One was on the right and one on the left. Probably we had to go that way. I estimated that the track we were looking for would be by the light on the left. We stumbled towards it. We were quite scared. Neetu had woken up and was sobbing. My wife had broken a strap of her sandals and her feet were covered with slush. She was on the verge of tears.

'Tonight will be the end of me,' she sobbed. I tried to comfort her even though I was dejected and afraid.

'I can see a house and I can see some cattle. Let's ask for help,' I suggested but my wife shrank back fearfully.

'All right. You hold Neetu and I will go and find out,' I said.

I reached the house, called out and a dog barked from inside followed by a voice asking, 'Who is it?'

A man in his thirties came to the door.

'Brother, I have to go to Rampur to the home of Pandit Ram Nath. I am his son-in-law. I decided to take a shortcut through the fields but have lost my way.'

'You took the wrong direction. You have to go the other way.'

'Who is it, Surjit beta?' A woman's voice called from inside.

The young man explained and a middle-aged woman came out to the courtyard.

'Bring him in. If he is a relative of Pandit Ram Nath then he is no stranger to us. We belong to the same village but since our fields were here we built our home here. Are you married to the older girl, Dulari?'

'No, I am married to Parvati, the younger one, and we live in the city.'

'Just come inside,' she said and turned to her son, 'why are you blocking his way? Move aside.'

Surjit laughed and made way for me. Seeing as there was no danger I asked Parvati to go in first.

'Oh! My dear Paro, this is your uncle's home. Come in, why you are standing outside?' She said moving forward to pat Parvati's head.

Quickly Aunt Kartar Kaur seated us on cots, and washed Parvati's feet according to the fine gesture bestowed on travellers on foot in some northern parts of the country.

'You silly girl! It is unwise to set off from home late in the evening. Is this the way to attend your sister's wedding? Girls come a few days earlier to help their mother out. But now you too have become a city girl...'

Next, our hostess ordered her daughter-in-law to warm milk for us. After we had drunk the milk she asked Surjit to guide us to our destination. She said, 'You could have stayed here tonight but Parvati's family will be concerned. Today is the day for all relatives to get together. Just guide them to the village, Surjit.'

Surjit picked up a staff and a torch and said to my wife, 'Sister, let me carry my nephew.'

But Neetu got scared and buried his head in his mother's shoulder.

'Don't worry, I will carry him,' Parvati said.

'You cry baby, I am not holding a stick to scare you but...' Surjit did not complete the sentence.

He then led us out of the house. Lighting the way with his torch, he got us safely to the outskirts of the village.

∽

The train moved over the bridge on the Beas, making a din.

'You made a big mistake forcing your way into the train,' the guard said sternly, 'what if I throw you off the train and get you arrested?'

'Sir, forgive us, please. We had no other way. That is why we got into the train.'

'You could only think of your compulsions, what about ours? What if I am caught? Won't I lose my job? The times are bad...the whole atmosphere is poisoned... Who knows who you people are? If some mishap were to happen how would I explain it?'

In a way, the guard was right. I looked at the young man whose face resembled that of the PE instructor from my school. What if he was one of them?

Seeing me looking at the Sikh boys, the guard felt that I was being suspicious of them and questioning the guard's decision to let them board the train.

'Now these boys told me about their plight and I could not refuse them. One or two people may be all right but a whole bunch of them...' the guard said, then lapsed into silence.

'Thank you for your kindness. We are indebted to you...' I said.

After this there was silence. As the train lurched along, I started wondering about the circumstances of the boys. What story did they tell the guard?

∽

The guard was gazing outside and the worldly wise, middle-aged Sikh gentleman addressed us, making sure the guard would hear what he had to say, ' We should offer something to the guard sahib—at least pay the fare.'

He glanced at the boys sitting next to him and then at Jugal and me before taking out a ten-rupee note from his pocket. Jugal and I also gave a ten-rupee note apiece and the two boys a twenty-rupee note to the Sikh.

The guard was now looking at us. Seeing the boys give a share, he said, 'Not from the boys. Return the twenty-rupee note.'

The Sikh got up to hand the money to the guard but the latter called out to one of the two railway employees and said, 'Murari, you take the money.'

When Murari pocketed the thirty rupees, I felt relieved for a moment. I shut my eyes and tried to relax. But suspicion was plaguing me. Was the guard afraid of the two boys?

I felt the face of the older Sikh boy merging into the face of the PE instructor who would torment me at school. The face seemed to be spreading out over the whole coach. I could hear the teacher shouting, 'Our days are at hand!'

Harcharan and the other masters at the school rarely said anything to anyone in public. Perhaps, when they were with the others of their community, they might have indulged in such talk but never at the common table. The talk there would embrace all. No one spoke like the menacing instructor who had vented the other day, 'Now they are killing our young Sikh boys in false encounters just like the butcher Mir Mannu of the eighteenth century. But never mind no matter how many they kill many more come forward... Where are the courts now? It is police rule all the way... The police are the law... They are the witness... They are the judiciary... They are the killers and such is the story of our democracy!'

On hearing him, the Maths teacher, Naresh, took me aside and said, 'What are they wailing for? They are out to kill everyone, be they policemen, witnesses, judges. No court is going to try or punish them... As for their day... it has always been their day... Whichever party rules the state, the chief minister has to be a Sikh. The country's president is a Sikh too... Important ministries are with them... They have high ranks in the police and the army... Just compare the percentage of their numbers to the posts they hold... What, then, is their problem?'

To cut him short for he was just not stopping, I laughed and said, 'It certainly is their day! They shoot one here and another there...'

∾

The two boys sitting on the crate were completely silent. The younger one had just uttered a word or two the entire journey. It seemed to me that my fears about them were unfounded.

But fear of another kind returned when the guard said, just as the train passed the Manowal station, 'It is not possible to drop you at Amritsar station. When we get there we will be questioned and so will all of you. The police may even round you up.'

The train slowed down on entering Amritsar. Just as it reached the twin gates of the railway crossing next to the Golden Avenue it slowed down even further.

'Okay, everyone, time to get off. The exit is at ground level,' the guard announced. Although the light of the moon was quite bright, the guard flashed his torch on the track ballast sliding past the open door and ordered us to jump out.

'Hurry! Move out!' he said.

I was closest to the exit. I put my feet on the steps and carefully got down on the rail track. In seconds, Jugal also stepped down. The others too got down at short intervals. We did not look back, although we felt uneasy walking along the rail track at this hour. If we were caught we could have been accused of anything. 'Are you tampering with the tracks? Is it your intention to derail the train?'

I turned to Jugal, 'Let's leave the track and head to Dande-Teende settlement.'

We started walking briskly. The truth was that I was still afraid of the two Sikh boys who had travelled with us. Who knew who they were? There was something mysterious about them and their silence seemed ominous.

I turned around and saw that the two were following us. Our middle-aged Sikh companion seemed to have headed off in a different direction. When I noticed the Sikh boys were behind us I began to panic. I told Jugal, 'Let's walk faster. These boys look dangerous...'

Just then I overhead the boys talking to each other. One said, 'Let's run and catch up with them.' It was the voice of the younger boy. I thought they would catch up with us and fire their pistols 'bang bang'. The bullets would pierce our backs and pass through our chests. I strained my ears to hear what they were saying, 'Let's call out to them...' It was the older boy's voice.

Afraid, Jugal and I walked on without exchanging a word. The two boys were walking so fast that they had almost caught up with us. I was just about to tell Jugal that we should make a run for it when I heard them call out, 'Babuji...' I was so terrified that my legs refused to move. Jugal stopped as well.

'You moved away so fast without taking us along,' the older boy said, 'Actually, my aunt, this boy's mother, passed away at about three in the afternoon. We explained our situation to the guard and he let us travel in his compartment.'

When I heard this words failed me, but I was still afraid.

The younger boy said, 'Come on, let's keep moving.'

I just stood there fear-struck. Seeing me stand motionless, the older boy explained, 'We are afraid of walking to the city on our own lest the CRPF or the police shoot us down because we are Sikh. These are trigger-happy times. No one stops to ask before firing. If you are with us, we will be safe.'

As he spoke the shadows of fear surrounding me started fading away. The blood that had frozen in my veins thawed and started flowing again.

Now unafraid, I began walking and asked them to relax and follow me.

◈

As I walked on I felt that I was Surjit who had led the way for my wife, son and I many years ago in the dark when we had to reach my wife's village for her sister's wedding. I imagined that I was carrying a staff in one hand and a flashlight in the other.

I felt I was living up to my name, Rajkumar, and walking fearlessly in the forbidden fourth direction.

A PLACE TO LIVE

GOPIKRISHNAN

Translated from the Tamil by Vasantha Surya

October 1980, I got married. Tara and I moved into a portion of a house on a small lane in Mylapore. There were several dogs and puppies, cows, buffaloes and calves, plenty of dust, mud and slush all along the lane, as well as cattle dung and, if you walked very close to the edge, kid shit. At night, for twenty days a month, the street lamps were not lit.

'Home' was a single room, and 'window', a small opening devised to let in light. There was no door. A little light managed to enter the room. Fresh air was a rare thing. When it rained, water poured in through the opening. Rainwater is clean...

To dry our laundry, we had to go to the house owner's terrace. There were two latrines—one for the owners, the other for the tenants. The only thing that would come out of you in that latrine was vomit. Any corporation pay-and-use latrine was far superior in comparison. There was only one water pump, and the water that came out of it could not be used for drinking. For that, there was a tap out on the street from which a pot could be filled. A decrepit old servant woman performed that chore for us, for which she received a monthly wage of five rupees. I really don't know why it should be so, but physical labour is poorly paid in our country. I couldn't afford to pay her more myself. So I was in the wretched position of aiding and abetting the exploitation of labour that our society invariably sanctions. Whenever I set eyes on that ancient creature, I felt guilty. Just to get rid of that feeling I gave her thirty paise tea-money at least twice a week.

The bathroom was a remarkable arrangement. Behind the narrow passage which led to the pump (of which I spoke earlier) was a little bit of empty space, bordered on one side by the back of the wall of the latrines. From the outside you could see the pump. A door was, for the landlord, an unnecessary expense. If you wanted to take a bath, you had to put your bucket down at the spot where the wall of the latrines met the wall of the narrow passage, so that anyone peering in from the outside could see half the bucket. Anyone who wanted to enter the bathroom was supposed to check if the bucket was visible. Then they were expected to call out, 'Who's there?' or 'Who's inside?', either in a kindly or an aggressive tone of voice, as they chose. How the bather revealed his or her identity from inside the bathroom was another remarkable arrangement. If it were a man, he had to announce that he was the husband of So-and-so, and give his wife's name. For example, I would say, 'Tara's husband!' If it were a woman, she would say her name. If she were a mother of a child, she would say, 'Such-and-such's mother!'

Despite all this, an awful thing happened to me once. An elderly lady, Ambujammal, who lived in the portion of the house opposite ours, suddenly came in while I was bathing. As though a ghost had just given her a ringing slap, her face instantly changed expression and she left in a hurry. She could have left the matter there. Instead, she went and told Tara, 'Tell your husband to wear a jatti when he's bathing!' A clear case of concealing one's own wrongdoing by blaming someone else! The news spread through the whole building. It so happened that such a calamity had never befallen any of the other men. But the landlady immediately issued an order: All men must wear jattis while bathing. It became terribly embarrassing for me. From my earliest years I had always bathed naked, and it had never occurred to me that there was any harm in it. Now, from the uproar these people were making, a general opinion seemed to have formed that I had treated Ambujammal in a particularly despicable fashion. It produced a monstrous feeling of guilt, and for a week I went about with my head bowed. Then a bright idea occurred to me. I began to sing Hindi songs loudly while bathing. I don't know at what unlucky moment I began this practice but the very next day, just as I was singing away, I heard the landlady demand in a ringing voice (the voice of a woman with landed property, after all—how else would it sound?), 'Who's that singing in the bathroom?' Not only my enjoyment of Hindi songs, but the simple pleasure of taking a bath turned bitter for me.

There were times when I would have just got back from the office, when all of a sudden the landlady's daughter would be assailed by some doubt or other about her English lesson. She was doing her higher secondary certificate course. For a while I would have to clear her doubts. It was my misfortune to be the best educated person in that building.

Ambujammal and her relatives vacated their portion of the house and new tenants arrived, two unmarried youths. One evening, when I returned from the office, the landlady stood in the doorway and said, 'Thambi, I must tell you something...' startling me somewhat.

'What is this, pa...so shocking! Did you see it?' she went in, 'You know those two new fellows? They are wearing only jattis, and talking to your wife! And she is responding to them! Laughing and laughing! Just control her a bit, pa. Times have become so bad!' Within an instant I brought myself to a state of internal calm, simultaneously summoned to my face the expression of turmoil that the landlady expected to see on it, and said, 'Is that so? How awful! I'll go and ask her about it,' and went into the house.

I didn't say anything to Tara. What was there to say? Maybe if those youths happened to have no clothes on at all while gossiping with Tara, something would have struck me as being not quite in order. These youths were the sort who are only fit to reside in men's lodges. In such places this sort of thing is common.

Before I got married, I had stayed in a lodge, too. Although I hadn't been as wildly 'progressive' as these fellows, I had often been a witness to such sights. There was an elderly man staying in one of the rooms of that lodge. He was quite pleasant to me. Once or twice I had fetched him tiffin from the hotel downstairs. My roommate even asked me about it: 'Why are you doing this sort of thing, as if you're an office boy or something?' But poor man, he was all alone in the world, a pensioner, and very old besides. I told myself, it's nothing much, just whatever little help I can offer. Apparently the old gentleman usually got up at four-thirty in the morning, bathed and washed his clothes and went off to the temple. One day I happened to wake up at four forty-five. I drank a tumbler of cold water, lit a beedi, and came out of my room. The tea stall downstairs opened only at five. How was I to spend fifteen minutes without drinking tea? Maybe the tea stall would open a little earlier today.

Grappling with that problem, I went towards the stairs. The old gentleman's room light was on. Happening to turn around, I saw him stark naked on his way to his room from the bathroom. Realizing that I had seen him, he ran to his room and locked the door.

I felt really disgusted. First thing in the morning a glimpse of the wide blue sky, or perhaps the face of a pretty woman might have brought some joy to my heart. (Though of course, laying your eyes on a pretty woman so early in the day is a rare event.) All through that day my stomach kept heaving and lurching at the memory. I thought of telling my roommate, but didn't. If I had told him, he'd have told others, and that fine bit of news would have spread all over the lodge. Then everybody would have looked at the old gentleman in a certain way, he would have discovered the reason he was at the receiving end of the peculiar looks and, if he had been of unstable mind, he would have agonized over whether or not everybody knew what he had done. As a result he'd have become mentally ill, to dispel which he would have had to visit psychiatrists and take tranquillizers for the rest of his life... I would never have forgiven myself. No! It's wicked to harm a fellow male. Although the psychology I had studied in college had not been of great benefit, it did, at times like this, come in useful. Left to myself, though, I hated psychology. All that poking and prying and turning things over and over! The romance of life utterly dies out. Psychology's a curse, it prevents an ordinary man from relishing any experience!

Another day the landlady did it again. She complained that Tara talked to the Muslim Saibu who lives in another portion. I was furious.

It was on the tip of my tongue to demand, How about you...aren't you talking to me? I suppressed my anger and went inside.

And Tara, too, she had to go and blurt out something to me—that Premila, from the neighbouring portion, always slept in the nude. She told Tara, and Tara told me, and for two nights I was in dire distress. Visions of Premila's naked body, which I had never set eyes on, kept appearing before my mind's eye. They made me very uneasy and proved beyond any doubt that I was a scoundrel. It's not that I want to rationalize this vileness of mine, but Premila, and equally Tara, are completely tactless creatures.

I felt very sorry for Premila's husband—I had seen the man. Premila worked as a typist. It seems her fingers used to ache, and her husband would pour warm water over them and massage them. Well, I did the same work as Premila did, but my fingers didn't give me any such trouble. Could it be, perhaps, that they had cast-iron keyboards in the office where she worked?

In the adjacent portion lived a young woman named Swarnalatha. She wanted to know what MBBS stood for. She asked me about it through Tara and I replied. I could have left it at that. Through Tara I asked her if she had a desire to know what other academic acronyms stood for, and she said yes. I took the time to elaborately write down the full versions of about thirty degrees and fellowships, and gave them to her (through Tara, of course).

Who knows how our esteemed Madam Landlady got to know of this? The very next day she told Tara, 'What business does that girl have with your husband? What's all this—don't you have any idea what is what? Such a complete ignoramus! Suppose something bad happens? Right in the beginning you should cut it off! This is trouble. You don't know about such things. I am older than you. I'm only saying it for your own good.' Madam Landlady was the pinnacle of wise counsel.

Soon Swarnalatha and her family vacated their quarters, and a new family moved in. A middle-aged lady with an infant, a ten-year-old boy, and a fat man. The man was her 'visiting husband'. He came once in two days, stayed for a little while and went away. The lady was his third wife. The other two wives were alive, he lived with every one of them, each in a different house.

I was quite amazed. A man requires formidable talent to carry on this kind of thing. That 'raja' had not only a 'rani' but two 'harem girls' as well, whom he had honoured by marrying. The 'raja' ran a printing press. He had mortgaged it, and along with two wealthy gentlemen was now producing a movie—*Woman of Fantasy*. The rumour went that he slept with some sexy actress or other and then took pleasure in telling one or the other of his 'wives' how much he had enjoyed the experience. The rumour also went that his better quarter would tell him jokes about sex and he would award her prizes for them, depending on their quality—the large hearted man! I had seen the man: he used to look at me as if to say, Pooh! Are you a man at all! What a runt!

One day when I picked up the latrine bucket there was a scorpion in it. I abhor killing pests. My rather loud announcement of the scorpion's presence being heard by the Saibu, he arrived with a broom in his hand and pounded it to death. He gave me a glare as though I were a mere speck; his look said: you impotent fellow! Be that as it may, there's no denying that the Saibu was quite a brave fellow.

∞

November 1981. A baby girl is born to us. Tara stayed at her parents' house for three months and returned home on Pongal in January 1982. At the time of the baby's birth, I had been a total wreck, seized and shaken by all sorts of horrible fears: Would the baby be born dead? Would Tara herself die? It was my friend Ramesh who dispelled my delusions and bolstered my confidence. Only when Tara returned with the baby did I become myself once more.

Under a corner staircase that led up to the house owners' living quarters was a vacant space, with a door leading into it. This 'room' fetched a rent of twenty rupees. An old lady had lived there for a long time. Everybody called her Ayyappan Mami. A married woman, with all the auspicious signs, though nobody knew anything about her husband, she eked out her days working as a cook in a Brahmin household. She would bathe very early in the morning, and when she returned from the bath, she was a sight to see: striding along with the lower part of her sari lifted and tucked high up around her middle in what appeared to me to be a very inelegant fashion. Nobody was supposed to touch her: she was madi, ritually pure. As for the passage, it was extremely narrow. If anybody approached her, they had to squeeze in their bodies, and allow extra space for Mami to pass through without being touched. The tribals of Australia have a certain custom: the son-in-law should never set eyes on his mother-in-law. If that happens, the son-in-law must at once turn aside and go in another direction, or hide in the bush. Mami's behaviour brought to my mind this 'avoidance behaviour'.

Suddenly one day, the landlady took pity on us. 'Why do you have to struggle like this, cooking with your stove on the floor!' she cried out. How very considerate of her, I marvelled. She arranged for a structure somewhat resembling a cooking platform to be constructed for us out of a mixture of cement and broken stones. She also raised the rent by fifteen rupees bringing it up to one hundred and fifteen. She must have only spent about fifty rupees to have the the platform made, and now we would have to pay an extra fifteen rupees a month, indefinitely! We had not found it inconvenient to cook on the floor. We had not wept and wailed about not having a platform to cook on.

One fine day, the landlady raised the advance to five hundred rupees. For everybody. She didn't play favourites. Somehow I put together two hundred rupees and handed it over to her. This was to be deducted at the rate of twenty-five rupees a month from the rent. What a tolerant perspective she must have had, to make such a generous gesture! We were to get our money back! Never mind the interest.

That the electric light bulb was allowed to be kept on between six and nine in the evenings was something to be happy about. When we heard her shouting—'Lights off! Lights off!'—at eight forty-five, we had to get up at once and switch off the light, even if we happened to be eating our meal. At night, because we closed our eyes and the whole world became dark for us, the sight of all the insects and rats scampering about could not throw us into a panic. 'Install your own electricity meter, if you want! If you're going to do that, first of all you have to hand me a deposit of two hundred and fifty rupees.' The landlady's reasoning was so rich, it beggared mere logic.

The landlord was a very good man who drank every day. He was a meek soul. What else could he do with a wife like that? Drink certainly protected him from the problems of the external world.

∽

November 1982. A holiday. A yen came over Tara to dress a little stylishly. That's the way she is: every once in a while she likes to do something different. She put my shirt on over her sari petticoat and left our room to throw out the garbage. The landlady let out a terrifying yell. 'What kind of dress is this? This is a house where respectable family people live! Go wear your sari!' I found this really galling. I didn't think Tara had done anything wrong at all. In this, too, there was a double standard. When her friends came to visit Premila, she'd greet them loudly, bubbling over with friendly feeling as she cooed, 'Hi, Chandru! Hi, Jacob!' Her affection would break all bounds and fairly flood the place as she all but enfolded them in her arms and ushered them in. I'm not saying any of this is wrong, yet it somehow rubs you the wrong way.

Tara is an authentic pativrata—like those great ladies of the past, the mythical paragons of virtue and chastity. I would certainly have liked to install a statue of Tara right next to the Kannagi statue on Marina Beach, but this lofty aspiration of mine still retains the dimensions of a mere daydream because of a scarcity of resources.

How would I fulfil my desire then? The more I thought of that landlady who was trying to do all she could to brand such a woman as Tara with the title of 'whore', the more intolerably it embittered me. 'We will look for another house.' From the way her face altered, I guessed it came as a bit of a shock to her.

Then commenced the long drawn-out procedure of looking for a house. Three weeks, many houses, and two brokers later one house seemed somewhat suitable. The rent was a hundred and forty, the advance a thousand, for just a room and kitchen. We liked it. At first the landlord said, 'You look like Brahmins, we're non-Brahmins. Will "that kind of thing" suit you?'

Even if you're bushman who slaughter and skin and skewer a goat, suspend it over a fire to cook it, and then eat it all up, it doesn't matter—the house suits us, we thought to ourselves.

I said, 'That doesn't matter. We are Brahmins, all right. But we eat meat. Everything will be okay.'

Next question: 'Are you Iyers or Iyengars?'

Summoning up all my forbearance I stated that our caste did not have such complicated divisions, explaining that there could even be Charis and Iyers and Raos in one and the same family. It reminded me of the first interview I attended after college. After asking my name and my educational qualifications, the official asked me, 'To what community do you belong?' Somehow I felt a furious urge to harass him. They had called me for the interview at ten in the morning. The interview began at four in the evening, but the important personage who was interviewing me didn't even offer a simple 'sorry' for the delay. Then there was another irritant: between my chair and his swivel chair was a large desk. There was not the slightest possibility of my hand reaching his cheek. Quite calmly I replied: 'I am a cobbler-Brahmin of the tribe of Todas, from the Annamalai Hills. In my hurry to reach my interview on time, I forgot to put a caste mark on my forehead. So, in order to atone for that misdemeanour, at least three times during the time I was waiting to be called up, I prayed to my family deity for forgiveness.'

That official must certainly have had the hide of a rhinoceros. He didn't understand my taunt, I had him quite neatly trapped. 'But you don't look at all like it!' he said wonderingly. 'Have you seen any Todas?' I demanded. When he answered, 'No,' I at once countered, 'Then how can you tell? External appearances are nothing but an illusion!' It was only then that Rhinoceros began to understand that I had been making fun of him. Yet he wasn't certain, so he began to turn over my certificates.

From my SSLC certificate he must have understood what my caste was. He went into a fit of rage. 'You give extremely impertinent answers. If you're behaving like this right at the time of the interview, who knows how you will behave when you start working here?' I, too, was getting angrier and angrier. I enquired if there was any drinking water in the room. Taken by surprise, he pointed to the water filter in the corner. Very slowly I drank three glasses of water and returned to my chair. 'Prevention is better than cure,' I told him. 'Please be so good as to refrain from asking the next unfortunate person what community he belongs to. I offer you my heartfelt thanks for your having wasted my time. May your deity give you some wisdom,' I gave him my blessing and went out thinking to myself that in our country a Gandhi should be born at least once in twenty years.

∞

December 1982. The third week. The 'house entering' ceremony was performed with all necessary rites. We moved in. Several times we had centipedes. At night mosquitoes reigned supreme. One night there was a snake in the neighbours' portion. Emitting loud screams, they managed to catch it and burn it alive. The landlord was a witness to this event. 'It's just a little snake, isn't it? There's a tamarind tree at the back, that's why,' he said placatingly, and went away. As far as he was concerned, it was a serious matter only if a hooded cobra or a giant python turned up. True, not all snakes are poisonous, but when one of them bites a person we have to wait and see if he drops dead or not, before this wisdom about snake biology can come to us. Besides, being human, our own survival is more important to us than the survival of our fellow creatures. What a convenient excuse for man to let loose his violence. And yet how supremely happy it makes us to think of ourselves as devotees of non-violence, as incarnations of peace. But shark meat puttu tastes so delicious!

∞

1983. Soaked through by the rain, the walls of the adjoining portion of the house gave off electric shocks. Two highly prized novels in my literary collection were eaten and digested by termites. There is no commandment forbidding termites from consuming literature. Our neighbours vacated their premises.

1984. It seems a Brahmin family is coming to live in the adjacent portion. It seems we may eat fish, eggs, etc., only in strict secrecy. We have to be particularly careful on Fridays and Tuesdays, it seems! Though in Tara's view, every day of the week is god's day. The number of Hindu deities being very great, and since it is a sin to eat non-vegetarian food on sacred days, we did not find it too difficult to cope with this problem. Boiling an egg for the child every day was enough for us. Cooking fish or meat once a month was more than enough. How sins may be turned into virtues if we refrain from committing them on some days is something I still don't understand.

The new neighbours were a bank executive (a man of obvious substance) and his family. The Man-of-Substance asked the landlord, 'Will your house leak in the rain?'

'If there is even a single drop, you may take a slipper and beat me!' said the old man, with emotion. Why not give the Man-of-Substance one of my slippers, I thought, trembling with eagerness.

The new tenants were a musically-endowed family. There were two little girls. When the wife of the Man-of-Substance saw her two children playing with our child she remarked, 'Girl children come from Lakshmi's lucky glance!' I felt comforted that they were such nice people to talk to. But the lady failed to sweep the house-front and make the kolam when it was their turn to do that chore. She also refused to wash the latrine. They were Brahmins, it seems. I couldn't say anything. As the proverb says, you can go on picking faults, but it doesn't get the job done. So Tara herself did those chores for them. When my child was playing so affectionately with their children, how could one take them to task?

One day I heard the landlady telling that lady in a low voice, 'Those people? Oh, only last month they got a fan put in. Before that they had nothing like that!' What the landlady had to gain by letting others know that we had only recently become somewhat well-off, I couldn't understand.

The house was not comfortable. There was not the slightest chance of fresh air finding a way in. It took two months for the Man-of-

Substance to become conscious of the fact that fresh air is a dire
necessity for an asthmatic. Seems he could take a decision on anything
only after profoundly examining it through direct experience. They
cleared out, like the rest.

   After a month another family moved in. Let me end with what
follows: 1984. It was Gandhi's birthday, a national holiday. Having
woken up at four in the morning, I had made myself some black
coffee and drank it. I was holding Sundara Ramaswamy's *The Story of
a Tamarind Tree* in my right hand, and with my elbow on the pillow,
had started reading from where I had left off. Something black came
from behind me, got into the gap between my elbow and the rest
of my body, raced towards the door and disappeared. After a brief
interval I realized that the apparition was a big rat. It was now five.
I wanted some tea. The tea stall to which I usually went would have
opened by now. I switched on the light in the passage. In the glare
I saw a gigantic house lizard, very close to the switch, just before it
suddenly streaked upward. I got a bit frightened. I didn't mention
all this to the landlord. Only if I happened to encounter a creature
the size of a bandicoot or a monitor lizard would it have produced
any effect on him. Besides, I was quite aware that he wasn't exactly
feeding and bringing up all the rats, lizards, centipedes, cockroaches,
mosquitoes and termites in the place. He was not guilty of any action
except that of keeping himself alive, and for that he didn't need to
take any particular effort.

   I have never believed in gambling. Or in private property. As I
drank tea at the stall that morning, I decided to buy a lottery ticket
at once. I would continue to buy one once a month. Some time or
other I was bound to get lucky. I was seized by the greedy desire
to build a house of my very own, where I wouldn't have to put up
with anyone else. I'd get pest control down every six months and
live in peace, free from insects and vermin. It was some time before
I became aware that my tea was over. Exasperated with myself for
having squandered a small but immediate and tangible pleasure I
ordered another tea and drank it, this time savouring it fully before I
turned homewards. That I'd begun to believe in such a wrong thing

and that too without regard to the sacredness of the day, made me feel rather contrite. Should a man start believing in gambling on Gandhi's birthday?

Please don't ask me what my address is and get me into trouble with my landlord. Until I win a lakh of rupees in a lottery I'll just have to stay in this house.

HUNGER

KOLAKALURI ENOCH

Translated from the Telugu by C. L. L. Jayaprada

S ometime early in the morning or last night, a bullfrog had died on the road. A car or a lorry must have run over it. Its four legs were pinned to the earth, its belly had burst open like a tomato, and a medley of its guts, blood and flesh had splattered on the road. The back and the belly of the creature were stuck together, pressed to the ground. This frog would never jump or leap again, it would never croak when it rained or flooded. Nor would it stir or cry when the sun shone or when it was cloudy. It must have arrived here, jumping and leaping vigorously. What had it wanted to eat? What had it wanted to achieve? Now it lay dead.

∞

Chinni was a seven-year-old from a village in which the shacks had been built on the left side of the road. She sat still and aimlessly watched the road. What she wore barely resembled a skirt and a blouse. Dirty, darned over and over again, her clothes were falling to shreds now because there was no cloth left to hold the stitches. She was pretty. The snot below her nose could, no doubt, be cleaned. The dirt on her body could, no doubt, be washed off. What of her hair—it could be brushed and neatly oiled. What of her clothes—one could get new clothes and she could wear them. If she had flowers in her hair, she would herself look like a flower. Even without any of these, Chinni was a pretty girl; she had pleasant features and sparkling eyes!

　　Now and then a car or a lorry passed by. The farmhands emerged from the village chatting noisily, swinging their staffs. Occasionally, a fierce wind blew. A boy appeared on the road that Chinni was staring at; he came from the side of the village where the cement houses were, across the road from the shacks. He was eating a banana. In his left hand, he held another banana. He was clearly enjoying the banana he was eating, biting it, licking it, nibbling it, bit by bit. Chinni watched him, drooling. Her eyes sparkled with hope. She watched him intently for a couple of seconds. She came to her feet. Dragging her feet, she walked slowly across the road to the boy. He slowed down but did not stop. He continued to eat. Now it was hard to tell whether he was really eating the banana or merely licking it and pretending to eat it for it did not seem to be diminishing in size.

Chinni looked into the boy's face. He returned the glance. She kept staring. He did not turn away. She watched the fruit in his mouth, the fruit in his hand, her glance shifting from his mouth to hand, hand to mouth, looking straight into his eyes, begging him wordlessly. He turned away as if he had not got the message.

'Can't you give me some?' Chinni asked, but the boy paid no attention.

'Give me a little!'

'Why?' he drawled.

'A little?' she pleaded.

'No, don't I want it? I won't give you any,' he said.

'A little, a small bit?'

'No.'

'Just a little.'

'I won't, I said.'

'Just as much as an ant's head.'

'No!'

Chinni's mouth watered, her eyes welled up. Her heart turned to water. A wave of misery swelled within her. She collected her spirits, stretched out her arm and tried to snatch the banana from him like an eagle. Like the mother hen that protects its chicks, he shielded the banana from her and dashed into the village located on the right side of the road. Chasing him, Chinni stumbled and fell on the cement road. She grazed her elbow, and her forehead was streaked with dirt. Chinni got up with tear-filled eyes. She glanced at the boy. He showed her the banana as if to offer it to her, but then stuck out his tongue, and, making a face, walked into the village.

Chinni stopped crying, wiped her nose, eyes, forehead, and elbow with the edge of her skirt, and flopped down under a tamarind tree, trying hard not to cry. It has been three days since she or her mother, sister and little brother had eaten anything. They were all starving. Chinni, her sister and brother had drained the water in the pot by daybreak. Her mother did not stir out of her bed; she was heavily pregnant, about to give birth and extremely weak. If her father got the day's wages they ate, otherwise they filled their bellies with water. If he returned home, they at least had water to drink, otherwise it was complete starvation. Her father had not come home for three days.

Her elder sister at least carried some water home like their father. Her mother would send her sister to the neighbour's to borrow a measure of rice. But they had neither. Everybody who lived on the village on the left side of the road had to scrape a living and nobody had anything to spare. On learning this, Chinni was seized by a fit of anger. She had taken to going to houses where she could smell rice cooking, or see smoke rising from the hearth. She would circle these houses, peep in and say to herself, 'They ate rice, washed the vessels, and turned the rice pot upside down to dry.' She had done this for the last three days, weeping silently.

That night her belly smouldered sleeplessly like a haystack on which an ember had fallen accidentally. Chinni felt death would be a relief to the suffering of an empty stomach in the monsoon. Earlier, whenever Chinni felt hungry during the night, she had been content to wait for the day in the hope that it would bring food. But for three successive dawns, she had awoken hungry. When day was about to break again, Chinni felt more miserable than happy. She could not bear to give hunger its irrevocable victory.

When she had lain curled up in hunger last night, it had rained on the hut like a curse on a poor man. She shivered in the cold on the wet mat she lay on, as hunger gnawed her until dawn. She woke up early in the morning and felt miserable. Her emaciated belly was visible to everyone in the village.

∽

Now, pulling her arms and legs up against her empty belly, with her cold body and wet clothes, she sat under the tamarind tree with an aching heart. The sun had not yet risen. Perhaps it was afraid that if it rose it might have to give witness to the vagaries of fate. A huge cloud rested on the hill that loomed behind the village it seemed hesitant to release more rain, as though afraid of being shrunk, melted, or annihilated.

'Chinni!' A harsh voice called out.

Chinni looked up. In front of her was the brother of the boy who had kept on eating the banana. Chinni was frightened.

'Can't you reply?' he asked, glaring at her.

She muttered, 'What do you want?'

'Did you snatch the banana from him?'

'No.'

'Tell the truth!'

'No.'

'If you lie, I'll pinch your cheeks.'

'No'

'Chchir!' he snarled at her. 'How dare you harass him? You dirty little bitch.' Furiously, he continued to abuse her. Chinni was about to break into tears.

'Beggar. Scoundrel.'

'You are one!'

'How dare you? What do you mean by that? Say it again, I'll slap you hard.'

'You are one!' she uttered the words again.

He kept his word as if he would otherwise lose his claim to the lineage of the legendary Harishchandra, known for speaking the truth. He slapped her hard on the cheek. A little girl, her little belly fastened against her backbone after suffering gnawing hunger for days. Chinni fell to the ground and even the earth hurt her. If she cried out 'Amma', her mother would not hear. Even if she had heard, she would not have come to her rescue. Even if she were to come, she would not have said anything to him. There was no question of hitting him back. If she were to hit him, she would suffer greater humiliation. Her father was not home, so he would not come. The boy's brother had no trouble and went away safely.

Chinni felt an ache in her belly as if her guts had knotted up. She could not even muster enough energy to get up from where she had fallen. The boy had done her a service by slapping her hard enough to make her forget the hunger, which had gripped her like a demon and had been haunting her like a ghost for the last three days. The blow filled her belly, abating her hunger.

The breeze whipped about lightly. There was a drizzle, a shower. But the cloud on the hill had not moved, it lay there like a shopkeeper sitting tight in front of his cash box. There were no raindrops under the tamarind tree. The night before, rain had washed the road clean and it was not yet dirty. Raindrops fell now and then like water dripping from just-washed hair. The bell from the higher elementary school beside the village rang urgently. Affected by hunger, cold, and the blows she had received, Chinni looked up bewildered at a father taking his toddler son to school and hung her head.

∽

Her father was not home. Until the other day, they had starved because he had no work when it rained. When her father had left home, the stove was damp and had not been lit since. For a twenty-five-kilometre stretch, flooding streams and rivulets had breached the road at several places. To clear the way for traffic, it had to be repaired at once. The supervisor had come searching for labourers, and her father had gone along with him three days ago. He had not returned since.

Chinni did not know whether the road was repaired or when her father would return home. She got up. Her legs were wobbly, she swayed like a madman, a drunk, one possessed. A gust of wind slashed her back. Hunger scorched her guts. The thought of the bruise on her elbow, the slap on her cheek, and the mud on her forehead drove her to a frenzy. More than the injuries themselves, the manner in which they had been inflicted on her brought tears to her eyes.

Just as swollen eyes are emptied of all tears after persistent sobbing, so it had stopped raining, as if the skies had no more energy to shower or drizzle. A lorry carrying boulders from the quarry was approaching, rattling as it came. Chinni looked at the lorry, at first uninterestedly, then with curiosity, and later with hope. When the lorry drew close, shuddering loudly, she stepped forward. The lorry was inching forward steadily with a full load, like a woman heavy with child. When the lorry was level with her, Chinni ran out in front of it as if possessed. The driver saw her and cried, 'Hey!' The owner saw her and cried out, 'Rai!' Shrieks and shouts. The lorry stopped with a screeching of brakes. The lorry was there. Chinni was there in front of the lorry. Within an inch of it! Chinni hung her head and just stood there, biting her nails as if she were innocent. When she saw two pairs of eyes from the lorry fixed on her, she writhed, hunger deepening within her.

'Who are you, miserable stray? Do you want to die?' shouted the driver.

'You wretch! You want to die and kill us too?' the owner cried.

'Out, out,' the driver yelled pushing her.

'Out, out,' added the owner, shoving her.

And so Chinni was back under the tamarind tree. An old tamarind tree, a tree that seemed to have stood there forever. The back of her head rested on the trunk. The tree shed drops of water like a mother weeping at her daughter's suffering.

The road looked washed and wiped clean, the water drying up. Wild shrubs on the roadside had caught leaves, bits of papers and other waste. They looked muddy with layers of dirt. On the side of the road, rainwater had carved runnels into the sandy soil, undulating like an emaciated man's ribs.

By the time her sister and brother showed up, there were no tears in Chinni's eyes. Her eyes had dried up like the water in wells during summer. 'Why are you looking so dirty?' her sister asked curiously, looking at her muddy body. Chinni was silent. 'Can't you talk? Did you not hear me?' Chinni did not reply. Her sister looked into her face intently. Chinni lowered her head. Her brother grabbed her shoulder and shook her.

The clothes of her brother and sister were worn and patched, their hair was unoiled like straw. Water dripped from their heads and cheeks. The little fellow was shivering with cold. 'Amma is groaning. She has been calling out, "Chinni, Chinni!" Come, let us go home,' he said.

When she heard the word Amma, Chinni began shaking. She wanted to cry, thinking of Amma near delivery, unable to stir out of bed. She had no food, nor did Amma. She could move about, but her mother could not. She was better off. Chinni could not bear to see her mother's pain. If she did, she would not be able to control herself from breaking down. No energy to cry, her heart ached, though she remained dry-eyed. Water trickled from her sodden hair, down her cheeks and disappeared. Drops from her head disappeared into her lips. Pushing up her hair with both hands, she glanced at her brother and sister by turn.

Her sister was ten. She helped Amma with household chores. When Amma fell ill, her sister had taken over all her work. She bathed her younger brother and Chinni, wiped them dry and dressed them in fresh clothes, if there were any. She loved Chinni and her little brother and shared with them whatever she could buy to eat. After giving them both what she had, she would sometimes go around the whole day chewing on her empty mouth. If a handful of rice was left at the bottom of the pot, she would quietly give it to Chinni and her brother.

On the night their father left home with the construction gang, Amma had given all the rice that was left in their shack to the elder sister without keeping anything for herself. She in turn gave it all to Chinni and her brother. Chinni, too, did not feel like eating. She felt sorry for her brother. He had greedily gobbled down the few mouthfuls given to him. It was over even before his little belly filled. He drank water and cuddling up to Amma, fell asleep warmly in her bed. Chinni and her sister also went to bed but could not sleep because their father was away. Her mother told her elder sister, 'See! The little one has also grown to be like you. Have you seen her giving food to her little brother without eating any herself? It doesn't really matter whether we have anything to eat or drink, your affection for each other is more than enough.'

When she heard these words, Chinni was happy, but can hunger help one to be happy? Her sister and mother fell asleep but Chinni could not sleep. Spotting the eyes of a cat in the dark, Chinni shut her eyes tightly and did not open them until daybreak. Before she dropped off to sleep, Chinni thought about her little brother. He was a silly little fellow. He could not play a single game. He could not even hop properly. He drooled and barely spoke twenty words a day. He was barely three! He would not stir out of the house unless accompanied by both his sisters. His tottering gait was cute, his lisping and stuttering words, too, were quite endearing.

∽

Almost a year ago, children playing on the same road were running from tree to tree. Some adults scolded them but that did not stop them from playing. They all cheered Chinni, saying that only she could run across to the other side of the road, touch the tree and come back before the lorry got there—only she had the guts to do this. As usual, Chinni dashed across the road, touched the tree and turned back, running as fast as she could. She did not see how close the lorry was. The children were shrieking. She could not make out whether this was out of delight that she had returned before the lorry, or whether it was a warning that the lorry was closing in on her. She heard a loud shriek. That was the last thing she heard. When she opened her eyes, everything had gone quiet. When she saw her mother and father, Chinni felt like crying. When she heard that she was out of danger but had lost a lot of blood, Chinni felt happy, not knowing why.

The lorry owner had waited until Chinni came around. When she regained consciousness, a great weight had lifted from him, as if he had offloaded a full lorry. Much relieved, he had driven away. From that day onwards, the lorry owner had paid Chinni's family a hundred rupees a month for four months, and given her food as compensation for six months. Those days Chinni enjoyed heavenly delights, lying on her simple jute cot. When she woke up, someone or the other served her food and looked after her. They ate only after she had eaten.

A hundred rupees a month for her sake! More than what her father and mother earned. This money was a symbol of the union of darkness and light when the lamp of her life breath had flickered terribly. This money was a wildflower that had sprouted on a grave. This money was the price, the measure of the earth that mingled with human blood. This money was the flag that showed the nobility of a rich man and the servility of a poor man.

Her parents who would have loved the child even without this money, loved her all the more because of the money. This money brought them happiness. Chinni felt proud that she had earned the money, and that she had repaid her parents' debt.

In Chinni's view, food meant pouring rasam on a fistful of rice. It was the most desirable food until then. She had never known that there could be any other kind of food. She did not know that bread and eggs could be her daily fare, nor did she know that delicacies such as bread and butter or bread and jam existed. When she tasted the food the lorry owner brought from town, she realized how ignorant she had been. When she ate bread and eggs, her tongue had felt like a garden blossoming with luxuriant, colourful flowers. When she ate bread and butter, she felt as if she were gliding effortlessly over slush, her body had felt like cotton wool. When the bread and jam slipped down her throat, it was sweet and sour, soft and hard.

When she removed the skin and ate grapes, they had disappeared down her throat, belly, and inner parts like a stone thrown into a well sinks slowly out of the sunlight. When an orange, a sweet lime, or a country orange was peeled, its seeds removed and the pulp put in her mouth, the juice overflowed, swelling like a spring, spreading a pleasant taste all over her throat. An apple eaten in the same way tasted like cream. There was no need to chew, no need to bite, no work for her teeth. It melted in the warmth of her tongue and slid down her throat. When she ate bananas of different varieties, centuries of hunger seemed to just disappear.

A piece of jalebi made her mouth water sweetly. When she chewed on a Mysore pak, each tooth came alive as if it had witnessed a great revelation. When she ate a laddu, it tasted like ambrosia from the crumbling foundations of heaven itself. When she put a scoopful of spicy boondi into her mouth, satisfaction spread along every nerve.

Varieties of biscuits: sweet, salty, pungent, and hot—Chinni soon gathered that man had scooped out all the tastes god had created and filled biscuits with them. The others in the house ate whatever was left after Chinni ate. It was a stroke of good fortune that in Chinni's house they were able to eat such good food for six long months.

Every day Chinni stood on the road waiting for the lorry, leaping up in joy whenever it came. When she took home the food given by the owner or the driver, she saw fortune in the lorry, god in the owner, and joy in her mother and father. All this made her extremely happy.

After six months, when the gash on her forehead disappeared, no more fruits came her way even when the lorry did. Even if the owner smiled, he did not give her sweets. Every time he stopped the lorry and enquired, 'Are you well?' and drove off, she was miserable and cried. Gradually, the lorry ceased to stop.

Her stomach revolted when she had to go back to eating red chilli pickle with her taste buds that had grown used to bread, when she had to drink rasam or other sour things with the throat that had swallowed fruit juices, when she had to eat ordinary sambar and rice with the tongue that had tasted sweets. Hunger was a gift given by god. Gradually, hunger cured the nauseous feelings that regular food evoked in her. She got used to her daily fare, although at times she craved the luxuries she had eaten for a while.

Chinni had waited for the lorry to stop for the last six months and was disappointed. Why had the lorry owner fed her so well for such a long time? Why had he suddenly stopped doing so? She thought hard and tried to find the answers to these questions but came up with nothing.

What could she do to get the rich food again? For six months,

this question had churned over and over again in her little brain.
What could she do?

⁕

On the night that she had lain hungry for three days, when she had
been tempted by the boy with the banana, and had been slapped by his
brother, the answer to the question that had been obsessing her flashed
through her mind. Hunger burned her insides, the cold tightened its
grip on her skin. When the house shook under the lash of the rains,
her Amma groaned. Her father was away but all these were swamped
by the excitement her insight generated. She was unable to sleep that
night. She was more anxious than the sun for daybreak. She got up
as the darkness faded, went to the road, looked up and down, and
went back home at least ten times. At last she reached the tamarind
tree and sat under it from nine o'clock onwards.

The sun still seemed to be snoring under a tightly wrapped
blanket. Hiding and flitting out from behind the hilltop, a big cloud
came into view like a recruiting officer with small clouds trailing it.
The wind blew fiercely and pushed the clouds forward. Suddenly it
began to rain, the raindrops falling like well-aimed bullets.

Chinni did not stir from where she sat. She did not move even
when the slanting rain slammed into her body. The children playing
on the road ran home. In the village on the right of the road, where
the concrete houses were, except for the roar of the rain, not a mouse
stirred. In the village on the left, the rain seemed vengeful. On both
sides of the road, the village was deserted. Not a soul to be seen.
Rain everywhere. On the hill, on the fields, on the houses, on the
trees, on the road, rain all over. It rained like the universal truth. As
the sky poured down rain, the earth threw up a great chill. The cold
and the rain were Chinni's only companions.

The leaves had become heavy, the branches heavier and the trees
hung their heads, drooping like a poor man in despair. A nearby
haystack, soaked with water shrank until it looked like a starved belly.
Chinni watched the road intently. When she saw the lorry coming like
the sun breaking through the clouds in the morning, joy exploded

in her. The same lorry that had become familiar all the year around. As the lorry drew level with her, every drop of blood in her body broke and leapt out.

The lorry, like the owner's goodness, was approaching. It looked like mother's love, like god's kindness coming face-to-face with her. It approached like bread, fruit, laddus, and biscuits, like food filling an empty belly. Chinni came to her feet. The lorry was closing in on her, moment by moment. Her hope grew; her blood surged within her, as if her hunger was being satisfied. The loaded lorry moved forward heavily. The rain slanted. A blanket of dimness from the sky to the earth. Daytime, but the village was silent. Not a soul stirred.

The lorry was almost upon her. Chinni ran across the road. Until then the driver had not seen Chinni. Then he saw her, a smiling Chinni. When he recognized Chinni's face, he became glum. The cheroot that the owner was smoking, slipped from his stiff fingers when he saw Chinni, a smiling Chinni running in front of the lorry.

Chinni kept smiling. There was no happiness in that smile, only despair, hunger, pain...no life in the smile, no radiance. That smile was not a smile. In that smile was sorrow, misery, despair, prayer, request, and a plea!

In the past it had been the driver's habit to smile back at Chinni. This time he did not. It was a ritual for the owner to respond to her smile with an answering smile. He did not do so either. The driver's hands shook, his legs shook. The fully-laden lorry surged forward. It was raining, the road was slippery. The driver pressed down the brake. The lorry did not stop. The brake did not respond.

Chinni was in front of their eyes. Pretty Chinni, smart Chinni, Chinni who had narrowly escaped death, Chinni whom the driver was very fond of. The owner's heart trembled. His nerves stretched until it seemed they would break. It seemed to the driver that his limbs were no longer obeying him, his hands turned the steering wheel of their own volition. The lorry swerved but did not stop.

Chinni saw the lorry swerving. But she could not bear to think of the ambrosia-like lorry, that lorry that provided food, escaping from her. She turned in the same direction the lorry turned. She moved where it moved. She stood in front of it, obstructing it.

'Chinni!' howled the driver. He turned the steering wheel again. The lorry swung on to the road again. He stepped on the brake forcefully. With a screech, like the groaning of an old man, the lorry stopped. Chinni was not in sight. Now she fell in the middle of the road. The last time she had fallen by the side of the lorry. This time she fell in front of it. The lorry had not been able to stop in time. Chinni thought she was losing consciousness, and she did.

Something hit her belly. Was it the hand of her mother or her father? Would she see them when she came to? Would Amma caress her hungry belly? Chinni no longer felt anything. The lorry was there. The road was there. Chinni was on it. At last its brakes worked and the lorry stopped. It moved while stopping. Stopped while moving. One of the front wheels felt something like a stone obstructing it; it climbed over it, and down the other side. The minute the lorry stopped, the driver and the owner leapt out on either side.

Chinni was nowhere to be seen. From under the lorry, blood mingled with rainwater and flowed red into a roadside ditch.

∽

In the middle of the road, its belly ripped open, blood splattered everywhere, its legs fastened to the road, flattened like a dosai, a bullfrog. A big bellowing frog. One that had cried, leapt, jumped, thought, wept, laughed, and one that had been troubled by hunger. And one, which, with its stomach severed, was hungry no more.

LINGERING FRAGRANCE
ISMAT CHUGHTAI

Translated from the Urdu by Tahira Naqvi

In the half darkness of the room a faint shadow was slowly advancing towards Chamman Mian's bed.

It was now at his feet. Was there a knife in the attacker's hand or a gun? Chamman Mian's heart began pounding in his chest. His toes became rigid. The shadow bent over his feet but before it could launch a full-fledged attack, Chamman shot up like a pole and the next minute his hand gripped the attacker's neck.

'Chiin', the shadow emitted a weak sigh and Chamman Mian toppled the enemy to the floor.

There was a loud jangle. Chamman dived under the bed.

'Who the hell are you?' he yelled.

'Ji...it's...me...Halima...'

'Halima? Oh.' He came out quickly and sat down on the carpet. 'What are you doing here?'

'Ji...nothing.'

'Who sent you? Don't you dare lie to me now, I'll pull your tongue out if you do.'

'Nawab Dulhan sent me.' Halima trembled.

Oh! Pyari Ammi and his mortal enemy! His thoughts began to scatter. For several days now his mother had been eyeing him strangely, whispering something in Nayaab Bubu's ear (Nayaab Bubu is a witch, the wretch) and Bhaijan had also been smiling mischievously at him. This was a joint conspiracy.

All sorts of things happen in nawabi families. His granduncle had tried several times to have Abba Hazoor poisoned, had set ruffians after him, so that he could take over his wealth and devour it all. Rafaqat Mamun had been poisoned by his real uncle from his mother's side, his favourite maidservant having administered the poison. To hell with such an inheritance.

Perhaps Pyari Ammi wants to hand down all her property to her older son. She has brought in her own brother's daughter as her daughter-in-law, hasn't she, and perhaps that's why she's after him.

Chamman Mian had no interest in land and property. Beating up tenants, threatening to throw them out of their homes and obtaining revenue from them by hook or by crook, having their animals forcibly auctioned—he hated it all.

Oh you can trust no one in this world, but how terrible when your own mother becomes your enemy! Always telling him to do this, not do that—don't study so hard, don't play so much, don't live so...

'Where's the knife?' Chamman Mian asked, bending down on his elbows.

'Knife?'

'Hands up!' Chamman Mian said, as if he was a secret agent.

'Uh?' Halima looked confused.

'You fool, raise your hands.'

When Halima lifted her hands, her dupatta slipped off.

Feeling self-conscious, she hastily brought her hands together.

'That same roguish behaviour again? I say, raise your hands!'

'But why?' she asked shyly.

'You wretch, where's the knife?'

'Which knife?' Halima was irked.

'What was in your hand then?'

'Nothing, I swear by God, nothing.'

'So why...why are you here then?'

'Nawab Dulhan sent me,' Halima said in a whisper and, lowering her eyes, began playing with the bead on her nose ring.

'Why?' Chamman Mian became fearful.

'To massage your feet.' She leaned against the bed.

'May God forgive me! Get out of here,' he said, flustered by

Halima's mischievous look.

Halima's face collapsed. She sat down on the carpet and with her head between her knees, broke into sobs.

Chamman Mian swore. 'Why are you crying, you stupid girl?'

Halima's weeping intensified.

'Halima, please Halima...for God's sake, don't cry, just leave...I have to go to college early tomorrow.' Halima continued crying.

༄

Ten years back Halima had been crying just like this. Her father was lying face down on the ground, blood oozing from his mouth. But the blood was very red, mixed with pink globs of flesh that Baba spat out every day with his phlegm.

Clutching him to her bosom, swaying from side to side, she lamented and wailed. Then people wrapped Baba in a white cloth and took him to the hospital. No one comes back from hospitals.

And she had been crying just like this on the day her mother deposited her under Nawab Dulhan's bed, filled her jhola with grain and didn't look back at Halima as she left.

Fed on leftovers Halima grew up in the servants' quarters, was raised playing in filth and garbage among chickens and puppies. She wasn't even allowed to crawl into Nawab Dulhan's courtyard.

Halima, undaunted, continued to live. Nayaab Bubu's twelve-year-old son Jabbar would beat the wretch mercilessly. Sometimes he would scorch the sole of her foot with red-hot tongs, at other times squeeze the juice of orange peels into her eyes, or take a pinch of Khala's snuff and stick it up her nose. Halima would sneeze for hours making noises like a toad, while the whole house roared with laughter.

Even now he didn't desist from teasing her. If she went up to the veranda to run an errand, he would pinch her, tug at her nose ring, or pull her plait. He was very devious. After all, he was Nawab Sahib's son and had always been pampered by him.

Nayaab Bubu was a bondmaid, full of allure and appeal at one time. Nawab Sahib, that is Chamman Mian's father, had fallen head over heels in love with her. Every now and then he would threaten her with marriage, but she was very sharp.

Whether a bondmaid is married or not, it makes no difference; she never becomes special. Women of nawabi families would die rather than allow her to sit with them. There isn't enough force in the two words recited by the Qazi to bore a hole through a stone or resolve the issue of survival.

Nayaab Bubu had a great life in the mahal. Instead of becoming the second wife and rival of the Begum, she worked hard and became her special confidante and friend. Worked her magic with Nawab Sahib in such a way that he allotted a reasonable income and some gardens to her son, Jabbar. All the servants were terrified of Jabbar. He strutted around the house dressed in a silk shirt and English trousers. He was a chauffeur in name, but actually exerted authority over everyone. Bubu on the inside and Jabbar on the outside—anyone who was unfortunate enough to come between them could not escape being pulverized.

⁂

Halima was still crying.

When Chamman scolded her she was shattered. Exhausted, he tried to appease her, and she melted. He took her cold hand in his and lifted her up from the floor. She clung to him as if she would fall apart. Oh God! The cold, magical winter night, the thundering storm, and the distraught Halima in Chamman's inexperienced hands!

His friends had enlightened him about the many tactics one could use to deal with girls, but call it stupidity or bad luck, Chamman had always regarded their sex chatter as nonsense and ignored it. He was intimately familiar with nothing besides his course texts and cricket. In the chilly winter night, Halima, a sizzling ember, scorched him. It was as if his hands had got stuck to glue.

He leapt back from her, as if a knife had stabbed some part of his brain. He was shaking with anger.

The storm outside was continuing to rage and Halima's sobs were causing a tempest.

'Halima, don't cry, please.' Helpless, he came and knelt in front of her. He wanted to place his own head on her bosom and weep uncontrollably, but was afraid that he would not be able to extricate himself from there. He wiped her tears with his shirt-front, helped her up and before she could understand what was happening, pushed her out of the door and quickly bolted it from the inside.

But his sleep had been washed away by Halima's tears. Trembling, Chamman Mian lay awake under the quilt till daybreak. Outside, the restless wind tangled with the trees, thrashed about, moaned.

∽

Nayaab Bubu turned her head for the salaam and raised her hands for dua. Then, folding the corner of the prayer mat, she got up and quietly opened the door of Jabbar's room and peered inside. A glimpse of her son's handsome body filled her eyes with tears of maternal pride.

She went in on tip-toe. Gulbahaar, the new bondmaid of Chamman Mian's father, Nawab Farhat, who was also Jabbar's father, used to secretly come to Jabbar and leave behind signs of her nocturnal visits. Today, as usual, her dupatta was trailing from under the quilt. Nayaab Bubu pulled it out. The wretch, she would have their noses chopped off one day. May God save Jabbar from the evil eye, he looked just like his father.

Suddenly she felt apprehensive. Was the father's bondmaid not equivalent to one's mother? She would feel so much better if she could get a fatwa from Alim Sahib. It wouldn't be fair to suffer in this life and then have to contend with hellfire in the next. It was not Gulbahaar's fault, really. On the one hand was the ageing Nawab Farhat stricken with haemorrhoids, and on the other this strapping youth. How she had cried last night. And the boy doesn't worry about the door being left open! If Bubu were not such a light sleeper, who knows who might see them. God alone takes care of everyone.

Nayaab Bubu had bought bondmaids specifically for Jabbar. One became sick, the other ran off with the sweeper's son. She had caused them a great deal of distress, that harlot! Girls from decent families weren't so depraved.

She had been tempted to ask Nawab Begum to give her Halima quite a few times, but she couldn't muster up enough courage to do so.

'No, Halima is for my Chamman,' Nawab Begum insisted. And today her resolve would be carried out. In any case, Jabbar didn't like meek and mild girls – like his father he wanted a sizzling hot pepper.

Mumbling to herself, Nayaab Bubu arrived in the bondmaids' quarters and felt her heart leap in her chest.

Halima was curled up in Sarwari's quilt. She prodded Halima's anklet with the tip of her shoe, and lifting a corner of the quilt, pulled it off.

Alarmed, Halima woke up and quickly started pulling her dupatta out from under Sarwari's sleeping form.

Bubu's eagle gaze rapidly travelled all over Halima's body. Halima lowered her head and began to pick at the stitches on the quilt.

'Hunh?' Bubu placed a hand on her hip and asked, 'What did I tell you?'

'Ji, Bubu.'

'So?'

Halima remained silent.

'You wretch, speak to me, what did he say?'

'His feet were not hurting.' Halima lowered her head.

'Hunh!' Fingering her prayer beads, Bubu turned around.

∽

Flowers bloomed in her heart. By God's grace, the only person left now to continue Nawab Farhat's line was Jabbar. It wasn't the older son's fault, it is God's will. The unfortunate Sanobar had been fated to live only this long. Barely fourteen when she was presented to the young man. What a delicate girl she had been, thin and slender. Had she been in a household with parents she would have been raised lovingly, received the care of a mother and father. She would have left her father's home one day, the melodious notes of the shehnai echoing in her ears, gone to her in-laws' house where two hearts would become one, a home would come into being, a new world would be created.

Since childhood, Sanobar had wanted to be a bride, always playing the game of 'Brides' with the other bondmaids. She looked so convincing as one that she made people laugh. She was a pretty child. Small-boned, of compact build, delicate hands and feet, small teeth, eyes illuminated like a goddess. How much Nayaab Bubu had wanted her for Jabbar but Nawab Begum stubbornly refused. She was a bondmaid from her maika, she had been specially procured from her maternal uncle for her son.

Who says Sanobar didn't become a bride? Bubu was from a long line of bondmaids, she understood very well that every woman longs to be a bride. Does she cease to be a woman just because she's a bondmaid? A heart beats in her bosom as well, she too has desires. She made sure the maidservants got their due. Early in the evening she had Sanobar bathed and dressed in a pink suit, broke off henna leaves with her own hands and had them crushed—the colour came out dark and deep on the unfortunate creature's hands and feet. Rubbed with fragrant oils, her hair was braided with a twill maubaaf and she was doused with attar from head to toe. Her friends whispered in her ears, teasing her. When Hashmat Mian lifted her up the miserable creature also pulled her dupatta down to form a tiny veil.

Fourteen-year old Sanobar who, when she set eyes on Hashmat Mian's face had set eyes on the angel of death, became pregnant within a year. All day long the pale, sickly, frail child lay on her stomach and vomited. Oh God, how girls are pampered in their parents' homes. The in-laws also go out of their way to be nice. In the days when she was well she would offer up a faint smile but only after Hashmat Mian begged and pleaded. Made him grovel for every kiss. When she fell from grace, he was revolted by her. It was the custom in the mahal that when cows became pregnant they were sent away to the village and brought back after they had calved. When they became useless, bondmaids and maidservants were also sent away to the village, and after they delivered they would leave the babies behind so that the constant yelping of these puppies would not cause a disturbance in the house.

They would create a great fuss, these unfortunate women, and would bellow like cows for their calves. When their breasts became engorged they would develop fevers and then be handed some begum's baby, be given the benefits accorded to wet nurses, and forgetting their own child they would become attached to the baby they were nursing. But women in nawabi families were not going to breed like goats and cows just to keep the bondmaids happy, so for the most part they would weep and wail and become dry, and then be put to work again...but Sanobar took a stand and said she was not leaving. Nayaab Bubu tried her best to explain things to her but she fell at Nawab Begum's feet. Bubu was worldly-wise; she hated these bondmaids because she hated herself, but she also felt sorry for them. Sanobar's time had come, but she wouldn't budge, she continued to give her favours to Hashmat Mian. One day, for some reason, she lashed out at Nawab Hashmat. He became livid, kicked her so hard that she was flung down next to the drain. That kick caused great damage. For three days she bellowed like a buffalo, then the infant died in her belly. If a doctor had been called in the situation would have become unmanageable—as it was, there were enemies everywhere. On the third day Sanobar breathed her last in the darkest corner of the servants' quarters.

Sanobar had surely been a most effective magician. Who knows what spell she had cast before dying, but it was four years now since Hashmat Nawab had remarried and was still childless. So many treatments, innumerable amulets and charms, vows made at shrines, lamps lit in temples, but Dulhan Begum did not conceive—and there was no hope that she would. Who knows whether it was true or not, but their enemies said that the young man had kicked the girl in the stomach when she was full term, and for this he had become impotent. That is why Dulhan Begum suffered attacks of hysteria and dashed off to her parents' place every other day. It is said her aunt's son is a very good doctor and he is the one treating her. It has also been said that there's something brewing between them as well.

∽

Nayaab Bubu heaved a long sigh, tested the hot water for Nawab Begum's morning wash by dipping her elbow in it, and made her way to her bedroom.

There was a time when Nawab Begum couldn't stand the sight of Nayaab Bubu's face, but Bubu fell at her feet and convinced her that she was Nawab Dulha and Nawab Dulhan's bondmaid. She wasn't some family harlot nor had she been bought for pennies; who knows how many generations of nawabs' blood coursed through her veins. Finally Nawab Begum gave in. In any case, this was no longer considered such a terrible thing; all the men in the family go around sampling tasty morsels. Nevertheless, Nayaab Bubu never exceeded her limits. She would listen to Nawab Sahib's sweet talk and disregard it. When he became involved with Munawwar Mirza, she actually helped Nawab Begum in managing that front. Instead of being happy at Begum's impending disinheritance, she wept and lamented with her. Her relationship with Nawab Begum was indestructible. Who was this harlot who had come along to divide the inheritance?

Nayaab Bubu backed Begum and worked astutely behind the scenes. Begum tied a rakhi on Tarhadar Khan's wrist and he became her brother. Tarhadar Khan then left for Paris with Munawwar. After Munawwar had been dispatched, Nayaab Bubu adorned the bridal bed and dressed Begum up like a ride. Along with the flowered jewellery on her wrists and feet, she also dazzled her ears with two gems on how to make Nawab Farhat happy, and then, clasping Jabbar to her bosom, spent a sleepless night in her chamber in the servants' quarters.

From that day on Nayaab Bubu didn't give up serving Nawab Begum.

When Nawab Begum saw Bubu enter with a long face she became worried. 'Is everything all right?'

Bubu haltingly narrated the whole story. The ground shifted from under Begum's feet. Right away Jabbar was sent with the car to fetch Hakim Sahib.

Hakim Sahib said, 'No need to be concerned, Dulhan Begum. The boy is inexperienced, he's young. Still, I will send some herbal preparations along with necessary instructions to the young man. Something else to consider, respected lady, is that it could be a case of revulsion. Sometimes the desired object is presented in such a way that there's no attraction. It doesn't mean that the digestive system is not working.'

'I already suspected that there was something wrong with the girl, she's not fit to satisfy the tastes of young nawabs, skinny, sickly creature that she is. I say, give the wretch to Nawab Baqar. He has said several times that Hashmat Mian likes his pair of English bloodhounds, he'll happily agree to an exchange.' Bubu started pressing Begum's calves.

'Oh no, I'll poison the wretch, but I won't hand her over to that leper, rotten from head to toe, the vile creature.'

It was unheard of that a bondmaid should visit a master and return unharmed the next morning.

One must think carefully and wisely. Why make a suggestion that might pit brother against brother? For this reason clever begums divide the property very carefully so that no one can demand the other's bondmaid. It's like a legal decree, this family decision.

'I'm tired of this boy,' Nawab Begum said. 'Almost nineteen, and never has he flirted with a maidservant. Our brothers, the moment they were ten or eleven, engaged in all kinds of mischief, and at sixteen or seventeen were ready for serious action. I say, Nayaab, did the wretch bathe properly or did you send her off to my son smelling of turmeric and garlic?'

'My dear lady, do you take me for a novice? By God's grace these hands have prepared all kinds of bondmaids for the bedchamber. I swear by Imam Hussain, if a young man glimpses even the heel of one of my bondmaids, he'll forget the fairies of *Koh Qaaf*. Remember, Hashmat Mian had been enamoured of that English girl and it was Sanobar, whom I had readied for him, who won him over with her wiles.' Her skills questioned, Bubu was offended.

Then, 'My dear, dear Begum, your son is better than the best, but the times are bad. A few days ago Afzal Nawab bought two bondmaids at an exorbitant price. The police found out and wouldn't let him leave the house. Bribes were paid, the family protested that the girls were poor, were receiving charity from them, but they were sent off to some home or the other. Fifteen hundred rupees down the drain! It's difficult to get new bondmaids these days.'

Even the outbreak of World War III would not have caused such a commotion in the mahal. The story leaked out slowly, rumours spread, and there were hissing serpents everywhere. How long does it take for talk to travel from one mouth to another? Those who heard the story beat their breasts in mock despair.

'Oh my, oh my, Chamman Mian!'

Afzal Mian heard the news as well and, pyjama flapping and mouth red with betel juice, he arrived and went straight to Chamman Mian to bring him to his senses.

'Oh my, we had no idea what the story was or else we would never have put our neck in a noose with your Bhabi. My beloved, it's not too late even now, your servant is here.' There was a time when he had fallen head over heels in love with Chamman Mian, but Bare Sarkar had threatened to kill him and only then had he sobered up. Chamman couldn't stand him.

'Shut up! It's not what you think. The truth is I don't like all this—I mean, it is not permitted without a nikah.'

'But my dear man, a bondmaid is permitted.'

'Not permitted at all.'

'This means that our ancestors were all sinners? You're the only one who is pious and upright?'

'I think that...'

'You think nothing, my dear. Have you ever studied the tenets of faith?'

'No, but...reason tells me this is not right.'

'Well, your reason has slowed down, my dear. Who knows what other nonsense your brain will come up with.'

'It is a crime in the eyes of the law.'

'We don't believe in the law created by non-believers, we lower our heads in obeisance to the decree of God, who is the Greatest. We treat bondservants, male and female, as members of our household. Look at Nayaab, she's ruling like a queen, her son doesn't want for anything; in fact all the bondmaids are putting on weight. Yes, it's true you've been handed shrivelled, dried-up goods, so take Sarwari then, she's as large as a fatted lamb.'

'Oh, shut up.'

'Now, look here, what's the real story?'

'There's no real story. Will you please stop bothering me?'

'All right, if that's what you want. Who can save you from being ridiculed? It's your decision. And, my dear sir, you probably don't know that your fiancée—'

'I don't have a fiancée...'

'Not now perhaps, but you will soon, and Hurma Begum is becoming quite friendly with that good-for-nothing Mansoor.'

'So what am I supposed to do?'

'Shall I tell you? I'm on my way to the bazaar, I'll send the bangle-seller here to cover your wrists with bangles, what else?' and he broke into a loud guffaw.

'This is all ignorance, all this talk stems from ignorance.'

'So our venerable ancestors were ignorant?'

'They might have been, how would I know?'

'Look, don't be stupid. Our elders would have started this custom for a good reason, it's a custom that is still being observed in our families. If they have a bondmaid, young men don't go astray, they are protected from all sorts of bad habits, they stay healthy.'

'These are all schemes put in place to legitimise adultery.'

'You are speaking like a non-believer, you are insulting our faith and —'

'Oh, please, stop this nonsense—you, guardian of faith, indeed. This is the only thing that's left a deep impression on your hearts.'

'You're stupid and also...insolent! You can go to hell, for all I care.'

∽

At night, when dinner was served, Nayaab Bubu ceremoniously offered Nawab Chamman a spoonful of Hakim Sahib's potent concoction wrapped in silver leaf. The night before, Chamman had torn up the paper with Hakim Sahib's directions without reading it and despatched Sarwari with a scolding. At this moment he felt like drowning in the largest serving dish. Knocking the spoon with his hand, he got up angrily and went to his room. The whole world thought he was impotent!

All the religious and literary texts he had read till now clearly indicated that if a relationship existed between a man and a woman without their being married, it was to be regarded as adultery and sin.

Outside the wind was howling again. A thin branch whipped against the window pane again and again, as if seeking a safe haven. Chamman fell asleep with great difficulty. Cool drops fell on his feet and he woke up with a start. His heart was beating wildly.

Halima had placed her face on his feet and was sobbing.

He pulled his feet away quickly. The same storm of tears. This girl had teamed up with the enemy, they were bent on ruining him.

'Now what is it?' he scolded.

'Am I so repulsive that I can't even touch my master's feet?' she moaned.

'Look, what is this nonsense? Leave my room, please.'

'No, I won't. I'm a bondmaid, not a leper. The entire mahal is cursing the day I was born. I'm being ridiculed; people are saying you find me repellent, that I'm not fit for you.

Beginning tomorrow, Sarwari will be appointed to serve you.'

'I will turn the wretch away, I don't need anyone to serve me.'

'You'll need her, Hakim Sahib says that—'

'Hakim Sahib talks rubbish, he's a stupid idiot!'

'What should I do then?'

'Go to sleep, it's late.'

'Day and night are the same for me. But why don't you do me a favour and bring me some poison?'

'Why should I bring you poison, you fool? What kind of talk is this? Suicide is a sin.'

'In that case I'll burn in Baqar Nawab's fire, he suffers from fevers, Chhote Mian.' A river of tears brimmed over again.

'What's all this about Baqar Khan, the wretched man?'

'It's all about him. You'll accept Sarwari, I will be sold to him in exchange for a pair of bloodhounds that cost eighteen hundred rupees.'

'Oh my God, what is all this nonsense?'

'Baqar Nawab is wasting away, the cleaning woman was telling Bubu. Bubu doesn't like me anyway, because I hit Jabbar with a shoe once.'

After Halima explained the situation in detail, Chamman Mian began shaking with anger. He was overcome by the desire to comfort Halima, dry her tears with his shirt, but was terrified that if he touched her he wouldn't be able to hold back.

'Do you want to marry me?' he blurted out.

'Oh my God! Everyone knows that Hurma Bitiya has been engaged to you since childhood.'

'And you?'

'I'm your bondmaid.'

'You're my bondmaid, but your mother was not a bondmaid, your father was not the child of a bondmaid, you're from a Sayyed family, Halima, and your father was a farmer.'

'Halima...Halima, listen...' He caught both her hands in his. 'Listen, I'll tell Pyari Ammi today that I won't marry Hurma, I'll marry you.'

'Marry me?' Halima pulled her hands from his grasp. 'Oh my God, you're talking like a child. Do you know what fate awaits those who fall in love? Sadiq Sahib was going to marry his bondmaid and the older Begum Sahib had her poisoned. The poor thing, how horribly she suffered for three or four days, she just wouldn't die, the wretch. If this is what you have decided, then you can strangle me with your own hands.' And she took his hands and placed them around her neck. What ensued was just what Chamman had feared. Halima's body was like glue, Chamman's hands were stuck fast.

'Go...go, Halima...my dearest Halima...go please, go...' and he gathered her to his bosom.

'Uff! How cold your hands are...Halima...'

'Warm them then, my lord!' She unbuttoned Chamman Mian's shirt and placed her small cold hands on his wildly beating heart. Sobbing, weeping, two innocent, inexperienced children melted into each other. Outside the breeze was swaying gently like a new bride walking on tiptoe. Everything Chamman Mian did was irrational and bizarre. Everyone laughed at him—you play with toys, you don't worship them. Nawab Begum heaved a long sigh of relief in the morning when Bubu came in, lowered her head, presented salutations, and offered hearty congratulations. It was eight o'clock and Chamman

Mian's door, by God's grace, was still shut.

And when the young man left for college, Nawab Begum saw the proof with her own eyes and offered two rakat prayers in gratitude. Halima had developed a fever and was lying face down in her chamber. Bubu teased her with risqué jokes every time she walked by. The entire mahal echoed with the news that Chamman Mian had accepted Halima, while the other bondmaids went about their business looking sullen and disappointed. Halima was fortunate that she had found such a handsome, innocent bridegroom. (In their personal conversations the bondmaids customarily consoled themselves by calling their masters 'bridegroom'.) Chamman Mian had always felt uncomfortable in the presence of girls, but having touched Halima just once he was good for nothing else. The moment he had an hour's break he would dash home, and he started making excuses to friends who came to visit on Sundays, the only holiday of the week. 'I have to study,' he would say, and when he studied he had his head in Halima's lap. Every full stop on the page was followed by a kiss.

'Illiterate girl! If you had studied a little you could have faired my notes for me.' And sitting next to him, Halima is writing 'ABCD' on the floor with charcoal.

'Come on, fill my fountain pen with ink, my dear.' Her hands, nose, face and dupatta were soon smeared with ink, and on top of that, tears. Such a silly girl.

Arrangements like these were very grand in the mahals. Young men were allotted separate rooms and bondmaids were not expected to do any other work. Halima had been trained by Bubu. She insisted on helping Nawab Begum with the wash in the morning, didn't give up cleaning and arranging the paandan, filling it regularly with fresh betel nuts and chuna.

'My dear girl, just go and take care of your Chamman Mian,' Nawab Begum would say, trying to keep her from doing all this, but head covered demurely, Halima would continue to press her feet. She's a mother-in-law after all, it's her son, isn't it, who kisses the bondmaid's feet.

New clothes and jewellery are bestowed upon the bondmaid. She enjoys the independence of having her own house and if she wants, can quickly go to the kitchen and cook something fresh. The gardener's wife brought Halima a basket filled with flowers and fragrant champa bracelets, but Chamman Mian didn't like the idea of sprinkling the bed with flowers.

'It makes me sad, lying on top of flowers, it's actually very cruel,' and he would gather all the flowers and drop them in Halima's lap.

Nayaab Bubu was parroting the same old chatter: the moment Halima's nausea begins she will be finished. When men lose interest in their wives, what hope can there be for a bondmaid? Seeing Chamman's passion, Bubu narrowed her eyes with pleasure.

'I'm thinking, we should have a nikah during the month of khali. Feroza Begum seemed a little indifferent this time,' Nawab Begum said, assured now of Chamman Mian's manhood.

'A curse on the rumour-mongers in the family, but it's been said that Hurma Bitiya has become quite liberated,' Bubu informed her. 'May there be worms in the mouths of those who say this, but it's some friend of Arshad Mian's, he often comes to the house.'

'Hai, who told you this?'

'Tarahdar Khan's wife visits frequently, it's her aunt who goes there to teach embroidery to Maryam Bitiya, and she was saying they're playing with a racket and ball all the time. God willing, there won't be any impediments to Chamman Mian's education, so if you ask me the sooner he's married to Hurma, the better.'

'But the boy won't let me touch the subject! He says he will have a nikah with Halima and no one else. I told him that if he spoke such rubbish again, by God, I would kill myself.'

'Ai, Begum, this is all rubbish. What connection is there between the words and deeds of these nawabs? Assess the situation and do what's best. Within a week he'll be on the straight and narrow again. Already I can see that the girl looks sickly.'

No secret in the mahal could be hidden from Bubu. She guessed immediately when cows, buffaloes, perhaps even mice, became pregnant.

'Pyari Ammi, is Halima going to the village?' Chamman finally decided to ask without beating about the bush. Halima had been crying constantly the last few days.

'Yes, my dearest boy, and Nayaab is going with her. I've told Ammi Hazoor that she must send some lemon pickle for you.'

'But Pyari Ammi,' Chamman said, 'why are you sending her? Who will take care of my clothes?'

'Sarwari can do it, and Latifa.'

'If Sarwari and Latifa touch any of my things...I won't stand for it. But why are you sending Halima away?' Chamman complained.

'Because I want to. Who are you to interfere in my affairs?'

'But Pyari Ammi—'

'Mian, I'm still alive! When you've dumped me in the grave you can do whatever you want.' Sparks blazed in Pyari Ammi's eyes. 'Your father never interfered in the internal affairs of the mahal, what right do you think you have to do so? Have you ever suffered in the past that you should be afraid you will now? Bubu decides what to do with the bondmaids.'

'Pyari Ammi, Halima is not a bondmaid, she's my life, she's the daughter of a Sayyed. You were the one who sent her into my heart and now you want to separate nail from flesh. Why? What blunder have I committed?' He wanted to say all this, but his voice was choked by emotion and lowering his head, he got up and left the room.

Halima couldn't stop her tears from flowing, was angry with herself. She wanted to spend her last few days in the mahal, celebrating. Who knew what life would be like after this. She had four days left and for these four beautiful days she had planned four sets of clothes with much thought. The smell of attar sickened her, but she controlled her nausea and doused the bed with fragrance. Washed her hair and wafted it over the smoke of fragrant herbs, refreshed the fading henna on her hands and feet, and covered her wrists with bangles because Chamman Mian enjoyed breaking them. No matter how many he broke, she still had some left to remind her that she was a bride.

'Aren't you sad at the thought of going to the village?' Chamman asked her when he saw her flushed and glowing. His own heart was bleeding.

'No.' Bubu had told her not to cry on any account.

'Why not?' he demanded angrily.

'I'll be back soon.'

'How soon?'

'In a few days.'

'How many days will that be?'

'Just six or seven months.'

'Six *months*?'

'Shh...speak softly.'

'I'll die without you, Halima.'

'God forbid, may all your ill fortune fall on me, my lord. God will send me back to serve you, I know. Not all girls die, Sanobar was special. Bare Sarkar kicked her in the stomach so her baby died.' She clapped her hand on her mouth in alarm. What was she saying?

'Baby?'

'No, no, Chhote Mian...I...'

'Swear by me...' Chamman placed her hand on his bosom.

'No, oh God, no.'

'Liar, Halima!' He quickly lit the lamp and looked at her, then lowered his head guiltily. Sat still for a long time. A child, his child, the child of a living human being. He was filled with feelings he hadn't experienced before, he wanted to leap up, break off all the stars shining in the sky, and fill Halima's lap with them.

'When will it be born?' he asked.

'Maybe in six months,' Halima said shyly.

'My results will have been announced by then,' he tried to change the subject.

Halima's heart sank. How will the sounds of the poor creature's crying travel from the village to Sarkar's ears here? If she were shameless and thick-skinned like her mother, she would allow the baby to grow up with the bondmaids. The father wouldn't even recognize the child. If it's a boy he won't be a son, he'll be a slave. Iron clothes, polish shoes. If it's a girl, she'll be sent to the village to spend her life waiting hand and foot on someone.

Halima's tongue had a lock on it. Bubu had said, 'If you try to influence the young Nawab, you wretch, I'll have you ripped into pieces and fed to the dogs.'

'Halima, you won't go to the village.'

'Please, don't talk like this.'

'I won't let you go.'

'Oh God, my innocent Sarkar.'

But he didn't let her continue. Bubu had said that a man is repelled by a pregnant woman, but what kind of man was this who made love to her exactly as he had the first time? The next day Chamman Mian bunked college and began going from door to door with his one-man petition.

'Bhai jaan, why is Halima being sent to the village?'

'Mian, this is the tradition of the mahal.'

'She's not cattle, she's the keeper of my child.'

His brother's face burned with anger. 'Look here, you're crossing all limits. Aren't you ashamed to say things like this in my presence?' And he left in a rage.

✍

Men don't interfere in mahal politics. When pyari ammis want, they provide their sons with skilled bondmaids to serve them. When they think the bondmaids are becoming a threat or are useless, they send them away. Another bondmaid is brought in to replace the one who has been discarded. The relationship with a bondmaid is only physical, respectable men don't develop emotional bonds with them.

'Afzal Bhai, please tell Pyari Ammi not to send Halima to the village,' he begged his cousin for help.

'My dear man, are you crazy? A pregnant woman isn't good for your health. Why are you so upset? Other arrangements will be made, don't worry,' he chuckled.

'I don't want other arrangements.'

'Don't forget you're getting married to Hurma Bibi in December.'

'I won't marry Hurma.'

'If Halima goes to the village, I'll quit college,' announced Chamman Mian.

'Oh, so the young man has become obstinate?' The Begum's

blood boiled. 'If he can be stubborn, I know how to respond. I will not allow that miserable Halima to stay here another day even if my dead body is being readied for burial. No more day after tomorrow or after that, Nayaab, start making preparations this very minute. I swear by the Holy Prophet...'

'Najam Bitiya is also expecting, by God's grace, and after she delivers the plan is to leave for England.'

'Why are you bringing this up? May God bless my daughter.' Najam was Chamman Mian's sister.

'But she won't take the baby with her to England, and it's not proper for Dulha Mian to go alone. If that wretched Englishwoman starts pursuing him again all hell will break loose.'

'Ai hai, Nayaab, what are you trying to say?'

'Najam Bitiya and Halima are just a few days apart. By God's grace, even if it's a matter of one week, it will be all right.'

'I see.' Nawab Begum began to understand. 'Najam Bitiya will be saved all the bother. When she leaves for London, Halima will be able to nurse her baby. The child will get good, natural milk.'

'Whatever you say, Begum Sahib. But what if she's not well taken care of in the village...Halima is very delicate. If she stays where I can keep an eye on her, she'll be under my thumb. I'll keep her under control and at the same time, the young Nawab's demands will also be met.'

'I don't want to give in to his demands,' but Begum was beginning to soften.

'As you wish, but I say that it's only a matter of time before Mian loses interest. Then we'll have our way and also earn his gratitude.'

But Chamman Mian was proving both Nayaab Bubu and the laws of nature wrong. Mad enough to have embraced a bondmaid— no young man from the Nawab's family had ever exhibited such shamelessness. All day, he read one book after another with intense concentration on prenatal care and raising children, and his pocket money went on vitamins and tonics for the bondmaid. What a waste!

Seated in the courtyard, Halima was busy embroidering Chamman Mian's kurta. She knew why she hadn't been sent away to the village, but didn't want to shatter Chamman Mian's dreams.

Meanwhile Chamman Mian was getting extremely nervous, he had never seen a pregnant woman at close quarters. He had heard that Najam Baji was also expecting but she lay in bed all day, moaning, her enormous body covered by a quilt.

He was afraid that Halima would burst. When he didn't find answers to his fears in books, he dashed off to Farkhanda Nawab.

Everyone in the family thought ill of Farkhanda Nawab because, many years ago, she had suffered badly at the hands of an ill-fated romance. But her husband, Ashraf Sahib, was in the police and sooner or later everyone needed him; for this reason, the family was forced to be nice to her. Actually, the other Begums were jealous of her because she was very erudite. And her son Na'eem and Chamman Mian were good friends.

Chamman Mian didn't have the slightest idea that Pyari Ammi had asked her to come on Friday for advice regarding jewellery for the bride. Farkhanda suppressed a smile and assured Chamman that when she came on Friday she would take a look at his Halima.

She got out of the car and headed straight for Chamman's room. First she scolded him for being so nervous, then said, 'Halima is fine. She is not going to burst. Don't give her fatty foods, but fruits and milk instead.'

'Tasleem, Phupi Jaan.' Halima pulled her dupatta down demurely just as Farkhanda was leaving.

'May you live long, gudiya,' And Farkhanda quickly exited the doll's house.

In Begum Nawab's room she saw the jewellery and was silent.

'Arre Bi, tell me what you think, why are you so quiet?'

'Bhabi Jaan, the world is changing, Hurma is a very nice girl, but...'

'Yes, yes, go ahead, say she's very fashionable and this jewellery is old-fashioned. Well, I'm going to get some new things from Bombay.'

Things should have been brought out into the open but Farkhanda Begum seemed ill at ease. Then came the excuses: she had a meeting to go to, etc. After she had left Nawab Begum and Bubu wasted no time in disparaging her.

When Nayaab Bubu went with the jewellery to Hurma she found that Feroza Begum was away visiting a friend, and Hurma was playing a game with racket and ball. Nayaab Bubu showed her the jewellery and said, 'Rani Bitiya, see if you like it.'

'Oh, but why do I have to approve Halima's jewellery?' Hurma said off-handedly, turning to run a brush through her short hair.

'Arre, God forbid, Halima is just a bondmaid.'

'Really? But the baby is Chamman Mian's, isn't it?'

'Baby?' Bubu broke out in a sweat. 'Which baby?'

'Farkhanda Khala was saying that...'

'Oh no, my child...that is...Tauba, tauba, the girl is so difficult. Your mother isn't here so you think you can give this old woman a hard time.' Seething, Bubu got up and left.

℞

'How much he kicks, the rascal!' Placing his hands on her taut stomach, Chamman was marvelling at nature's wonders. 'Why are you so aloof, Leemo?' Overcome by love he called her Leema, and after that she became Leemo.

Chamman wrapped her in the quilt and burying his face in her body, inhaled deeply. How fragrant she is, like a Dussehri mango! He never tired of her but it's selfish to be so demanding. She was quite worn out. No, he wouldn't touch her now. Time, please stand still, don't look back, don't look ahead because there's darkness behind and ahead of us. Who can trust that which is ahead?

'God help us, how Halima has betrayed us,' Begum Nawab dipped her finger in honey and plopped it into her granddaughter's mouth. 'Nayaab, is your wretched mouth a coal pit? You said both would deliver at the same time. Najam is weeping hysterically. She doesn't want to nurse the baby and your Halima hasn't delivered yet. You said you would send Halima's baby to the village and Halima would take charge of this one. What will happen now?'

Nayaab couldn't bear to be wrong. Under any circumstances. How could this two-bit bondmaid have had the guts to upset her whole scheme!

Halima was squeezing some orange juice. Chhote Sarkar would be returning soon after winning the match. Bubu was staring at her, just as an eagle eyes its victim before pouncing on it. She looked furious.

'Halima, come here,' she called harshly. Halima trembled.

'I see, so this is what you've done.' Bubu glared at her from top to toe.

'Speak up, you wretch, whose is it?' she demanded, as if seeing her swollen belly for the first time.

'This...this orange...'

'Not the orange, you wretched creature, this watermelon,' she said, smacking Halima's stomach with her fan.

Halima was stunned. Until now no one had referred to her pregnancy. She stared in dumbfounded amazement at Bubu.

'Will you say something or do you want me to hit you on your face, you sly wretch?'

Halima's tongue was glued to her mouth. If someone had chopped her up into little pieces, she still wouldn't have been able to utter Chhote Sarkar's name. His sin was her sweetest blessing.

'Why don't you speak, you damned woman?' Bubu slapped her so hard that the ring on her finger pierced Halima's cheek and drew blood.

༈

Chamman Mian was scoring one hit after another. The entire field echoed with applause. When Chamman Mian held the silver cup, surrounded by the sound of clapping, he felt it was Halima's smooth and silvery stomach beating in his hands.

As usual, Chamman Mian ran to his room as soon as he got home and called out to Halima, but when he didn't get a reply he picked up the cup, and perspiring heavily, went to his mother.

'Ai, Mian, where did you bring this lota from? It's quite beautiful,' exclaimed Bubu.

'It's not a lota, Bubu, it's a cup.'

'Oh, my dear son, please call Hakim Sahib, tell him I'm getting terrible cramps in my legs again,' moaned Pyari Ammi.

'All right, Ammi ji. Bubu, will you please tell Halima to get out my cotton kurta, it's very hot.'

When he returned after making the phone call, Bubu motioned that his mother was asleep.

'My clothes?'

Again Bubu gestured that he was not to worry.

'Where's Halima?' When he came out after his bath he saw that Sarwari was putting the drawstring in his pyjama.

'I'm asking you, where's Halima and you're not replying,' he roared.

'Oh God, I don't know. She must be in the servants' quarters.' Sarwari was all made up today.

'Servants' quarters? Go and tell her to come here.' He snatched the pyjama from her hands.

Sarwari smiled and started removing the buttons from the discarded kurta and putting them on the freshly starched one.

'Arre, you witch, didn't you hear me? Get out of here!' He snatched the kurta from her and flung it down.

'Bubu sent me.'

'Bubu sent you? Why?'

Sarwari lowered her eyes and giggled.

'You miserable creature!' Chamman swung his racket at her. Her anklets tinkling and body swaying, a coquettish expression on her face, Sarwari walked out of Chamman's room.

Five or ten minutes passed. Feeling agitated, a towel wrapped around him, Chamman sat down, idly turning the pages of a magazine. After another fifteen minutes he lost his cool.

'Is there anyone around?' This was how he called for Halima.

Sarwari reappeared with full coquettish armour. Chamman's heart sank at the sight of her malicious smile.

'You witch, tell me the truth, where is she?' He twisted her braid around his wrist and pulled it tight.

'Oh my God, I'm dead! Help me, mother! Sarkar, she's in the servants' quarters!'

Chamman let go of her and his whole body started shaking. He put on his slippers and dashed out.

'Arre, Mian, for God's sake, stop, where are you going?' Sarwari ran after him. 'It is not for men to go there!' But Mian was beyond listening. He ran into Nayaab in the veranda.

'Bubu, tell someone to call the lady doctor.'

'Oh my, Chhote Mian, put on some clothes first.' She turned to Sarwari and scolded her. She had wanted to send Latifa but Sarwari had begged her to let her go instead.

'Ai, Mian, why?'

'Bubu, send Jabbar with the car, a phone call won't do.'

'But why, Mian?'

'Halim...' His throat became dry. 'Halima...she is...'

'No lady doctor for her, we'll get a mem from England. Shameless hussy! These servants and bondmaids have become too big for their boots. You should go, your friend Na'eem Mian called, it's his birthday. Sarwari, you wretch, go and take out Mian's churidar-pajama and sherwani.' She was about to walk away, then, 'Oh yes, Mian, you made me forget what I was going to say. Your Pyari Ammi is not feeling well, so stop by at Hakim Sahib's on your way to Na'eem Mian's. I'll tell Jabbar to get the car.' And she strode out.

Flustered, Chamman returned to his room, sat down, then jumped up and got dressed quickly without giving much thought to what he was wearing. He had seen many bondmaids die, been haunted in his dreams for months by the sight of Sanobar's corpse. Halima was also delicate like her.

He went straight to his older brother. 'Bhai jaan.'

'What is it?' He was playing chess with a friend.

'I...there's something...I want to talk to you about,' he tugged at his sleeve with trembling hands.

'Just wait Mian, let me finish this game. Look at this great move! I say, Mian Quddus, save your castle.'

'Bhai jaan,' Chamman felt he was dying. He waited about ten minutes but for Chamman it was as if centuries had passed.

'Arre, my dear boy, you won a cup! Congratulations.'

'Bhai jaan, Halima...she...please send for a doctor.'

'I see. Well, the doctor will come if she's needed—'

'No, Bhai jaan, Halima will die. Please do something.'

'Do you think I'm God that I can prevent a death that has been fated? And aren't you ashamed, running around like this for a bondmaid? Control yourself. She's giving birth to a bastard—what will you call her if not that, will you say she's virtuous?'

'Bhai jaan...she is...the...'

'Why are you fretting? Without a nikah the woman is immoral, an adulteress, fit to be stoned. Better for her to ˌdie. The world will be a cleaner place without one such as her.'

'But I'm complicit in the sin, too.'

'So, what do you want me to do? Go and atone for your sins, why pester me?'

Pointless talking to someone so dense. If it had been anyone else saying all this, Chamman would have cracked his jaw. But he was so used to being respectful to his elder brother that he swallowed his anger, hung his head, and left.

Chamman battered at every door as if crazed. He pleaded with his father, but Abba Hazoor had been so singed by the wretched Gulbahaar that the very mention of the word bondmaid made him jump three feet in the air.

'How dare you admit to your foul deeds with such brazenness in my presence! First you step into the gutter and then you want to drag the whole family into it.'

Chamman rubbed his eyes on the soles of Pyari Ammi's feet, but she became hysterical. Would that she had become deaf before hearing something like this, or blind so that she wouldn't have had to see this day dawn.

He beseeched with folded his hands before Chacha Mian.

'God forgive us! Let her die, the wretch, I'll give you my Mahrukh, a real firecracker. Why are you bent on destroying yourself over a sickly bondmaid? All because of the nonsense you've been reading in those useless books.'

People were smiling, making jokes at his expense, and he was sitting on the cold stony floor in front of the servants' quarters and weeping. An eighteen year-old boy was acting like a baby, crying uncontrollably.

Abba Hazoor was livid. If Begum hadn't stopped him, he would have skinned Chamman alive for this humiliation to the family. The day he heard that his older son, Arjumand, had got rid of a bondmaid, his bushy moustache had quivered with the weight of his smile. The oldest son couldn't have children and if Chamman went this way, where would an heir to the property come from?

No one had ever seen a spectacle like this, nor heard of such an occurrence. The servants were sniggering, the bondmaids giggling openly.

And inside, lying on a sagging rope-bed, Halima was cooing like a pea-hen. Her hands were bleeding from constantly rubbing against the rough hemp of the bed.

'Hai, Sarwari, he's sitting on the wet floor, tell him to get up from there, God forbid that he should catch a chill.' If her labour pains had given her some respite, she would have gone and forced him to get up. But the pains, coming in waves, were racking her heavily perspiring body. She bit her lips so that Chamman Mian wouldn't hear her voice, but the heart hears everything. Chamman Mian didn't want to live, he wanted to dash his head against a stone so that his pain would cease. Suddenly someone called out his name and pulled him back from the depths of despair. He got up, picked up his bike from the porch, and without bothering to change his mud-spattered clothes rode off, barely avoiding a collision with the gate.

'Hai, my beloved son.' The Begum regained consciousness and beat her chest.

'Ai hai, Chamman, is everything all right?'

Covered in mud from head to toe, his face drenched with tears, Chamman was weak from weeping. 'Halima...Phupo...'

'Is she all right?'

'She's dead, she's dying...Phupo...no one listens to me, no one.'

'Ai hai, you're so stupid! I told you to inform me immediately. I'll call the ambulance right away, she'll be taken to the hospital. Who can fight with the elders?'

'It was my final exam today, when I came back I found out that... that...Phupo, she'll die, she must be dead already.'

'No, no, she won't die, stop worrying, my boy.'

When Farkhanda Nawab's car arrived with the ambulance behind it, a storm broke out in the mahal. Begum immediately went into the throes of hysteria and pretended to be dying. Nawab Sahib loaded his gun and came out thundering, but retreated when he saw the police car behind the ambulance. The family had not had to deal with such a display of public humiliation even when Manjhle Nawab's property had been seized by the court.

Without wasting a moment, Farkhanda Nawab forced her way straight into Halima's chamber.

Chamman picked up the blood-soaked Halima in his arms and the scene was set for mourning in the mahal.

The next day, with just one stroke of his pen, Chamman relinquished all his ancestral rights. It wasn't as if he had earned them with years of hard work and so he felt no regret. He signed everything and anything that was placed before him and so was disowned.

∽

He now lives in a dilapidated house on a narrow street. Teaches racket ball in some school and attends college. He can be seen riding a bicycle often, dressed in frayed trousers and a shabby cotton shirt. Sometimes a boy with light-coloured eyes is spotted on the carrier of the bike, wedged between household rations.

The child is from his bondmaid.

Who knows if he has had a nikah with her or not!

NOTES TO THE STORIES

Seed: Mahasweta Devi
'Bichhan' first appeared in *Nairitey Megh* published by Karuna Prakashani in 1979.

The King's Harvest: Chetan Raj Shreshta
'The King's Harvest' first appeared in *The King's Harvest: Two Novellas* published by Aleph Book Company in 2013.

Signs: Nirmal Verma
'Ishare' was first published in *Madhyam*, a Hindi Sahitya Sammelan publication in 2002.

The Period of Mourning: Bolwar Mahamad Kunhi
'Iddath' first appeared in the short story collection, *Akashakke Neeli Paradey*, published by Kamadhenu Publishers in 1999.

Bulbuls: Habib Kamran
'Bulbul' appeared in a volume of stories titled *Aevil Baana* published by the author in 1994.

The Deepest Blue: K. R. Meera
'Karineela' was first published by Rainbow Books in 2005.

Jumman: Shripad Narayan Pendse
'Jumman' first appeared in the short story collection *Jumman* published by Mouj Prakashan in 1956.

The Witch: K. K. Mohapatra
'Daa'ni' was first published in the literary journal *Nabalipi* in October 1999 (Puja Special Issue). Subsequently it was published in a collection of stories *Chora O Anyanya Galpa* by Friends Publishers in 2001.

A Place to Live: Gopikrishnan
'Kaaninilam Vendum' was first published in *Ovvatha Unarvukal* in 1986.

Hunger: Kolakaluri Enoch
'Aakali' first appeared in *Oorabaavi* published by Jyoti Grandhamala in 1983.

The Fourth Direction: Waryam Singh Sandhu
'Chauthi Koot' was first published in *Samdarshi* in 1988.

Lingering Fragrance: Ismat Chughtai
'Lingering Fragrance' was published in *Ismat: Her Life, Her Times* by Katha
in 1979.

NOTES ON THE AUTHORS

 Bolwar Mahamad Kunhi (b. 1951) is a short story writer, novelist, playwright and scriptwriter. He is the first writer to introduce the Muslim ethos and culture into creative Kannada prose. He is also the first Indian writer to be conferred the central Sahitya Akademi Award twice and the first Kannada writer to receive the Bala Sahitya Puraskar. The Karnataka Sahitya Akademi has honoured him three times. A recipient of numerous other national and state awards, Kunhi, is considered to be one of the finest writers of Kannada literature today.

 Chetan Raj Shrestha (b. 1978) is a trained architect specializing in conservation architecture. He was born in Gangtok, Sikkim, and has lived in Darjeeling, Bengaluru, Mumbai and Sydney. His debut work of fiction, *The King's Harvest*, won the Tata Literature Live First Book Award 2013. His second book, *The Light of His Clan,* was published in 2015.

 Despite his mother tongue being Sourashtra, **Gopikrishnan** (1945–2003) wrote in Tamil. His short-story collections include *Mudiyadha Saman* (The Impossible Equation, 1999), *Thooyoen* (The Puritan, 2000), *Maanida Vaazhvu Tharum Aanandham* (The Happiness that Human Life Offers, 2002), *Ovvatha Unarvukal* (Feelings Unbecoming,1986) and a novel, *Ullaeyirundhu Sila Kuralgal* (Some Voices From Within,1983). He also published a small handbook of social work called *Samoogappani, A-Samoogappani, Edhir-Samoogappani*. He contributed significantly to the field of translation and to the preparation of CRE-A's Tamil-English Dictionary.

His stories are significant for the way they present the unpredictability and the monotony of life and also its injustices and disparities in a light-hearted, at the same time poignant, vein. The element of humour with its undercurrent of pathos and righteous indignation is the hallmark of his works.

Habib Kamran (1927–2007) worked in the School Education Department of Jammu and Kashmir Government as teacher/administrator. He started his literary career as a novelist, but did not publish anything in his lifetime except a collection of Kashmiri short stories, *Aevil Baana*. His short stories have been published in anthologies and literary journals in the original Kashmiri as well as in English translation.

Ismat Chughtai (1915–1991) the grand dame of Urdu literature, was a novelist, short-story writer and essayist who represented the birth of a revolutionary feminist politics and aesthetics in Urdu literature in the twentieth century. Although a spirited member of the Progressive Writers' Movement in India, she spoke vehemently against its orthodoxy and inflexibility.

Kamalakanta Mohapatra (b. 1951) is a writer and translator who has published a novel, two collections of short stories and a book of essays in Odia. He has translated selected works of Isaac Bashevis Singer, Jean-Paul Sartre and Gabriel García Márquez in Odia. He has collaborated with Leelawati Mohapatra and Paul St. Pierre on a number of translations into English, notable among them are *The HarperCollins Book of Oriya Short Stories, Ants, Ghosts and Whispering Trees: An Anthology of Oriya Short Stories, JP Das: Sundardas, Bijay Mishra: The Gravediggers* and *Gopinath Mohanty's: Dark Loneliness*.

K. R. Meera (b. 1970) is an award winning Malayalam writer. She worked as a journalist for the *Malayala Manorama*, but resigned to focus on her writing. Her first short story collection, *Ormayude Njarambu,* was followed by more short story collections, novellas, novels and children's books. She is the recipient of multiple awards, including the Sahitya Akademi Award in 2015 for her most famous novel *Aarachaar* (*Hangwoman*). It was shortlisted for the 2016 DSC Prize for South Asian Literature and won the Kerala Sahitya Akademi Award in 2013, as well as other regional awards.

Kolakaluri Enoch (b. 1939) is a distinguished scholar, critic and Telugu writer. His collection of short stories *Oorabaavi* is considered the first volume of Telugu Dalit Short stories. He taught Telugu literature for decades in SKD University and is a former Vice-chancellor of Sri Venkateswara University, Tirupati. He has won the following awards: the Padma Sri and 29th Moortidevi Award of Bharatiya Jnanpithin 2015, and has received multiple honours from AP Sahitya Akademi. A unique mark of his writing is that Dalit and socio-economic issues remain in the background against which human dramas of compassion and cruelty take place.

 Mahasweta Devi (1926-2016) was a noted social activist and Bengali writer. Her first book, *The Queen of Jhansi*, was published in 1956. She has published twenty collections of short stories and close to a hundred novels. Besides contributing to almost all the leading Bengali periodicals in the last twenty years, she also started a journal named *Bortika* to enable those who were not part of the 'literary' class in Bengal to gain access to literature; ordinary people, not acclaimed 'writers' wrote in the journal, and working class women were especially encouraged to write. Her efforts and activism following the death in police custody of Budhan Sabar, a member of the so-called 'criminal tribes', led to the formation of the Denotified Tribes Rights Action Group, and resulted finally in the removal of the nomenclature 'criminal tribes' from government records as well as reform in policies involving these once-criminalized communities. She won several literary prizes including the Sahitya Akademi Award in 1979 for her novel *Aranyer Adhikar*; the Padma Shri in 1986; the Jnanpith Award in 1996; the Ramon Magsaysay Award for Journalism, Literature and the Creative Communication Arts in 1997; and the Padma Vibhushan in 2006.

 Nirmal Verma (1929-2005) pioneered the Nayi Kahani movement in Hindi literature in the late 1950s with his iconic story 'Parinde'. He wrote five novels, eight collections of short stories and nine volumes of essays and travelogues. A much loved and well decorated writer, his honours include India's highest literary award, the Jnanpith in 2000, India's third highest civilian award, the Padma Bhushan in 2003, and Sahitya Akademi Fellowship for lifetime achievement in 2004.

Shripad Narayan Pendse (1913-2007), popularly known as Shri Na Pendse, was a celebrated Marathi novelist. His novel, *Rathachakra* received the Sahitya Akademi Award in 1963. As part of the UNESCO Collection of Representative Works, in collaboration with the Sahitya Akademi, his novel, *Garambicha Bapu* was translated into English as *Wild Bapu of Garambi*. As a recipient of the Rockefeller Foundation Scholarship, he toured England, France and the USA, and met many well-known writers. He has also written plays. His short story collection titled *Jumman* was published in 1956, and his autobiography, *Shri Na Pendse-Manus Ani Lekhak*, in 1974.

Waryam Singh Sandhu (b. 1945) is a celebrated Punjabi short story writer. He received a Sahitya Akademi Award for his short story collection, *Chauthi Koot*, which was also made into a national-award-winning film of the same name by Gurvinder Singh. He has five collections of short stories. He holds a Doctorate in Philosophy from Panjab University, and taught Punjabi in Lyallpur Khalsa College in Jalandhar. He now lives with his family in Canada.

NOTES ON THE TRANSLATORS

C. L .L. Jayaprada (b. 1954) retired from Andhra University as professor of English after teaching various literatures of the world in English and Translation Studies for three decades. A bilingual translator, she published several Nobel speeches and Australian stories in Telugu translation as she did Telugu stories in English, in *Indian Literature, Sarasa, Chandrabhaga, JSL, Journal of Literature & Aesthetics, South Asian Review* and *Routes*, a British Council book. The story in *Routes* titled 'Foxtrot' on Anglo Indians in India won her the Jyesta Translation Award. Her published books of translation include *He Conquered the Jungle, Stories of Tenali Raman* and *Purusha Ahamkaraniki Sawal*. Sahitya Akademi brought out *Kalipatnam Rama Rao's stories Yagnam and Other Stories*. Tirumala Tirupati Devasthanams published her *Savitri* in Srinivasa Bala Bharati Series in 2013.

Ipshita Chanda (b. 1961) teaches in the Department of Comparative Literature at the English and Foreign Languages University, Hyderabad. She has been ICCR Visiting Professor of Indian Culture at Georgetown University (2013-2014). She has authored *Packaging Freedom: Feminism and Popular Culture* and *Selfing the City: Women Migrants and Their Lives in Calcutta* and coedited *Shaping the Discourse* (with Jayeeta Bagchi) and *Locating Cultural Change* (with Partha Pratim Basu). Her translations include *Bitter Soil*, a translation of Mahasweta Devi's selected stories; *The Glory of Sri Sri Ganesh*, a translation of Devi's *Sri Sri Ganesh Mahima*; as well as translations of Sukumar Ray's plays and Satinath Bhaduri's *Dhorai Charit Manas*.

J. Devika (b. 1968) is a teacher and researcher at the Centre for Development Studies, Kerala, a writer, translator and feminist. Her main areas of interest are the history of gender, development, culture and politics of Kerala. She employs an interdisciplinary approach in her research, and many of her articles have been published in international, national and regional journals. Her most notable translations include short stories by Sarah Joseph and K. R. Meera, and the autobiography of Nalini Jameela. She translated K. R. Meera's *Aarachaar (Hangwoman)* which won widespread acclaim.

Keerti Ramachandra (b. 1947) is a teacher, editor and translator, who translates from Marathi, Kannada and Hindi into English. Her translations have appeared in several journals and magazines. *A Dirge for the Dammed*, her translation of *Zadazadati* by the Marathi writer, Vishwan Patil was shortlisted for the Crossword Award, 2016. She has also received the A. K. Ramanujan Award for translating from Kannada and Hindi. Her most recent work was a translation of U. R. Ananthamurthy's *Hindutva or Hind Swaraj* with Vivek Shanbhag. Besides teaching, she has also conducted workshops in translation. She comes from a family that speaks Marathi, Kannada and Hindi, and has lived in Chennai, Delhi, Mumbai, Dubai and Kolkata.

Leelawati Mohapatra (b. 1952) is an author and translator. She and her husband, Kamalakanta Mohapatra, are considered to be among the best translators of Odia literature today. She worked in the Indian Revenue Service, but resigned to concentrate on her writing. She cotranslated *The HarperCollins Book of Oriya Short Stories* and *Ants, Ghosts and Whispering Trees: An Anthology of Oriya Short Stories* and *Kanumamu*, a satirical novel written by Laxmikanta Mohapatra. She is author of *Hanging by a Tail*.

Neerja Mattoo (b. 1938) taught English in the Government College for Women, Srinagar, before retiring as principal. She was awarded a British Council Visitorship to the University of Oxford and the HRD Ministry's Senior Fellowship in Literature to work on Kashmiri women poets. She has published three books of translations of Kashmiri short stories into English—*The Stranger Beside Me*, *Contemporary Kashmiri Short Stories* and *Kath: Stories From Kashmir*. She has also published a well known cookbook, *Sal: A Feast of Kashmiri Cuisine*.

Nirupama Dutt (b. 1955) is a poet, translator, journalist and literary critic. She writes in Punjabi and English. She has published an anthology of poetry, *Ik Nadi Sanwali Jahi*, for which she received the Punjabi Akademi Award. She translated *Poet of the Revolution: The Memoirs of Lal Singh Dil*, Punjabi short stories in a volume called *Stories of the Soil*, Gulzar's anthology of poetry, *Pluto*. She wrote the biography of Punjab's Dalit icon *The Ballad of Bant Singh*.

Paul St. Pierre (b. 1945) is a Canadian translator and professor. He is currently adjunct professor in the Department of Linguistics and Translation at the University of Montreal. He taught in translation programs in Canada for over twenty-five years. Along with the Mohapatras, he has co-translated *Ants, Ghosts and Whispering Trees*. He has published and edited several translated works and anthologies, as well as written extensively on translation theory and practice.

Pratik Kanjilal (b. 1964) is a translator and journalist. He is publisher of *Little Magazine,* an independent publication featuring the best of contemporary South Asian writing. He is Books Editor and leader writer with the *Indian Express*. Earlier, he has worked with the *Economic Times, Business Standard* and *Down to Earth*. He has also been a columnist with the *Hindustan Times, Free Press Journal* and *Time Out*. He was awarded the Sahitya Akademi Translation Prize in 2005 for *The Last Wilderness*, a translation of *Antim Aranya*, Nirmal Verma's last novel. He also received the first New York University Prize for Hyperfiction in 2008.

Shanta Gokhale (b. 1939) is a novelist, editor, translator, playwright, columnist and performing arts critic. Her two novels in Marathi, *Rita Welinkar* and *Tya Varshi,* won the Maharashtra State Award for the best novel of the year in 1992 and 2005, respectively. She translated her novels into English as *Rita Welinkar* and *Crowfall*. She has also translated many works of Marathi drama into English, most notably the plays of Vijay Tendulkar, G. P. Deshpande and Mahesh Elkunchwar. Her translations of Marathi literature and involvement with Marathi theatre have greatly helped to introduce the Marathi literary world to the non-Marathi reader. She was awarded the Sangeet Natak Akademi Award in 2016 for her overall contribution to the performing arts.

Tahira Naqvi (b. 1945) is a translator, writer, and Urdu language lecturer in the Department of Middle Eastern and Islamic Studies at New York University. She has translated the works of Saadat Hasan Manto, Munshi Premchand, Khadija and Ismat Chughtai into English.

Vasantha Surya (b. 1942) moves between journalism (over 300 articles and reviews), poetry (*A Word Between Us*, *The Stalk of Time*), children's books (*Mridu in Madras*, *Eklavya*) and translation (*A Place to Live*, an anthology of her translations of classic Tamil stories). She has also translated six Tamil novels (the latest being *Koogai* by Cho Dharman), poetry for Tamil Dalit Writing as well as some translations of the works of Rilke and Brecht from German into Tamil. *The Ballad of Budhni* is her translation of a full-length folk poem from Bundeli Hindi.